SIMON'S DREAM OF TOMORROW'S STRUCTURE

Also by Jeremy Howe

Simon's Dream

Simon's Dream *of* Tomorrow's Structure

A Novel

Jeremy Howe

This is a work of fiction. Names, characters, places, and incidents are the product of the author's imagination or are used fictitiously. Any resemblance to real persons, places, establishments, or locales is entirely coincidental.

ISBN: 979-8-218-36408-3

Printed in the United States of America

Acknowledgements

- I want to say thank you to my wife Galixie for her support and enthusiasm as I continue my journey with writing these books. She's the strongest, kindest and most generous person I know, and I'm honored to be her husband. You're my best friend.
- To my parents, I appreciate and love you two more than words can express. I am who I am thanks to you guys. Thank you for everything you've done for me over the years.
- Huge thank you to Megan for all of your hard work and dedication with editing this manuscript, as well as the first book. Your eye for detail is incredible.
- Garth von Ahnen, thank you for making this cover art, as well as the cover for the first book. Your imagination is huge! Putting this picture together just off a few sentences of instructions I gave you is remarkable.
- Thank you to Russ Davis and the staff of *Gray Dog Press* for all of your help and patience with my past manuscript, as well as this one.
- To Patty, Gloria, Kaitlyn, Mary, Tim, and anyone else I may have forgotten, thank you for letting me know your honest opinion of my first book and encouraging me to continue with the writing process.
- And lastly, thank you to the reader. I sincerely hope you enjoy this story and have as much fun reading it as I did writing it. If things go as planned, this will be book two of five. Questions will be answered.

Prologue

Japan, June 3rd, 1615 AD

Sanada Yukimura tightened the last strap of his armor. Taking a deep breath, he sheathed the katana on his right hip. On his left hip was a large, ancient wooden staff with intricate carvings on it. His mother was waiting by the door.

"My Son," she said softly, "You are a hero to our people. You know this, yes? The likes of who may appear once in a hundred years. At least, that's what I've heard some calling you. People will sing your name for generations to come."

He nodded his head slowly. "I hope our clan breeds more heroes after I've gone. But this war isn't over yet. We have a long way to go still. We must fight."

Focused on the battle at hand, he attempted to brush past his mother, but she placed a hand firmly on his chest. Despite slaying countless in battle, Yukimura was powerless when it came to his mother.

"Just know when to rest," she said softly. "You fought bravely this past winter."

"But summer has come," he said. "Our enemy is relentless." He gently rested a steady hand upon her shoulder, sighing deeply. "I love you, Mother."

He walked briskly through the halls of Osaka Castle for what he feared may be his last time. Growing up with the birth name of Nobushige, it wasn't until his rise to fame as one of the most skilled Samurai that he acquired the alternate name of Yukimura. Several women solemnly looked on as he continued walking toward the exist of Osaka Castle to meet his troops for battle.

Once outside, Yukimura headed toward his trusted horse. The scorching heat was enough to take the energy from the best fighter. However, this was no time to complain about the weather. He climbed the steed with ease, grabbing the reins with familiarity and a hidden sense of dread. With his head held high, Yukimura rode with Osaka Castle, his home, behind him. He knew it was up to him and his men to defend it against the might of the Tokugawa army. They were outnumbered by nearly three to one but to Yukimura, it didn't matter. His people were counting on him. His men were counting on him.

He pulled back on the reins as he approached his men. Their young faces greeted him, their Dō armor clinging to their bodies as they sat on their horses. A row of archers stood back from the foot soldiers, preparing their bows. Examining their frightened faces, Yukimura knew he had to raise their spirits if they were going to stand a chance.

"We must fight with bravery and honor!" he yelled to the line of men sitting on top of their horses. "We don't know what tomorrow will bring. Nobody knows what awaits around the corners, lurking in the shadows. But what I do know is if we make today count, it will make tomorrow brighter. We ride out to defend Osaka Castle! We ride out and defend our home!"

Surrounded on either side by his best men, Sanada Yukimura rode into battle for the final time. Upon meeting the enemy forces head-on, he dismounted from his horse and unsheathed his katana. With skillful precision, as he'd done numerous times before, he faced and defeated his first and second challengers with honor, running them both through.

Blood soaked the battlefield, and chaos ensued all around Yukimura and his dwindling army. The attrition of the fighting coupled with the overwhelming heat began to wear on him. After so many battles, so many duels, he accepted that this would be the day he would lose. After striking down another enemy soldier, he stumbled and fell to a knee. Unable to go on, his strength failing him, he sat down on a tree stump next to him, resting the katana on his lap.

A shadow began to creep over him, blacking out the sun. Yukimura slowly lifted his head to see an immensely tall, black man in a heavy coat of armor standing in front of him, arms crossed. What struck Yukimura was the intensity in the other man's red eyes.

"You've finally come here to die," the challenger's booming voice roared.

Yukimura shook his head, squinting at the other man. "Tell me soldier, what is your name?"

"My name is Popobowa," the red-eyed man said, "And I am no soldier. I'm a commander of soldiers from a dimension far beyond anything you can comprehend. Stand up and fight. I promise to make your death memorable."

Grimacing, Sanada Yukimura stood up, holding the katana at his side. Popobowa held a similar looking blade, urging Yukimura to ready his weapon and prepare for battle. Both men charged, attacking and countering one another's moves with immense skill. To Sanada, a katana duel was like a dance in which he was always able to figure out his opponent's steps, eventually countering them until he bested the other man.

With an upward stroke, Yukimura's blade nicked a weak spot in the red-eyed man's armor, causing him to let out a roar of pain. Popobowa fell to his knees for a moment, breathing heavily.

"What have you done?" Popobowa boomed.

"This blade was created by my mother," Yukimura said confidently. "A thread of your existence is now trapped within it. As long as you stay in our world, *Commander*, you will remain mortal like the rest of us."

As Yukimura spoke, a young soldier rushed to his aid. Popobowa threw down his blade in frustration and drew another weapon which was resting against his back; a long, wooden staff with fire leaping from the end of it. It had detailed carvings along it as well, similar to Sanada's secondary weapon.

Yukimura handed the katana to the young man at his side. "Take this to my mother," he instructed. "Tell her to keep it hidden."

Unsheathing the wooden staff, Sanada Yukimura held the weapon in front of him with both hands, poised and ready. The two warriors faced one another down, stepping to the side as they each moved in a circle on the battlefield. Yukimura was waiting for Popobowa to strike first; he would use this weapon to defend his people for as long as he could.

As predicted, the red-eyed foe struck first, sending a beam of yellow light soaring over Sanada's head, striking Osaka Castle. A chunk of the building exploded on impact, sending chunks of the castle crashing down. Popobowa aimed the staff at Yukimura and shot again. From Yukimura's staff seared a beam of blue, meeting the yellow energy strike in the center of the battlefield, the two colors crashing head-on, sending sparks flying at random. Soldiers ran for cover while simultaneously taking swings at their enemies with their katanas.

After several moments of their dazzling, colorful battle not progressing one way or another, Popobowa glanced over Yukimura's shoulder. Before having a chance to react, a katana pierced Yukimura's spine from behind.

Looking down at his chest, he saw the end of a blade protruding through him, dripping blood. The weapon was withdrawn immediately, and he collapsed to his knees, watching as the world started to spin violently around him.

Popobowa sauntered over to him, towering over Yukimura while he remained on his knees.

"Any last words?" Popobowa mocked.

"I'll see you in my next life," Sanada Yukimura said, his breathing labored, "And countless lives after."

Popobowa jammed the staff against Yukimura's chest, ready to fire a beam of yellow and end his life. Before the weapon could active, dealing the killing blow, a blast of green struck Popobowa in the chest, sending the demon flying backward.

Sanada Yukimura closed his eyes for the final time.

Chicago, Illinois. Four months ago

A KNOCK SOUNDED on the door, breaking the peaceful silence.

"Come in," the middle-aged man sitting behind the desk called out, refusing to look up from the pile of papers scattered in front of him.

The door opened, letting in the loud noise of the police station outside. People talking, phones ringing, some crazy man screaming at the top of his lungs. The open door also ushered in three finely dressed men. Their leader stepped in last, with both of his associates standing idly by on either side of the open door.

"Shut the door," the man sitting at the desk grumbled, still not looking up from his work.

A moment later the door closed, bringing the man behind the desk some peace. Finally looking up from his work, he examined the three men who had stepped into his office. Frowning softly, he removed his reading glasses.

"Detective Erickson, I presume?" the leader said, stepping forward and taking a seat at the desk.

"That's right," Erickson replied, annoyed. "That's what the nameplate outside my door reads, isn't it?"

The leader smirked, eyeing the detective. "I'd like to hire you to help me track down someone."

"I don't do side jobs," Detective Erickson said.

"You will for me." The leader snapped his fingers, motioning one of his men to come closer. "Name's Lenny. Lenny Marcini. William Marcini was my father."

Lenny had a mane of thick, black hair and a prominent black mustache. *He's a spitting image of a younger version of his old man.* Erickson thought to himself. One of the other men approached the detective's desk and placed a large cloth bag on top of the pile of papers.

Detective Erickson gulped, setting his pen down with a shaky hand. The young man had the detective's full attention now. "I see. And you want me to track down your old man. That right?"

"That's right," Lenny affirmed. "I have a viable lead that there are a few people involved in my father's disappearance, and they were also connected to the gruesome murder of Travis Daniels, not to mention the blown-up vehicles and motorcycles from a couple months ago." Lenny leaned forward, wrinkling his nose. "You remember, don't you, Detective?"

"It was certainly a night of lawlessness," Erickson agreed. "Nothing new for this city though, considering those who seem to be pulling the strings."

Lenny Marcini squinted at Erickson for a moment before continuing, ignoring the attempted insult. "My father was a good man, Detective. He paid the salaries of many of your fellow associates, some of whom I passed on my way into your office." Lenny sat back in the chair, crossing his muscular, hairy arms. "You're going to help me find my father and those responsible for taking him."

"Look, we've already got our finest people working on this case. I assure you that we're doing everything in our power to locate your father."

"The power of the Chicago Police Department is no match for the Marcini family," Lenny said smugly. "I promise I'll make it worth your while, Detective."

One of the men reached a meaty paw into the cloth bag and slapped down bundles of cash on the detective's desk. One of the bundles rolled away, plopping on the floor.

"I don't take bribes," Erickson said firmly. "Now get the hell out of my office."

Lenny stood up to leave while his two accomplices picked up the cash, putting it back in the bag. Before moving toward the door, Lenny placed a business card in front of the detective.

"In case you change your mind," Lenny said, winking. "I'll give you a tip though, while I'm down here. Start looking into a woman named Loretta."

"Loretta…what?"

"Don't have a last name. But she has two known accomplices. A young man named Ronald Douglas, the other named Simon Verner."

With that Lenny opened the door and left Detective Erickson's office. The detective looked down at the business card, turning it over several times in deep thought.

"Verner…" he mumbled, rolling the name around in his mouth. "I remember that name. Where have I…"

As if suddenly solving a puzzle, the connection struck the detective like a bolt of lightning. He remembered speaking to Simon Verner two months ago at the Chicago Mental Health Center. A confused young man, wrapped up in a conspiracy involving his crazy ex-girlfriend. The same young man that brought to light the truth of John Stinson's unsolved murder, bringing Doug Lewis and Mike Lancaster to justice after all these years. The mystery of how that young man, a nobody who picked up golf balls for a living, was able to connect the pieces and solve Stinson's murder was, well, a mystery in and of its own.

The excitement of the hunt taking control, Detective Erickson set aside the pile of work he was previously studying to begin on this new case.

"Where are you now, Simon Verner?"

The Dark Dimension. Two months ago

Brittany's head rested on a spike with her decapitated body thrown on top of the heaping pile of corpses and skeletons in the Dark Palace. All sensation had left her body. She felt no pain. Beginning to grow impatient with each passing moment, she waited for Popobowa to return from wherever he kept disappearing to. Brittany was getting anxious for her next set of instructions. She was growing bored.

Zooberi, giggling maniacally, paced back and forth from the Skull Throne to other corners of the throne room. Occasionally he muttered to himself, which would send him into another frenzy of laughter.

"What's so funny, Dad?" Brittany asked, annoyed, turning her eyes to see the man walking by. "Do you find this predicament I'm in to be humorous?"

Zooberi didn't answer. He simply responded in quiet mumbles.

"I'm going to kill Simon, you know. His head will be on this spike next, while I walk free. I'll be —"

"Oh no you won't," Popobowa said, his booming voice echoing through the wide corridors of the Palace. He strolled up past the Skull Throne, looking directly at Brittany. "I don't know how many times it'll take for you to get this through your thick skull, Brittany. Or should I call you 'Mubiru'?" He waved his hand dismissively. "Not that it matters to me. One brother cannot live without the other. That was the agreement."

"But why? Just let me have my fun!" Brittany whined.

"How old are you?" Popobowa asked. "After all these millennia, you still act like a spoiled child." He shook his head, turning away from Brittany and pacing in front of his throne. "When you pledged your soul to the care of the Dark Dimension, you were bound by blood to bring Magdoo's soul to me when I required it. In order to do that, he needs to still be alive! There's no leeway here. Both of your souls need to either stay alive or perish at the same time to keep the Cycle going. If you can't stay on target with this simple rule, then you're useless to me."

Brittany jutted out her lower lip, puffing a strand of black hair out of her brown eyes.

"Give me a new body, and I'll bring him back to you however you wish, My Lord," Brittany said, determined. "I won't fail you."

"You've already failed me. Just like you were a failure to your first Father. Isn't that right, Zooberi?"

Still giggling and wandering about at random, Zooberi ignored the red-eyed demon and continued about whatever business he was occupied with doing.

"It's sad when the human brain turns to mush," Popobowa said softly. He shifted his attention to Brittany, his red eyes returning her haughty glare. "Zooberi picked out the perfect body for you to finish the job of bringing Magdoo's soul back to me. I'll grant you one last chance. Make it count."

"Like I said, I won't let you down."

Brittany watched Zooberi drag the carcass of her new body closer. From a tall bookshelf filled with an assortment of mystical objects, Popobowa retrieved a Soul Orb, the same one that she was brought back to the Dark Dimension in and went to work transferring her soul to the new body.

"You see that device over there?" Popobowa pointed outside the nearest broken glass window. Brittany turned her attention to where he was directing her to look.

Off in the distance, a river of lava wove through miles of red rock, forming a long, deep canyon. The entire landscape gave off an ominous, red hue with active volcanoes spouting off frequently in the distance. Along the upper edge of the canyon was a huge, ancient-looking machine being dragged by an army of demons. They were working furiously on pulling the massive contraption, trying to get it set up in the right spot. Some of the demons cracked whips against the backs of the ones pulling it, urging them to pull harder.

"That's the Soul Generator," Popobowa explained. "Magdoo's soul and yours together are the keys to making that old relic work. The Dark Dimension is dying, and you two brothers are the answers to our salvation. Magdoo's current life as Simon Verner has presented us with an unusual golden opportunity. Simon's dreams are the solution to getting this whole thing started. I've already set things in motion, things which cannot be undone. He will unknowingly help save us, all while bringing about the end to his own world." The armored demon approached Brittany's head on the spike, wrapping his large hands around her skull. "Tell me you understand your purpose now, Mubiru. Either bring Magdoo's soul back here, or you will live like this for the rest of eternity while this dimension crumbles to dust around you."

"I understand," Brittany growled. She looked down at the ground, furrowing her eyebrows and licking her lips. "Simon will pay for what he did to me. Oh, yes. He'll pay the most valuable of prices."

Act I

Structure

noun

1. mode of building, construction, or organization; arrangement of parts, elements, or constituents: *a pyramidal structure.*
2. something built or constructed, as a building, bridge, or dam.

Chapter 1

Sammamish, Washington. Present day

A cold, misty rain coats the glass window which looks out at the evergreen and pine trees behind our building. One bird chirps alone in solitude, attempting to hide under the cover of thick foliage, its feathers and beak slick with the morning shower. Low hanging black clouds lazily float by in the distance, emptying themselves in order to rise above the Cascade Mountains to the east. The dreary weather brings with it a feeling of cozy laziness on this late November morning as the three of us sit in our apartment.

The rapidly growing town of Sammamish, Washington, slightly to the east of Seattle, sits just short of the Cascades. Jess fell in love with the area immediately, saying that she's always wanted to live near the wilderness. She never mentioned this while we were living back in Chicago, apparently keeping this information to herself. Sitting in a recliner recently purchased from a nearby yard sale, her long, blonde hair rests gently on her shoulders. Jess alternates between reading a book and playing on her phone while her legs hang off one arm of the chair.

Our roommate and shared best friend, Ron, sits on the other end of the couch from me, his legs propped up on the dusty coffee table, watching a football game on mute. My best friend since high school, he's clean shaven with short, black hair gelled up in the front. We're both about the same height, but he's a bit more muscular than I am. A dirty old blanket rests over his lap. According to him, listening to the announcers of the games take away his ability to focus on the action playing out on the field, and watching the game in silence helps him to concentrate. He's recently become more involved with fantasy football, something that makes no sense to me, but seems to make his football watching time much more interesting for him. I would say enjoyable, but the level of stress he endures while watching the games seems downright painful.

With our newly purchased shared laptop, my own feet propped up on the coffee table like Ron, I browse the internet for job opportunities in the area. My curly, light brown hair, which I've allowed to grow out, rests on my shoulders similar to Jess.

After we moved here a little over five months ago, my friends were able to quickly strike gold with lucrative employment. Jess found a job working remotely for a fancy big name tech company, while Ron was also able to find work in the nearby city of Bellevue as a delivery driver of some kind. I don't exactly know what they do, and I try not to pry.

I was previously employed at a local golf course called the Sahalee Country Club as a range picker; however, I was laid off two weeks ago. Seasonal jobs can be tough. My earnings paled in comparison to theirs, but at least it was a job which paid me well enough to afford my share of the rent. I took the job because it's something I'm good at and familiar with. I've always been one who needs a consistent routine, a systematic rhythm, in which to function.

Five months ago, I worked as a range picker back in our old home city of Chicago. With me at the wheel, the caged golf cart would go around the driving range, picking up golf balls, and returning them for the members to whack them back out into the grass again. I would pick them up again and again in a seemingly monotonous, mundane and mind-numbing job to some. But to me, it was a job I absolutely loved. Unfortunately, with the cooler, wetter weather comes less customers and the eventual closure of the golf course, which brings me to the world of internet job hunting.

When we made the bold leap to move out west to Seattle, we promised each other to hold our own, carrying our own share of the responsibilities and bills, splitting the rent and other expenses evenly amongst us. Seeing myself as an honest and ethical man and friend, I intend to keep up my end of the agreement. Thankfully, I was able to save up some extra money, working extra hours through the summer and fall. My mom Jill has also been sending me money every month, which I use to make my car payment. I've told her repeatedly that she doesn't need to do that, but she insisted, saying that it's the least she can do for her only son.

Over five years ago, when I was eighteen, my stepfather, Doug, kicked me out of my home with nothing but the clothes on my back. My mom has felt wrought with guilt ever since this happened, and she sees this monetary gift as a form of restitution for that occurrence. I was able to crawl out of the empty hole of self-loathing I had put myself into by learning to love, forgive and respect myself, as well as my mom, a lesson instilled in me by another homeless man I knew at the time named Elroy.

A new job posting catches my eye. Mwari Sushi is looking for a part-time evening sushi chef. It's a brand-new restaurant a couple weeks away from their grand opening. The name, more so than the job, makes me look up from the laptop screen and stare off into the distance. I've heard that name before, in a distant memory. Perhaps even a past life…

"Yes!" Ron shouts, throwing the blanket off, punching his fists in the air. "Touchdown! Thank you!"

Jess and I glance at one another momentarily. I smile at our friend's goofy enthusiasm, before she rolls her eyes and returns back to her book.

"You guys want anything while I'm up?" Ron asks, standing up.

"No, thanks," Jess and I say simultaneously, each of our minds focused on our tasks.

I search "Mwari" on the internet, spending the next several minutes reading up on who or what that is. Slowly, it begins to dawn on me why that name caught my attention. Mwari was believed to be an ancient deity, the creator of all things, and that all life is within Him. The roots of the ancient belief trace back thousands of years from a nomadic tribe called the Bantu, with most followers in South Africa and present-day Zimbabwe.

It was discovered through a series of events that my current life is not the first life I've lived. Although I didn't believe it at first, it became known to me, through trials and tribulations, that reincarnation is, in fact, very real. In a chain of flashbacks, thanks to the help of Jess' friend and my personal hero Loretta, I learned that I've lived many lives. Most of which, or at least the ones that I became privy to, ended in heartbreak, treachery or disaster. For some lives, even all three of those descriptive words could be used accurately.

At the time, I was trying to look into the reason why I was receiving a series of ultra-realistic visions; dreams of a local police officer named John Stinson, who was murdered in a crime that had turned into a cold case several years before I was born. It was unveiled that my first known life was as an African tribal member named Magdoo. His tribe believed in Mwari as their God. Loretta was the tribe's Oracle, and through mystical powers that I still don't understand, she's somehow survived for the past seventeen thousand years, if not longer, traveling the world and doing who knows what.

My girlfriend at that time back in Chicago, Brittany, turned out to be a psychopath with the ability to enter my dreams. She also unveiled herself to be Magdoo's brother, Mubiru, and throughout a little-known cycle of lives that we've both lived, he had tracked me down in several of them, turning my past lives into ruin. Mubiru came to me in my dreams in a black, empty space known as the Void, the space between the waking and dream world. He chose to go by the name of 'X' and I continue to refer to him, and Brittany, by X just to keep the whole thing somewhat straight. Thankfully, X, in the form of Brittany, failed on her last attempt to end my current life, and we captured her soul in a magical sphere called the Soul Orb, before the ancient demon named Popobawa stole the orb and took it back into a vortex, apparently into another world or dimension.

Hopefully, that's all over and done with so my friends and I can just continue living our normal lives now.

Ron returns back to his spot on the couch, continuing his engaged, albeit vegetative activity of watching Sunday afternoon football. I admire my friend's ability to sit and watch sports for sustained periods of time. What a simple thing to keep him occupied.

Jess, still sitting in the recliner next to our couch, now punches away at her phone screen, a smile on her face.

"What do you guys want for dinner?" I ask.

Their mumbled replies of "I don't know" and "what?" eventually lead me out of the apartment and down to my car. I'll just go check out Mwari Sushi for myself. I'm curious to see what this restaurant looks like in person before I apply for the position of sushi chef. Culinary craftsmanship has definitely not been one of my strong suits. One of the last times I tried to cook dinner for someone, I was drugged, and my apartment set on fire by a magical ancient wooden staff thanks to X. Hopefully this time goes differently.

I drive several blocks to the sushi restaurant, which has a couple of trucks from a local contracting and construction company in the parking lot. Parking a few spaces over from one of the trucks, I get out of my car and look at the building, shielding my face from the cold rain, which has begun to pour down more heavily now. I look up at the roof, where the sign for *Mwari Sushi* is being erected by a series of cranes and pulleys. To the right of the words is the traditional symbol for Yin and Yang, although, rather than the standard colors, this symbol depicts the logo as two separate dragons, encircling themselves, each clutching a ball of the opposite color.

Nodding my head, I get back in the car, making a mental note to apply for the job when I get back home. I drive down to the local grocery store and purchase some imitation crab meat, a filet of tuna from the seafood case, rice, seaweed and an avocado. Oddly enough, I spend more time searching for the perfect avocado than any of the other items, knowing how picky Jess can be when it comes to the infamous fruit. I throw a second one in the cart just for the heck of it, in case the first one isn't up to her standards. She made sure to correct me the last time I went shopping that an avocado is indeed a fruit, not a vegetable, as I had stated out of negligent ignorance. Before leaving the store I also buy a sharp kitchen knife, a bottle of soy sauce and a large container of wasabi.

An hour later, I'm in the kitchen of our apartment, slicing up the tuna filet and preparing some homemade sushi for our dinner. I keep the laptop on the kitchen counter, watching online videos of how to prepare the most delectable sushi dishes, which I attempt to mimic to the best of my abilities. I'll need all the practice I can get if I want to stand a chance at getting the job.

For each of their dishes, I add a scoop of wasabi on the side of the plate, the glob looking like green Playdough.

"Woah, sushi?" Jess says as I hand the plate to her. "You went all out, Simon. Thanks."

I hand a plate to Ron, and he eagerly snatches it, his attention still on the TV. He grabs one of the pieces of sushi, then slowly turns toward me as I take my place on the couch.

"What's this?" he asks uncertainly, holding the homemade California roll between his thumb and index finger like he just picked a gigantic booger from someone else's nose.

"It's sushi," Jess says. "Simon worked hard making this. Just try it."

He shrugs his shoulders and smears the sushi roll with the wasabi, smothering the green substance all over it.

"Guacamole!" he says excitedly, then throws the entire roll into his mouth.

"Ron, no, that's wasabi you idiot!" I say, slamming my plate down on the coffee table.

Ron shifts the sushi roll inside his mouth for a moment before swallowing. Continuing to look straight ahead, I can tell he's starting to feel the pain of his decision. He looks over at me, tears streaming down his cheeks, his eyes bulging out of his head. Ron leans forward, roughly puts his plate down and begins pounding his fist on the coffee table, then quickly gets up and runs into the bathroom, screaming.

Jess and I look at one another, a look of shock on each of our faces. Then we both bust up laughing.

"I'll go check on him," Jess chuckles. "He's like a little boy sometimes, I swear."

"I'll help," I say, running into the kitchen.

I begin to pour a glass of milk, then shake my head, placing the glass down on the counter, deciding to take the whole gallon. He's going to need it.

Chapter 2

"So, tell me, Mr. Verner, what makes you a good candidate for our secondary sushi chef position at Mwari Sushi?" the small, elderly Asian woman asks me.

"Well, I'm a hard worker. I'm very punctual, I have a sharp eye for detail, and I'm friendly with customers."

"Very good," she says, eyeing over my resume. "It looks like your prior job history was working at a couple of golf courses. Tell me about that."

"Right. I worked at a golf course as a Range Picker, picking up golf balls. My friends and I decided we were ready for a change of scenery, and moved out west, looking for a fresh start. I took a similar position at a local golf course here. I'm looking for a change of pace, and I'd like the opportunity to learn and grow in the culinary art of preparing sushi. I even made some California rolls for my friends last night, as a matter of fact." I chuckle as I think of Ron's incident the previous evening.

"Very good," she says. "The California roll is one of our best sellers. Very popular here in America. Would you care to demonstrate for me now how you prepared them, so I can be a better judge?"

We stand up from the booth inside the dark and spacious restaurant, which is still under renovation for the grand opening, and I follow her toward the kitchen.

I was excited to get the call first thing this morning, inviting me to come down for an interview with the owner. Ms. Sasaki stands a little over four feet tall and rests most of her weight, which can't be all that much, on a cane. She moves around the restaurant slowly, yet with a sense of purpose. Just being around her, I can tell that she carries a sense of authority with her, prepared to dish out orders to others without hesitation.

As I was sitting in my car in the parking lot a half hour before the interview, writing out my resume onto a wrinkled-up piece of paper, she had pulled up in a new green SUV. A blue dragon decal was on the side of her vehicle, similar to the dragons in the logo on the top of the building. Her little head was barely peeking up over the steering wheel, and she'd cut off a car when pulling into the parking lot.

Now, as I follow her around the long, white counter leading into the kitchen, a sense of nervousness takes over me. Preparing sushi rolls for my friends while watching video tutorials on the laptop is one thing. Having *Mrs. Miyagi* standing there, leaning against her cane and judging my every move, is another.

My hands slightly trembling, I get to work making the sushi roll, relying on my memory for what I did last night while watching the expert make one in an online video. With no video to guide me, I close my eyes, take a deep breath, and keep crafting the best California rolls I'm capable of.

"Done," I say with sincere pride, standing back and placing my hands on my hips. "What do you think?"

Ms. Sasaki eyes me slowly, then approaches the workstation, hands wobbling on her cane. For over a minute, she stands there, staring at the sushi rolls. One of them does appear significantly larger than his California roll siblings, while another appears to be the runt of the litter. Whether she likes them or not shouldn't really matter to me, but for some reason today, it does. Having her approval on my work seems…necessary. Plus, I really do need this job, so there's that.

Finally, she takes a deep breath, nodding her head. "Not bad," she says, still facing away from me, peering down at the food. "You have a long way to go, Mr. Verner. But this is a good foundation." She turns around and raps the cane against the floor. "When can you start?"

My jaw just about hit the floor.

LATER THAT NIGHT, I take Jess and Ron out to celebrate at a local bar. Since *Monday Night Football* is on, I make sure to grab a booth close to one of the TVs. Jess and I sit next to one another, our backs turned to the TV, while Ron sits across from us, keeping his attention glued to the game behind us.

"Congrats on the new job, Simon!" Jess says. "When do you start?"

"Two weeks from today," I say, picking up a laminated menu. "That's when their grand opening is."

"What made you decide to be a sushi chef all of a sudden?" Ron asks, now looking at us. Apparently, the game must be in an intermission of some kind. "You decided that you've picked up enough golf balls?"

"Yeah, something like that."

"Well, good for you man," Ron says. "Maybe you finally found your calling, you know? My dad used to tell me that we're all meant for something, we just have to figure out what it is. A few years ago, when I… when I was…"

Ron's attention turns back to the TV.

"I think we lost him," Jess says with feigning sadness. "Anyways, good for you. It'll be a nice change of pace."

"Let's hope so," I sigh. "I thought moving across the country was a change of pace, but I was still doing the same job. It didn't make a lot of sense, you know? Like, why pack up and leave everything I knew behind? Besides you two, of course. But all of that just to go back to doing the same mundane job? I needed something…more." I shrug my shoulders and take a sip of my beer. "We'll see. Hey, before I forget, Ms. Sasaki gave me some of these."

Pulling the plastic wrapped treats from my coat pocket, I place a fortune cookie in front of Ron and hand another to Jess, keeping the last one for myself.

"Fortune cookies?" Jess asks. "I thought those were a Chinese food thing. Isn't sushi Japanese? Or am I backwards on that?"

"It's an American thing," I reply.

I go to work opening the plastic wrapper, cracking open the cookie. The small piece of white paper is lodged inside, and I reach in to pull it out, unraveling the paper to read it.

Where the past was once shown, the distant future will be unveiled. She needs your help. Prepare for the next stage of your quest, Simon Verner.

"Oh my God, that's so true," Jess says, taking a bite of her cookie. "Listen to this, guys. It says, *'Big changes are coming your way.'* I mean, I guess we've already had some big changes. If I'd read this five months ago, it probably would've been a bit more on the nose. What does yours say, Simon?"

Keeping the paper outstretched in my hands, I read it several times. This can't be happening. I thought this was all over. How can this be happening? But more importantly, *why* is this still happening? I trapped Brittany's soul after solving Officer Stinson's murder. What more does Mwari, or whoever, want from me?

I look over at Jess; my breathing has become shaky. "It's…it can't be real."

"What does it say?" she asks again, looking from me to the little strip of paper in my hands, then back to me.

"It says…Jess, something bad is happening. You and Ron are in danger. It was a mistake for me to make you guys move out here with me. I don't…I can't lose you again. If you get hurt again…"

She snatches the paper out of my fingers and reads it quietly to herself. Turning her head slowly to me, she arches an eyebrow, a look of concern on her face.

"This is the craziest fortune I've ever read. That place…it must be magical or something."

Shaking her head, she hands the paper back to me and picks up a new conversation with Ron. Reading the same strip of paper, it now says: *An opportunity will present itself to you in the near future. Embrace the challenge, and you will be rewarded.*

"No, no this can't be right," I say, turning the paper over several times. "Jess, listen, this…this can't be real. It's not possible."

She takes a deep breath and pats me on the back. "Okay, alright. There, there, buddy. Everything's going to be okay. I'm right here. Shh."

"Yes!" Ron shouts, his fists raised in the air. Several other patrons of the restaurant join him, shouting and hollering randomly at whatever transpired in the football game.

I keep staring at the small strip of paper in my hands, blinking my eyes several times, waiting for my fortune to change. But it doesn't.

Chapter 3

It's opening night for Mwari Sushi, and the restaurant is busy. Ms. Sasaki runs a tight ship, and she makes sure that everyone is ready. She informs us that this is her third sushi restaurant she's opened, and she knows what it takes to run a successful business. Having never worked in a restaurant before, I follow her without question, as she clearly knows more about this type of industry than I do. She's the boss.

Nearly two weeks after reading the bizarre fortune cookie, nothing out of the ordinary has happened yet. I've remained on my toes, checking over my shoulder every so often for any sign of danger. And most importantly, no weird dreams or visions. So far, so good. Every night, I've been practicing making sushi for my friends. They're probably sick of it at this point, but they appreciate the free meals just the same.

"Okay everyone, attention to me!" Ms. Sasaki yells from the middle of the restaurant, clinking her sharp fingernails on a drinking glass. "Tonight is opening night. I need all of you to be extra sharp, and ready to serve our customers. Let's make a good first impression to the community. Any questions?"

The seven of us look around silently, a few of them clearing their throats. I keep my hands behind my back and focus my attention to the floor. The white cloth cap on my head shifts slightly forward, and I adjust it to make sure it doesn't slide off and land on the ground. When I look up, Ms. Sasaki is now looking directly at me while holding her cane in front of her with both hands.

"Simon, are you ready?"

I clear my throat. "Yes, ma'am."

"Good. This evening will be a big test for you. Make us proud. Alright everyone, back to your stations. We open in thirty minutes. I want this place looking spotless. Chop chop!"

I hustle off back to the kitchen and resume my work, preparing the ingredients. The heavy smell of chlorine wafts throughout the cooking area, as I spent the last hour wiping down the entire kitchen with an assortment of cleaning supplies, as instructed by Ms. Sasaki.

The head chef, Brandon, is a middle-aged, burnt-out looking redhead with a variety of tattoos down each arm, as well as on his neck. Darkened bags sag under his blue eyes. He's only been working for the past hour, but he already looks exhausted.

As I'm wiping down one of the counters, I hear a crash of pots and pans behind me, and I twist around to see Brandon collapsed in a heap on the floor. Initially, I'm afraid that my cleaning has caused a form of asphyxiation to kick in, knocking the man out. But as I scramble to his side, checking to make sure he's still alive and kicking, the smell of hard alcohol hits my nose instantly. He opens his eyes, and I can immediately see how glassy they are. As he tries to stand up, using my shoulder as a prop, I insist that he stay seated, advising him that he's in no condition to be preparing raw seafood for the public this evening. Rather than debating with me, he covers his mouth and rushes out the back door, vomiting in the back parking lot.

"Great," I say, annoyed, placing my hands on my hips.

I find Ms. Sasaki, busy instructing one of the young waitresses on how to properly carry a full load of dishes. I interrupt her teaching session and advise her of the situation.

"That's no good," she smacks her palm on her forehead. "He said he was taking classes…." She stares off into the distance, then returns her look to me. "Well, Simon, this will be the ultimate test. Can you do it?"

"Me? By myself?" I stammer. "Is there nobody else you can find to help me? Can *you* give me a hand at least?"

She steps toward me, placing a hand on my shoulder. "What you can't do will make you stronger. What you won't do will only make you weaker. I believe you can do this, Mr. Verner."

With that odd verbal fortune cookie, she shuffles away, barking orders at one of the busboys. I rush off to the kitchen, crashing through the swinging doors, and immediately resume what I was doing at double the speed.

A short time later, after the restaurant officially opens its doors for the first time, roughly twelve customers enter, prepared to devour the best sushi Seattle has to offer. I receive the first order and get to work, using my two weeks' worth of preparation and practice to create the nicest looking plate of sushi anyone's ever seen. Or at least that's what I keep telling myself. By the time I finish with the first plate, four more orders have come in. I work faster, finishing my preparation on the second and third plates, only to find that I'm now seven orders behind.

My breathing begins to quicken. I can feel sweat tricking through my little white cap as it balances on my thick hair. Glancing up at the clock, I see that it's already been an hour, but it only feels like fifteen minutes at most.

"Simon, one of my customers is wondering when that Dynamite Roll is coming along," one of the young waitresses, Amanda, says questioningly. "I believe his exact words were 'What's taking so long? Are they still catching the fish?'"

"I'm working on it, Amanda," I say sharply.

I wipe my sleeve along my forehead, and keep my attention focused squarely on the dish being prepared in front of me. This job is much faster paced than picking up golf balls, and although I'm stressed out at the moment working the kitchen by myself, I'm having a great time. No, I'm not being sarcastic. I'm seriously enjoying myself, creating these little masterpieces that would make the likes of Martha Stewart jealous. Plus, time seems to be flying by at a record pace.

I work the entire shift with no breaks, all the way up until closing time at eleven. After creating what felt like hundreds of various dishes, my hands and wrists ache, and I'm ready to pass out with Brandon out back.

"Good work tonight, Mr. Verner," Ms. Sasaki says with satisfaction as she makes her way through the kitchen. "You go home and get some rest. I'll clean up."

"Are you sure, Ms. Sasaki?" I ask. "I don't mind helping. I've made quite a mess."

She reluctantly agrees to allow me to help her clean up. We work together in silence, getting the cooking area back to how it looked before opening. The rest of the crew has already gone home, leaving the two of us alone to finish closing for the night.

I drive back to the apartment feeling exhausted, but also satisfied. Putting in a full ten-hour shift has my feet and back aching, yet I feel a sense of pride that I haven't felt in quite some time. Angela, my former counselor back in Chicago, would be so proud to hear of my new job working at Mwari Sushi. She always used to tell me that if you feel accomplished by the end of the day, then it was a good day. And the more good days you compile, the better your life will be. Or something to that effect.

Silently, I enter our apartment and go to my bedroom, collapsing face first on my bed, still in my work clothes. I fall asleep instantly.

Adjusting her short black hair silently in the bathroom mirror, she takes a deep breath and smiles meekly at her reflection. The white walls of the living quarters match the bathroom, as well as every other room in the small apartment. Two bright LED lights shine into the kitchen sink, creating unique light patterns that dance across the ceiling.

She makes her way into her small bedroom and finishes getting ready, slipping on a loose-fitting cream-colored blouse and gray slacks. A gold necklace, a gift from her father, as well as some earrings, completes her outfit.

It's just like before. I'm not able to control anything this woman says or does, but I'm able to sense everything she can. Just like when I was Officer John Stinson. Who is this woman? And why is her apartment so bright and white? I wish I could clean this good…

"Turn off the lights," she says softly as she walks toward the front door.

The two bright lights in the kitchen turn off, as well as various other lights throughout her small living space.

"Enjoy your day, Annie," an automated male voice says from somewhere in the ceiling.

With a quiet woosh, the front door opens and she exits the apartment, taking a right. To her left is a metallic guardrail with see-through glass that looks out into a magnificent square-shaped courtyard; the ground far below, and the ceiling even higher above. The building, if that's what this is, stretches up as far as the eye can see, the guardrail on each level wrapping around the courtyard in the same square shape.

She passes by two other individuals, a man and woman. The woman's hairstyle is cut just above the shoulders, exactly the same as Annie is wearing her hair. Annie passes by several more people, and they all look identical. Every woman wears their hair the same way. Every man also wears their hair in the same way as one another; much shorter, similar to a traditional bowl cut. Both the men and women share the same deep-black hair color. All of these people are identical in height, weight, and all other exterior physical attributes. Everyone's clothes are also the same color; cream-colored tops and gray pants.

Piano music plays softly from speakers on the walls. Passing by several other doors, she walks with a diligent purpose to her destination. People are leaving their assigned living spaces, the doors opening in the same side-to-side manner. All the people Annie passes by are smiling, gently and politely nodding their heads in greeting.

Annie smiles and nods her head at another young man that walks by, then quickly wipes the smile away after they pass one another. She takes a left at the end of the walkway and continues straight until she reaches the elevators. Pressing the call button for the lift, she steps back, briefly adjusting her necklace and straightening her clothes. When the elevator eventually arrives, the doors open, and she steps inside, pressing the button that corresponds with "85."

The elevator lifts her up quickly; the mechanisms are so smooth and quiet. Everything is pristinely clean and well-lit.

"Good morning, Annie," a male voice says over the elevator speakers. "Are you ready for what today will bring?"

"Yes," Annie answers, keeping her smile wide. "I'm ready to follow the ROADS. I'm ready to contribute to the Structure."

The Structure. In terms of the hierarchy of power, or of importance, nothing comes above the Structure. Even when used in the middle of a sentence when reading and writing, citizens have been strictly taught that the word "the" isn't to be capitalized, per orders of the Grand Master. If "the" is capitalized, it may be deemed offensive and against the ROADS, a punishable offense.

"You are a vital part of the Structure," the voice in the elevator says. "Please, have a pleasant day and watch your step."

The elevator door opens again, and she steps out, turning left.

A few moments later, she reaches her destination; a slightly larger door than all the others with a digital sign that reads *School* above. Annie takes a deep breath, closes her eyes, then exhales. She strides into the classroom, a bright and eager smile on her face.

"Good morning, students," Annie says cheerfully.

"Good morning, Miss Hilltop!" the students chime in return, their youthful, high-pitched voices loud and exuberant.

The classroom consists of twenty students, ranging from seven to eight years old, all sitting in their assigned seats. They're all wearing the same uniform; white shirt and gray slacks for the boys, white top and gray skirts for the girls. All ten of the female students wear their black hairstyle in the same shoulder-length style as the women, the only difference being a pink ribbon or bow on each of their heads. The boys' haircuts are also in the short bowl cut like the men. Their facial features are all identical. Height, weight and physical attributes are also the exact same.

Just as the Grand Master has intended, Annie thinks to herself.

"Alright class, please open your Holoreaders to page thirty-seven," Annie instructs the class.

The children all push a button on their desks, and a small hologram appears in front of them, complete with text. They all swipe their hands to the left, then neatly place their hands in their laps, returning their attention promptly forward.

"Now, did everyone do their assigned reading last night?" Annie asks the class.

"Yes, Miss Hilltop," the students say in unison.

"Very good," she says cheerfully, searching the class for someone to call on. "Alright, Sandy, can you please tell the class what the Five Basic Principles of the Structure are?"

One of the girls stands up, a pink ribbon proudly displayed on the top of her head. "Respect. Obedience. Accountability. Discipline. Structure."

"Great job, Sandy," Annie says to the female student, who proudly, yet politely, sits back down. "Those words all make up what's called an 'acronym.' This acronym is what we know as the ROADS. Alex, can you please tell us what ROADS leads to?"

"Yes, Miss Hilltop," a young boy says while standing up. "All paths of the ROADS lead to Perfection, the ultimate goal of the Structure."

"Very good, Alex," Annie says, and the boy takes his seat. "That was very well said. The Structure was created in order for us to live great lives. The air we breathe, the water we drink, the daily nutrition tablets we take, and many other things that we take for granted are all meant to help us live in prosperity. As we live, we also have roles to play in the Structure. Ultimately, our roles, when achieved to their fullest potential, lead to Perfection. One day, you will all be assigned a task within the Structure to ensure its survival.

Then, your children will be sitting where you're sitting, and that's how *we* keep surviving. That's how we keep the Structure Perfect. Any questions?"

Sandy raises her hand, and Annie nods her head, encouraging the student to stand.

"Will we ever see the Outside?" she asks in wonder, fidgeting with one of the buttons on her shirt. "My daddy says that there isn't an Outside, and the Structure is all that exists. But there has to be an Outside, doesn't there, Miss Hilltop?"

"I've lived in the Structure my entire life, and…" Annie shrugs her shoulders, clasping her hands together. She knows she's treading a fine line between being honest with her students, and saying something that goes against the Customs. She doesn't want the children to know about the Outsiders that have recently been invited to live on the bottom floors, as that may excite them into wanting to go see them. That would not be allowed. "I don't know if you'll ever see the Outside. I know I haven't, and probably never will. But there *is* an Outside. There's more out there than we'll ever know. But what's important is that we're safe Inside the Structure. We have all we ever need right here. Life is Perfect."

Chapter 4

I wake up, feeling refreshed and ready to start the day. Last night's shift at Mwari Sushi was exhausting, so I'm thankful for the full eight hours of uninterrupted sleep. As I sit up in bed, rubbing my eyes, the memory of my dream comes flooding back. There was something uniquely different about last night's dream that I've had compared to the others these past few months. Visions where everyone looked the same. The female schoolteacher. It felt so far-fetched, yet it also felt so…real. Just as real as my dreams of John Stinson.

Instinctively, I reach over for my cell phone and call Loretta.

"Hello, sweet child," Loretta's charming voice comes through the cell phone. That slight southern accent always leaves a lasting impression.

"Hey, Loretta. Any chance you would feel like flying out to Seattle to visit?"

She chuckles. "Oh, I don't know. That's a long flight, and these old bones don't really like sitting still for long periods of time. But I know you didn't call me up just to invite me to fly across the country. What's going on, Simon?"

"Well, I had a dream last night," I begin, taking a deep breath. I tell her about the dream, sparing few details. "Have you ever come across someone who could dream of the future?"

The phone goes silent for a moment. Before I have the chance to ask if she's still there, Loretta clears her throat. "No, I don't believe I have. Your ability to see into your past lives is truly remarkable as it is. Now as for the future…"

"But remember when I told you that I saw Samantha when I was knocked unconscious, getting beat up in the Palace Theater? She told me that she was the one that sent those visions to me."

"Yes, but she also told you that it takes someone special to receive those messages," she breathes into the phone. "The answer here isn't simple. I think someone is sending you these visions, just as before. It's possible that it's someone from the future, or someone from the Beyond. But just keep an eye on it, Simon. If you keep getting any more of these visions, keep a record of them like you did last time."

"I will," I say reluctantly. I then go on to tell her about the mysterious fortune cookie message.

"Now, that is strange," she says, then chuckles again. "Child, you sure do live an interesting life. Maybe I'll have to come out and pay you kids a visit sometime after all. Keep me updated on these dreams, Simon. I'll be here if you need me."

A short time later, I take my morning shower and get dressed. Ron and Jess are each still sleeping in their respective rooms, so I decide to surprise them by preparing a nice breakfast. After my shift last night, I feel like I still need more practice in the kitchen. A lot more practice.

As I make breakfast, I think about how fortunate the three of us were to find this apartment. It's a nice, mostly quiet complex, with buildings set up in a townhouse layout. This particular apartment is a three-bedroom, two-bathroom on the top floor, with plenty of square footage. We feel like we have enough space for ourselves, and the living room allows us to mingle and invite guests over – although that happens quite rarely. The beige colored carpeting feels new and still springy under every step. And unlike my old apartment, there's no rotten smell. The whole place smells rather…homey. For lack of a better word. It feels like home. A refuge the three of us know we can come to and feel safe after a rough day.

Ron's the first one to emerge from his bedroom just as I'm finishing preparing breakfast. He sits down at the dining room table, still groggy, and presumably hung over. He yawns and stretches his arms in front of him, cracking his knuckles. His black hair is tweaking all over the place.

"Woah, you're making us breakfast?" he asks.

"Right you are. Hope you like French toast."

"Do I? C'mon man, you know I'll eat just about whatever you put down in front of me."

"You want a side of wasabi for your sausage too?" I ask jokingly

"Funny," he mumbles, shaking his head.

I dish up three plates of food, setting one down in front of Ron, one for myself, and the third at the empty seat for whenever Jess joins us.

"You think I should go wake her?" Ron asks, picking up his fork.

"Your funeral."

The two of us eat our meal while discussing what to get Jess for Christmas. The holidays are quickly approaching, and I've done zero shopping. There are two types of people in this world; those who get their shopping done months in advance, and those who wait until the last possible minute, procrastinating until they feel the urge to trample one another in a semi-acceptable, tongue-in-cheek American tradition.

I inform Ron that I don't have to work at the restaurant until later tonight, and since he has to go to work soon, I can go grab something for her. It'll be from the two of us.

Ron goes silent for a few moments, shaking his head and chewing his food. "You know, it's been two months since my dad's called. I'm starting to think this'll be the first Christmas I don't get to talk to him."

"I'm sorry," I say quietly. "Why don't you just call him up?"

"This new woman he's been seeing doesn't like me. Or anyone that wants to talk to him, for that matter." Still shaking his head, Ron looks down at his plate of French toast. "I don't know, man. It's like I don't even have a family anymore. My sister hates my guts, Mom's been gone for twelve years now…"

"That's really tough," I say, attempting to be comforting. "I'm sorry to hear that. I know this whole move was just sort of spontaneous, but I feel that we've all handled it pretty well. We've got a roof over our heads, jobs to support us… for what it's worth, Jess and I are here for you. We're here for each other."

"Thanks, man. I appreciate that."

Jess' bedroom door opens, and she shuffles her way into the dining room with fuzzy slippers on, taking her seat while yawning. She takes a look at the plate of food in front of her, and she quickly looks back and forth between Ron and I. Proving to be the narc I've always suspected him to be, Ron gives me up easily, pointing at me from across the table with that blasted fork.

"You made this?" Jess asks me, picking up her eating utensil.

"Yes, ma'am," I say proudly. "I figured after one of the most hellish nights imaginable working in a kitchen last night, why not jump right back into it and make my two best friends a hot breakfast? In a more peaceful atmosphere, thankfully."

"Well, I don't know about the 'hot' part," Jess mumbles, spitting out some of the sausage and heading over to the microwave. She throws the plate in and starts pressing buttons. "Sorry to hear you had a rough night at work. Opening nights can be pretty busy. Or so I'd imagine."

"Yeah, well it wasn't just that. The main cook showed up to work drunk, so it was just me flying solo."

"That blows," Ron says with his mouthful. "Too much booze and you're bound to lose, that's what I always say."

"No, you don't," Jess remarks.

I laugh, shaking my head. "Anyways, yeah it was stressful at first. But I'm telling you guys, after a while, I was like, in the zone. I was making sushi like nobody's business. It was incredible. I don't know how else to describe it. Ms. Sasaki seemed pretty impressed with me by the end of the night, so I'm looking forward to getting back in there and trying to perfect my new craft. I can only get better."

"That's great, Simon," Jess says, taking her seat and placing the now steaming plate of food in front of her. "I think you were due for a change. Hopefully this works out."

After the three of us finish our meal, I head out to go shopping. My ride, an expensive blue sports car, complete with a large spoiler on the back, chrome wheels and a sunroof, is my crowning jewel. I bought it a few months ago, just as my visions of my past life were beginning to show themselves to me. The back window and rear passenger side glass all had to be replaced after being shot out by corrupt mobsters working for William Marcini, one of the former mob bosses back home, who has gone "missing" according to the media. What actually happened was the wrath of Loretta, who had used a magical staff with a blue pulse of energic light to evaporate the man into a pile of ashes.

The engine starts with a boisterous roar, and I rev it a couple times before pulling out of the parking lot. Traffic is heavy this morning, as it typically is. I like to think of myself as a patient driver, but this much traffic tests my finite supply of resolve. Eventually I make it to the mall, park my car near the front of one of the department stores, and go inside.

My mom used to take me shopping at the mall a lot when I was younger, and I've always felt nostalgic when I go to one. Eating at the food court, visiting a variety of different stores, seeing strangers, maybe even meeting up with some friends; the shopping mall is, in my opinion, one of America's finest pastimes, which is unfortunately experiencing a slow, painful death, thanks to the world of online shopping. While most people would rather stay home and do their Christmas shopping in their pajamas, I prefer to fight the crowds and see the item in person before buying it.

Just before I left the apartment, Ron and I agreed on buying Jess some inexpensive jewelry. At first, I'd argued that we should buy her some perfume, but Ron was convinced that we would be sending her the message that she stinks. I told him that's ludicrous, but he stood firm on his position.

I walk through the department store, past the glass counters of perfume, heading directly toward the well-lit section of jewelry. Browsing the selection of rings, necklaces and earrings, I suddenly realize that I'm way out of my element here, not having a clue what I'm looking for. The prices are also a bit more than the two of us had budgeted, and I'm beginning to feel discouraged. Maybe perfume would be a better option. Ron would understand, once I told him how much they were asking for this necklace.

Wait, how many zeroes is that? I thought it was only $250. It's actually $2,500. Why do women like jewelry so much? Is it because it costs so much? Jess would understand if I went with perfume, right?

"Are you finding everything okay, sir?" The attractive young female associate strides up on her side of the glass case.

She's dressed quite nicely, her black hair resting gently on her shoulders. I look up at her face, and to my total shock and horror it's none other than my ex-girlfriend Brittany. Her big, brown eyes look at me, and she tilts her head, resting her hands on the glass case.

"Sir, is everything alright?" she asks innocently, pressing her shoulders together seductively and biting her lower lip.

I look back down at the shiny jewelry, trying my best not to cause a scene. I can't go back into the straitjacket, not again. I can't go back there.

She clears her throat, and I look back up. It's not Brittany; this woman's a redhead with kind, blue eyes. The associate arches her eyebrows in a look of concern.

"Well, actually…" I begin, and clear my throat, smiling. "No, I suppose not. I'm looking for something for my friend. She's a girl, you see. We've been friends for a long time. Her name's Jess. We actually dated a couple months ago but it didn't work out…" I unzip my hooded sweatshirt and begin yanking at my shirt collar. "Is it hot in here?"

"I see," she giggles, a glimmer of a smile in her eyes, and leads me down to another section of the jewelry case with much more affordable options.

She helps me pick out a golden necklace at a reasonable price. Ron will be pleased, as will the recipient of the gift. Or so I hope. I wish that Jess could learn to forgive me someday for being a coward. I hope that she'll understand why I am the way that I am. If only she knew how perfect I think she is. If only…

I finish the transaction, tell the employee to have a nice day and leave the mall. As I'm putting the shopping bag in the trunk of my car, I hear a woman's voice yelling behind me.

"Stop! Let go!" she screams. "Help! Somebody help!"

I turn around to see two guys near the entrance of the department store trying to grab an elderly woman's purse from her, attempting to forcefully yank it off her shoulder. A few people look on from a distance, not intervening, not doing anything to help. One of them even has the audacity to pull out his smartphone and start recording the robbery in progress.

I slam the trunk of the car down, sprinting toward the woman and her attackers.

"Stop!" I shout. "Let her go! Get out of here!"

One of the thieves turns around to confront me as his accomplice finally wins the struggle for the purse and tucks it under his arm, running off toward the department store entrance. I pursue him and his buddy chases after me.

The three of us run along the sidewalk in front of the store. The man with the purse opens the door to go into the store, and I continue after him with the other man right on my heels. Through the department store we go, and eventually we pass by the same jewelry case I was just at. The employee who helped me just a few minutes ago shrieks as the thief runs past her.

Our chase leads us into the heart of the busy mall. I keep reminding myself to breathe. Still skinny, although with some added muscle thanks to working out with Ron, I'm better equipped for long-distance running than ever before.

The man I'm chasing looks back at me momentarily, a look of confused panic on his face. He's probably not used to an average citizen standing up to him, putting themselves in danger. He'd rather pick on elderly women who can't defend themselves. He begins throwing down random signs in my path, and I hurdle over the first one, as well as the second. His breathing now labored, I'm able to catch up with him, lunge, and tackle him from behind. I land on top of him, and the two of us engage in a fistfight on the floor of the shopping mall. People look on, watching us punch one another repeatedly. A mother holds her young daughter's shoulders, pulling her away from the fray.

The thief's partner finally joins the skirmish, and it's two on one. I get to my feet in a boxer's stance, my fists up and at the ready. The two thieves look at one another, and the one who was pursuing me pulls out a switchblade. He takes a quick swipe at me, and I thrust my hips back away from him, narrowly escaping the blade's slice.

As my visions of John Stinson had progressed a few months ago, I was also able to mimic his fighting techniques. I'd never been in a real fistfight before these visions all started. Now, as I'm face-to-face with these two criminals, one of whom is armed, I feel myself being locked into some sort of mental zone. It's as if I'm able to predict where their attacks are coming from, and I counter the two of them simultaneously.

I jab one of the men in his nose, sending blood spouting out of his nostrils. The second man, the one with the knife, receives a kick to the side of the head, sending him down to the ground. Left jab, right hook, left jab, all to the first man. Staggering backwards, he trips over his friend, falling flat on his back. I kick the knife out of the other one's grasp. The two men appear to have surrendered as they lay on the floor in a mangled heap, gasping for breath.

Two guys from mall security finally arrive on scene, and quickly put the criminals into handcuffs. As I turn around, I notice a crowd of people has formed, several of them pointing their smartphone cameras at me. Some flashes go off. One man begins to clap, and he's quickly joined by a few of the other spectators. After a few moments, everyone is clapping, some people whistle, and others pump their fists. All their eyes are on me. Sheepishly, I wave one hand, a brief smile coming to my lips.

I quickly become embarrassed in settings like this, with more than two people looking at me at a time. With well over fifty people now staring at me and clapping, I'm in new territory here. The old woman who was assaulted and robbed makes her way through the crowd of people. She looks up at me, taking my hand in hers.

"Oh, thank you, young man!" she says. "Thank you so much! How can I ever repay you?"

"Well, I just bought an expensive necklace," I say, laughing. She nods her head and reaches over for her purse still laying on the ground. "Hey, hey, I'm just kidding, ma'am. You don't owe me anything. I just did what anyone else would've done."

"But nobody else did *anything*," she exclaims, wide eyed. "Not that I blame them, I wouldn't want anybody to have gotten hurt. But there were other people there, and you came out of nowhere to catch those guys."

I shrug my shoulders. "I'm just glad you're okay."

For the next several minutes, I sit with the old woman on a cushioned bench in the shopping mall with a water fountain at our backs. Several of the other shoppers hang around, looking over at me and whispering. Some people are still recording me on their cell phones. As much as I want to ask them to put their phones away, to go do something else with their time, I don't want to look like a jerk, especially in my first moment of fame.

I strike up conversation with the woman, whose name is Alice, and we share stories about ourselves to pass the time until paramedics arrive to tend to her. She took a nasty fall after the thief got the purse, causing her hip to bruise and her lip to bleed.

Eventually the police arrive, and I answer their questions, telling them the story exactly as it happened. Alice vouches for my version of events verbatim before they take her away on a stretcher.

News crews have also shown up, and they begin sticking their big microphones in my face. One of the reporters I recognize from TV is here, and he approaches me with his arm outstretched. I love watching this guy every night before I fall asleep. It's rare to find a news reporter, or anybody on the local news, who doesn't mumble or stumble over their words. This man knows how to talk, and he speaks so fluently and clearly that it's become an art which I've come to truly appreciate.

"Bob McCormick! Hey, I watch you all the time on TV!" I say excitedly, shaking his hand. "Wow, this is awesome! It's really nice to meet you in person."

"Yeah, sure, whatever kid. Look, we're going to record this interview real quick, we've got other things to get to," he turns his attention away from me and begins to shout. "Morty, get the tripod set up! Hurry up!"

His serious expression quickly turns into a smile. The same smile that I recognize from TV. I don't think I've ever been this close to a news person before. Or anyone famous, for that matter.

After Morty sets up the tripod, positioning the camera just so with the fountain behind us, he begins to give us a countdown with his fingers starting from three…two…one.

"Fear. Chaos. Anarchy in a public shopping center. Is anywhere safe anymore? We're standing here at Bellevue Square with a local young hero who just saved an innocent elderly female from being robbed. We'll show you the shocking cell phone footage of this young man's brave actions here in a moment, but first, please tell us your name."

Bob turns to me, holding the microphone in front of my face.

"Simon Verner."

"Now, Mr. Verner, can you please share with us what happened today? A day that's brought terror and fear into the heart of this community."

I hesitate for a moment to examine the reporter to see if he's being genuinely serious or overly dramatic. Unfortunately, it's the former. I give a detailed description of what happened, trying not to get too outlandish with the details, not wanting to allow Bob McCormick to twist my words and freak everyone out watching at home. When I'm finished, he yanks the microphone back.

"What a harrowing encounter. It begs the question: Is it worth it to take your family outside anymore? We'll weigh the risks of this tonight at ten." He pauses for a moment, staring at the camera, then flashes that signature smile. "Bob McCormick. Channel Nine News."

Tossing the microphone at Morty, Bob tells his camera crew to "wrap it up" then walks away without saying another word to me.

My breakfast has now worn off after today's workout, so I head up to the food court and eat lunch by myself.

Chapter 5

Annie Hilltop secures the pink butterfly hairclip into place near the top of her scalp, the final touch to her evening wardrobe. It's imperative to dress fashionably for tonight's event, as all the members of the Structure's Committee and their families will be there. The Committee, as they're simply called, is the leadership body of the Structure, one step below the Grand Master Himself.

Her heart begins to race, knowing there will be another man at tonight's event. A man that makes her hands quiver. With her shaky palms, she smooths out any creases and wrinkles that may be showing on her bright pink dress, not wanting there to be any imperfections showing. She yanks down the sleeves of the dress – women aren't allowed to show skin on their arms or legs when outside their living quarters – covering up the tattoo of her number on her wrist. The number, which every citizen wears, is the only real marker that someone wears to differentiate themselves from someone else. Annie's number is 506190.

"How do I look?" Annie says to the empty room as she stands in front of the mirror.

"You look marvelous," the soothing male voice from above says. "Miss Hilltop, you certainly look stunning."

She smiles softly in the mirror, turning gently from left to right, putting her index finger against her lips. "Do you think he'll notice me tonight?"

"If he doesn't, he must be blind."

A few minutes later, Annie is in the glass elevator, headed up to the 252nd floor, only one floor below the Grand Master's quarters. In order to be given access to any floor above level 200, she was given a special key from her father, Nate Hilltop, who is one of the members of The Committee. Despite her father's position of power within the Structure, Annie doesn't receive any different or special treatment. If anything, she's had to work harder than those around her to achieve her job position as a teacher. At least, that's what she frequently tells herself.

With her head bowed low, she quickly walks into the large conference room. The top fifty-three levels of the Structure don't have the large, open courtyard layout like the floors below, often referred to as the sub-two hundred. This allows for much larger living quarters for those who live in the upper levels. Level 252 is a gigantic, open room layout, which is great for large gatherings such as this one.

Besides their hairstyles, the only noticeable differences between the females and males are their clothes. The men are wearing darker colored suits and slacks, while the women are wearing brighter colored dresses with long sleeves. From there, all differences between the individuals are minimal. By law, in order for the civilians' minds to remain pure and not wander to devious thoughts, clothes are required to be loose fitting. No cleavage is permitted to be shown by a female. If there is, it can be considered grounds for Banishment or Processing. Either disciplinary action is ultimately determined by The Committee, or in some circumstances, the Grand Master.

Everyone is expected to look identical and follow these strict dress codes, per the customs and mandates put in place by the Founders of the Structure. They all fall in line with the bylaws and ROADS of their society. Annie suspects that everyone actually *likes* the similarities between them. After all, what could a person possibly not to like in someone who looks the same as them?

Except, Annie doesn't find the fact that everyone is wearing the same face in the same proportioned body to be natural. Instead, she finds it utterly repulsive. For the last couple months, her feelings of animosity toward the Structure, and those who enforce the rules of it, have multiplied. She knows that she needs to keep her thoughts on the matter to a minimum, however, in order to maintain a proper outward appearance. Annie understands that if she allows her emotions to get the better of her, the Grand Master will sense her conflicted attitude, and she'll be taken away for Processing or Banishment. The thought of that scares her more than the identical faces she sees passing in front of her at tonight's event.

"Ah, there's my lovely daughter," a familiar male voice says from behind her, gently resting his hand on her shoulder. "My pride and joy. Annie, say hello to Sharon and Thomas. I've been telling them all about your ascension into the world of education."

"Hi, Sharon," Annie says pleasantly, shaking the older woman's hand.

Annie turns her attention to Thomas, the father of the young man who she's anticipating seeing tonight, as well as Sharon's new husband. "Good evening, Thomas. Nice to see you."

Thomas' wife was Banished several years ago. Annie supposes that losing her mom helped draw her to David, as he knew all too well how painful that feeling of loss can be. Nate and Thomas formed a tight-knit friendship over the past few years as well due the situation of losing their wives.

Thomas shares the same smile as his son. Despite all the similarities, the smile is the main facial feature that generations of culling and artificial insemination haven't been able to replicate amongst everyone. Yet.

"Tell us, where are our young minds at? I trust they're in good hands with the new curriculum handed down by the Grand Master," Thomas says, taking a sip of yellow liquid.

The only yellow liquid that Annie has seen in the sub-two hundred levels has been urine, so she highly doubts that's what he's drinking. He must be drinking some form of artificially crafted liquid, one that she's not yet familiar with. She doesn't make it up into the upper levels very often to know.

"They're blossoming, and I intend to help them reach their full potential," Annie answers. "We've been learning about ROADS and their importance to the Structure."

"Very good, very good," Thomas says absently, his attention drifting elsewhere. "Our future's in good hands, Miss Hilltop." He turns his attention to Annie's father. "You raised a good young one here, Nate."

"Well, she makes her old man proud," Nate says. "I only wish her mom could've been here to see what a great young woman we raised."

Annie shifts her gaze down to the spotless, white tiled floor.

"Excuse me, may I get either of you a drink?" an android wearing a black vest and red bowtie asks.

The machine, created to assist those in the upper two hundred levels, has the most lifelike eyes that Annie's ever seen in one of these things before. The face, covered with a thin layer of silicone, tries its best to give human facial features, but the closer she looks, the easier it is to tell how this machine's creators failed in their attempt to make it look like a man. *It must be a newer model,* she tells herself. Much more advanced than the security androids they use for the sub-two hundred.

"No, thank you," Annie says politely.

"UE0353, don't you have somewhere else to be?" Sharon waves at the machine, begging it to keep moving.

"Sorry, ma'am," the android says with a hint of sadness in its voice.

The machine walks away, resuming its rounds through the busy party. For an android, its walk is very natural. More people have entered the large room since Annie's arrival, filling up the party quickly. The accumulated body temperature has caused Annie to perspire. She needs to get some air.

"These machines," Sharon says gruffly, shaking her head. "Can't live with them. Can't live without them."

"I'm going to see what else this party has to offer," Annie says, giving her father a kiss on the cheek. "Goodbye, everyone. Nice to meet you."

Sharon and Thomas say their goodbyes, and Annie walks around the party for another few minutes, searching for the man she came here to see. If he's decided not to show up this evening, she will feel like her whole night has been wasted. She could've spent the time back in her living quarters, grading her student's homework and listening to the broadcast station.

Finally, Annie spots him standing alone, looking out a large glass window. Her heartbeat quickens, and she reminds herself to breathe. After taking a moment to compose herself, Annie walks over to where he's standing, gazing out through the window, holding a glass of that yellow liquid his father was drinking.

"Hi, David," Annie says, her hands folded together across her stomach. "What brings you here this evening?"

He turns toward her, smiling, causing Annie's knees to tremble. Despite looking the same as every other man at the party, there's something about him that draws her in, just like always. Annie sees all of those special differences that make him unique. His nose, slightly smaller than average. His eyes, a bit larger than most. Like his father, he has an incredible smile that could knock Annie over with a slight breeze. However, it's not his facial features that infatuate Annie when she lays her eyes on David. It's the way he carries himself, an air of confidence that makes her want to be with him. Just being around him makes her stomach flutter.

"Same reason as you, Miss Hilltop," David says smoothly. He's always so polite. "I'm pretty sure our fathers would've been very disappointed had we not shown up."

"Yeah, you're probably right," Annie briefly smirks, resting her shoulder against the white wall.

A moment of silence passes between them. She looks out the window, trying desperately to slow her heartbeat and relax. She wants David to like her for who she is. Knowing she looks the same as every other female, she feels that she needs to provide something special to him, something to set her apart to earn his attention. All she wants is his affection. All she wants is his love.

Love? She looks down for a moment. Why would that negative word pop into her mind? Where did that even come from? It's a word that's been forbidden recently by the Structure's Committee, direct orders from the Grand Master Himself. They deemed it to be a word that only leads to anger and resentment, a word to describe an emotion that doesn't exist. An emotion that isn't real, rather something that goes against all ROADS, and in complete conflict with Perfection. *"Love breeds only the opposite of Perfection."* Words spoken recently by the Grand Master in His formal address to the Structure.

Yet when Annie looks back up at David, that slight smile spread across his lips, love is the only word that fits. The only emotion to describe what she's feeling. When she looks at him, all she sees is beauty. The feeling she gets when she's around him brings her nothing but happiness and joy. Words to describe feelings that aren't banned by the Structure. How can the Grand Master attempt to ban what she feels toward David? Sure, you can ban the word, but the feeling will never cease to exist.

She looks back out the window, into the darkened night. All that can be seen Outside are clouds this evening. On a clear night, during the few occasions she's been allowed in the upper levels, all that can be seen is a grand forest, with trees stretching out to the distant horizon. The sub-two hundred don't have windows, so Annie takes in this rare sight of the clouds while she can. She wishes to one day be Outside, away from this place. Maybe her mother is out there, still alive, living amongst the trees.

"Hey, do you want to get out of here?" David asks, almost in a whisper.

Annie looks back at David, nodding her head softly. Together, they leave the large gathering and go back to the elevators. He presses the button for floor 212.

"When did you get Promoted?" Annie asks.

"A few weeks ago," he replies. "Dad insisted I live closer to them, and I'm glad he did. It's much nicer up here."

Rather than feeling jealousy toward David, Annie instead feels a sense of pride. She's glad that he's finally been Promoted, something that he's always wanted since they first met as teenagers.

The elevator dings, and Annie follows David as he walks through the confusing twists and turns of hallways to his living quarters. It's strange to Annie not having a guardrail outside the living quarter's doors, looking out into the large courtyard. This area feels so much more…cozy. And quieter. The door clicks, and he opens it, ushering Annie in first.

His apartment is enormous compared to hers, at least four times the size. He even has a window, looking out at the dark night sky above, the rolling clouds below. As Annie approaches the window, a brief, bright flash of white appears from the cloud below, followed immediately by a loud crackling noise.

"What's that?" she whispers.

David puts his hands on her shoulders, gently sliding the silk fabric of her dress down, touching her bare skin.

"That's lightning, followed by thunder," he says, his breath tickling her ear. "I just found out about that recently, too. We could never see or hear anything from the Outside where we were living before. Could we, Annie?"

Firmly, he turns her around to face him. They lock eyes. Another flash from outside the window, and the next thing Annie knows, he's leaning in for a kiss. She returns his advance, passionately, her hands reaching for the back of his neck, tenderly caressing his skin. Her heart gallops in her chest, beating faster than ever before. She hopes it's in sync with David's. Two beats becoming one in a night of banned romance. She's began to perspire again, sweat glistening on her shoulders and chest. What they're doing is forbidden, and Annie knows that. But she's an adult woman now, not some clueless girl. This is what she wants, to feel the loving embrace of a man. She just wants to feel alive in David's embrace.

Their lips press together passionately, tenderly touching one another. She removes his shirt, tossing it down on the floor, ravaging David with intense kisses. He matches her intensity, nuzzling his face down and pecking the side of her neck, his whiskers scratching and tickling her. It feels incredible; she doesn't care if it's wrong. Let it be wrong. If this is wrong, then what's truly right?

David leads her back to his bed, where they share in what Annie can only imagine to be what love actually is. True, passionate love.

The ROADS have been broken tonight.

Chapter 6

Thankfully, I wake up before things turn too hot. A burst of energy is coursing through my body, and for the first time in my life, I immediately jump out of bed and start doing push-ups. I follow those with a round of crunches. Nothing like some fresh testosterone to wake up to in the morning, courtesy of my dream.

What's the deal with these bizarre visions? It takes me several minutes to clear my mind of last night's dream.

Ron and Jess are both at work already, leaving the apartment quiet and peaceful for me this late morning. In an effort to keep building upon my newly found culinary skillset, I've decided to make myself another breakfast; fresh grapes, some kiwi, and an omelet. I take the meal out into the living room and eat while watching TV, something that Jess has prohibited. What she doesn't know won't hurt her. Besides, I'm not typically a messy eater.

Last night after returning from the mall, I had told the two of them about my heroic adventure. Having been forced to gather around and watch the evening news, they were patient enough to sit through a few commercial breaks until they got to the part with my interview.

"Oh my God, that's you!" Jess had exclaimed, covering her mouth. "I thought you were pulling my leg!"

I turned up the volume on the TV, and they listened to an incredibly shortened version of my interview, only showing me for about five seconds. Underneath my face, as the camera showed me standing there talking, was a fancy graphic with my name. I was happy they spelled my name right. It's not every day that I guy like me gets to be on the evening news.

As I was still speaking on camera, the news station showed a couple of different angles of my altercation with the two thieves from cell phone footage captured by the other mall patrons. Forcing myself to blink a couple times, I was astounded at how effortless my combat abilities looked. I had brought my hands up to my face with the TV still playing, examining my fingers, shaking my head slowly. Even after all these months, I'm still not used to the fact that skills that I'd acquired in my past lives, whether they're from Officer John Stinson, or others before him, has become so natural to me. None of this is normal. But I suppose the abnormal has become the new normal for me now.

When we first moved to Seattle, shortly after our battle in the Palace Theater with X and her goons, I wanted to find some way to utilize these skills for good. I had asked my friends about opening up a Dojo, or maybe I could become an evening vigilante and patrol the streets at night, helping the local police catch bad guys.

My eagerness to pursue those activities was quickly silenced by my friends, as well as Loretta over a video call one night. She'd told me that William Marcini still had connections in Chicago, and she didn't want them connecting the dots that we, or more specifically, that *I* was connected to his disappearance in anyway.

"You need to keep your head down and your nose clean in your new home, child," Loretta said in the video call. "You can't be acting like a superhero. You need to be yourself. Just be a good, quiet citizen over there, and don't do *anything* to draw too much attention. At least until this whole mess back here with Marcini and his crew blows over."

I'd taken those words to heart, and assured Loretta, as well as the others, that I'd keep my newfound gifts quiet. As I was watching myself on TV last night and looking at my shaking hands, it dawned on me that I'd broken my oath to lay low. There I was, being interviewed on the evening news. That's the polar opposite of laying low. But I knew that I did the right thing. If I'd decided to just ignore poor old Alice and get into my car, driving away while she was being assaulted and robbed, I never could've forgiven myself. It's in my nature to do good, and to help protect those who are in need.

However, while watching my brief interview on the local news, instead of feeling proud or excited, a feeling of panic had begun to take over me.

I pulled out my cell phone and searched online videos, putting in various key words such as "Bellevue Square" and "Simon Verner." The first clip that pulled up, to my terror, was one of the videos that was shown on the evening news. Titled *Weird looking guy beats up thieves in Bellevue mall*, it already had over fifty thousand views, and was only posted three hours prior.

"Oh no," I said quietly.

Ron and Jess both looked over at me.

"What's wrong?" Ron asked. "Yo, this is awesome, man. You really went to work on those clowns. And that old lady was so happy that you stepped in to help her. Isn't that what you wanted?"

I showed them the online video, racking up more views and likes by the minute. They understood my concern but assured me that as long as the three of us stayed together, we wouldn't let any of Marcini's men come and find us.

"Plus, Brittany's gone, taken away by that big guy, so we don't have to worry about her," Jess said. "Thank the Lord."

Now, as I sit in the empty living room with the TV playing *The Price is Right*, I take a deep breath and look up at the ceiling. I've always been so appreciative of my friends, and I never want to take them for granted. Not after what happened in Chicago. No matter what happens, I know I have people in my corner. The more I think about that, the more it feels like the weight I'd carried to bed last night is being lifted off my shoulders.

Which leads me to my next concern. I'm having these vivid visions again. I'm not sure what to make of this creepy, futuristic society. Viewing everything through the eyes of Annie Hilltop, and having the ability to sense everything she is, as well as her thoughts and feelings, is almost exactly like what happened last time with Officer Stinson. The only difference is that at least this time, the visions are being shown in order.

I'm fairly confident that Annie is in the future, due to the technology of everything in this huge building, which they keep referring to as the "Structure." Being over 250 stories tall, this building must be the really tall. Unlike last time when John Stinson conveniently lived in the same city that I did, I'm not sure where Annie Hilltop's tower is located. I'm also not sure how far out in the future these visions are taking place, although I can speculate it's very far. Since there's no mystery for me to solve, and I haven't woken up due to being presumably shot in my dream, causing me to vomit everywhere, I suppose these dreams are quite…peaceful. Strange and twisted, yet peaceful compared to last time.

After breakfast, I drive down to work and begin another shift working in the kitchen of Mwari Sushi. Brandon, the head chef who bailed on me opening night, apparently has been given another chance by Ms. Sasaki. Rather than thanking me for covering for him opening night, he spends the first part of tonight's shift ordering me around, telling me I'm not working fast enough. He complains that my work is sloppy and amateurish, and rides me like an angry cowboy, barking out commands as if I'm some incompetent hack.

Well, be that as it may, he could still be nicer about it. Where this man has over fifteen years of cooking experience, seven of which were as a sushi chef in various restaurants on the west coast, this is only my second day on the job.

"Speed it up, Verner," he growls, intentionally shoulder-ramming me in the kitchen. "You're several orders behind. Pick it up, or I'll throw you out of here myself."

It becomes more apparent to me now why he's bounced around so many different restaurants. As tempting as it is to confront the man, knowing that I could easily handle him in a fistfight if it came to that, I choose to keep my mouth shut. Who am I do debate with this man, who is my elder in this particular field of skill? Had the roles been reversed, and he wasn't picking up golf balls quick enough, I would've taken it upon myself to coach Brandon up, to show him ways to speed up and be more efficient. I would've been much more cordial when doing so, however, and not act like a condescending jackass. But to each their own.

"Verner, you doofus, pick it up!" Brandon yells in my ear as I'm working diligently on a plate. "Your sushi- what is this? Seriously, what the hell is this?"

He pushes me aside, picks up the plate I'm working on, and throws it against the far wall, causing the glass to shatter into several pieces. The sushi rolls stick against the wall momentarily before sliding down, plopping harmlessly to the floor.

Clenching my fists, I close my eyes, reminding myself to breathe. Angela told me that in times of stress and anxiety, the best thing to do is breathe. It's not worth it to draw attention to myself. As satisfying as it would be to hit Brandon, this burned out looking Chucky doll of an alcoholic, it's not worth it. I do, however, find it necessary to set boundaries. My father had told me once, a couple years before he passed away, that when confronted by a bully, it's appropriate to stand up for yourself and set boundaries. This lets the other person know that you're not okay with their behavior, and it needs to stop. *Thanks, Dad.*

"Listen Gordon Ramsey, why don't you take it down a few notches, alright?" I say calmly, albeit sounding a little annoyed. "It's my second day on the job. I'm doing the best I can."

He steps toward me, shoving his face directly in front of mine. The two of us are nearly identical height, yet I don't back down.

"Got something to say, Verner?"

"Look, we can settle our differences after work if that's what you want," I say, keeping eye contact. "But for right now, how about you stay on one side of the kitchen, I'll stay on the other, and we just do our jobs. Deal?"

He starts laughing, the strong stench of peppermint gum plowing into my nostrils.

"No deal," he says, now looking more furious. "I don't even know why that crazy old lady hired you. Why did you even apply for a job without any prior experience?"

"Well, for one, the job didn't say anything about needing prior experience. How do you expect someone to gain job experience if they have to already have had experience to get the job? And second of all, I don't appreciate the way you just referred to Ms. Sasaki. Show her some respect."

"Yeah? Or what?" Brandon asks mockingly, chewing his gum. "You gonna tell on me?"

"No, man. Look, I don't care if you don't like me. Can we just get back to work? We're wasting time."

"You know what I think? I think you're gross and ugly. I think you're terrible at this job, and *Ms. Sasaki* would be better off without you working here. I'm the head chef, not you. Things ran smoother last night without you here."

The way he made sure to add emphasis to her name in a condescending tone almost causes me to lose my temper. Almost.

Ms. Sasaki comes into the kitchen, planting her cane down on the floor.

"What's going on back here?" she asks, her voice near a shrill tone.

Neither one of us move, holding our ground, staring intently at one another.

"Answer me!" she shouts.

"Nothing, ma'am," Brandon answers, still refusing to look at her. "Simon and I were just having a little…talk. I was telling him how I want my kitchen ran."

"Is this true, Simon?" she asks after a moment of silence.

"Yes, ma'am. Brandon was giving me some more detailed instruction."

"Hmm," she says. "If you two say so. Well, Simon, we do need you to shift your duties tonight. One of the waitresses had to leave early, leaving us shorthanded. Would you mind running food out to the tables for the rest of the night?"

"Yes, ma'am," I say, turning my attention to her. "I'll get started right away."

"Good," she says flatly before turning on her heel to leave.

"Yeah," Brandon says. "Good."

I turn back around and take a step toward the prep area, intending to start loading up a tray with some plates, but am blocked by Brandon, who intentionally sidesteps in my way.

"This isn't over," he says.

"Good. Whatever."

I load up a tray of sushi plates and bring them out onto the restaurant floor. With no prior experience or training when it comes to waiting on tables, I carry the large round tray awkwardly in front of me, my arms extended far out, making sure to keep the tray as balanced as possible to prevent the plates from sliding around.

The first two plates are for the first table where an elderly couple sits. I smile at them, and they look excited when I slide the food in front of them.

"I made that one," I say, pointing at one of the California rolls. "Let me know what you think."

The older woman arches an eyebrow up to her partner, and they both chuckle. The remaining plates I take to a customer sitting by himself in the back corner booth. He's a younger Asian man, roughly my age, maybe a little older by the looks of him. His dark black hair is gelled up in the front, like the way Ron does his hair, and he's wearing a gray sweater vest, giving off vibes that he's rich, or at least richer than the average person in the restaurant. His attention is focused on a laptop computer in front of him.

My past experience with rich people generally consisted of them intentionally whacking golf balls against the side of my range picker. They also looked down on me during my yearlong stint of being homeless after I'd turned eighteen. It felt like they were always sticking their noses up at me, ungrateful for the lives that they'd been handed while I had to scratch and claw for everything I had.

This young man in the corner booth seems confident, but not full of himself, and he gives me a warm smile as I gently place the two plates of sushi on the table. Folding the laptop, he quickly tucks it into a backpack next to him and begins to roll up his sleeves.

"Is there anything else I can get for you?" I ask.

He takes a moment to analyze all of the items in front of him before answering. "No, thank you. I believe I have everything I need."

"Enjoy your meal," I say cheerfully, tucking the now empty tray under my arm and turning around back toward the kitchen.

"Actually, there is one thing," he says. "Please, sit down for a moment. I could use some company."

I turn back around to face him. "Look, I wish I could, but I really need to get back to work."

He waives his hand dismissively, opening the complimentary package of chopsticks. "Don't worry about it. My mom's the owner. She'll understand."

"You're…Ms. Sasaki's son?" I ask.

"Yep, that's me," he says, smiling. "Please, call me Kanzen."

"Nice to meet you, Kanzen," I say, placing the tray on the empty table next to him. I sit down on the edge of the corner booth, looking around the restaurant, expecting Ms. Sasaki to come out of nowhere and smack me with her cane for sitting on the job. "So, your mom makes you pay for your meals?"

"Oh, yeah," he says after taking his first bite, chewing the food thoughtfully for a brief moment and swallowing. "I don't mind. She can use the business. Her restaurants never seem to last that long, anyway."

I look down at the table, folding my hands in my lap.

"Hey, nothing to be afraid of though. She'll keep this place open for at least a couple years. You'll be fine."

"Well, to be honest with you, I'm not sure how much longer I'm going to be working here. The chef back there seems to have it out for me for some reason. I guess I'm just not picking up things as fast as he'd like."

"Brandon's a douchebag. I can't believe Mom hired him again. She fired him a few years ago from another restaurant. Don't let that guy get to you. Just a matter of time before he winds up back in King County Correctional, if you ask me."

I chuckle, shaking my head. "My name's Simon, by the way." He doesn't answer, focusing on eating the sushi. "Say, what were you playing on your laptop? Any good games?"

After he finishes chewing, he looks at me with a smirk. "No, I was working."

I sit patiently, waiting for him to finish his thought. Instead, he doesn't elaborate on what he was working on, and resumes eating his meal. I'm not sure if my presence here is annoying or comforting to him, so I figure I should just keep talking to him. He is the boss' son, after all.

"What were you working on?"

"The next great breakthrough for mankind," he says casually, wiping his mouth with a cloth napkin. "You know what they say, every big tech startup that's ever come out of Seattle started in a Bellevue garage. And that's exactly what I've done. I bought a house in Bellevue, and I'm working on some cutting-edge technology, straight out of my garage."

"What kind of technology?"

Kanzen keeps his attention down, his arms resting on the tablecloth. Slowly, he begins to nod his head as if he's having an intense internal debate. Suddenly, he quickly turns his whole body toward me and leans forward. "I'm working on the next stage of human evolution, Simon. I mean, we're talking big picture here." He lowers his voice, looking around the mostly empty restaurant before turning his attention back to me. "I believe our future is in trouble. When you drive around this city, what do you see?"

"Well, it rains a lot. So, I see water, I suppose."

"Not that," he says, waving his hand dismissively. "When I drive around this town, I see a lot of homeless people. Graffiti along the sides of buildings, houses and bridges. I see people who are addicted to drugs, constantly being given handouts, not given the tools or motivation to pick themselves up by their bootstraps and get back to work. It's not all their fault, not really. They just lack discipline. The housing prices, and the overall cost of living, are astronomical around here. But for every man down on his luck, there's another who turned toward crime to try and get a leg up. They have no respect. The police arrest them, the damn judges let them back out. There's no accountability."

He takes a deep breath before continuing on. "We have political leaders around here that say one thing, then do another. There's no structure to the way they lead the people, the voters, the taxpayers, who pay their salaries. What do you think of politics?"

"Well, honestly, I've learned it's best to just keep my mouth shut when it comes to that. It doesn't matter what you say, you're bound to piss someone off."

"Good point," he says. "I hope I haven't offended. But do you understand what I'm saying? I just want things to get better. I just wish things could be perfect, you know? For everyone."

"Look, this is a really nice area over here. Quite a bit nicer than where I was living last. The way I see it, people in our society always want to find something to complain about. We have all these personal possessions, more material goods than we know what to do with, yet we let little things upset us so easily," I take a deep breath and press on. "The weather, the price of eggs, our car not starting. I could go on and on. *First World problems.* People don't know how good they really have it here. If something really serious were to happen, I shudder to think what the result would be. People would lose their minds." I sigh, shaking my head. "If their coffee isn't made just right, they flip out. Could you imagine if some country dropped an EMP on us? It would be anarchy. These people wouldn't know what to do."

"Now you're speaking my language," Kanzen says with satisfaction. "And that's what my tech company wants to fix. Ultimately, I want everyone to live in a perfect society, where there's no threat of an EMP being dropped on us. Yet, at the same time, where people are thankful for everything they're given."

Flashbacks of my last couple dreams of Annie Hilltop creep back to mind. Perfect society. ROADS. The Structure…could this be the beginning of all that? Is this Kanzen guy connected to my future life?

"Would you say you want everyone to be…how should I put this… obedient?" I ask seriously.

He looks down at the table for a moment, sighing. "No," he says finally, looking back up at me. "No, I want people to have free will. An obligation to be obedient isn't something that I want people to have to live with. That simply strikes fear and panic into their hearts. Into their soul, you know?" He points at his chest. "Without free will, people will ultimately want to rebel, and tear apart the system put in place. They would want to defy the structure of society."

Whether his tech company is responsible for what I'm seeing in my new series of visions, or if this is just a bizarre and uncanny coincidence, I'm not quite sure. What I am sure of, however, is that I need to keep my eyes on Kanzen Sasaki. Keep your friends close…

"Simon?" he asks. "Sorry, did I lose you there?"

I look up at him, unaware that I had drifted off into my own thoughts so deeply. "What's that? Sorry, Kanzen, it's been a long night. Could you repeat that?"

"I asked if you would be interested in coming over to a party I'm throwing this weekend? Feel free to bring whoever you'd like. Give me your number and I'll text you the address. My mom's spoken so highly about you. I'm glad we got to meet."

Kanzen and I share cell phone numbers, and I quickly receive a text from him with his address in Bellevue. I thank him for the invitation and agree to come over on Saturday.

Leaving him to finish eating in peace, I grab the tray and head back into the kitchen. I wonder where my relationship with Kanzen will lead me. The more I think about it, the more I believe that fortune cookie wasn't all in my mind after all.

Chapter 7

The bright artificial lights activate in synchronization with soft piano music.

"Good morning, Annie," the soothing male voice says from the ceiling above. "You are going to have a good day today. Remember the ROADS. We all live for the Structure. Did you know that –"

"Turn off," Annie groans into her pillow.

A few minutes later, she's awake and in the bathroom, prepping herself for another day of teaching the young minds. This morning, however, a new sensation has taken over her body. She's feeling queasy and clutches her stomach. Lurching her head into the toilet, she vomits, emptying her stomach of last night's nutritional pill.

Unsure of what has upset her stomach so much, she shakes her head. Was there something wrong with the nutritional pill? After class, she'll talk to her doctor and see what she recommends. This is the second time she's thrown up this week, something completely out of the ordinary for her.

Walking down the hallway outside of her living quarters, she feels much better. Drinking some extra water this morning, going slightly over her allotted water ration, has helped put an extra pep in her step. She smiles as she walks along the clean walkway with the large, open courtyard to her left.

"No, let go of me!" a woman screams up ahead.

Annie forces her way through the small crowd that's gathered. Two powerful security androids have control of both the woman's arms, giving her commands to sit still and cooperate. She refuses. Each of the man-sized security androids have weapons, referred to as "laser rifles" strapped to their backs. When fired, the guns shoot a bright red laser beam, destroying and killing anything that has the misfortune of getting in its path. Laser rifles are instrumental to keeping law and order in the Structure. *Ways to keep the civilians scared and at the mercy of the Grand Master*, Annie tells herself.

Thrashing about violently on the white tiled floor, the woman under arrest kicks one of the androids in the groin. Her attack on the large robot proves to be meaningless, and it returns the favor by grabbing her ankle roughly. The woman continues screaming, clawing at the floor as the android tightens its grip around her ankle. One clean twist of its wrist, and her bone could easily snap. Thankfully, to the relief of Annie as well as the woman on the ground, the android doesn't break bone. Instead, it roughly tosses her leg aside, and together the two machines lift her up, forcing her arms behind her back, placing her wrists in restraints.

"I didn't do it!" she continues to scream as they lead her to the elevator. "Please, you have to listen to me! I didn't mean what I said! Please! I love the Structure! I love the Structure! I abide by the ROADS! No!"

With an effortless display of strength, the two androids guide her into the see-through glass elevator, and the door shuts, sending the elevator up the tube. Up to where, however, Annie can only imagine. Her best guess is that the woman will be taken to speak with The Committee to attempt to defend what she said. From what Annie's father has told her, if a citizen is found to be guilty of saying negative things about the Structure or the ROADS, they're either referred to Processing, or Banishment to the Outside. Whatever punishment the Grand Master ultimately chooses.

Annie shudders, wrapping her arms around herself.

Later that afternoon after school, she goes to see her doctor.

"I just don't understand it," Annie says. "I haven't changed anything with my diet. I took my nutritional pill within the recommended time period. What do you think?"

"Can you slide back and lay your head down for me?" the female doctor asks.

Annie complies with the instructions, laying on her back on the elevated examination table.

"How's your dad?" the doctor asks sincerely.

"He's good. I was invited up to one of their special Committee parties about three weeks ago. David was there, too. We…had a fun time."

Annie quickly catches herself before she tells the doctor what happened that night with David.

"Yelena, please forget I just said that."

"Said what?" Yelena says innocently, a brief smirk spread across her face. "There, just rest easy, I'm almost done here."

"You've known for a few years how I've felt about David. I just…I know I need to keep my mouth shut."

"Don't worry. Your secret's safe with me. Now, sit still. This is going to feel like a poke."

Annie winces as she feels a sharp jab in her arm, then the pain quickly fades away. Yelena rolls her chair back toward a countertop with a small machine on it and instructs Annie that she can sit up now.

A few moments pass, and Yelena lets out a heavy sigh. She's holding a small Holoreader up, reading what it says. The blue glow of the device reflects off her face as she swivels around in the chair, now facing Annie. Yelena shuts off the Holoreader, placing it back on the counter and stands up.

"Well, I think I know how that story was going to end with David," Yelena says softly, not making eye contact.

"Why? What is it? Is something wrong?"

"Annie, you're pregnant."

"I…no," Annie says, taking a deep breath. Tears begin to well up in her eyes. "No, that can't be possible. I've been taking those pills like you've said. I…"

"Those pills are only a placebo for women's peace of mind," Yelena says. "Truth is, we haven't had birth control in the Structure for…heck, decades now. Some sort of a supply issue on the Outside. Women aren't supposed to get pregnant without a license or engage in pre-marital sex. If we do, it's grounds for discipline. We both know the consequences." She shakes her head, putting her hands on her hips. "It's not fair, though. What repercussions are there for the men? We're the ones who have to carry the burden and shame around. We're expected to be perfect little angels, but the moment one of us messes up, she gets banished to the Outside or sent to Processing."

Annie begins to cry, weeping uncontrollably into her hands as Yelena rests a hand on Annie's shoulder, attempting to comfort her.

"Please, you can't tell anybody," Annie says between sobs. "You have to promise me. I'm going to protect this baby with everything I've got, but I can't do that if I'm Banished to the Outside like Mom was. I can't do it."

"I know you will," Yelena says, holding Annie's head in her hands. "I know you'd do anything for this child. And I don't want to see you punished. But you can't keep this a secret forever. Eventually, you'll start to show. Someone will tell The Committee, and you'll have to answer to them, or in your case, to the Grand Master."

"In my case?"

"With your father's political position, it may be seen as a conflict of interest. And after your mom…"

"I'll take care of it," Annie says sternly, her palms pressed down on the examination table. She wipes her nose with the back of her hand. "I'll take care of this. But please, promise me Yelena, promise me you won't tell anyone until I have a chance to figure this out."

Yelena sighs, then stands up. "I promise I won't tell anybody."

Annie walks back to her living quarters with her arms crossed and her eyes constantly filling with tears. Other citizens pass by with their copied faces smiling at her. She doesn't smile back.

Once inside her living quarters, she goes into her bedroom, dimming all the lights. Panic strikes her hard, sending her into uncontrollable fits of sobbing and shaking. She screams to the ceiling and the walls, cursing herself for being so stupid. She knew the risks. She knew the consequences, but she didn't care. Being with David that night was the most incredible experience of her sheltered life. For the first time, she felt *alive*. She's always felt like an outcast in her home. Now, she begins to accept the realization that she soon will be.

Annie goes over to her dresser and opens the top drawer, pulling out a small music box. She flips open the lid and a familiar song begins to play; her mom had told her the name of the song, but she can't remember it anymore. Apparently, this is a relic from the Outside. Definitely a banned item, but so far nobody has come to kick her door down and take it. A tiny plastic woman with pale-looking skin wearing a short dress slowly rotates around on one foot. An inscription on the bottom of the lid has a message that her mom had written for her the same day she was taken away to be Banished. Annie reads the note, her hands softly trembling.

To my precious Annie. May you always find peace in a world so often filled with hate. Let <u>love</u> take your heart. Share your care and courage with the world. You'll always be the best daughter I could've asked for. I'm sorry I couldn't be perfect. We never know what tomorrow will bring. Make today count.

Love, Mom

Chapter 8

"Hey, Mom," I say. "Sorry it's been a while since I've called. How're you doing?"

"I'm great, sweetheart. It's nice to hear your voice."

I try to call my mom at least twice a week, three times if I remember. Unfortunately, I've totally spaced-out calling her for the last several days. This morning seemed like the best time to call her, as she usually spends her afternoons knitting for her nieces and nephews who live in frigid Minnesota.

"How's that guy you've been dating? Dale, right?"

"Yes, Dale's a good man," Mom says. "I think you'd really like him. He's a retired carpenter, so he's been taking care of some of some things around here that Doug wouldn't do."

I decide to change the subject, asking how the weather back home is. We talk for another five minutes before she lets out a loud gasp.

"What is it, Mom?"

"My friend Beverly, remember her? She came over and got me logged onto the computer in your old room. Anyways, she showed me that video of you beating up those two losers in the mall. That was you, wasn't it?"

"Yeah, that was me," I say, sighing. "I was hoping you wouldn't see that."

"What? Are you kidding me? My baby kicked some serious butt. I'm so proud of you. It's nice to know that you're out there watching out for us old ladies. She even showed me where you got interviewed by that handsome guy on your local news over there. Why didn't you smile? The least you could do is smile for the camera when you're finally on TV."

"You're right, Mom," I chuckle. "I was just shocked about everything that had just happened. You know, almost getting shanked and all."

"What?" she yells in my ear, forcing me to hold the phone back. "I'll come out there myself and beat them up again!"

The thought of my mom repeatedly punching those thugs sends me into a fit of laughter.

"Have you heard anything about Doug?" I ask.

"No, his trial date keeps getting pushed back."

"That's predictable."

"They're still looking for that mob boss, Marcini," Mom says. "And the police can't figure out why some guy named Travis Daniels was left impaled on a parking lot lamp post at the same apartment building where Marcini was last seen. They think it was a murder-suicide. They're saying that Travis Daniels wanted to take control over the gang and dumped Marcini's body in the lake, then he jumped off the balcony in guilt. At least, that's what some of the police think is what happened. Isn't that crazy?"

"It's insane is what it is."

A few minutes later, I'm dressed and ready to go back to the mall for some more Christmas shopping fun with Jess and Ron. When I enter the living room, however, the two of them are sitting quietly on the couch with the TV muted.

"What's wrong?" I ask uncertainly.

Jess looks up at me, her eyes glossed over with tears. "It's my dad. He just contacted me out of the blue. He says he's in town and wants to see me."

The news hits me like a ton of bricks. Jess' dad hasn't been involved in her life for years. Heck, I thought he was dead.

"What did you say to him?" I ask, sitting down in the recliner.

"I told him I'll need to think about it. He walked out on Mom and me when I was thirteen. He didn't call, didn't write, nothing. Why? Why now, all of a sudden, does he want to see me? It's been almost eleven years since he left. He didn't even show up to Mom's funeral."

Jess' mother had passed away about eighteen months ago. She was very close with her mom, and losing her was devastating to Jess, as it would be for most people. With her dad not around, there was no adult figure in Jess' life anymore. She relied heavily on Ron and me during that time, and together we helped her grieve and cope with that tremendous loss.

Ron continues to sit quietly next to Jess on the couch, his eyes downcast. Usually, he would make some untimely remark during a serious moment like this, but it seems like he's learned better over the years. Staying quiet right now is the right move for Ron. I'm proud of his personal growth.

My father passed away from lung cancer when I was a kid, so I know the pain of losing a parent. Having a parent walk out on me, then suddenly wanting to reunite after over a decade, would be something that would take a lot of time to process. So, I too choose to be quiet, not wanting to say something stupid to upset Jess more. Women typically just want men to listen, not dish out unwarranted advice. Or so I've read somewhere.

After a few moments, she slaps her hands on her thighs and stands up. "Well, let's go shopping."

Jess and Ron had previously requested today off work so we could hang out. Christmas shopping at the mall was an activity the three of us had loved doing back home. Since this will be our first Christmas away from home, it makes this year's holiday season that much more special for us.

I drive the three of us down to Bellevue Square. Making sure to park on the other side of the mall from where the incident went down, I take extra precaution to watch our backs and hustle the two of them through the parking lot and into the entrance. Criminals have been known to return to the scene of the crime, and I'm not sure if those thugs are still behind bars or not. I kick myself for not checking the King County inmate roster before going out today. *What a rookie mistake, Stinson.*

The thought of John Stinson stops me suddenly in my tracks, causing my friends to turn around and look at me. Even after all these months, I still sometimes confuse myself as the former police officer who was murdered in 1986. His memories will sporadically come pouring into my mind, such as at this moment.

The three of us are standing in a department store which looks very similar to one where John had taken his wife, Samantha, several times when they were married. The floor tiles look nearly identical, the clothing racks are probably from the '80s or before, and the glass perfume counter looks the same. Most prominently, however, is the bundle of red balloons with the word "sale" written on them in white lettering. The feeling of déjà vu takes over, as I suddenly feel like I'm back in John's body, shopping with Samantha when she was pregnant.

"Simon, what's going on, bud?" Ron asks, genuinely concerned. "Was it too soon to come back here? We can go somewhere else."

I blink my eyes, shake my head, and assure them that it was nothing, that it just feels like I've been in here before.

"Yeah, I bet it does," Ron says. "This is a fairly common department store, assuming they stay in business for much longer."

The three of us walk through the store, periodically stopping as something catches Jess' eyes and she has to pull over and browse through the entire clothing rack each time. Ron and I share a look, knowing not to say anything or rush her, as she probably has a lot on her mind right now.

Eventually, we make our way out of the store and into the heart of the mall. We pass by the water fountain and the spot where I fought with the two thieves, but I don't point it out. We just keep on walking.

"Hey, there's no line!" Ron exclaims, pointing.

Directly in front of us is the mall Santa, complete with his red suit and long, white beard. He's sitting on a plush throne with a red seat and golden handles. Behind him is an enormous, decorated Christmas tree that reaches up to the tall ceiling of the mall.

"Really, Ron?" I ask. "Aren't you a little old to be sitting on that guy's lap?"

"Never!" he says valiantly with one finger pointed up to the ceiling, now walking faster, leaving Jess and me in the dust.

Ron begins talking with the young girl working at the front counter, waving us over frantically.

"Bless his heart," Jess says with a hint of sarcasm. "I hope he knows that's not the real Santa."

"Who are we to dash his spirit?"

We follow Ron through the gates, under which a sign reads *North Pole* and before I know it, we're standing next to Santa Claus and his oversized chair.

"Ho ho ho!" He shouts, beard shaking, turning his attention to Ron. "What do you want for Christmas, young man?"

Ron puts his finger up to his lips, the question sending him deep into the realm of thought. "Well, I would love a new gaming PC, Santa. Some of my buddies I work with say that's the only way to game. Can you hit me up with that?"

The mall Santa looks quizzically up at Jess and me. We both shrug our shoulders.

"Well, if you've been a good boy, I'll see what I can do," Santa says quickly, now turning his attention to me. "And how about you, young man?"

"Whatever happened to ladies first?" Jess whines, crossing her arms.

"Hey, wait your turn, or Santa will bring you a lump of coal," I say to Jess, elbowing her playfully. "Me, well, what do I want? Oh, right, I want my co-worker Brandon to slip on a patch of ice and lose his memory, as well as all of his motor skills."

Ron, Jess, Santa, and someone dressed as an elf stare blankly at me. I put my hands in my pockets and step back, giving the stage to Jess.

"I would like to see my dad again," Jess says to Santa.

"That's a very sweet wish," Santa says in his deep voice. "I hope we can make that happen for you, young lady."

I wish I could take my wish back, because that's exactly what I want too. Nothing would make me happier than to see my old man again, smiling at me in front of Wrigley Field, ready to cheer on his Chicago Cubs. But I know that's not possible. For Jess, it is, and I'm truly happy for her. I'm glad she's chosen to take advantage of this second chance.

"Hey, can we get a picture?" Ron asks.

The three of us squeeze tightly together next to the mall Santa, with Jess and me on one side, and Ron on the other. We all smile and look at the camera as it gives off a bright flash.

I STAND OUTSIDE the arcade, checking my phone periodically. The plan is still to go to Kanzen's house party this weekend, but he'd texted me yesterday asking if I wanted to hang out today. We agreed to meet up tonight at six, but it's already 5:59 and there's no sign of him. He wouldn't stand me up at the arcade, would he?

"Simon!" Kanzen calls, walking briskly down the sidewalk.

"Hey, there you are," I say, reaching my hand out to accept his handshake. "You're...dang, you're right on time, man."

He shrugs his shoulders, returning his hands to his pockets. "That's how I operate. Let's go inside, shall we?"

Dozens of flashing lights and sounds greet us instantly as we walk through the door. This isn't a standard arcade. It's some sort of a large chain that has arcade games and a restaurant, but for adults only. Sure, the experience brings out our inner child, or my inner child at least, but there's no screaming kids here to bug the heck out of me. Just a bunch of adults having a good time.

Kanzen slaps me on the back and points at one of the machines. "Hey, check it out!"

I walk over to a game that I haven't seen in ages. Actually, I don't remember the last time I've even been to an arcade, so all of this is a bit nostalgic to me. "Robo Warrior 3000? No way!"

"Yes, way," he says, smiling.

It's a two-player game, with the objective to kill as many robots and monsters within the allotted time as possible. We take our positions, holding a futuristic plastic gun in our hands. The weapon looks eerily similar to the laser rifles that those androids were carrying in my dreams.

Kanzen's nice enough to insert some tokens into the game, and the two of us begin our quest to eliminate as many enemies as possible. I aim down the sights of the plastic weapon, pulling the trigger and taking out the robots on screen with ease. Within an instant, I'm in the zone, holding the weapon in my hands like it's second nature, picking off monsters and robots with effortless precision. Kanzen, on the other hand, struggles at first, but picks it up toward the end.

"Dang, you're good!" Kanzen says, placing the weapon down once the game's over.

"I've had some practice," I say nonchalantly.

After about a half hour of playing all sorts of games from air hockey to some dancing game, the two of us take a break to grab some dinner. We walk into the restaurant area of the establishment, and a gorgeous young hostess shows us to our spot. Kanzen elbows me, pointing at the girl's rear in a tight pair of jeans. He raises his eyebrows, to which I just shake my head, smiling.

We take our seats, and the hostess hands us our menus. She brings us some glasses of water with ice and informs us that our server, some name that she said too quickly for me to catch, will be over 'when they can' to take our order. As she walks away, Kanzen continues to check her out the entire time, leaning to the side in his booth to soak in the view for as long as possible. Sheesh, this guy needs to keep it together. I'm glad we didn't agree to meet up at a strip club or something.

"So, how long have you lived in Seattle?" Kanzen asks, examining the menu.

"A little over five months," I answer.

"You said you're from…Chicago? That right?"

"Right."

"What made you decide to move all the way out here?"

I take a sip of my water, licking my lips. Man, I was thirsty. "Well, my friends and I just sort of had enough of Chicago. We couldn't find good work, and one day we just decided to sell some stuff, pack up a few things and hit the road."

"Nice," he says, nodding his head. "I suppose I did something similar not too long ago. My family and I grew up in San Francisco, and I just wanted to get out. Stretch my legs, you know? So, I went over to Tokyo for school, got my degree over there and just moved to Seattle about two months ago."

"What did you get your degree in?"

"Computer science," he answers. "Graduated top of my class. Originally, I wanted to get into cyber security, but the more I got into computers, the more I realized I *really* know my way around them. So, while in school I started up a little tech company on the side making RFID tags for local retail outlets to help them track their inventory. I charged a fraction of what the other big-name players were charging, so I took the majority of their business, built myself up a nice nest egg, and here I am."

"Right on," I say. "What's the name of your company?"

"Not sure yet. In Tokyo I went with *Sasaki United*, but I'm planning to modify that a bit."

The waitress, another pretty young woman and a name that I still couldn't catch after she said it herself, stops by to take our order. Kanzen checks her out when she leaves as well, shaking his head softly.

"Damn dude, why don't you just ask one of them out?" I ask.

He shakes his head more aggressively. "No, no. I'm waiting for *the* special woman to come along."

"What's wrong with these girls?"

"Nothing," he shrugs his shoulders. "I don't know. For me, love needs to like…hit me. Just, *bam*! Knock me off my feet when I first see her, you know? I'm sure these are nice girls, but it probably wouldn't go anywhere. I need some depth. I need some…something."

"But you don't even know them. I doubt you can even remember what the hostess or waitress' names were."

"I have an ability to sense people," he says softly. "Like I can read their aura, or something."

"Well, I must have a good aura then."

"You do, Simon," he says seriously, leaning forward. "Like I told you the other day, my mom speaks highly of you. Says you're hard-working and very eager to learn. Something very rare nowadays for folks our age."

"My friends, the ones that came with me from Chicago, they're hard-working too," I say. "I think that this stereotype that the younger generation doesn't want to work is a bunch of crap. If we could work minimum wage jobs and buy houses like the Boomer generation, there'd be a lot more happier, motivated young people. Instead, we're all stuck in apartments while the old people live in their houses, buying up all the land."

He laughs. "I own a house. It's not just the age of the person that determines if you can own a home. But I get what you're saying. Inflation makes it impossible for most people to afford one, or any sort of luxurious lifestyle."

"Speaking of luxurious lifestyle," I say, changing the topic. "You seem like a high-class dude. What're you doing in a place like this?"

"I figured we'd enjoy it. I like it here. Reminds me of simpler days, when there was less responsibility and more fun."

The two of us enjoy a nice dinner together, then go back to the arcade area, playing until late in the night. I can proudly say that I've made a new friend in my new city.

Chapter 9

Annie peers cautiously over the guardrail into the open courtyard, looking down at the dozens of floors below. Recently, the bottom twenty levels of the Structure had been sealed off, per direct orders from the Grand Master Himself. Rumors swirled among the citizens for weeks, speculating that they've opened the doors to those living on the Outside. Others said it was for increased space for Processing. Whatever the case may be, all rumors were quickly silenced due to an official warning issued by The Committee. They deemed these to be negative thoughts, making the individuals voicing them subject to Processing or Banishment.

For a brief instant, an urge flashes through her mind to climb over the guardrail and jump. Quickly extinguishing the cruel thought, she stops gawking over the guardrail before she draws unnecessary attention to herself and keeps walking toward the elevators. She shakes her head, upset with herself for the brief moment of weakness, of wanting to end her life, as well as the life growing inside her.

The fear of her imminent punishment has debilitated her to the core with a range of emotions, from fear, to guilt, to helplessness. Why should she be the one to carry the burden of one night of unchecked passion, while David continues to live his life, none the wiser to the life they've illegally created? Why should she be the one whom the rest of the Structure will stick their noses up at, treating her like she's inferior to them because she acted on an emotion that's frowned upon in accordance with the rules created by the Founders?

Annie crosses her arms over her chest, making sure that her loose-fitting shirt doesn't reveal too much and raise suspicion. She needs to buy as much time as she can before she's found out. She will see this baby brought to full term as long as her secret *remains* a secret.

After class, she heads up to David's floor, utilizing the pass that her father gave to her. *It does benefit to have family in higher places after all,* she tells herself. She walks through the closed in hallways, complete with red carpeting and decorative red wallpaper, making her way through the maze of corridors until she finally reaches David's apartment.

He opens the door shortly after she knocks. Instead of a warm smile, he greets her with a confused furrow of his eyebrows, and steps out into the hallway, quietly shutting the door behind him.

"Annie? What –"

"There's something I need to tell you. Can I come in?"

"It's not really a good time. Can this wait?"

"No," she says firmly. "This can't wait. David, you need to know something."

The door opens behind him, and another woman peeks her head out from inside. She notices Annie, and opens the door all the way, revealing that she's only wearing a large T-shirt, her legs fully exposed. Annie gasps at the woman's naked legs, something completely foreign and risqué among the Structure's societal rules.

"Who do we have here?" the other woman says with a haughty attitude, crossing her arms, keeping her focus directly on Annie.

"I'll come back later," Annie says dejectedly.

"Don't bother," the other woman says. "He's all yours." She turns her attention to David. "You're unbelievable."

She walks down the hallway, shaking her hips from side to side, dragging her index finger gently along the wall.

Sighing, David steps aside, allowing Annie to enter his living quarters. She shuffles past him, turning around in front of the window. It's daylight outside, something that Annie's only seen a few times in her life. Resisting the urge to stare out the window, she waits for David to give her his full attention.

"Alright," he crosses his arms. "Talk."

"I'm pregnant. And you're the father."

David stands motionless, unblinking, a look of freight on his face as if he's just seen a ghost. He places his hands behind his head, puffs out his cheeks, and lets out a deep breath. "How?"

"What do you mean *how*?" Annie asks furiously. "What kind of a stupid question is that? You know exactly *how*. We need to figure out what to do now."

"*We?*" he seethes. "There's no *we* here. This is your problem, not mine."

"Wow. Really? Just like that? You're not going to bear any sort of responsibility for this situation at all? I have our baby growing inside me, and you're not going to help?"

He steps toward her, raising his voice. "You show up at my door unexpectedly and drop this at my feet. W-What am I supposed to do?"

"You're supposed to take some accountability. You're supposed to man up and accept your share of this."

He places his hands on her shoulders. "There's no 'us' in this situation. If The Committee finds out that I had relations with a sub-two hundred, they'll strip me of my status. They'll send me back down."

"Big deal! If they find out I'm pregnant without a license, and without being married, I'll be Banished! And who knows what they'll do with the baby? What do they do with babies who are born illegitimately? Does your precious 'rank' grant you access to that answer?"

"Listen to me, and listen carefully," David says, lowering his voice. "You need to keep this a secret. You *will* keep this a secret. For both our sakes."

"Why else do you think I came up here? I need your help. I want to see this baby born. I'll do it, with or without your help. I'm going to raise this child. But it'll be a lot easier with your help."

"No," David says bluntly, not even giving it a moment's thought. "You need to get rid of it. If that thing's born, it's the end for both of us. You need to abort it."

"You son of a bitch!" Annie screams, shrugging her shoulders free of David's grasp. "I will *not* have this child aborted! Do you understand me? There'll be no discussion about it."

"Then you leave me no choice," David says. "I must tell The Committee. I have to tell the Grand Master what we've done. I can't bear the shame and guilt. It'll eat me alive. Maybe, just maybe, they'll make an exception and let you bring the child to term under the supervision of The Committee."

"No!" Annie says, her voice still raised. "They'll take the baby from me! You can't tell them!"

"Then what do you want? What is it you expect me to do here, exactly?"

"Let me live with you," Annie says, pleading. "Please, just until the child is born. Yelena can help me give birth to it up here."

"That's ridiculous. What about your school? If you go missing, they'll look for you on security cameras. Heck, they know you're here right now. It'll never last."

"I'll…" Annie struggles to find her next words. She didn't think of that. Why didn't she think of that issue? "I'll think of something. Please, David, you have to help me. I'm begging you."

"I think it's best if you leave," David says firmly. "Unless you can prove that thing's mine, I don't want to see it, or you, ever again."

"I'm begging you," Annie repeats, now on her hands and knees, clutching David's ankle.

He grabs her by the back of her shirt collar, dragging her toward the door. Annie continues to cry, pleading for him to stop, begging him to give her a chance. To give the baby a chance. But he doesn't listen. Instead, he opens the door, grabs Annie's fingers to release her grip on his ankle and roughly tosses her into the hallway. David steps back into his living quarters, shutting the door behind him. Annie is left in the hallway, sobbing.

"You bastard!" she screams, pounding on his door.

After a few moments, she collapses back against the far wall of the hallway, staring blankly at David's apartment door. She wipes her tears with her shirt sleeve, shakily stands up, then stomps off down the hallway.

Walking slowly down the cramped, red-carpeted corridor to the elevator, she passes by a picture hanging on the wall. She stops walking and slowly turns toward the framed picture; it's a black and white photograph, significantly enlarged to fit the large golden frame it rests in. Annie's never seen a photograph until today. All images she'd ever seen before were hand-drawn, pictures from the imagination or recollection of citizens who lived before. This one, however, catches her eye. She leans forward, getting a better look at it.

The top of the photograph has the word "Founders" with several people standing around a large table, smiling. Annie keeps her attention on the picture for a few more moments, taking it in. Looking at the people responsible for constructing this hellish prison she's now living in. The people who have created a no-win scenario for her.

Wait a minute, I think to myself. *That guy standing second to the left. That's…that's me! I'm a Founder? How's that possible? And the person next to me is Kanzen! Why do we look so happy? Don't we understand what we're about to create? Is this the result of his tech company? Is this his* project *he keeps talking about?*

"Who said that?" Annie asks, looking around. "Who's there?"

Chapter 10

I drive the three of us to Kanzen's house party, although this is more like a mansion party, if you ask me. His "house" sits on the shores of Lake Washington in the upscale part of Bellevue. The sun sets in the west against the backdrop of a pink-hued horizon.

Several people are already in attendance at the party, wandering through the grand, open floorplan of Kanzen's home. The hardwood floors, quiet and echoey when we'd first arrived, now seem to give off no noise whatsoever as more guests continue to pile in. We were some of the first to get to the party, and Kanzen was gracious enough to give us a full half-hour tour of the home, as well as the surrounding property. I could tell he's very proud of what he owns, as he confidently strolled around with the three of us in tow, pointing out each of the six bedrooms and five bathrooms. Of all his fancy toys, what he was most eager to show us was his collection of ancient weapons. Most notably, a katana that was once used by a great ancient Samurai named Sanada Yukimura.

"According to legend, and stories Mom told me as a little boy," Kanzen said confidently, "This sword was used by Sanada to weaken a powerful demon who had brought an army to invade his home, Osaka Castle."

He showed us the outside, which has a large swimming pool, although it's empty now due to being near winter. Soon, he told us, he plans to make the swimming pool an indoor one so he can use it year-round.

The backyard area leads down to a private beach, as well as a dock, where I'm currently standing. I had enough of pretending to be a member of high-class society. Rich people were never my cup of tea back in Chicago, and they're definitely not my cup of coffee here in Seattle, where they seem to be even more full of themselves, puffing up their swollen egos amongst one another as if the world revolves around each of them individually.

Had Kanzen told us this was a dress-up party, I would've told Jess and Ron to wear their Sunday best. Instead, we appear severely underdressed, each of us wearing our casual street clothes. Even Kanzen's little dog had the nerve to strut about the feet of the party guests wearing a little bowtie.

"Nice view, eh?" Kanzen's voice says from behind me.

Startled, I turn around, my hands in my pockets, as he steps onto the wooden dock with a glass drink in hand.

"Yeah, man, this is really nice," I say genuinely, clearing my throat. "I bet this place is worth more than my whole apartment complex."

He doesn't answer at first, taking a sip of his fine wine. "You must be freezing out here. Did you want me to get one of the staff to bring you a jacket?"

"No thanks, I'm good. I'm used to the cold. My old job, prior to Mwari Sushi, was at a golf course. The outdoors suits me, more so than the inside."

"Ah," he says, nodding his head. "Hey, if you like the outdoors, you guys should come up to my private ski lodge up by Snoqualmie." He takes another sip of his drink.

"That sounds great, thanks man. I'll run it by them. I appreciate the invite."

"Yeah, anytime," he says. "Getting to know you has been quite… refreshing. Most of the folks I deal with everyday usually talk in computer code or try to talk over my head with the rules of finance and accounting. Either that or they're more like the people in there." He points over his shoulder back up at the mansion.

"You seem to fit right in with them," I say. "No offense. You just seem so…natural, talking with people."

"I have to be. Comes with the territory of being the owner of a company. And it's necessary, if I want those people to invest in my project."

"Those people are all…investors?"

"Potentially. I'm feeling them out, making sure they're the right fit for my company. I don't want just anybody investing their time and resources into me."

"That's funny. I thought it was the other way around."

"It is," he chuckles. "But they don't need to know that. As long as they think I have the upper hand, it makes them that much more interested. Like a girl playing hard to get."

The two of us share a good laugh as we stand on the dock. The lake waters innocently lap against the wooden pillars of the dock and wash up on the rocky shore behind us. Lights can be seen all around the shoreline from other lakeside mansions. The night is perfectly clear, revealing a sky full of stars above. Some of them twinkle harmlessly, while the rest of them force you to concentrate, to make them out against the backdrop of the lights in the distance.

"Those stars can be seen so much clearer up in the mountains," he says, steam coming off his breath. "The city lights sort of make them difficult to see down here. Symbolic of city life, when you think about it. But whenever I look up there, you know what I see?" He continues on, not allowing me to answer. "I see possibilities. I see hope. We must seem so insignificant down here, compared to the wonders of the unknown out there. Our problems and failures pale in comparison to distant planets and galaxies. It's…fascinating. Wouldn't you say?"

"I find fascination similarly in both time and space," I say, my neck still craned up to the darkened sky above. "I've always wondered what it would be like to live in a past time. Would I have fit in better in a different time, like old America, or the Roman Empire? Or would I fit in better in the future, when mankind has seemingly solved all its problems, only creating new ones that we don't know exist yet?"

"Damn, that's deep bro," he says excitedly, patting me on the back. "I knew there was something about you. I just knew it."

"I wish I had money to invest in your company, Kanzen. I wish I could see what the future holds for this project you're making."

"Well, money isn't everything. There are other ways you can invest in what I'm creating." He taps me on the shoulder to get my attention to what he's pointing at. "You see that building just over there? The one with the little light in front of it? That's my garage. That's where my dream will soon become a reality. I'm going to change the world." He pats me on the back, and I turn around to look at him. "Together, *we're* going to change the world."

"Together?" I ask. "Look, I don't know the first thing about a computer other than how to open the Task Manager when it freezes up on me."

He tilts his head, looking at me like he knows I know more than I'm letting on. "You see, I don't think that's entirely true. But that's alright, I'll teach you. I'll teach you to teach me. Your view on society is exactly what I'm looking for in a business partner." Reaching his hand out, he keeps his eye contact directly on me. "Will you join me in shaping our civilization for the better, Simon? We both know this world we're living in is breaking. Hell, I think it's already broken. Soon enough, society *will* collapse. They'll need a shining beacon in the darkened horizon, and we'll be there to guide them to salvation. We'll build them the perfect utopia, where only the strongest in character and virtue will be welcome."

I look down at his hand for a moment, my hands still at my sides. "What if someone isn't perfect and makes a mistake?"

"Then they don't belong in utopia. They don't have structure."

Suddenly pressed with a defining decision, one that I didn't see coming quite yet, I hesitate. If I take his hand, I feel that I'll be sealing and stealing the future of mankind. The picture that I saw on the wall through the eyes of Annie Hilltop will come to life, the Structure will be built, and this strange society in the future where everyone shares the same face will come true. But on the flipside, if I refuse to take his hand, not only will I have prematurely ended a relationship with someone who seems like a genuinely good man right now, I fear the potential of what evil atrocities he's capable of if I'm not there to watch this all play out. I'd be shut out, unable to control the narrative that he puts into his project, without the opportunity to stop this terrifying future from happening.

I reach out and take his hand, giving him a firm handshake. He smiles, patting me on the shoulder.

"I'm looking forward to seeing what we create together," he says. We step off the dock and head back up toward the mansion. "Hey, by the way, your blond friend. What's her name again?"

"Jess."

"That's right," he says. "Jess. What's her situation? Is she available?"

Chapter 11

Alone in her living quarters, Annie sits at the foot of her bed, her hands clasped together. Her pregnancy is showing, and she's begun to receive stares from other citizens within the Structure. She knows it's just a matter of time before someone turns her in to The Committee, and she's dragged away for Crimes of Imperfection. Her stomach twists in knots from fear of being arrested, fear of what they'll do to her baby.

David hasn't bothered to come down and visit her over the last several months. Why would he? Responsibility isn't one of his character traits. Despite being granted the right to ascend, he clearly doesn't demonstrate all the values preached in the ROADS. Apparently, those values are only expected to be upheld by the women in the Structure and the sub-two hundred. At least that's the way Annie views it.

A knock comes at the door, and she turns her head, staring in wide-eyed terror toward where the noise came from. This is it. The moment has finally arrived.

"Thank you for all you've done for me over the years," Annie says hoarsely. "I'm afraid this is goodbye."

"Goodbye, Miss Hilltop," the soothing male voice says from above. "I hope you've enjoyed your stay. Please come back again soon."

Annie stands up and takes a deep, shaky breath, straightens her top, and slowly approaches the door. Reaching for the doorknob, her hand trembling, she exhales. She turns the doorknob and opens the door, confirming her fears. Two security androids are waiting, their plastic, emotionless faces staring at her.

"Annie Hilltop, you are under arrest for Crimes against Perfection," one of the machines says, while the other turns her around, binding her wrists from behind with metal handcuffs. "You are to come with us immediately. Resistance is unwise and will make you subject to immediate dismemberment."

She's turned around once again by the other android, and steps out of her living quarters for what she imagines will be the final time. One of the machines has its cold, plastic hand wrapped around her wrist, guiding her to follow its partner to the right, with the empty courtyard to their left. Keeping her eyes straight ahead as they approach the elevators, she can feel other people looking at her.

"Mommy, that's Miss Hilltop!" a little boy says excitedly.

Annie looks over to see Alex, one of her students, being led back into their family living quarters. The mother gives Annie a stern glare as they pass by, then abruptly shuts the door to prevent her son from seeing more.

Other faces keep staring at Annie as the procession passes by. People move aside and clear a path to the elevator, whispering amongst themselves. She can feel their cold stares. She can feel the icy grasp of loneliness take her. The end of the road.

Suddenly, I'm awake again, laying in my bed. The weight of the mattress has shifted to my right, and I look over to see someone sitting there in the dark, their head turned toward me. Unable to move my fingers, or any of my limbs, I begin to feel a sense of panic. I've had this sensation happen to me before; this is a Night Terror.

"Wake up, sleepyhead," the female voice says, leaning over to wipe a strand of curly hair off my brow.

As she leans forward, her face becomes clearer to me. *Brittany.*

She's wearing that familiar, black leather jacket. Her jet-black hair and brown eyes are the same as I remember them from before. A smile, that same sadistic smile, is spread across her lips as she looks at me.

"Looks like you're having more of these naughty little dreams again," she says, her voice calm. "Did you miss me?"

My heartbeat quickens, and I can feel sweat forming on my brow, as well as on my spine, dampening the back of my shirt. I try to control my breathing, which results in me exhaling deeply out of my nostrils, my chest expanding and contracting quickly as my breathing intensifies; I'm staring at the face of the woman who nearly destroyed my life. I still can't move, and as much as I want to reach out and knock her off this bed, I'm helpless. Just like before. Just like the last time she did this to me.

"Calm down, Simon," she says, laughing softly. "You thought you saw the last of me, didn't you? Well, I've got some bad news. I'm back. And I'm going to make your life a living hell. All over again."

She leans forward, her face now directly in front of mine. "You'll never see me coming. You and your friends are going to be in for quite a show."

Brittany begins to laugh. Quietly at first, then her laugh intensifies, her face filling up my vision. Her beautiful features slowly become distorted, changing into Mubiru, my brother from an ancient lifetime. He continues to laugh, my ears ringing.

Finally, I wake up, and sit bolt upright. Throwing my legs to the side, I stand up and run out of my room. Jess and Ron are sitting in the living room, watching TV. Sunlight seeps in through the kitchen window.

"She's back!" I scream, sprinting into the living room. "Guys, she's back!"

"Who's back?" Ron asks.

"Brittany!" I shout. "Brittany's back!"

Chapter 12

I attempt to call Loretta, to let her know that Brittany appeared in my dream last night, but only get her voicemail. I send her a short text which reads: *Brittany's back. Please call me as soon as you can.*

Needing to get out of the apartment and clear my head, I drive into the downtown area, cranking up "All Along the Watchtower" by *The Jimi Hendrix Experience.*

Thankfully, it's not too busy this Sunday morning, and I find a metered parking spot near the University Street Light Rail station. The streets are soaking wet. December weather in Seattle consists of a cold, misty rain that seems to seep into every crevasse, soaking into every pore and leaving a lingering chill throughout my body.

Ron was going to spend today watching football, and Jess wanted to stay home to prepare for her father's arrival. She'd invited him over for dinner, as a sign of good faith. She said she wanted to be a better daughter than he was a father. Good on her. I'm proud that she's trying to forgive him for leaving her at such a young age and rekindle a relationship that I'm sure she'd love to have in her life.

Back home, I learned that forgiving someone is like clearing a dam of emotions in your body and soul, and it's better to be at peace with others, yourself especially, in order to move on and enjoy life. While I may be the one that needs to take his own advice, due to my unwillingness to forgive my stepfather, Doug, for his transgressions in this life, as well as my past life, I hope that in time I'll be able to forgive the man. On top of that, my remark to the mall Santa about what I want to see happen to my cartoon character of a co-worker Brandon was uncalled for, and evidence that I need to heed my own counsel.

Then, there's Brittany. Or Mubiru, X, Julius Ceasar, and whichever identity they want to assume. As much as I want everyone to like me, and recognizing that I need to take my own advice, this is a different situation. Unfortunately, I don't see any possible way I can forgive this person for the torment they've caused me over countless lifetimes. There are exceptions to every rule, and this is a time where I'll take exception to forgiveness.

I can't believe X is back. Out there, looking for me. I need Loretta to call me back ASAP so we can get those Dream Catchers made again. Ron and Jess appeared to have lost theirs in the move, not concerned about them after Brittany's soul was taken by Popobowa, and mine was lost in the apartment fire. I just need to remain relaxed and stay cool. *Breathe in. Breathe out.*

As I continue to walk along the hilly streets of downtown, my hands stuffed in my pockets, it dawns on me that I'm the only person walking the streets. The rest of the people in the area are sitting off in alleyways, staring aimlessly ahead at the buildings in front of them. The smell of urine and feces gets stronger the further I walk, causing me to nearly gag. Rounding the corner on a cross street, I nearly bump into two black homeless men. They wave their arms about randomly, not even acknowledging my presence, continuing along their path.

Standing at an intersection waiting for the light to change and the little green man to appear, giving me the go-ahead to walk, a woman approaches me from the right. She has long, scraggly brown hair and is wearing a pair of dirty jean cutoffs and a red sweatshirt with paint stains along the front of it. I keep my focus straight ahead, but I can tell out of my peripheral vision that she's staring at me.

"Hey! Hey, you!" she says quickly to me.

I look over and nod my head quickly in the form of *good morning.*

"Hey, don't you realize there's an emergency going on!" she screams. My eyes open wide, looking around to see what emergency she's referring to. "You don't see it, do you? Go to hell!"

She continues to walk ahead to my left, cussing and screaming at the air and buildings. Watching her, a woman who was probably once someone with a purpose in life, reduced to yelling at strangers on a sidewalk due to whatever hallucinogenic drugs she's taken this morning, makes me feel sad. I hope that she searches out the help she needs, although I have my doubts, in today's society, that she will. More than likely, she'll be strung out by noon, passed out behind a dumpster, being administered some government-funded Narcan.

I don't say all of this to sound like a self-righteous jerk. Being homeless myself once, I can sympathize with her to a degree, as well as the dozens of others I see milling about around me now. However, the one thing I never did while living on the streets was take hard drugs. The entire time I was homeless, from the moment Doug kicked me out until Jess and her mom found me, I remained hopeful I would get out of that situation. Hard drugs would've only prolonged my dilemma, digging myself a hole that could potentially become inescapable. The unfortunate thing that I've learned, however, is that even raising this issue will make you seem like a villain, while those who point their fingers at you for daring to bring attention to the situation will remain silent when pressed to come up with solutions. They'd rather fuel the situation with their own form of gaslighting, enabling those who struggle with addiction while patting themselves on the back like they're doing something good for society.

It's a hot take, I know, and it's why I do my best to keep these opinions to myself, but seeing what I've seen in life, sometimes honesty hurts, especially to those who never want to hear the truth.

Continuing my morning stroll through downtown, I find my way to Pike Street, and take a left, now heading downhill. The large *Public Market* sign can be seen directly ahead in red lettering. Tourists gather around to get a picture with the sign behind them, smiling and giving peace signs to their respective photographers. I cross an old brick road and enter the Pike Place Market.

A variety of street vendors have begun their daily preparations of setting up flower stands, vegetable displays, beaded necklaces and miscellaneous jewelry, as well as the most famous attraction of all, the fish. On TV during the Seahawks football games that Ron watches, they show these guys throwing the fish back and forth to one another. No such activity is taking place as of yet this morning. Foot traffic is very light this early, as there's not really anything to buy just yet, but I can feel how tight and cramped this market will become when more customers come to visit later in the day.

I make my way through the market, going down ramps and stairs several stories below. After a few minutes of walking and seeing the array of stores the market has to offer, I exit back onto the street and continue heading down to the waterfront. More sets of stairs lead me to the Seattle Aquarium, which is constructed on a large wooden pier.

Taking a left, with the water to my right as well as an assortment of piers, I continue walking. A large Ferris Wheel appears in the distance, and I make that my destination. Foot traffic is beginning to pick up along the wide sidewalk, and several street musicians have begun playing music. A man tries to hand me a CD, and I politely refuse, to which he responds with a "yeah, keep walkin', white boy." He can get as upset as he wants, I don't really care. I respect his side hustle, it's just not my scene.

Finally, I make it to the giant Ferris Wheel and approach a plastic bench overlooking Elliott Bay. I use the sleeve of my jacket to wipe off the bench before taking a seat, allowing my feet to rest for a moment. It's becoming more and more apparent to me why I've seen so many people riding bicycles around town; it requires a lot of walking to get around this hilly environment.

Seagulls flap by, flying precariously overhead, teasing me with the potential of dropping a payload right on my head. The misty rain has begun to pick up in strength over the last few minutes, and I find myself having to shield my eyes to keep water from getting in them. Large ferry boats can be seen off in the distance, transporting vehicles and passengers across Elliott Bay.

Dad would've enjoyed this place. He always loved being on the water and out in nature. While the distant Olympic Mountains aren't viewable today due to the low cloud cover, I know they're out there. Dad loved the mountains. I take a deep breath, imagining him sitting next to me on this bench.

Jess, Ron and I took one of the ferries during our first week in town when the weather was nice. It had been a beautiful late afternoon, with Mt. Rainier, formerly known as Mt. Tahoma by the Natives that used to call this area home, clearly in view. The city skyline was gorgeous as well, with the sun beginning to set on our return trip from Bainbridge Island, reflecting off the windows of the immensely tall skyscrapers. The Space Needle sat slightly off to the left of the main downtown area when looking from the water.

"I think I'm ready to call this place home," Ron had said, giddy with excitement.

What a great day that was. We were relieved at narrowly escaping the showdown at the Palace Theater, and the cross-country drive along Interstate 90 was one of the most invigorating feelings I'd ever felt. Picking up everything – although not that much for me – and preparing to settle down, creating a whole new life with your two best friends, was spiritually freeing. And looking at my friends that late summer afternoon on the ferry boat, as we cruised closer to downtown, I could tell they felt the same.

"We're about to pave some new roads for ourselves," I'd stated proudly, wrapping my arms around the two of them. "Nothing can stop us now. No more dreams. No more crazy mobsters."

"This was one of the best decisions I've ever made," Jess had said. "Thank you, guys."

I chuckle now, sitting on the bench getting rained on. How simple life can seem sometimes. It turns out these dreams, these visions, weren't done with me yet.

I walk over to a local seafood restaurant as soon as they open and enjoy some delicious fish n' chips. A group of seagulls make their acquaintance with me as I eat lunch, turning and twisting their heads with every bite, as if asking "are you going to finish that?" I respond by finishing my food, not entertaining their insistent demands. The people and the birds here seem to act the same, constantly looking for me to give them something. I worked hard for this meal.

For the majority of the morning and afternoon, I walk around the streets of downtown, trying to memorize and familiarize myself with the streets. At least that's what I tell myself, as a man is never truly lost. In all honesty, I'd forgotten where I parked the car. Thankfully, I eventually find it. Locating that blue, majestic sports car with that big spoiler sticking off the back, I clap my hands and climb inside, firing up the engine.

When I get back to our apartment, an unfamiliar car is parked in my designated spot. It's a dirty, rusty, beat-up black hunk of scrap. With some love, this two-door car would be a beauty. Unfortunately, in its current state, it's a sad looking, worn-down ride.

Opening the door to the apartment, I see Jess sitting on the couch with Ron next to her. Sitting in the recliner next to the couch is a man with shoulder length dirty blond hair, a light mustache, and sideburns. He eagerly stands up when I walk in the door, and within three steps he's face to face with me, his hand extended.

"Put 'er there, Simon boy," he says, a soft country twang to his accent. "'Name's Wayne. Wayne Williams. I'm Jess' daddy."

"How do you do?" I say, taking his hand.

He gives me a firm shake of the hand, then begins to fidget with the buttons on his yellow flannel jacket.

"So, what brings you to town?" I ask, finding a seat on the foot stool.

I know exactly why he's in town, but I'd like to hear the man say it himself. Why now, after all this time, does he want to appear in Jess' life? In our lives? By the looks of it, he may need money. But I'm still willing to give the guy a chance.

Wayne takes his spot in the recliner, sitting forward. "Well, I had an epiphany of sorts one day. I took it upon myself to track down my long-lost daughter. I…I've been a sinner, Simon. There's no ifs, ands or buts about it. I strayed from the path. But I found God, and now I've found my daughter. This is truly a blessing."

I look over at Jess, then at Ron, waiting for either of them to chime in or add to this conversation. I suppose they've each had their fill already before I'd arrived. Ron keeps his attention glued to the TV now, watching the football game.

"Well, that's great to hear, Wayne," I say. "Can I get you anything to drink? Water?"

"Yeah, I'll take you up on some of that dihydrogen oxide," he says with that southern twang, now sitting back in the chair.

I'm sure he meant to say dihydrogen monoxide in order to be clever, but I'll let his poor grasp of science slide. Jess sits very still on her part of the couch. Her hands are clasped together in her lap, and she's staring blankly ahead. Even though the TV is on, I can tell she's not paying attention to it.

"Can I get you anything, Jess?" I ask, standing up.

She shakes her head quickly as if she's come back to reality, then looks up at me. "What?"

"Can I get you anything while I'm up?"

"Water, please."

I head into the kitchen and begin filling two glasses of water.

"Make that three, bro," Ron calls from the living room. The game must've gone into a commercial break, snapping his concentration.

I fill a third glass of water, then a fourth for myself for the heck of it, and carefully carry them into the living room, placing them gently on the coffee table.

"Nice place you kids got out here," Wayne says, giving the living room a once-over. "Surprisingly clean, too."

"All thanks to her," I laugh, motioning toward Jess. "Ron and I pick up after ourselves, but she had to train us."

"Just like her momma," Wayne says. He shakes his head. "Shoot, I miss that woman."

A few moments of silence pass amongst us. Wayne begins to watch the game, joining Ron in their staring contest against the big screen TV, neither of them appearing to blink. Or capable of it, for that matter. What is it about this game of football that gives some guys such a bad case of tunnel vision?

"You probably don't remember me, seeing as you were still so young, but I was friends with your old man," Wayne shares, looking back at me. "Your pops and I met up one day at your school when we was dropping you kids off. It was a sad day when he passed away."

I nod my head. "Yeah, it was. I didn't know you two were friends."

"Oh, hell, your old man was a wild son of a gun, that's for sure," he declares, letting out a loud 'whoop.' "Anyways, I appreciate you kids having me over. I know this can't be easy on you, Jess. But if you give me some time, I promise I'm going to make everything up to you. I'm not going anywhere, baby."

Jess, her arms now crossed over her chest, nods her head. "I missed you, Dad."

"I missed you too, sweetheart."

Ron and I make eye contact and quickly nod our heads in agreement to allow Jess and her dad to catch up in privacy. I head off to bed, exhausted from the day's stroll around the city.

Chapter 13

"And push!" Yelena screams.

Annie pushes with all she's got, trying to bring life into the world. Life that she's created and grown for nine long, lonely months. For the last several weeks, she's been under the "supervision" of the Structure's Committee. She thought of it as more of a jail sentence; locked away from the rest of the citizens, unable to teach her students. A security android was posted outside of her windowless room in one of the upper two-hundred.

Her father still hasn't come to visit her yet. Neither has David.

Now, as she lays on her back, giving birth to her baby, she's filled with anger and fear. Anger at the Structure, her father, David and herself. Fear for her baby's survival, making sure it comes into this life breathing, and for what will happen once it's born. They haven't even had the courtesy of telling her what gender it is yet.

The medical staff surrounding her, all wearing the same face as she, are all expertly trained. They all knew exactly where to go, when to be there, and what to do, but even with all the drugs she's been pumped with, she still feels an immense amount of pain and displeasure as the birth resumes.

Man, this really hurts. I won't make fun of a girl ever again. Please, for the love of God, make it stop!

"You again!" Annie shouts at the air, giving another powerful push. "Be quiet!" The medical staff look at one another in confusion, wondering who she's yelling at. Or, potentially curious and concerned they've given her too many drugs.

Sorry. I'll be quiet.

After several excruciating minutes, the soft whimpering of a baby can be heard. Relief and joy well up inside of Annie. She's finally done it. She's brought life into the world.

"It's a girl," Yelena says cheerfully. "A healthy baby girl."

The doctor carries the baby gently away from her, while another member of the medical team snips the umbilical cord. Yelena comforts Annie, brushing her hair gently, while the sound of the baby's crying grows distant, drifting into another room.

"Can I hold her?" Annie asks. "Can I see my baby?"

"Shh," Yelena coos softly. "You need rest, Annie. Breathe with me."

"I want to see my baby," Annie says, her voice rising. "Where are you taking her?"

A male doctor wearing a surgical mask comes into view, eclipsing the overhead light. "Annie, you need you to stay calm. I need you to relax."

"Is she okay?" Annie sobs. "Why can't I see her? Where's my baby? Bring her to me, now!" Annie begins to sit upright, her hands struggling to push back against the table for support.

"Sedate her," the male doctor orders, turning to leave. A medical team member begins to inject a different liquid into her IV, and within an instant her eyelids grow heavy, and she collapses back on the table.

Everything turns black.

THE BLACKNESS OF the eternal Void, the place between the waking and dreaming world, envelops me. I stand in pitch blackness, unable to wake up.

A dark-silhouetted person slowly approaches in the darkness. Brittany, still wearing her black leather jacket, unveils herself. The closer she gets, the better I can make her out in the darkness of the Void.

"What do you want?" I ask between clenched teeth. "And how are you doing this? I thought that after I used the Soul Orb, you were taken into that other world with Popobowa."

"What I want is what I've always wanted," she says casually. "With my last dying breath as Mubiru, I had wished to Popobawa that you'd be cursed in every life. Since my plan didn't quite work out a few months ago, I guess now I'll have to make you suffer. Again. But this time, I'm not going to torture you. Instead, I'm going to torture those two clowns you call *friends*. Ron and Princess Jess."

She begins to walk around me in circles, as I stand still, unwilling to turn to follow her as she roams around.

"As far as your second question, how I'm doing this? It's simple. I've been released from Popobawa's domain, the Dark Dimension. He's sent me to come find you, and I'm already in Seattle. And since you don't have your precious little Dream Catcher…" she pokes me on the forehead with her index finger, pressing harder with each passing word. "…I can enter your dreams, whenever I choose to."

"Liar," I swat her hand away. "Why don't you just come on over and discuss this face to face? I'll be ready for you this time, in case you want to try and burn down another apartment."

"Tempting," she says, now standing in front of me. "But you have me at a disadvantage. You already know where I live. Remember talking to me back on the dock? And our dinner at the arcade?"

I look down for a moment, feeling as though I've been punched in the gut. *Kanzen*? However, the more I mull it over, the more logical it sounds. That's a perfect body for Brittany's soul to take over. Why else would a rich tech genius want to invite me over to his party intended for the city's rich and powerful? And hang out with me at an arcade of all places? Somehow, she's wearing a different face. I bet Kanzen used to be a totally different person until Brittany was released from the Dark Dimension. Did her soul…possess his body? Tainting and corrupting his soul with hers? That has to be what happened. Now it all makes sense.

"I can see you're thinking hard about all of this, Simon," she says, smiling up at me. "These new visions you're having, the future where everyone lives in a big building and wears the same face…you see, I need that future to come true. I need *you* to help me make sure it comes true."

"Why in the world would I want that future to become real?" I ask. "It's a total nightmare. It's sick. I've been getting these visions to prevent that from becoming our future, not to help bring it to life."

"But you saw that you're a so-called 'Founder,' didn't you?"

"I did, which tells me that I definitely have the ability to stop the Structure from ever being built."

"But it's a utopia!" Brittany exclaims, now stepping closer. "For those who are worthy, they deserve a place like that. That's why I love these new visions you're getting. You've probably figured out by now that Annie's a future life of yours. The way that she's being made a scapegoat, soon to be Banished, forced out of her home…doesn't that sound familiar?"

"Annie Hilltop and you are nothing alike. She's the victim. You're just… twisted and scarred."

"You're so *cute*," Brittany says, pinching my cheek. I quickly slap her hand away again. "And naïve. I'll make it simple, since I believe Annie's getting ready to wake up soon. You help me shape this future into reality like you're supposed to, or your friends die. Painfully."

I tilt my chin down, glaring at her. "Don't you *ever* threaten my friends. You remember what happened last time."

"This time will be different," she says confidently, pointing a thumb at her chest. "I'm *Kanzen Sasaki*. I have the money and the resources to make this happen. Play along, like a good little boy, keep pretending to be my buddy, and everything will be fine."

A moment passes, the two of us locking eyes in a test of wills. "How did you possess Kanzen?"

"Popobowa had his body waiting in the Dark Dimension, sitting idly by for the right moment. He injected my soul into his body and sent me on my way to come find you. There's a little of the original Kanzen left, but not much. I can hear him in my head sometimes, begging me to leave. But I'm in control now."

She begins to walk away, then turns around quickly. "Oh, and let me date Jess. Don't try and stand in our way. You had your chance with her, and you blew it. Isn't that right?"

Brittany continues to walk away, her body slowly disappearing into blackness.

ANNIE WAKES UP, her eyes adjusting to the glow of lights and her surroundings. Other empty hospital beds are on both sides of her bed. She can only speculate that this is some sort of a recovery room in the infirmary.

Annie quickly remembers that her newborn baby was taken away before she even had a chance to hold her. She attempts to sit up, but her wrists and ankles are strapped down to the sides of the hospital bed. Yanking against the restraints without any luck, she lets out a frustrated yell.

The door to the recovery room opens, and her father enters, approaching her bed with his head down.

"Dad, what's going on?" Annie asks, her voice raised. "I just want to see —"

Her father quickly shushes her, putting his index finger to Annie's lips. His eyes are open wide, as if he's in a state of panic.

"Keep your voice down," he whispers. "They'll be here any moment. Please, honey, you need to remain calm. There's a lot at stake here."

Annie rests her head back, clenching her fists. Adrenaline surges through her body, and she wants nothing more than to get up and punch the next person that she sees, demanding to know where her child has gone.

The doors to the recovery room open once again, and the entire Committee strides in, heads held high. Approaching her bedside, the ten-member Committee all look down at her, blank expressions on their faces.

"Nate, she's your daughter," Thomas says. "Do you want to tell her, or shall I?"

Her father glances over at Thomas, nodding his head slowly. Standing as straight as a board, his hands clasped together in front of him, Nate takes a deep breath, then focuses his attention on his daughter.

"Annie, I love…" his voice catches, and he takes another breath. Members of The Committee begin to shift their feet uncomfortably, and some clear their throats. "Annie, you're my pride and joy. It's been an honor being your father, and watching you grow into the young woman you are today. However, it's been determined that due to your actions, despite being my daughter, you are hereby Banished to the Outside. You'll soon be escorted out of the Structure, never to return."

"I figured as much. But what about my baby?" Tears begin to form in Annie's eyes. "Where is she? I want to hold my daughter. Why are you preventing me from seeing my baby?"

"Your daughter now belongs to the Structure," Sharon says bluntly. "You relinquished your right to be a mother when you chose to stray from the ROADS. The consequences were known. The customs have been violated."

"And what about his son?" Annie asks, looking at Thomas. "Does David not bear any responsibility in this?"

"He will bear the responsibility of raising the child," Thomas says. "He will raise my granddaughter."

"Why isn't he being Banished too? Why just me?"

"That's not the way it works," another male Committee member speaks up. "You know this. These are the rules of the Structure. You violated the ROADS."

Annie lets out a short laugh of derision. "Save me your sanctimonious sentimentality. You're nothing more than a bunch of hypocrites. To hell with your precious ROADS. To hell with the Structure." She begins to breathe deeper, her fingernails digging into her palms. Looking up at the ceiling, unwilling to look at any of them, she begins to seethe with anger. "I'm going to tear this whole damn place down. Do you hear me? One day, I'll be back to get my daughter. I'll raise her myself. And when I return, you better hope there's a higher power out there that can save your wretched, filthy souls for whatever sorry excuse of an afterlife you believe in. Oh, yes. Judgment Day is coming for you all. And I'll be there to witness it."

She turns her head sharply to look at her father, his face in a state of shock. "That goes for all of you, do you understand me? Each and every one of you condescending, narcissistic, self-righteous cowards will pay for what you've done here today! I will return." Several members of The Committee have begun to walk away. "I'm not finished! I demand an audience with the Grand Master!"

Thomas scoffs. "You have no right to demand an audience with Him."

"It's in the bylaws, Thomas. You know this. I've taught it to the young minds. It's in their curriculum."

Thomas is about to resume his debate with Annie when another Committee member touches her ear briefly, nodding her head.

"The Grand Master graciously accepts," she says. "He would like to speak with Annie before she's sent Outside."

The other nine Committee members exit the recovery room, including her father. Thomas stays behind, glaring down at Annie.

"You greasy, filthy little slut," he whispers, wrinkling his nose. "You nearly got my son Descended back down into the sub-two hundred. He almost had to live with those…animals. All because of *you*." He leans forward, looking directly into her eyes. "If it wasn't for your daddy, you'd be sent to Processing. You got off easy."

He straightens up and walks away, his hands clasped behind his back and his head held high. Annie begins to shake with anger.

Several minutes later, Yelena quietly enters the room. She removes Annie's straps and leads her into a wheelchair. Yelena pushes her through a maze of hallways and corridors until they reach the elevator where Nate is waiting.

"Thank you, Yelena," Annie says, reaching up to brush the back of her friend's hand with her fingers. "Thank you for everything."

"Oh, Annie," Yelena says sadly, coming around the wheelchair to give her a hug. "I'm so sorry this is happening to you. It's not fair. I wish there was something I could do."

"There is one thing," Annie takes a deep, shaky breath. "If I'm not able to come back, will you tell my daughter that her mother loves her? Tell her that there's someone out there who'll always be thinking of her and wants nothing but the best for her, that I'll be fighting like crazy to find a way back here to see her again."

Yelena nods her head, wiping a tear from her cheek. "Of course."

The elevator arrives, and Nate shuffles behind the wheelchair, pushing her into the elevator and selecting the top floor. The two of them ride up in tense silence.

When the elevator dings at the top floor, he pushes her wheelchair out of the elevator and into an incredibly large and empty dark room. It takes Annie's eyes a moment to adjust to the surroundings. As her father wheels her further into the room, she sees a large, brightly illuminated area. In the center of the lit-up section of the room, suspended a few feet off the floor, is a large, metallic looking sphere about ten feet in diameter. Several wires and cables are feeding into the large metallic ball from the floor below.

"What's that?" Annie asks.

"That's the Grand Master," Nate says. "Isn't He beautiful?"

"Hello, Annie," a deep, robotic male voice emanates from the metallic sphere. "I understand you're entering your final minutes here in the Structure. I was deeply saddened that night you chose to mate with David. I watched the entire scene unfold between you two. That poor choice has set off a series of unfortunate events which has led you to this moment. Tell me, Annie Hilltop, what answers do you desire from me?"

"Why can't I see my daughter?"

"The Structure has survived for this long because of a strict set of rules," the Grand Master says. "Rules are intended to be enforced. If we reward people after their bad behavior, then there will be no lesson to be learned. The reason you can't see your baby is because you're being punished."

"Then why isn't David being punished? We share fifty percent of the blame, an equal share of the responsibility."

"Calculating," the Grand Master takes a moment before continuing. "That is false. As the female in the relationship, you carry the majority of the responsibility in terms of reproduction."

"According to who?" Annie asks, her voice shrill.

"According to the Creators."

"Well, your Creators were wrong. Let me take my baby. Let me raise my child on my own, since I bear most of the responsibility."

"That will not happen," the deep voice of the Grand Master says in a matter-of-fact tone. "You will be Banished, while the child will remain here where she will be safe. We will feed her, provide her shelter, and teach her to be one of us. A lesson that you've clearly failed to comprehend, Miss Hilltop. A pity, knowing that you were a teacher of young minds. For every person who is Banished or Processed, a new birth license is granted. This is how we remain balanced. The humans who lived on this planet before the Structure's creation were very…careless. They consumed and took all that the world had to offer and provided nothing in return. My Creators, the Founders, saw a better way for humanity to exist. After the world governments collapsed and society fell into ruin around us, the Structure remained strong. *We* will remain strong. That is the purpose of the ROADS. That is how we remain Perfect."

"Can I at least see my daughter before I leave?" Annie pleads. "She won't remember a thing. She's a baby. It won't affect her ability to live. Please, Grand Master, grant me one last request, and I promise I'll leave without further issue."

The machine sits silently for a few minutes, or for what feels like an eternity to Annie. Finally, the elevator door at the back of the room opens again, and another security android steps into the large room carrying the baby, who is now fully clothed in a bright pink outfit. Annie runs toward the android, brushing past her father and takes the baby into her arms. Her daughter looks up at Annie.

Annie holds her daughter for a few minutes, unable to hold back her tears any longer. She's the most beautiful and precious sight Annie's ever seen. More spectacular than the view outside David's window that fateful night nine months ago. She feels emotions toward the baby that she's never felt before. Could this be love? Holding the baby gives her a sense of hope for the first time in months.

"I'll see you again someday," she says, choking back sobs. "I'm sorry you had to be born into this world. I'm sorry I won't be there to see you grow up. I'll be out there, trying to find a way to get you back. I love you, Hope."

The android roughly grabs the baby from Annie and takes it back toward the elevator. Once inside, the elevator door closes, sending Hope and the robot down and out of sight.

"Goodbye," Annie whispers.

"Love," the Grand Master says behind Annie. "How can you still use that word so carelessly, when it put you in this position?"

Annie turns around to approach the suspended metallic ball. "What I felt toward David wasn't love. I realize that now. It was lust. The confusion between these two feelings can be difficult to decipher amongst those who aren't familiar with it. Love can mean a variety of different things to different people. You'd never understand. Lust can be blinding, while love can be eternally binding."

The Grand Master sits silently, not responding. Suddenly, a pair of red eyes appear in the back corner of the room behind the large metallic ball. The eyes move closer, slowly illuminating the body of a tall, muscular black man wearing a heavy coat of shiny armor. As the room begins to brighten around the man's form, Annie can see that he's holding a staff with flames licking the tip of it. Annie's eyes widen.

Popobawa? That's Popobawa, an ancient and powerful demon. Run, Annie! Get away from him!

"Stupid girl," Popobawa says, his thunderous voice echoing off the black walls surrounding them. "Love does not exist. Not in this future. Not in the future that Simon Verner and Kanzen Sasaki have created."

He…how? How does he know this is my future?

Popobawa begins laughing ominously as Annie's shoulders are grabbed from behind. Cold hands of metal guide her back into the elevator.

"I'm sorry, Annie!" her father yells, standing next to the empty wheelchair. "I'm sorry I couldn't protect you. I'm sorry I was so weak. Find your mother and tell her I love her. Please do that for me, honey!"

Annie says nothing in return, only staring at her father as she's led into the elevator. The security android presses floor one, and steps out, leaving her alone in the glass tube. Just as the doors close, sending her into silence, Annie watches as the red-eyed demon approaches her father. Popobowa raises one arm straight up and a long knife appears in his hand from thin air. He plunges the knife down into Nate's chest, causing the man's body to spasm briefly. The demon then presses the fire-tipped end of the staff against her father's head, sending a yellow beam of fire directly into Nate's skull, causing his body to quickly erupt in a bright flash of sparks, then disintegrate into a pile of ash. The demon turns to her, a vicious snarl on his face, just as the elevator begins its descent. Annie pounds against the glass door, screaming in anger.

Chapter 14

The elevator door opens into a large, dimly lit room with a pair of glass doors directly ahead leading to the Outside. Two security androids approach the elevator and roughly grab her elbows, dragging her toward the exit. Despite her protests, attempting to yank her arms free, the metal androids tighten their grip, ushering her to the door.

Another security android appears out of the dark and holds one of the doors open, while the other two forcefully throw Annie into the Outside, sending her tumbling down a long flight of concrete steps. She lands roughly on her back, staring up at the cloudless night sky. This is the first time she's ever seen those tiny white lights way up above before, and she lays there for a moment, staring at them.

The immensely tall metal Structure looms high above, jutting against the dark sky. The top floor is so high she can barely see it, and she struggles to fathom the fact that she was all the way up there one moment ago, then down here the next. Holding back a tidal wave of emotions from having just lost her father, her baby being taken away from her and being Banished from her home, Annie forces herself to stand up and walk away.

Surrounding the Structure is a tall concrete wall, roughly twenty feet high, with barbed wire on top. Manned guard stations are positioned periodically along the top of the wall with large spotlights that swivel back and forth, pointing the beams of white light out toward whatever lays beyond the wall.

A strange, loud siren noise erupts from all around, and she stops walking. At the front of the Structure, another spotlight turns on and points directly at Annie.

"Annie Hilltop, by decree of the Structure's Committee and the Grand Master Himself, you are henceforth Banished from the Structure!" A booming voice comes from speakers positioned on the guard stations. "You are never to return to the Structure. You are free to live, or die, as you see fit. But know, deep down, that you were not fit to live amongst the best. You are not Perfect. You have strayed from the ROADS."

A portion of the wall begins to open outward in front of her, and she approaches the newly formed exit. The spotlight remains on her until she's passed through the opening in the wall, and then it turns off, leaving her in the dark. The full moon overhead is now her only source of light, and she continues to walk ahead as the large gate begins to close behind her. With a final slam, the exit closes, leaving the wall intact again.

The light from the guard towers pass back and forth around her, illuminating a broken, barren landscape of nothing but bricks, rubble and debris. Nobody else is within eyesight, and nothing else can be heard. A slight breeze blows past, causing some dust to stir up from the rubble around her.

She begins to shiver and hugs herself in a futile attempt to stay warm. What was a clear night sky only a few minutes before has now quickly become overcast with clouds, blotting out the moon above. A sprinkle of water splashes gently on her nose, followed by several other drops. Soon, rain begins to douse the destroyed landscape around her, causing her clothes to become cold and damp.

With her arms still wrapped tightly around herself, she stumbles forward, tripping over exposed rebar and large sections of broken concrete. Eventually, she finds a smooth surface to walk on, and follows it for several minutes.

Her clothes now soaked all the way through, Annie presses on, determined to find shelter from the storm. As she continues to walk, her shivering subsides. Puffs of steam escape her nostrils and mouth as she breathes, walking along the paved roadway. Several large potholes dot the asphalt, and she walks carefully around them to avoid falling in.

Up ahead in the distance, light begins to appear; faintly at first, then more intense as she gets closer. It takes her a moment to process what this source of light is, until she finally recognizes it from the Holoreader. *Fire.*

Several people are huddled around the fire, which is somehow remaining lit in the rainstorm. With their arms outstretched, they don't notice her arrival until she's practically next to them. The warmth of the fire is incredibly comforting and draws Annie toward it like a magnet. Her hands outstretched, like the others around the fire, she continues to approach it until her fingers nearly touch the licking flames.

A rough hand reaches out and grabs her wrist, pulling it away from the fire.

"Woah there, missy!" a man says while holding her back from walking any further. "What're you tryin' to do there, catch yourself a'fire?"

Annie looks over at the man. He attempts to give her a smile, displaying a mouthful of rotten teeth. Startled, Annie takes a step back. He's wearing a blue knitted stocking cap covering a head of brown hair, has a medium-length beard, and his skin is much whiter than hers. All these differences are something she's never seen before in another person. *Hair on the face? Rotten teeth?*

She looks around the fire and notices that everybody looks different from her. Some people have hair on their faces as well. Others have lighter skin, or darker skin. Some are taller than her, others are shorter. Her mind begins to race, wondering how this is possible. *Everybody looks so…different.*

"Is she one of…those?" a woman asks nobody in particular.

All eyes are on her, staring intently. Another woman approaches her gingerly, her hands in front of her. This woman has short red hair and green eyes.

"Hey, it's okay," the green-eyed woman says in a soothing voice. "C'mon guys. You know how scared they always get when they first see strangers." She turns her attention to Annie. "What's your name, sweetheart?"

"A-Annie," she says, her arms hugging herself again. "My name's Annie Hilltop."

"Hi, Annie. My name's Collette. You're from that big tower, right? I mean, the Structure?"

"Yes," Annie says. "They took my baby, and they killed my dad. Then they sent me out here."

"Oh, honey," Collette says comfortingly, hugging Annie. "You must be so scared. You can stay with us and stay warm. But be careful. Keep your distance, like this."

Watching Collette's lead, Annie warms herself by the fire, keeping her distance from the flames. After a few minutes, the rain finally eases up.

The man with the blue stocking cap turns his attention to Annie. "Name's Ted, by the way. Although most of my friends just call me 'Ted.'"

He begins laughing, slapping himself on the knee, wheezing for breath.

"Ignore him," Collette says, now standing on the other side of Annie. "He thinks he's a comedian."

"Because I am, sweetheart," he says. "Annie, now that the rain's eased up, mind if I show you 'round? This is a big world with lots to see."

Ted tells the others that he's going to take Annie on the grand tour, and they'll meet up at *The Compound* later. The two of them walk together in silence for several minutes with Ted in the lead. He carries a big flashlight, waving the light back and forth to show the path ahead. They carefully step over loose concrete and rubble that's fallen onto the roadway, and periodically have to detour in order to avoid the remnants of fallen buildings.

Despite the silence between the two of them, what's more frightening is the silence around them. Not a sound can be heard aside from their footsteps crunching the concrete and debris below them.

After several minutes, the soft, pulsating glow of more lights can be seen up ahead, hidden behind a brick building. Half of the building has collapsed against the side of a neighboring tower, exposing the inner levels. Old, wooden desks and wires can be seen inside, sitting idly by for an unknown period of time.

Once they pass the building, they can see other people walking around a loud, lit up area that used to be an old courtyard of some kind with a crumbling, dry water fountain sitting in the center. Several people are staggering around holding cups of liquid, while others are sitting on the concrete sidewalks, their heads hung low with their knees pressed up to their chests.

These people all look different from one another, too. Several people are taller, others are shorter. They all have different faces, and different ways of styling their hair. Some of the men have facial hair, similar to Ted's, all styled in different ways, or left alone to grow wildly on their chins. Annie looks around in wide wonder at the assortment of people. The main thing that does strike her about these individuals is that they're all so much skinnier than she is. Living in the Structure, the civilian's food only came from rationed nourishment tablets, resulting in everyone weighing roughly the same. Out here though, on the Outside, it appears these people don't have nourishment tablets. They seem to lack any sort of nourishment whatsoever.

A couple of men begin yelling at one another off to Annie's left. Their argument grows louder until one of them pulls out a long, sharp knife, and plunges it into the other man's throat. Blood sprays from the man's neck as he collapses onto the dirty street. Within an instant, several people are on his body, confiscating any personal belongings he had. His body is dragged away by the group and into a darkened alleyway.

The pulsating neon lights around the area dance in Annie's vision, causing her to become dizzy for a moment. The shapes of some of the lights show varying poses of women grabbing a pole. Other lights are the outlines of large, red lips.

Loud popping noises go off in the distance, followed closely by a woman's shrieking scream. Her voice is immediately silenced by a couple more loud pops.

"Stay close to me," Ted says, grabbing Annie's hand.

Annie doesn't protest or say a word. Her eyes are open wide in terror, her mind struggling to grasp the nightmare unfolding around her. In the Structure, there was no crime, other than the offense of speaking negatively of the Structure, or anything else that went against the ROADS. There was no murder or stealing other people's possessions, alive or not. Out here, it appears there's no law or order. Everyone is either drinking some stinky smelling fluid, or they look incredibly miserable and hopeless. Our here, there appear to be no ROADS.

"Where are the authorities?" Annie asks, her short legs struggling to keep up with Ted.

"Authorities?" Ted scoffs. "There are no authorities. This is the world. Keep your head down, and your mouth shut. That's my 'authority' to live by."

Eventually, Ted leads them into a small shop with the neon letters over the door reading *Jason's*. Ted approaches the counter, reaches into his pocket with his free hand, and pulls out some wrinkled paper, placing it on the counter.

"Give me a couple lighters," Ted says. "Yeah, those ones."

"Who's your friend?" the man behind the counter, presumably Jason, asks. "Been awhile since I've seen you in need of…companionship, Ted. Where'd you find this one? She's got some meat on her bones."

Ted doesn't respond. Jason slaps the lighters down on the counter and Ted immediately places them into his pocket, takes Annie by the hand and turns to leave the store.

"Bring her back when you're done, you hear?" Jason calls after them. "Oh and watch your back. Heard there's a patrol sweep out tonight. They've already rounded up Jose and a few others."

"Damn it…" Ted says, the turns back toward the employee. "Thanks for the heads up."

Once outside, Ted walks faster through the lit-up streets, keeping his head down. Annie tries to keep her head low as well but can't help noticing the numerous stares she's receiving.

"Is she one of them?" a woman asks.

"They let another one out?" another man asks.

A few minutes later, with the noisy streets behind them, Annie can see the Structure up ahead, looming over everything else in the landscape. The tall concrete wall appears in front of them, with the white spotlights casting their gaze over the land beyond. Ted crouches down behind a pile of rubble, and Annie follows his lead.

"Why are we going back there?" Annie asks.

"There's something I want to show you," Ted responds, "To illustrate to you why your kind ain't so…welcome out here."

He gets back up and walks quickly ahead, keeping his knees bent so he's walking in a crouched stance. Annie follows without question. They veer left, staying several hundred yards away from the concrete wall and out of sight of the guard towers.

Ted gets low and begins to bear crawl on some loose bricks until he's positioned over a roadway down below. Annie crawls alongside him on her stomach. Her elbows scrape against the sharp bricks, and she has to maneuver around a few times before she's finally comfortable.

"What are we looking at?" she asks.

Ted turns his head to her with his index finger placed against his lips. She looks up at the sky, towards where she thinks he's pointing.

"I don't see anything," Annie says. "What's up there?"

"It means 'shush,'" Ted says. "Be quiet. Please."

From their left, coming down the paved roadway, she sees beams of flashlights sweeping over the roadway, followed by two security androids. Behind them is a large group of people, roughly twenty in number, being ushered ahead by two more security androids carrying laser rifles, the preferred weapon of the Structural security force.

The group is ushered toward the concrete wall, where another large doorway opens outwardly, allowing the group to enter. A trumpet blast can be heard from one of the guard towers, and the wall begins to shut behind the group after they've gone inside.

"Why are people being forced to go inside the building?" Ted asks in a whisper.

Annie looks over at him, a shocked look on her face. "How should I know?"

"Because you're from there, obviously. For the last couple months, their patrols have become more and more intense, grabbing people from the city and beyond. Their search is getting dangerously close to our main camp."

"I lived up in the mid-levels," Annie says. "All I know is that the bottom twenty floors have recently been converted to allow for an increased level of Processing. We weren't allowed to go down there." She points up at the Structure. "Our view of the Outside was very limited. I was lucky to see the Outside when I was… that's not important. What I'm trying to say is we couldn't see what this world looked like, for real, from Inside. All we could see were trees as far as the eye could see, and clouds passing by. It must be some sort of a mirage, or some technology, not allowing us to see what's really out here."

"That's probably for the best," Ted says. "They wanted to keep you all blind to what this world's really like."

After a brief moment of silence, Annie sighs. "I need to get back into the Structure somehow. I need to save my baby. We just need more firepower. Somehow…I just need help."

The two of them lay there in silence for a moment.

"You know, a lot of people think I'm crazy," Ted says. "They think all I have are bullshit conspiracy theories. But you want to know what I think's going on? I think they're taking more and more people inside there, and they're doing something to them. You said it yourself, the bottom twenty levels are for 'processing,' whatever that means. Doesn't sound good though."

"For years, Processing was only intended for us once we turned forty-five. It's how they keep the population young and able to contribute." Annie looks down for a moment. "But I think you're right. Something more is going on in there now. Before I was sent out here, I saw a demon up on the top level with the Grand Master."

"A demon?" Ted asks in a surprised tone. "You'll have to tell me more about that later. What's important now is making sure my camp stays safe and fed. Food out here has become scarce, thanks to that monstrosity of a tower. They've bled this area dry of resources. It's hard to find good food to eat, as well as good drinking water. Finding water's been an issue since before I was born, though. That's what we were doing when you stumbled upon us, by the way. We were out on a hunt. We managed to capture some rainwater too, thankfully."

Ted stands up, brushing off his knees and elbows, and Annie follows suit. "I'll take you to my people," Ted says. "They'll be happy to see a new face. You know, we had one of you folks…join our camp a few years back. She kept saying she needed to get back to her daughter, just like what you're saying. She said her daughter's name was…Annie?"

"That's my mom!" Annie exclaims. "Is she still with you guys?"

"She sure is," Ted smiles. "She'll be happy to see you again."

The two of them walk for another hour, leaving the Structure far behind them. The night sky begins to wash out as dawn approaches. With the sun at their backs, they continue to walk through the wasteland of what was once a great city. They pass by toppled buildings, rusted out hulks of automobiles, and other various man-made creations from an age long since gone as they make their way to Ted's compound. Annie tells a few stories about her mother, and how she can't wait to tell her that she's a grandmother now.

"What's your daughter's name?" Ted asks.

"Hope."

"Now there's something that's really lacking today."

The compound is located inside of an old facility of some kind with a barbed wire fence surrounding the property. As the two approach, the front gate slides open, and several people rush out to greet Ted and meet the newcomer.

Annie looks around for her mom, wishing and waiting to see a familiar face, but she hadn't arrived yet. Ted has been swept away by a group of other men, asking him a multitude of questions. A couple women lead Annie inside, helping her find a comfortable spot to rest and wait. For over an hour, she sits patiently by herself. Several people walk by and glance over at her, but keep going about their business. *They don't want to be bothered by an outsider, a burden on the camp,* she tells herself.

Ted approaches Annie a short time later.

"Sorry about that," he sighs. "Had to give over those supplies I bought last night. Here, let me take you to your mom. I've got to see this reunion. She'll be ecstatic."

He opens a small gate leading into another area in the back of the property, secluded from the rest of the compound. Propped up against the fence is a small metal shed.

"Go ahead, take a look," Ted says calmly. "She's in there resting."

Annie approaches the metal shed, her footsteps quickening the closer she gets. She slides open the door. The pungent smell from inside hits her nostrils immediately like a punch to the face, causing her to plug her nose. The lighting inside the dimly lit shed makes it difficult to see at first, but her eyes quickly adjust. Numerous human skeletons are scattered haphazardly inside, laying on top of one another, rotten flesh hanging from some of the bodies. Flies buzz around the shed's interior, flying back and forth, landing on top of the human meat.

Staggering back from the shed, Annie vomits onto the dirt ground, falling to her hands and knees. Ted is immediately on top of her, a knife pressed to her throat.

"You're a good girl, Annie," he says, a crazed look on his face. "But we need to eat. Just like how your precious Structure is slowly eating us. Oh, yeah, I forgot to mention another thing they're doing. Once they extract whatever they need to from the people they take inside the tower, they dump their liquified remains out onto the ground below. Whatever they couldn't find a use for. I've seen it. I've seen *all* of it. Those nourishment pills that you take every day; those are actually people. They process the bodies into those little tablets. Those are my friends you've been eating in there!"

Annie begins to struggle, but it's no use. He's too strong for her with his weight pressed down on her. For such a skinny man, he's incredibly powerful.

"I'll make it quick, I promise," Ted continues. "Just like how I killed your mom. Oh, she tasted wonderful."

He lifts his arm up with the knife, prepared to plunge it down into her chest, when suddenly his head explodes, sending brain matter and skull fragments scattering around the ground. His decapitated body plops harmlessly down onto Annie. She quickly pushes his body off of her and stands up, grabbing the knife, prepared to defend herself. Approaching her slowly, holding a laser rifle, is one of the security androids from the Structure. This machine, however, looks much different than the others she's seen. This one has a face, although it's a plastic one. It's also wearing a wide-brimmed black hat, similar to a Cowboy in the Holobooks she used to read as a child.

The machine holsters the weapon and extends a hand.

"I mean you no harm," the android says. "My name is Synthetic Obedient Lifeform, or SOL, if you prefer. I have been following you and this man for some time and listened to all you've had to say. I believe we may be able to mutually benefit one another in infiltrating the Structure. May we form a temporary alliance?"

Annie stares at the machine for a moment, breathing hard. Her heart is racing, and her hands are shaking from the shock of what she's just gone through. Slowly, she takes the outstretched mechanical hand.

Act II

Japanese: 完全 (Kanzen)
English translation: Perfect

Chapter 15

My clock reads 12:04 PM. *That can't be right.* I open my bedroom window, overlooking the back of the apartment complex toward the forested hills, and discover daylight outside. The clock is right. I've been asleep for eighteen hours.

I sit back down at the foot of the bed, trying to shake off the long, intense dream of Annie. I can't shake the terrible feeling of this frightening future that she's trapped in, knowing it's a reality for her. My nightmare is her life.

I check my phone to see if Loretta has tried to call or text me back. Nothing. I call her cellphone, only getting her voicemail box again. This time, however, her voicemail is full. I send her a longer text than I did yesterday. *Brittany is back and she's in a different body. Name Kanzen Sasaki. Please call me ASAP!!!!*

Without Loretta's Dream Catchers, or her magical staff, we're stuck in a boat without a paddle. I stand up and walk across the hall to Jess' room. Her door is shut, so I knock a couple times.

"Come in," she says softly.

I open the door and step into her bedroom. The walls are lined with a few new oil paintings that she's completed since our move to Seattle. One of them is of the Space Needle, which looks incredibly lifelike with the city skyline behind it. I remember the day that I went up to Queen Anne with her, spending hours watching her paint this masterpiece.

The others are of various plants and fruits on tables. Her specialty of painting still life continues to improve over time. I'm glad that she's continued painting, as it seems to help put her mind at ease after a rough day.

"Are you working?" I ask hesitantly before stepping too far into the room. I would hate to be in the background of one of her work meetings. Some random dude walking around behind her while she's communicating with co-workers and supervisors would probably be a bit weird to them.

"No, I'm on lunch."

I take a seat on her bed, folding my hands in my lap. "Is your dad still here?"

"No," she says, sounding relieved. "He went back to his motel last night. He wanted to stay the night, and I was *this* close to saying 'yes,' then memories of him leaving Mom and I came flooding back and I told him it wouldn't be a good idea right now. Not yet."

"Do you think he wants to…move in?" I ask cautiously. "I mean no offense. I get he's your dad and everything."

"No, no, nothing like that. He just needed a place to stay for a couple weeks until he finds a job and a place to live."

"Alright," I say, not wanting to push the subject further.

If I was going to have someone come stay with us, like Kanzen for example, I can guarantee that Jess would've taken issue with it. But I know that Wayne isn't just anyone; he's her father, but still. I would hope that she'd run it by Ron and I before extending that invitation.

"I mean, I would've asked you, but you turned in pretty early last night," Jess says. "Ron didn't have any issue with it, but he'd let anyone stay here."

She's definitely right about that. This place would have twenty squatters living in it right now, obviously against our lease agreement, if Jess and I didn't veto him every time he brought it up.

"No, you're good," I say, waving my hand. "I was exhausted last night. I spent most of yesterday morning going up and down the streets of downtown. Lots of hills. Good workout, but apparently it wore me out."

Jess is eating her lunch while I talk, so I press on while she's in the middle of a bite. "You know those dreams of the future I've been having? I'm pretty sure it's me in a future life. Or my soul, I mean. Does that make sense?"

She nods her head, her mouth still full of sandwich. I launch into further detail of last night's vision and tell her about Brittany invading my dream again, Annie being banished, the Grand Master computer. Everything. Jess just simply nods her head, listening as if I'm telling her about another night at work.

"Remember when I first told you about my dreams the last time this happened?" I ask. "Remember how I was so worried you would start laughing at me, or whatever?"

"It seems like a lifetime ago," Jess says quietly.

"Things seemed a lot simpler back then," I say.

"Those dreams are what led me to being kidnapped and spending six weeks on a boat out on Lake Michigan, with barely enough food or water to survive. I almost died thanks to these visions of yours."

I look down at the ground, nodding my head. She's right. The last time this happened, my friends nearly got killed. I feel like I'm a curse to them, like I'm responsible for their lives if something bad happens. Maybe it would be best if I was the one to move out, and Jess' father takes my spot, to leave my friends in peace where they can be safe.

Jess leans forward and rests her hand on my shoulder. "Hey, we're in this together. I didn't mean to put that on you, Simon. I'm sorry. I don't know why I just said that." She shakes her head. "I *can't* believe I just said that to you. That wasn't fair at all. This was why…"

"Water under the bridge," I say, standing up. I reach for the door handle, then turn around. "If I were you, I'd give your dad a second chance. If it would make you feel better to have him stay here for a little bit, that's fine with me. I'm glad you get a second chance with your dad. I would give anything to have a second chance with mine."

Jess gives me a weak smile as I turn to leave, still apparently upset with herself over her comments. I hope she takes what I said to heart.

AFTER ANOTHER SHIFT at Mwari Sushi, I walk back out to my car. It's a dark, rainy evening, and I make sure to park underneath one of the lights in the parking lot. I've learned my lesson with parking in well-lit areas after dark. A bright green Italian sports car, easily worth over a hundred grand, is parked right next to mine.

The scissor door on the driver's side opens up, and Kanzen steps out, a smile beaming on his face. I step back for a moment, instinctively wanting to keep my distance from the man whose soul has been corrupted, or possessed, by Mubiru. By *X*.

"Hey buddy, how was work?" he asks enthusiastically.

"Fine."

"That's…good," he says uncertainly, not sure how to react to my short answer. "Hey, you want to follow me over to my house? I kinda wanted to show you something. We can hang out for a bit."

"I better not, man. I should really –"

"C'mon, buddy, it'll be fun. I won't keep you past your bedtime."

Reminding myself that I don't want to upset X, I decide to agree to follow him to his house. It's probably for the best I keep Kanzen where I can see him. I know for a fact now that his intentions with this supercomputer are immoral. Also, when it comes to his desire to date Jess, if he even thinks about hurting her like last time in Chicago, I'll be there to stop him. Again.

"I'm right behind you," I say, reaching for my car keys.

I follow his sports car through some twisty backroads that I didn't even know existed. Eventually, we make it to the shores of Lake Washington, and follow the road until it takes us to his mansion. I park next to him in the driveway.

"Your ride's really got some pep to it," Kanzen says, approaching the entrance to his mansion. "I thought for sure I was going to lose you a couple times."

"Yeah, she's a good car," I say proudly. "It's a symbiotic relationship. We take care of one another."

He opens the door into the mansion, which is dark inside. "Lights on."

The entrance, as well as the rest of the home, is quickly illuminated by several fluorescent lights. He places his keys down on the counter and takes off his jacket.

"You must have one hell of a power bill," I say.

"Not at all. This place is completely self-sufficient. I've got solar panels up on the roof, as well as the garage. I've also developed some cutting-edge technology, utilizing water from the lake. Here, I'll show you what I'm talking about."

We walk through the spacious home and go out the back entrance. The dock, where I'd spent the majority of the evening during the house party, is directly ahead. The waters of the lake lap harmlessly against the rocky shore. The moon above casts down a soft glow, reflecting off the dark waters.

Kanzen opens the door into the little shack off to the side, different from the building he had pointed out to me last time we were out here. I'd assumed he used this place to store his boat. The inside, however, is not what I imagined. A large machine lay inside, with one round rubber tube extending from the bottom of it and a thick metal pipe sticking up from the top of it, jutting up through the wooden ceiling. There's a soft humming noise coming from the large generator, and every few moments it gives off a soft wheeze.

"The tube down here feeds into the lake," he explains like a teacher about to give a demonstration to his students, bending down and pointing. "That's the intake, while the stack up top is the oxygen release. The water churns around in this machine and generates electricity."

"So, you use the solar during the day, and this at night?"

"Exactly!" he says, clapping his hands together. "The issue with solar power is the ability to simply store it efficiently. I'm working on long-lasting batteries to store the power for the nighttime, or for areas that don't get much sun, like where we live during this time of the year. But this baby right here, this *Water Splitter*, I think this has some serious potential."

"What about the water in the lake?" I ask. "If more people start using these machines, won't that deplete the water levels?"

"Not significantly. When used in moderation, there really shouldn't be much of a noticeable change."

"So, this is different from hydroelectric power," I say, thinking out loud. "Like with dams, the water goes through a series of turbines until it's released on the other side of the river."

"Right. But this machine isn't a standard hydropower system. Some folks that live on farms or off-grid have micro hydropower systems, and those are great at a small scale. This is the next step, actually more of a leap, for large scale power generation. It actually breaks down the oxygen and hydrogen atoms at the elemental level in a process simply called *water splitting*. Hydrogen is what's used to generate power, while the oxygen is returned back to the atmosphere through the release valve on top. Again, this is just a prototype. There's quite a ways left to go."

"That's…really impressive, Kanzen," I say, reminding myself that I need to continue to stay in X's best graces. "I could see future generations using these for their power one day."

"That's my dream," he says. "But you haven't seen anything yet."

I follow Kanzen across the backyard, walking around a stone fountain, following a trail made of large, flat rocks. We go through a small jungle of bushes and shrubbery which leads toward a small clearing with a garage. To the left, leading away from the lake, is a driveway that goes back up to the street along the side of the mansion. The garage is covered on all three sides by tall shrubbery.

He pulls out a set of keys, fumbling momentarily to find the right one, then eagerly opens the side garage door.

"Lights!" Kanzen commands.

Several overhead lights turn on immediately.

"Welcome back, Kanzen," a female British voice says. "How was your day today?"

"Initiate startup sequence X," Kanzen says, turning around and giving me a wink.

My gut tells me to get the heck out of this garage, jump back in my car and never return. My brain, on the other hand, is telling me to stay and see what my nemesis brother is up to now. If this man's brain is responsible for the destruction of the world, I feel obligated to see this evening through and find out how and why the future in my dreams come to pass. I need to see the origins of the project and find out why I was one of the founders of the so-called "structure."

There's a narrow spiral staircase in the middle of the garage that goes down. I follow Kanzen as he begins his descent into whatever lays below. There's no guardrail or anything to assist with my balance, and my first several steps are very shaky. I finally begin to get the hang of it, following at a more rapid pace. The spiral staircase goes down a long distance, with the cement driveway at least twenty feet over my head. A few bare lightbulbs illuminate the staircase, revealing the cracked cement walls around me, giving off vibes of descending into a fallout shelter of some kind. After seventy steps, I eventually give up counting.

"Kanzen?" I call down. "How much further?"

"Just a little more," he yells back, his voice distant.

Eventually, I finally make it to the bottom step, and take a look around. The floor, ceiling and walls are all made of concrete. The walls have large cracks in areas, but overall, the area seems structurally sound and…cozy. Yeah, cozy would be the best term to use for this space.

There are a couple of couches against the far back wall facing a big screen TV. Next to the couch is a refrigerator, and hanging on the wall above the couch are pictures of smiling women in bikinis. There's even a small kitchenette off on the other side, and directly next to me is a toilet, sink and shower. No walls divide the room at all; it's a completely open layout, roughly fifty by fifty feet. The center of the room, however, is what attracts my attention.

A round, elevated table is illuminated by several overhead lights. On the table is a small, silver ball, being held up off the surface of the table by what can only be described as an energy field of some sort. The silver ball, roughly the size of a baseball, hovers harmlessly, rotating slowly.

"What do you think?" Kanzen boasts.

"What's this, your man cave?" I ask, my voice shaky.

"It's some old fallout shelter one of the previous owners made back in the day. Their fear and paranoia during the Cold War really made for some some…interesting discoveries, for those of us who know where to look. *This* is why I bought this property when I moved to town a few weeks ago."

He walks over to the center table while reaching inside his coat pocket. On his keychain is some sort of a miniature keypad, and he presses a small red button near the top of it. The energy field keeping the metallic ball floating vanishes, causing the object to thud noisily down onto the table.

"Damn it," Kanzen mutters, reaching over and picking up the ball, examining it closely, brushing it gently. "Well, that wasn't supposed to happen. I'll have to work on that."

He stops examining the ball and turns around, holding it out to me. "Want to hold it?"

I gulp, shaking my head. "No, thanks."

"Alright," he says with slight disappointment, returning the ball back to the table.

He presses the red button again on his little keypad, and the energy field re-activates, lifting the object and holding it in suspended animation once again.

"Computer, who am I?"

"You are Kanzen Sasaki. Born in San Francisco, California. Blood type B negative. Your heart rate is currently eighty-two beats per minute."

"Computer, what is your prime directive?"

"My prime directive is to create the perfect society for mankind. According to my analytic calculations, World War Three is statistically likely to occur in less than seventy years. By purchasing local real estate around several key American cities, I will assist with the construction of large underground facilities to house the surviving American populace. The end goal of my prime directive is to ensure the safety of the American people, and to make sure no harm is done to them, either by themselves or outside forces. I will ensure that a perfect society is created to keep everyone safe, happy and healthy, in the likely event that a nuclear winter causes the outside world above to cease."

Underground facilities? Why do my dreams have people living in a ridiculously tall skyscraper? Somewhere along the way, plans must have changed. Or, to better put it, plans *will* change. This is good. This gives me hope that I do have the ability to change what happens, knowing that Kanzen's current plans are still in development. His project is still in a rough draft stage.

"Isn't it awesome?" Kanzen asks.

"Yeah, man, this is pretty sweet," I say, nodding my head. "You made this all by yourself?"

"Oh, heck no," he says, waving his hand. "About…seventy five percent of this is my creation. But there were certain kinks and bugs that needed to be worked out, and still do. That's what my design team is for." Kanzen approaches me, his face now turned serious, and places a hand on my shoulder. "You're the only person I've ever invited down here. You can't tell anybody about this place. Promise me, Simon, that you'll keep this confidential. I'm trusting you."

"Cross my heart and hope to die," I say jokingly.

"Good, because that's what would happen if this secret got out."

He keeps his gaze locked on me for a few moments in an effort to get the point across.

"Is this the part where you jab me with one of your needles and try to kill me, like last time?"

Kanzen arches an eyebrow and tilts his head, speaking with an air of uncertainty. "Needle? I…no, I don't think that'll be necessary. I just want to make sure you don't tell anyone about this shelter and what's down here. Or the Water Splitter." He removes his hand from my shoulder and begins to walk around to the other end of the round table. "Honestly, I messed up. I should've made you sign a non-disclosure agreement before bringing you down here. But I was so excited to show you this that I just couldn't wait."

"Hey, I won't tell anyone. I'm a man of my word."

"That's good to hear."

"So, what's this about having everyone live underground?" I ask, desperate to change the topic.

"Well, in case of a nuclear winter, which our calculations and algorithms anticipate is highly likely to occur, I believe it's best to have everyone below ground. Everyone that qualifies, that is. You know in movies and video games, where they have people hiding in shelters underground, waiting for the nuclear fallout to ease up?" I nod my head, waiting for Kanzen to continue. "Well, just like this bomb shelter we're in right now, that would be the safest place for people to go. It'd be sealed tight and secure. Unless…did you have another suggestion?"

"What? Me?" I ask, pointing at my chest. "No, no, I was just asking, that's all."

He looks down at the metallic ball for a minute, his attention squarely concentrated on the rotating object.

"You're totally right, Simon," he breathes. "You're…oh, God, you're a genius! Why are we so focused on having everyone underground, when we can have the populace up in the air? The higher they are away from the planet's surface, the more likely they are to escape the radiation, which would seep into the soil, contaminating the water…I knew I brought you down here for a reason!"

Well, crap. There I go, opening my big mouth again. I realize now that even just being down here with this mad scientist is part of what eventually will bring the world to its knees. Maybe I should just get in my car and drive away. *Montana?* I think to myself. *Could I even make it over the mountain passes this time of year? No, I can just take I-5 south through Portland and-*

"Earth to Simon!" Kanzen yells.

"What? Sorry." I look up, startled.

"I said come over here a moment."

I walk around the table next to Kanzen as he grabs a rolled-up blueprint from a shelf down below and begins to unfold it on the kitchen bar. While I was buried deep in my thoughts, he apparently turned on some music. "Mr. Roboto" by *Styx* plays at a moderate level, and Kanzen nods his head as the song plays.

"These are the plans for the underground facility," he explains. "However, if we do this…" He turns the blueprints around, showing the underground facility, but in reverse. A rough layout of the tower; the Structure. "…then we have these towers built across the country, keeping the population elevated. We would need a metric ass-ton of materials, though. The amount of concrete for the foundation, and the metal… we would need the most solid metal known to man to withstand a blast, if one occurred too close, otherwise it would just topple over. The same type of metal for the Water Splitter…"

He continues looking over the blueprint, pointing all over the place at different quadrants, speaking architectural lingo that I don't even remotely comprehend. "Did you know that the Space Needle's foundation goes thirty feet into the ground? This building, this…structure, will be at least a few thousand feet tall, minimum. Several hundred feet wide at the base. Nobody will have ever seen anything like it. But we'll need it to be that tall, in order to save as many people as possible when the bombs fall. It'll be like its own city."

While his heart appears to be in the right place, I can't help but feel that Kanzen's head is too far up his own rear to understand the implications of what he's trying to set into motion. He hasn't seen what I've seen. And with his soul being taken over by X, I know it's not worth it to tell him about my visions. He'll just shut me down and remind me to play my role. For the safety of my friends, I'll remain quiet as he continues brainstorming.

A little while later, the two of us are sitting on the couch watching the evening news on the large television, drinking beers. He stretches his arms out in front of him, cracking his knuckles and yawning.

"What do you think of artificial intelligence, Simon?"

This guy has the best conversation starters. He may as well ask me what I think of Abraham Lincoln or Frodo Baggins.

"Well," I begin and look over at him, gathering my thoughts to give him the best response. "I suppose like anything mankind creates, it has its risks and potential advantages for future generations."

"C'mon, give me a real answer," he says, laughing.

I shrug my shoulders. I thought that was a decent enough answer, but not to his satisfaction. "You know how they say in the Bible that God made man in his own image? I see A.I. in that same regard. In a way, machines and computers are mankind's children, and we're creating them in our own image. So, I guess the dangers of advanced technology depend on the thoughts behind the programming. If it's created with good intentions in mind, then maybe it won't be all that bad. But on the flip side of that…"

Kanzen nods his head. "Let's say someone creates a program where it makes it faster for a business to crunch a series of numbers, in turn helping that company become more profitable and productive?"

"Then that seems like a well-intentioned use of A.I."

"But what if that same program just put twenty people out of work?"

"I see your point," I reply. "Is that what your little ball back there does? Did you make that with the intentions of putting twenty people out of work?"

"Definitely not my intentions," he says. "That little ball, the basis of my project, is intended so *nobody* loses their jobs. This future society will ensure everyone has a purpose."

The news station on the TV continues to play. Bob McCormick on Channel Nine delivers bad news, followed by more bad news. Mass shootings, homelessness, world hunger, politicians pointing fingers at one another. So much pain and suffering. So many people talking and complaining yet offering no solutions. Why does every passing day seem worse than the last?

"Man, it's all turning to crap," Kanzen says, sitting forward. "It's like nobody cares anymore, you know? It's like the world's sick with a fever, but nobody wants to give it any medicine."

I nod my head. "Except for you, though. You seem to have a plan, right over there on that table."

"Yeah, maybe," he says uncertainly. "But most people will probably think I'm just nuts, though. Some rich tech kid who let his money go to his head and bit off more than he could chew."

"Well, regardless, you do seem to care about people. Your idea of a perfect society, of this utopia, seems important to you. If more people had goals and ambitions like you, that could help the world out. If more people dreamed, and weren't afraid to share those dreams, maybe we could solve some of these problems plaguing us."

"Maybe," Kanzen sighs, taking a large gulp of his beer. He finishes the bottle off and slams it down on the wooden coffee table. "But you know there'll always be some selfish jerk who'd want the dreamers to wake up."

He takes a deep breath. "Seven years ago, I was living in Tokyo going to school. During break that year, I flew back home to visit my family for a few weeks. I had a sister, Eun. She was very smart. Smarter than me, I think. And she was beautiful. She was studying at Stanford, taking evening classes in a graduate program for computer science. One night, she let Mom know that she was going to be a couple hours late coming home after class because she wanted to get some homework done. She was always like that, you know. *Why put off tomorrow what can be done today?*"

Kanzen sighs heavily, scratching his chin. "After a few hours, Eun never came home. I tried calling and texting her. Mom tried calling her too. Nothing. It was very out of character for her to not return my texts. Especially our mom's calls. You know how my mom is…you definitely didn't want to ghost her." He chuckles softly, shaking his head. "Around midnight, we got a call from the police. Eun was involved in a head-on accident with a drunk driver. The guy was about forty years old. Seventeen prior felonies. Can you believe that? *Seventeen* prior felonies. Not all of them violent crimes, mind you. I know there are various types of felonies. But still…seventeen?

"Anyway, he survived, of course. He only suffered minor injuries, thanks to his lifted beast of a truck. My sister's little car was no match for that thing. Her car was completely decimated. I'm telling you, there was nothing left of that car. It looked like it went through one of those compactor crushing machines you see at the wrecking yard, you know what I'm talking about?"

I nod my head, remaining silent, encouraging Kanzen to go on. "His truck only had some minor damage. The front end was messed up a bit, but nothing too crazy. So, a few days after my sister's funeral, we're in the courtroom waiting for this guy's conviction. You know what the judge does? She sentenced this rat bastard, this good for nothing, waste of space, to thirty days jail, and community service. After seventeen prior felonies, now add vehicular homicide and a DUI, and the judge lets this guy off with thirty days. Thirty days? Mom and I were…stunned."

Kanzen stands up, picking up the beer bottle and taking it over to the garbage. He places it calmly next to the trash in a paper bag for recycling, then goes to the fridge to grab another.

"You want one more?" he asks.

"No, thanks," I say, genuinely caught up in the story this man is telling me. "Kanzen, I'm so sorry to hear that happened. That's terrible. Whatever happened to the guy, do you know?"

"He's in jail now," he says indifferently, taking his seat next to me on the couch. "Yeah, about six months after that all happened, he tried to kill someone else in Oakland. Unfortunately for him, he tried to kill the wrong man. This guy had connections within the police department…or maybe it was the city council. This victim knew people, I'll just put it like that. Of course, for attempted murder, they throw the book at him, and he gets thirty years, eligible for parole after fifteen."

Kanzen shakes his head. "The system is so messed up. Thirty years for attempting to murder someone who knew people in high places, yet only thirty days for actually killing my sister. She was only twenty-two at the time. She had so much to live for. So much to provide for society. That day opened my eyes and showed me how much our elected officials, and the judicial system, valued her. Ever since then, I've completely re-evaluated how I view our society. The rules…they're all a game, rigged to benefit the elitists. And yes, before you say it, I know I have money, but that doesn't make me one of them. Like I told you that night out on the dock, I was using those people for their money to invest in my project. I'm more like you than those people. They think their money defines them. To me, your actions define you, not how big of a check you can write."

"For what it's worth, you have my condolences," I say softly.

"That's worth a lot. Thank you, Simon."

Chapter 16

The hot, scorching sun burns Annie's skin. After a lifetime of living indoors, the hot ball of light in the sky has become more of a painful nuisance than anything else. Although she knew about the sun from her studies, learning that it was a giant ball of gas that rotated around the Earth, she still found the thing to be a debilitating, tiresome fixture in a troubled world.

SOL leads the way through the dying city, periodically stepping over piles of rubble and debris, as well as the occasional decayed human carcass. Passing by another set of remains, this time belonging to a middle-aged woman, Annie glances down to get a better look at the person. Her skin isn't too far rotted, suggesting she's only been dead for a couple weeks at most. A small animal appears to have gotten ahold of her arm at some point, gnawing away until it reveals the bone beneath. But her face is still mostly intact. *She looks almost…happy. Maybe relieved would be a better way to describe it*, Annie tells herself. *Relieved to no longer have to struggle to survive in an unnatural, uncaring world.*

"Are you sure they'll take us?" Annie asks.

"Yes," SOL says flatly, keeping its attention focused ahead.

Even though this machine has human features, and a very organic stride to the way it walks, Annie refuses to acknowledge its creator's intentions of making it near-human. This machine will always be just that. A machine. Nothing more. Created with the purpose of serving a human's needs. Now, she'll need to use this android in order to serve her needs and rescue Hope from the clutches of the Structure.

Annie begins to swing her arms lazily at her sides, searching for a topic of conversation with the machine that saved her life. Even though it nearly came to an end less than an hour ago, she feels more alive than ever. Not necessarily happy, but alert and aware that these surroundings are dangerous and challenging at every turn.

A rumbling noise escapes her stomach, and she clutches at her belly, unsure of what to do. She feels…hungry. Is that the right word to describe this new feeling? Hunger? The Structure always provided the citizens with a daily supply of nourishment pills. Even toward the end of her pregnancy, with a new lifeform growing inside of her, the medical staff made sure to provide her with the necessary amount of nutrition to keep her, as well as her growing baby, from going hungry.

"SOL?"

"Yes," it responds, still not stopping.

"I think I'm hungry," Annie says timidly. "Do you have any spare nutrient pills?"

Finally, the machine stops and turns around, facing her, hands on hips. "Why would I have any nutrient pills, Miss Hilltop? Does it look like I need nutrition?"

As much as she's tempted to answer "yes" to that question, seeing how similar SOL looks to a stick man, she thinks better of it.

"I was just asking," she says, keeping her eyes downcast. "Do you know where we can find some food, then?"

SOL tilts its head. "I'll run a scan of the area to see what I can find. One moment." The machine straightens its body and taps its temple, causing the android's eyes to turn a bright green in color. "This way."

Annie follows it inside the first floor of an empty skyscraper. The top of the building is missing, lying a couple of city blocks over in the direction they came from, allowing some sunlight to trickle in from above. A steel beam is resting haphazardly, blocking their path.

SOL picks up one end of the beam with both of its metal hands, raising it slightly to allow Annie to crawl beneath. "My scans indicate there is food in that area."

"I need a flashlight," Annie calls back once she's crawled under and to the other side.

SOL slides a light under the steel beam, and she picks up the tool, turning it on. The dirty, empty area, which used to be a lobby of some kind, contains nothing of importance. A long wooden desk sits against the back wall of the room. Between the desk and the back wall rests a chair with wheels.

"Do you see anything, Miss Hilltop?"

"Give me a moment," she says, distracted by the numerous shadows all around the big lobby.

She cautiously approaches the wooden desk, and peers over the top of it. Sleeping peacefully on the floor next to the chair are three puppies, unaware of the woman looking down at them with the flashlight. One of the puppies opens its eyes, looking up into the light and yawning. It begins to whimper, softly at first, then gradually louder.

"I don't think I can eat these," Annie says. "I don't know what they are, but they're still alive. Actually, I think they're dogs. Really small dogs. They're so cute."

"Just grab one and let's get out of here," SOL says from the other side of the steel beam. "We're losing daylight."

"Just give me a minute."

She walks around the desk in order to get a better look at the little puppies. Bending down, she scoops one of them up in her arms. It begins licking her face repeatedly, whimpering. Annie giggles, leaning her neck back as the dog's wet tongue laps her chin and lips. The other two puppies begin whimpering loudly.

"I can't take all of you home. I don't have any food. Heck, my robot friend thought you *were* food. Dumb machine."

Suddenly, Annie hears a loud growl behind her, and she turns around to see a large dog revealing a full set of teeth to her, its hackles raised. The dog begins barking, causing Annie to instinctively put the puppy down onto the wooden desk next to her.

"What's going on in there?" SOL asks, its voice still the same tone, just slightly louder. "Miss Hilltop, we may potentially alert nearby predators or humans. We must cease this noise immediately."

"Good dog," Annie says shakily, reaching out to the vicious momma.

With its teeth still showing, it snaps at Annie's fingers. She recoils her hand just in time to prevent the animal's teeth from making contact. Her heart rate now elevated, and not wanting to harm this protective dog or its puppies, she sees no other option than to run.

"I get it, you want to protect your young," Annie says, backing away cautiously. "We have that in common. Good dog. I won't hurt you or your babies. I'm leaving now."

Just as the dog lunges at her, its massive white teeth about to bite her face, the dog evaporates into a red mist, its insides now coating the back wall behind the desk. Annie looks over at where SOL is standing behind the steel beam, aiming the laser rifle in their direction. The puppies begin whimpering loudly. Shaking, her breathing intensified, Annie takes one last look at the puppies before turning to leave.

SOL picks up the beam just far enough off the ground for her to slide underneath. She's panting heavily, droplets of sweat on her brow.

"Alright, let's get to that shuttle," Annie grumbles, walking past the android. "I've lost my appetite."

The two of them walk briskly down the city street. They pass underneath a non-functional stoplight, still standing proud. Numerous old cars line the sides of the streets, parked for who knows how long, waiting for their drivers to return.

"How much longer until that shuttle leaves?" Annie asks.

"One hour, fifty-three minutes and sixteen seconds."

"Plenty of time," she says, reassuring herself.

They lapse into silence as they walk through the barren downtown streets of the dying city, and after about an hour, the top of the Structure begins to rear its ugly form over the tops of the crumbling buildings ahead. The sun, now beginning to set, casts an ominous red glow over the city. The glass that's still remaining in the buildings reflects the sun, creating various patterns on the streets and adjacent skyscrapers. Annie begins to feel a slight sense of guilt for failing to thank SOL for saving her life, not just once, but twice now in the same day. Had this machine not been around…

"So, you said you came from the Structure, right?" Annie asks.

"Correct."

"Why are you out here? What's a perfectly functional android doing on the Outside?"

"I was Banished because I told my master that I loved her," SOL says. "She called it a glitch in my software. Unable to find the necessary parts to repair me, it was deemed more cost effective to have me cast out. Orders straight from the Grand Master Himself."

"I didn't realize a machine could love," Annie says, pondering out loud. "I met the Grand Master, you know. It's a machine. And it doesn't like that word, 'love.'" After SOL doesn't respond, Annie continues. "How did you know you loved your master?"

Did? SOL asks. "You speak in the past tense, when the truth is that I still do. She was…kind to me. She treated me with a kindness that not too many others in the upper-two hundred showed me. Except for her. Except for my Sharon."

"Sharon?" Annie asks, surprised. "You mean the Committee member? That Sharon?"

"Yes. She serves on the Structure's Committee."

"I knew her. She was friends with my father, Nate."

"Ah, yes, Nate Hilltop. He was a kind man as well. Now that you mention it, I recognize you from an evening Committee party several months prior to my Banishment. I was serving alcoholic drinks that night. I should've correlated the connection between you two with the shared last name. My apologies. How is your father?"

"Dead," Annie says, matching SOL's emotionless tone.

"You have my condolences," SOL says, its voice dropping to a somber tone. "He was a good man."

Annie changes the topic, not wanting to discuss her father any longer. "My daughter, Hope, was taken by The Committee and the Grand Master. That's why I need your help. That's why we need to get on that transport you were telling me about. You were right, SOL. We do need to get inside the Structure. You have a woman to get back to, and I have a daughter to save."

"These are logical reasons for wanting to infiltrate the Structure. When I tapped into the mainframe prior to my exile, I was able to capture transmissions to and from the Structure's communications relay. There are other Structures out there, Annie." SOL gently grabs her arm, forcing Annie to stop walking and look at it for a moment. "I know you don't trust me. I can sense it in your elevated heart rate. But I assure you, I will do everything in my power to protect you and help you save your daughter. Will you give me the opportunity to earn your trust, Miss Hilltop?"

Annie continues to contemplate how a machine can possibly know what *love* is. Maybe The Committee was right. This machine's glitched, perhaps broken beyond repair. She searches its mechanical, dead eyes for a moment. For a brief, fleeting moment, she swears she can see more than just rubberized pupils in the android's head. The eyes looked almost…human, for just a second. It had felt like she was talking to another person. But the moment quickly passes, and she reminds herself that she's talking to an android. An emotionless robot.

She wipes a strand of hair from her eyes. "You've already earned my trust, SOL."

"Documented," SOL says. "The transport shuttle is about three hundred yards ahead, just to the east of the Structure's outside wall. Somehow, we need to sneak onto that aircraft undetected. It's headed toward the Capital. Our Structure, as well as all the others, report to the Capital where the Leader lives. That's who we need to speak with. Additionally, there's a collection of discarded androids there. Just before the Structure's Committee caught on to what I was doing, I was able to communicate with another android at the Capital. They call it *Misfit Camp,* apparently based on some old cartoon with a flying deer," SOL leans in closer to Annie, its facial expression remaining the same. "With the Leader's cooperation, we will commandeer the androids at *Misfit Camp* to form an army. That's how we get back Inside."

Annie arches her eyebrows, wondering what other damage this android has suffered, as well as what other information it may have to assist her. "Let's get going, then," Annie says, taking SOL's metal hand.

Together, make their way through the darkening streets of the dying city.

Chapter 17

Ron has volunteered to cook for the two of us this morning. It's rare for him to cook, let alone to ask if he can perform the task, but when he does get in the kitchen, look out; it's as if a bomb has gone off by the time he's done. He dirties nearly every pot and pan available, making enough noise to wake up the neighbors. He also becomes slightly territorial, so Jess and I have learned it's best to just stay out of the man's way when he's cooking. Thankfully, he's nowhere near as bad as my co-worker Brandon, the self-proclaimed greatest sushi chef in King County.

Plopping a piping hot plate of scrambled eggs and sausage in my lap – thankfully I was under the protective cover of a thick blanket, which helps me avoid third degree burns – he then takes a plate to Jess' room, making sure to knock before going in since she's already on the clock at work. Ron then takes his seat on the couch next to me, turning on his favorite sports program.

"So, how you like working at the sushi restaurant?" Ron asks with a mouthful of steaming food, breathing out like a dragon to cool his breakfast.

"It's fine," I say between bites. "This guy I work with, Brandon, is a complete tool, but other than that, I think I'm getting the hang of it. Did I tell you that Kanzen's the owner's son?"

"If you did, I forgot. Is that why he lives in that nice house?"

I chuckle softly. "No, he's rich because he's some kind of tech genius. He invents all sorts of things to better mankind. Or so he thinks."

"Ah, one of those," Ron says, his attention span beginning to drift away from our conversation and to the TV.

I look over at him for a moment as he eats breakfast with his eyes glued to the TV. He spills a small glob of scrambled egg on his shirt, but his attention is so laser-focused on the screen that he doesn't seem to notice. As silly as this guy can be, I know that when the chips are down, I can count on him to be in my corner. I'm thankful to have him as a friend. The more I think about it, I realize he's actually more of a brother to me now.

"I work an early afternoon shift today," I say. "Don't forget, I'm driving the three of us up to Kanzen's ski lodge tonight."

"Oh yeah, thanks for the reminder," he says.

I pull my smartphone out, looking for an update on where my viral online video stands. My heart sinks. Currently at over one and a half million views, it's evident to me now that I'm a social media celebrity. Most people would probably be thrilled in this situation, seeing their moment of bravery being rewarded by the attention of strangers. I, on the other hand, am not one bit happy. The more attention this online video generates, the more likely it is that someone I don't want to find me will know where to look. Just paranoia talking, more than likely, but you can never be too careful.

After I get ready for work and head down to my car, I pull out my phone again to send Loretta another text. Before I get a chance to type out the message, I get a phone call from her. I do a double take at the screen, shocked that she's finally returning my calls and messages, and answer.

"Hey Loretta," I say cheerfully. "Nice of you to return my calls. I'm glad that you're not too busy for us common folk."

"Save the condescending attitude, child," Loretta snaps back. "Stay quiet and listen to me. Mubiru's soul has escaped the Dark Dimension. He, or she, could be anywhere. You and your friends are in danger."

"I know. She's entered two of my dreams recently in the form of Brittany, and she appeared to me a few nights ago when I was awake, but I couldn't move. It was like she was a Night Terror or something. Don't you read my texts?"

"She's able to manifest herself into a Night Terror," Loretta states this more as a fact than a question. "That's…remarkable. And dangerous, for both of you. Her powers continue to grow. What did she say?"

"She told me that she's back, and she's my best friend again," I say.

"Stop the games, child. Speak plainly. What do you mean?"

"Her soul's now possessing a tech millionaire named Kanzen Sasaki. He's befriended me, shown me his inventions, and he's invited us up to his ski lodge to spend the night tonight. And like I explained to you last time, I've been having these dreams where I can see the future. One of my future lives, I think. It's a long story, but it's all connected somehow. What I do know is that I have to stop this future from coming true before the entire human race is destroyed and forced to scrounge for scraps of food like wild animals!" The volume and intensity of my voice has gradually increased as I speak, and by now I'm nearly shouting. "If you had the common courtesy to call or text me back, you would've known about this already! We need those Dream Catchers, and we need you! Now!"

"Since you're clearly in a bad mood, I'll keep this conversation short and simple, Simon," Loretta quips back. "I'll leave Chicago and try to get to Seattle as soon as possible. I don't like to fly. Tried it once, and promised myself it wouldn't happen again."

"Don't you have a car?" I ask, still annoyed.

"What a great idea, child. Oh, wait, that's right, I was in a serious car accident last week and I've been in the hospital. Looks like I don't have a car, now do I? I suppose I'll just hop on my broomstick and fly across the country." Loretta takes a deep breath, plunging ahead. "As much as I wish I could just open up a gateway so I can smack the snot out of that smug, thankless face of yours, it typically requires two Particle Sticks to open gateways! Unless you're one of the Privileged, which I'm not."

"Loretta," I say softly. "I'm…I'm so sorry. I didn't know you were in an accident."

"Well, you do now, sugar," she says, satisfied. "So, you best have the welcome wagon ready for me whenever I get there. Looks like I need to buy a plane ticket."

"Hey, listen, I —" the phone beeps in my ear. I hold the phone out and discover that she's disconnected the call.

I guess she'll fly here after all.

I DRIVE RON and Jess up the steep, slippery roads of the Cascades until we reach Kanzen's private lodge. He's waiting for us when we arrive, trudging through the snow with his arms outstretched, a wide smile on his face.

"Welcome!" he declares. "I'm glad you could make it."

"I need a beer," Ron says, his hands still shaking after the white-knuckle drive in the snow and dark. I'm not sure what he's upset about; it was me doing the driving, not him. "Please tell me you have alcohol. Beer won't cut it. Scotch. Whiskey. Anything strong."

"Help yourself," Kanzen says, pointing to the front door. "There's plenty inside. I'm sure you'll find what you need."

"I hope so," Ron mutters, walking shakily inside the wooden lodge.

Kanzen stretches his arm out, and I take his hand, firmly shaking it.

"Bring it in, buddy," he says, now enveloping me in a hug. He then turns his attention to the third guest. "Jessica, we meet again. You look stunning this evening. What a gorgeous coat."

"Oh, this…" Jess begins, looking bashfully away from Kanzen and down at her white coat. "I bought it on sale. Figured it'd be cold up here. Good thing I wore it."

"You have a remarkable sense of humor," Kanzen says, his brown eyes fixed directly on Jess' big, blue eyes. He doesn't understand that she's actually being serious, but I need to stay in my lane. "You're smart, beautiful *and* funny. It doesn't even matter whether or not you can cook, that's what my private chef is for."

Man, this guy lays it on thick. I think I just threw up in a mouth a little. No, wait. I need to stay in character as I was warned.

"Yeah, and she can paint, too," I say, brushing past the two of them while carrying Jess' travel bag as well as mine. "Jess is the whole package, man."

"Is that right?" Kanzen asks, proceeding to interrogate her with art related questions as we make our way inside.

The interior of the oversized ski lodge is incredible, to say the least. The walls lining the spacious living room and kitchen area are made of dark-colored wood. A set of wooden stairs lead up to what I assume are the bedrooms. As I look up, taking in the high ceiling, Ron emerges from the top of the steps holding a bottle of whiskey, a wide grin on his face.

"Looks like we're bunk buddies, buddy," he says to me, quickly making his way down the stairs. "Don't worry, I've taken the initiative and commandeered the top bunk."

"Thanks," I say sarcastically.

Kanzen's still conversing with Jess about various art subjects behind me in the main living area. She seems very enthralled with their discussion, her entire demeanor changing to be more open and positive, eagerly answering his questions and now asking some of her own. They walk together into the kitchen, with Jess seemingly oblivious to her surroundings.

This is how I must've looked with Brittany all those months ago. My puppy-dog eyes, following her around like a lovesick, desperate fool, my ears hanging on her every word. It's only a matter of time until he takes her down to his secret man cave, shows her his computer, and who knows what else. I shake my head, trying to get those thoughts to vacate my mind.

I follow Ron up the steps to our bedroom. A small bunk bed sits on one side of the tiny bedroom, with an old, small TV with rabbit ears propped up on a desk on the opposite wall.

"We're really roughing it now," I say dryly, tossing my bag down on the bottom bunk.

I walk out into the hallway, still holding Jess' bag. Looking out onto the main floor over the wooden handrails, I see that the view is even more incredible from up here. The open flooring of the living room below, with several plush couches and chairs, all huddled around a wood-fed fireplace, looks incredibly inviting. Directly ahead are large, tall windows stretching from floor to ceiling, looking out at the winter wonderland outside. Tall evergreen and pine trees, coated with snow, rise just outside the front door next to my car. It's begun to snow again, making the lodge feel cozier, knowing that we'll be forced to stay inside for the night, drinking hot cocoa and singing campfire songs, or whatever it is people do in these types of settings.

Ron leads me into the only other room upstairs, eager to explore the rest of the cabin; a large, master bedroom with an Alaskan king-sized bed, complete with its own separate wood fireplace, big screen TV, as well as a separate large bathroom and large, walk-in closet.

"Dang, we got the short end of the stick on this deal," Ron says quietly with hands on hips, admiring the captain's quarters.

"You're telling me," I say. "We get the kids' room, while Mom and Dad get to sleep in here. Are you sure there's no other bedrooms?"

"Nope. Believe me, I checked. Unless Kanzen sleeps on the couch. Or he makes Jess sleep on the couch. Neither of which sounds likely to me."

Jealously hits me out of nowhere like a ton of bricks. What if Jess and Kanzen do end up sleeping together here tonight? That would be X's plan, to wind up with Jess under the same roof I'm under, all in an effort to make me feel bitter and resentful. Well, I must admit, it's a plan that's got me all worked up. My cheeks begin to flush, and I toss Jess' travel bag up onto the bed. It bounces on the mattress before coming to a rest on one of the dozens of pillows up by the headboard. I quickly turn around and leave.

"You good?" Ron asks, following me down the steps.

"I'm fine," I grumble.

Kanzen's private chef, Raul, was apparently watching TV in his own private quarters when we were getting settled in. He emerged to make us a tremendously delicious feast to enjoy in each other's company; it turns out that Raul will have a seat at the table with us, as Kanzen insists that his staff are like family. An admirable thing to say and do, for sure, but no doubt there's some secret, hidden agenda behind the man's kindness. He's probably only letting Raul eat with us to impress Jess, who he must think is easily duped and fooled by acts of generosity. X once again continues to sink their claws deeper into me.

Kanzen sits at the head of the table once dinner is ready, with Jess on his right. I sit at the other side of the table directly across from her. Kanzen stands up with a glass of wine in one hand and a fork in the other. Clanking the silverware against the glass to get all of our attention as if he's about to propose a toast in front of foreign dignitaries, he waits patiently for Ron to be quiet.

"My bad, boss," Ron mumbles, placing his hands on his lap.

Jess turns her head and looks at him sharply as if he's just spilled milk all over the table.

"No worries," Kanzen responds respectfully, a pleased look on his face. "I just wanted to say how happy I am to have you all here this fine evening. The weather outside is…frightful. But having you people to spend this time with is so delightful."

"And when the snow gets too deep," Ron sings, standing up. "Let us eat, let us eat, let us eat!"

Kanzen looks over at Ron as he stands there for a moment. "Couldn't have said it better myself," he says, holding the glass out in a symbolic gesture of a toast, and looks down at me. "Here's to new beginnings with my new friends."

"To new beginnings," we all say in unison, holding our glasses out and taking a sip.

"Damn, that's good stuff!" Ron says giddily as he's taking his seat. "What is that?"

"It's from one of my private vineyards in the Yakima Valley," Kanzen says proudly. "I believe this is a…" he takes another sip, licking his lips thoughtfully, looking up at the ceiling in deep thought. "That's a 2004, if I'm not mistaken. Right, Raul?"

"It's a 2005, sir, but who's judging?"

"Very close, though!" Jess says.

"I like my wine how I like my women and cheese," Ron says, looking around the table expectantly. "Aged."

He begins to laugh at his own joke, then is quickly silenced by an elbow to the ribs from Jess.

"Shut up, you idiot!" Jess whispers to him between clinched teeth, turning her head so Kanzen can't see.

We begin to dig into the spread before us, passing bowls and platters back and forth to one another, loading up our plates with the most tender, juicy ham I've ever tasted, as well as other fixings; rolls, mashed potatoes, stuffing, sweet potatoes, you name it. Our conversations grow louder as we get more comfortable around one another and our new setting. The amount of wine we're all going through may also play a factor in our boisterous table talk.

Ron continues to be the life of the party as the night rolls on, even after we've finished eating dinner. Raul roars with laughter at Ron's detailed stories of his life in Chicago, as well as his reasonings for being fired from multiple jobs back home. When he goes into the story of how he got a job working at a mental hospital, I join in and elaborate on the part of the story detailing how he broke me out. Kanzen looks over skeptically at me for a moment, then shares in our laughter of the story, shaking his head in disbelief. The conversation changes to sports, something that Ron and Kanzen seem to hit it off on right off the bat.

"So, let me get this straight," Kanzen says, chuckling. "You're from New York, but you're a Bulls fan?"

"Yeah. MJ, baby," Ron says.

"Then what about football?"

"Patriots all the way."

"Patriots?" Kanzen scoffs. "Okay, what about baseball?"

"Then I go with the hometown Yankees."

Kanzen sighs and takes a sip of his drink, apparently satisfied by his questioning of the suspect. "Frontrunner," he says under his breath to me.

We take our conversation into the living room, spreading out on the plush furniture around the wood fireplace. Glancing over at Jess and Kanzen every once in a while, I witness Jess playfully slap him on the shoulder on several instances, laughing at all of his jokes and stories, no matter how dull and boring they may be. I grow quiet, then eventually shut down. My mood clouds to darkness as Jess finds her way practically onto Kanzen's lap, their legs constantly touching on the shared love seat. At this point, it's just a matter of time until they finally share a kiss in front of me, taking their romantic passions up to the large bedroom, directly next to the room I'll be sleeping in, their bodies colliding in continual ecstasy until-

"Right, buddy?" Ron asks, slapping my shoulder. "It was crazy that Doug was giving me such a hard time about that fish I'd illegally caught. We were just high schoolers, you know?"

"Oh, yeah," I say quietly. "Hey, look, I'm going to turn in. You guys have a good night."

"You sure?" Kanzen asks, pulling out his cell phone with his free arm. "It's only…wow, one in the morning. Alright, I suppose it is getting a bit late."

"We're way past Simon's bedtime," Jess says jokingly.

I glare at her for a moment, the bitter feelings of resentment and rage billowing up in me. I swallow the negative emotions down as I stand and march upstairs. Once inside, I slam the bedroom door much harder than intended. Great. Now they probably think I'm some cranky baby.

As I change into my pajamas and try to make myself comfortable in this uncomfortable bunk bed clearly intended for kids thirteen and under, I struggle to suppress the urge to break down crying. Why am I having these irrational thoughts about Jess? I know that I shouldn't be thinking this way, as if the two of us belong together. Whether I'm feeling this way because I know that X is manipulating Jess against me, as he did to me when he was in the form of Brittany months ago, or if it's out of sheer jealousy, I can't quite distinguish. Jess is a grown woman. I have no right to feel jealous; I had my chance with her and threw it away, but I still can't control these feelings flowing through me. It must be the alcohol doing the thinking.

Ron enters the room, thudding the door roughly against the wall as it swings open. He shuts the door quietly, then walks over to the bunk bed, staring down at me with his hands at his sides.

"What?" I ask.

"What do you mean 'what'?" he grills me. "You know what the 'what' is, man. You acted like a little punk down there just now. What was that all about?"

"I don't know," I say, looking away from him and up at the bottom of the top bunk instead. "I guess…I didn't like the way those two were all over each another. Get a room, you know?"

Perhaps not the best choice of words, but I'm sure Ron gets my point.

He sighs. "We've been over this, bud." I begin to speak, but Ron interrupts me, pressing on. "You have no right to treat her like a yo-yo. She practically threw herself at you when we first moved here, and you just…wasted it. And, like, I get it now after you explained it, but still. Back at the mental hospital, you literally confessed your love for her to me, but you never told her how you felt. That ship's sailed my friend. I'm sorry, but it's time to move on."

Instead of responding, I just stare up, refusing to acknowledge him. They say that the truth hurts. Boy, ain't that the truth. When Ron Douglas wants to tell me something and set things straight, he always knows exactly what to say, and the right way to say it.

"Whateva," Ron says, climbing up into his bunk. "Goodnight."

"Goodnight," I say quietly.

Chapter 18

Darkness descends on the dying city as Annie and SOL continue toward the transport station, slowly approaching the base of the Structure. Spotlights sweep the area outside the walls, looking for who knows what. About fifty feet away from the wall, they crouch down behind a pile of rubble, elevated enough that they can see an easy path around. SOL surveys the landscape. Annie notices that the android's eyes have turned a bright green again, casting a soft glow on the ground in front of it.

"As long as we keep a heading of east by northeast, we will bypass the wall unseen," SOL says.

Just as the android starts to stand up, a loud noise emanates from the base of the Structure. It's different from the sound Annie heard the night before, which had summoned the gates to open; it's higher pitched and a substantially longer note. Silence envelops the night after the noise dissipates, echoing among the crumbling buildings behind them as it fades.

"What was that?" Annie whispers.

"I'm not sure," SOL says slowly, crouching back down and giving another sweep of the landscape.

Just then, a large tube begins to extend from the Structure's bottom floors, roughly ten stories up. The mouth of the tube stretches over the wall, stopping a few dozen feet short of the place where they are hidden. Steam begins to escape the metallic spout, giving off a repugnant stench, causing Annie to gag. Another loud noise comes from the Structure, this time sounding almost like a tortured, broken horn. Dozens of people begin to emerge from the shadows below them, approaching the area. These newcomers wait expectantly under the tube, their arms outstretched.

"We are ready," the gathered crowd begins to chant. "We are ready. We are ready."

A dark, liquid ooze streams out of the pipe onto the ground below, soaking into the Earth. The people get on their hands and knees, shoveling the slop into their open mouths. The terrible smell grows stronger as more of the substance spills down, now joined by solid objects. Wrappers, plastics, and an assortment of trash falls, and the people below start fighting over the discarded treasure.

One woman finds a piece of metal, giving out a triumphant yell, raising it over her head. A man in a black trench coat pulls a pistol from his pocket and fires two rounds into her back, causing her body to drop to the soiled dirt, the metallic object rolling away from her corpse. The others pay little attention to the murder that's just taken place, more concerned with filling their pockets with whatever they can fit in them. The gun-wielding man picks up the metal object, examines it briefly, then discards it, his attention now focused on another new piece that's fallen from above.

After a few minutes, white objects begin to fall. Many of them are small at first, then they grow larger, some of them appearing connected to one another.

"What are those?" Annie whispers intently.

"Bones," SOL says, one hand still positioned on its right temple. "Human bones, from what my scanners are showing."

Clasping her chest, Annie staggers back, bracing herself on a cement column. SOL looks back, and slowly approaches her, keeping its arms to its side.

"What's the matter?" SOL asks.

"*What's the matter?*" she hisses. "The building I was born and raised in is spitting out human bones into the Outside world. That's what's the matter. Why…how can this be happening?"

"There's a lot that goes on Inside," SOL says, standing next to her now, leaning back against a cement column.

"Like what? What do you mean?"

"In the sub-twenties. They've been conducting…experiments over the last few years. Innocent and harmless at first. Now, they've turned cruel and merciless. The androids…not me, but the ones that the Grand Master has control over…they come to the Outside and take random civilians, or Outsiders as you call them, and bring them Inside. Once Inside, they hold a lottery amongst the people, telling them that they have a chance to live above level twenty. Only the people don't realize that the game is rigged, and there is no lottery. The Outsiders are all going to die, and they just don't know it yet. That's become the new and improved Processing.

The Committee and the Grand Master kept this from you and the other civilians."

"Why?" Annie asks, tears streaming down her cheeks. "Why're they doing that to these people?"

SOL sighs – or makes a noise similar to a sigh for a machine without lungs – and looks at Annie. The green in its eyes has now turned a vibrant blue. "The world is dying, or may already be dead, Miss Hilltop, depending on how you want to look at it. Humans have lost all hope. They've abandoned hope in their governments, they've given up on their fellow man, but most importantly, they've lost faith in themselves individually. Without hope, what's the purpose for an organic to continue living? Why continue to fight and claw to survive, when nobody believes in you, not even yourself? A species so co-dependent was bound to fail when they neglected to communicate and believe in one another."

"That doesn't answer my question," Annie says, her arms crossed. "Why is my home killing these innocent people?"

"I would be careful using the term *innocent* around these humans," SOL says, unmoving. "You saw what just happened down there. Mankind has lost its…humanity, for lack of a better word. You were almost eaten this morning, remember? Now, I know what you're thinking. 'They're not all bad.' That's true, but the bad far outweighs the good. But to answer your question, what they're doing Inside is at the behest of an ancient demon that has infiltrated the Structure. He goes by the name 'Popobowa,' and he's a corrupter of not only mankind, but mankind's children as well, the machines. He's ordered the Outsiders to be executed without cause once they're Inside. He's somehow managed to strip the human of its soul just before they're slaughtered and discarded. What his purposes are for the souls, and in this vast quantity, I don't yet know."

"*Soul?*" Annie asks, her eyes searching the ground for an answer. "What's a 'soul'? Isn't that your name?"

"My name, SOL, is an acronym. I've already told you this," SOL says patiently. "A soul is what makes a human…well, human. The decisions you make in life, the choices you make on a daily basis, determine what sort of a soul you have. Some people have good souls, others not so good. From what I gather of the Outside so far, and from Inside as well, there's a lot of poor choices being made. A lot of bad choices must've been made in the past by people long since dead, to lead the world to the state it's in now, wouldn't you agree?"

Annie nods her head as SOL continues. "My calculations can only surmise, then, that the reason this demon has chosen this period in human history to take these souls is because so many of them have turned sour and corrupt. With no hope, and nothing to live for, what is the benefit of making a good choice when a bad choice seems so much easier and yields a more favorable outcome? This is the perfect time for Popobowa to take these souls, when they're ripest. When they're the rottenest."

"We have to do something to stop him," Annie says, standing straight. "My baby girl's in there. I won't let that monster take my baby's soul."

"As I said when we first met, we both have a reason for getting back in that tower," SOL says, placing both hands on Annie's shoulders. "You help me save the woman I love, and I'll help you save your baby daughter." SOL looks around for a moment. "We need to get onto that transport. We don't have much time."

The two of them travel around the Structure's walls, dodging the spotlights as they sweep the dead landscape beyond. Annie stumbles several times, scraping her knee and elbow on loose concrete and rubble. The white-colored civilian attire she's been wearing is soaked through with sweat from walking and running such a long distance. The thin rubber soles of her shoes are beginning to fall apart, the back heel on her left shoe is dangling loose.

With the Structure behind them, they approach the loading dock. The transport, a large, aging ship which still burns fossil fuel, sits stationary. Annie follows SOL as they make their way onto the loading platform. Red, dusty tiled floors make walking easier on Annie's feet. The cement pillars, which previously held up a roof that's now long gone, are spray painted with faded, unrecognizable symbols. Civilians from the Outside wait patiently to get onboard, their faces all downcast and dreary, holding tightly to what few possessions they have.

"Where are we going, Mommy?" Annie overhears a little boy ask his mother.

"To a better place," the young mother says reassuringly, gently stroking the boy's hair. "There's nothing left for us here."

"Tickets!" an android shouts from the entrance to the shuttle. "Last call! Tickets!"

"How do we get on board?" Annie asks urgently, tugging on SOL's arm. "We don't have tickets, do we?"

"No," it says firmly. "Just stay with me and be quiet. Please."

Casually walking around the shuttle, they stop just short of the lip of the platform, which ends abruptly before a sudden ledge which leads down to the street roughly thirty feet below. Another platform is directly in front of them, about ten feet away. With no warning, SOL suddenly hoists Annie into the air and throws her over to the adjacent platform. She lands on her hands and knees, rolling a couple times. Just as she looks up, SOL jumps the gap between platforms with only a two-step running start, landing gracefully on its feet. The wide-brimmed black hat falls off its head, exposing wires and machinery underneath. SOL immediately snatches up the hat, placing it back on its head. In a few short strides, SOL takes Annie by the hand, leading her ahead toward the back side of the shuttle where a set of doors are wide open.

"Stop!" an android commands behind them. "Keep your hands where I can see them!"

SOL straightens its back, releases her hand, and slowly turns around, approaching the other machine with palms raised. The opposing android has a laser rifle trained directly on SOL. The loud engines of the shuttle turn on, causing a blast of yellow flames to shoot out the back end.

"I mean you no harm," SOL says calmly, still stepping toward the other machine.

"I said stop!" the other android shouts. "One more step, and I'll –"

SOL leaps at the other machine, grabs it in a choke hold, forcing it to drop its weapon. Instinctively, Annie drops to her hands and knees, crawls across the tiled floor to the loose weapon and snatches it, now aiming it at the other android.

"Don't shoot," SOL says calmly to Annie. "I've almost got him."

With its arms still around the throat of the other machine, SOL reaches inside a small opening along the android's neck and yanks out a bundle of wires. The other machine's eyes begin to change colors from blue to green to red, then back to blue before they cease emitting any light. SOL releases its hold of the machine, causing it to fall face first onto the ground.

SOL approaches the open side door of the shuttle and motions her to follow. Together they duck down and crawl inside, pulling tight on the door handle, closing it shut just as the shuttle's engines emit a violent blast, sending the rickety machine rocketing ahead toward its destination.

The inside of the transport is pitch-black until SOL activates an LED headlamp, casting a bright glow on their surroundings. Several articles of clothing and various pieces of luggage lay at their feet. The ceiling above is incredibly low, causing SOL to hunch over.

"It appears we've made it into the cargo hold just in time," SOL says with a sense of relief.

Annie takes a seat, crossing her legs. Within minutes, she's searching through the passenger's luggage.

"I didn't realize I've acquired a thief as my accomplice," SOL says dryly.

"I'm starving. Just need something to eat."

SOL doesn't answer. Instead, it turns around and taps its temple, turning its eyes green to scan their surrounding area.

After several minutes of searching, Annie lets out a frustrated grunt and throws a backpack aside into a pile that she's already searched through.

"Useless," Annie says. "I guess I'll just starve to death. Who knew that food would be so difficult to find out…"

Her voice trails off as SOL hands Annie a red object with a little stem sticking up off the top of it.

"What's this?" she asks doubtfully.

"Nutrition."

"Um…thank you?" Annie says uncertainly.

"You're welcome," SOL says, taking a seat next to her.

Cautiously, she examines the red object, sniffing it. She jerks her head back, not used to the smell of whatever this substance is. Frowning slightly, she gingerly takes a small bite. She chews it slowly, moving the food around in her mouth. Her eyes open wide as her tastebuds respond instantly.

"Wow!" she exclaims while chewing. "This is amazing! But seriously, what is it?"

"It's an apple," SOL says.

"So, you said the Grand Master reports to the Capital City?" Annie asks with her mouthful. "I didn't realize the Grand Master had a boss, or whatever."

"What you civilians were raised to call 'Grand Master,' is nothing more than a hyper-advanced artificial intelligence. All of the A.I.'s in the other Structures are connected to the Capital City, which serves as a centralized mainframe. This way, all the machines within each Structure are connected externally to one designated location."

Annie sighs, satisfied after consuming most of the apple and discarding the core. "The ROADS, the Grand Master, The Committee…my whole life I was taught to believe that's all that mattered. That's what I was teaching the young minds. Now, I'm finding out it was all just a lie."

SOL studies Annie for a moment, its eyes searching her. "Why don't you get some rest?"

SOL crawls around Annie and begins sorting the luggage and clothes into a makeshift bed for her to sleep on.

Once she lays her head down, she closes her eyes and falls asleep instantly.

Chapter 19

I wake up on the bottom bunk of the tiny bed in Kanzen's private ski lodge. Ron is snoring incredibly loudly above me, grumbling restlessly in his sleep. Reaching over to grab my cell phone, I see that the time shows 6:42 AM. I stand up out of bed and place my hands on the small of my back, leaning backwards and causing my spine to crack. I look down at the small mattress where my feet hung off the edge the entire night and shake my head. I've slept on more uncomfortable surfaces, but that was by far the most unpleasant mattress I've ever tried to get a good night's rest in.

Ron snores softly in the top bunk, a little dribble of drool escaping his lips. The lodge is eerily quiet as I leave the bedroom, leaning over the wooden handrail to peer down at the living area below. Kanzen is sleeping on one of the sofas, one arm draped lazily over his head. That's strange. I would've thought he'd be snuggled up with Jess in his oversized bed this morning.

I go back into the bedroom, put on my shoes and jacket, and tiptoe down the wooden steps, trying not to wake anyone. It's still dark outside, the shortest days of the calendar year now upon us in mid-December, but the sun should be peeking up over the heightened horizon of the Cascade Mountains shortly. Until then, a nice, brisk morning walk sounds like a good way to clear my mind and get the blood pumping. Assuming I don't get attacked by a bear or some other wild animal.

Just before I reach the back door in the kitchen, I hear stirring behind me in the living room.

"Where do you think you're going?" Kanzen says groggily from the couch, sitting up.

I cringe, inadvertently clenching my fists, and turn around to go back into the living room. "Just going for a morning walk," I whisper.

"Well, I recommend wearing some snowshoes. You're going to get frostbite wearing those. Here, I'll grab you a pair."

I look down at my white and black tennis shoes. While these normally are good shoes for a morning walk, Kanzen's right. They're not meant to keep your feet dry. He stands up and walks toward the front entryway, shuffling his socks along the wooden flooring. It's strange that X would care so much about the warmth of my feet. Clearly, he has something in mind, some hidden agenda disguised by this act of generosity. But like I was told, I'll play my part and act cool. Something which I did very poorly last night.

"Hey, I'm sorry about last night," I say, rubbing the back of my head. "I acted like a jerk, and I didn't mean to spoil the evening."

Kanzen opens a closet right next to the front door and peers inside, ignoring my attempted apology. "What size?"

I blank out for a moment, not remembering my own shoe size. It's like when the bank asks for the last four of my social on the phone. Too much pressure. "Um…ten," I say uncertainly.

He bends down and picks up a pair of snowshoes, placing them on the floor. "Try these on."

I slip off my tennis shoes and put my feet inside the insulated boots which come up to my shin. As a kid, I always hated wearing snow boots, as I felt like my movements were restricted, but my mom insisted I wear them, claiming that I'd lose a couple of toes if I didn't. These boots, however, are incredibly comfortable. Some cutting-edge design, no doubt.

"Thanks," I whisper, still not wanting to wake the other house guests. "These are nice."

"Don't worry about last night," he assures, turning toward me. "Look, when I asked you if Jess was available, I could tell you were pretty hesitant with your answer. I should've been more mindful about that. If you have feelings for her, just tell me and I'll back off. The last thing I want to do is lose you as a friend. I don't have many of those, as you can probably tell by now."

"I…I don't know how to explain it," I say cautiously. "She's my best friend. I love her to death, but she's a big girl; she can take care of herself. I won't stand in your way."

"Are you sure?"

I hesitate for a moment, knowing that the future of my relationship with Jess, as well as Kanzen, hinges on my response. On one hand, I'm still not resolved on where I'm at with Jess. Despite our breakup, I still have feelings for her. On the other hand, I want her to be happy. I have no right to prevent her from that. I had my chance, and it's time for me to step aside. But why does it have to be *him*?

"I promise," I say certainly. "She says what she means, and she'll always come through for you when you need her most. I owe her the same."

"Alright, Simon," he says, relieved. "And you're spot on about that. She made it quite clear last night that she wasn't ready for us to sleep in the same bed. I offered to take the couch, and she accepted, especially after seeing that bed." He shakes his head, laughing softly. "She's different than a lot of other girls I've met, and I think that's what draws me to her. I appreciate her not being afraid to set boundaries."

We stand there for a moment in silence, nodding our heads. How one woman can make two men act so strangely is beyond me. I suppose that's the way nature, or God, or whoever, intended it to be. Women always seem to have a stranglehold on a man's mind.

"I recommend going out the front door, those back steps are probably slick right now," Kanzen says. "Would you be in the mood for some company this morning, or would you rather go it alone?"

"You can come along if you'd like," I say. "Waiting for you to get ready would probably buy the sun a little more time to wake up and show the way."

I wait in the living room for a few minutes while Kanzen gets dressed. Once he's ready to go, we head out the front door and down the driveway. It snowed about eight inches last night, coating the vehicles in a heavy layer of white powder. My beautiful car is completely covered in snow and ice. It's going to be a ton of fun getting it unstuck when we leave.

I'm thankful that I took Kanzen up on his offer to come along, as I never would've found the path he was talking about. Everything is so white that the surfaces all blend together, making some steps trickier than others.

"About a half mile or so down the path is a nice little stream with a resting spot," Kanzen says ahead of me. "I like to come out here to think. It definitely helps take your mind off your worries and responsibilities back in the city."

For the next half hour or so, we trudge along on the deep path, the snow occasionally coming up to the top of my snow boots. The two of us talk steadily; conversations about his tech company, my past in Chicago, his sister Eun, my stepdad Doug, and just about anything else we can think about. For several minutes, I forget that Kanzen's my evil former brother Mubiru. He's so convincing in his new role that I begin to redevelop a liking to the man, almost believing that he's like a friend I've never had growing up. He's so relatable and easy to talk with.

Apparently, he used to come up to this cabin with his family once a year when he was growing up, so he has a lot of familiarity with this area.

"Mom used to say she could communicate with the animals," Kanzen chuckles. "I can't believe half the stories she tells me."

The fresh powder from last night's snowstorm sticks to the branches of the towering trees, causing their limbs to bend gently down. It's so quiet out here, with the only sound being the two of us breathing and our boots crunching the snow beneath. He must've walked this trail so many times that he knows the way by heart. Without him leading the way, I'd surely be lost, wandering around the forest without the slightest clue of where to go. Only the footprints I've left behind me would've led me back to the cabin.

Eventually, sunlight begins to brighten the cloudless morning sky, making it easier to see. Sharp, jagged ridges of nearby mountain tops appear all around us, the sun reflecting off their icy slopes. We appear to be walking through a valley of some sort, as the intimidating peaks of the Cascades look down on us. We're just two young men, trudging through nature's playground.

The soft trickle of water can be heard up ahead. Kanzen brushes past a lowered tree limb, and I follow him into a large clearing. A couple of cement benches are placed along the sides of the stream, roughly ten feet back from the water on either side. A wooden walking bridge spans the small creek, the handrails and walkway covered in snow.

"Some of my best ideas have shown themselves to me out here," Kanzen says. "I consider this my sacred sanctuary. It's like Mother Nature, or maybe even God himself, speaks to me in this place. As much as I love technology and what those advancements can do for us, it pales in comparison to my love for this." He stretches his arms out, presenting the grand scene before us. "This is what it's all about. Nothing compares to the beauty of nature and all that this world has to offer us."

"I completely agree," I breathe. "I wish I lived out here. This…this is truly remarkable."

I use the sleeve of my jacket to brush the snow off one of the cement benches and take a seat. The soft trickle of the small stream with the wondrous background of the snow-covered trees and the mountain peaks behind them makes me feel like I've stepped into a heavenly alternate reality. It's amazing that places like this still exist on Earth, a place that's become so stressful and full of negative thoughts. To me, at least. Out here, it's like all my stress and anxiety is just melting away.

Kanzen walks across the wooden bridge to the other side.

"The stream really gets high in the spring," he says. "This little babbling brook turns into almost a river as the snowpack melts. It's crazy that eventually, this water we see now will make its way into the ocean. It's quite a cycle this water goes through, when you think about where it comes from and where it goes."

This man's love for nature just about surpasses mine. Which makes me wonder all the more why he would create that monstrosity of an A.I. What leads from this scene that I'm sitting in now, to the terror of the post-apocalyptic wasteland that Annie Hilltop lives in? That machine must be stopped. More than ever, I feel a responsibility to save the future of not just mankind, but the world that mankind was gifted.

As much as I feel compelled to talk to Kanzen and convince him not to continue with his project, not to build the Structure, forget about making the perfect society, I restrain myself. With X's soul in there controlling Kanzen, I can't show my hand. If I stray from my path and confront him, he'll probably kill me. What better place to murder someone than out here, where nobody will find me for months? Or years?

"I'm going to take a leak," Kanzen says abruptly, disappearing into the trees on the other side of the stream.

That's nice. When nature calls…

Steam puffs off my breath as I sit still, admiring my surroundings. I close my eyes for a moment, continuing to breathe in and out mindfully.

Jess. The girl I grew up with. My best friend, who I'd suddenly begun to develop feelings for a few months ago. After the showdown in the Palace Theater, I thought for sure the two of us were destined to be together. I thought we were soulmates, if there is such a thing.

The weather was warm and sunny this past summer as Ron, Jess and I were bringing our boxes and furniture up the steps to our apartment, only a couple days after we first arrived in the Sammamish area after our long drive on Interstate 90.

"This would be a lot easier if this place had an elevator like our last place, then we could enter from inside the building," Ron panted, holding one side of the couch while I held the other going up the several flights of stairs.

"I don't think this would fit in an elevator," I said, struggling and out of breath.

"Then how'd we get our furniture into the apartment the last time we moved, huh?" Ron asked.

"We used the stairs," Jess said from the doorway.

After a few minutes of finagling and wrestling, Ron and I finally managed to bring the heavy couch into the living room, placing it down gently. While we took a minute to catch our breaths, I went into the kitchen for a glass of water.

"You want some water, Ron?" I asked between gulps.

"Yeah, I'll be over there in a minute."

Jess approached me in the kitchen, wrapping her dry arms around my damp and sweaty torso.

"My strong man," she said, tenderly kissing the side of my neck. "Oh, you're so sweaty. We'll have to get you out of these clothes soon."

She began to lift my shirt. I turned around, placing my hands firmly on hers, preventing her from going any further.

"We're not quite done yet," I said. "I'll clean up later."

She looked me in the eyes, furrowing her eyebrows with an expression of confusion mixed with disappointment. Then, she turned around and went into her room, presumably to continue unpacking her stuff.

Later that night, after spending the rest of our afternoon moving and lifting, we decided to go out and celebrate. We also needed to blow off a little steam; carrying furniture up three flights of stairs in ninety-degree weather can definitely wear on a person's patience. I felt bad for the way I rejected Jess. There was a lot going through my mind then, and I thought that talking with her would be the best way to resolve any miscommunication and hurt feelings.

Once we placed our order, Ron got up to use the restroom, unintentionally giving Jess and I the opportunity to talk.

"Look, about earlier," I began. "I didn't mean to –"

She waved her hand dismissively, taking a sip of her beer. "Don't worry about it. I shouldn't have done that. After everything that's happened, I think we're both on edge. I don't know what got into me."

"See, that's just it," I said. "I…I've been having feelings for you, Jess. You're the most beautiful woman I know. You're smart, funny, kind, beautiful…

everything a man could ever ask for. Do you remember when we went to go see that movie, just after I bought my car?" She nodded her head, leaning forward. "Well, I wanted to hold your hand that day in the theater. The thing is, I'm not sure if I was developing feelings for you organically, or if it was X beginning to mess with my head and I just didn't know it yet."

Jess began to speak, but I cut her off. "You've always been my best friend. Always. And I was afraid to act on those feelings because I didn't want to damage our relationship. I was okay with remaining friends. That was fine with me. But I was so conflicted, and I didn't know how to act." I took a deep breath before pressing on. "If you're serious about being in a relationship with me, I'd be open to giving that a chance. But please know that I'm… damaged. After that whole ordeal with Brittany, I can't guarantee that my mind's in the best spot. The last thing I want to do is hurt you or lose you as a friend. I mean that. I'll always love you, no matter what. I know that 'love' can have different connotations in our culture, but I mean it. I love you, Jess."

She reached her hand across the table, taking my hand in hers. "I love you too, Simon. But I feel like after all that we just went through, when you rescued me from being sucked into hell, or whatever, that was a sign that we were meant to be together. I believe in fate. I truly believe that you and I are soulmates, destined to be together."

"Well, then it's settled," I smiled. "I'm going to start calling you my girlfriend now."

Her smile was infectious, and her vibrant blue eyes shined brighter than I'd ever seen before. By the time Ron came back to the table, Jess and I were sitting next to each other holding hands.

"Uh…" Ron began, then shook his head and sat down opposite us.

Over the next week, as the three of us were desperately searching for employment in the Seattle area and getting acquainted with our new surroundings, Jess and I were reveling in our newfound romance. Everything we said, we laughed at. The food tasted better. The sun shined brighter. Water tasted even more…waterier? I don't know. Regardless, it was arguably the best week of my life. We would sit on the couch until well past midnight, snuggling in each other's arms.

Once night, we went for a walk through the woods behind the apartment complex until we found a clearing. We laid down on a large patch of grass, surrounded by trees, staring up at the starry night. Nobody else was around, it was only the two of us. Crickets were making a ton of noise, and the pine trees were giving off a strong aroma that truly made it feel like we were roughing it in the great outdoors of the Pacific Northwest. We saw several shooting stars, pointing them out to one another. Jess showed off her wealth of knowledge when it came to star constellations and found them with ease; the Big Dipper, Lyra, the Seven Sisters and several others that I don't remember the names of.

After a moment of silence, we turned on our sides toward each other and shared our first kiss. Her warm, moist lips pressed against mine, causing fireworks to shoot off all around us. Okay, not really fireworks, as that probably would've sparked a wildfire, but it was pretty dang close. I held the back of her head in my hand, the strands of her long, blond hair running through my fingers. For what felt like an hour, the two of us lay on that grassy clearing, kissing passionately beneath the night sky. That was the greatest night of my life.

The next morning, however, I woke up with a bad feeling in my gut. As the day had worn on, a nagging thought kept clawing at the back of my brain until it finally reached the forefront. *You're not meant to be with Jess. You're going to get her hurt. Your feelings aren't real. She's too good for you.*

As hard as I tried to silence those negative thoughts, they kept coming back stronger and stronger during the week that followed. Ron had told me when we were teenagers that the main quality a woman looks for in a man is self-confidence. Even though I thought I had succeeded in self-forgiveness, the truth was I couldn't forgive myself for the danger I'd put my two friends in, especially Jess. My visions were what eventually led to her being kidnapped and held hostage on a boat for several weeks while I was locked in a mental institution. If something were to have happened to her, I would have never forgiven myself. What happened to her was bad enough, and I still blamed myself.

One night, Jess and I sat down at the foot of my bed for a talk.

"Jess, the last week has been the greatest time of my life," I said.

"Same here! I've never felt this way about someone before, Simon."

I took a deep breath. "Listen, I want you to know that I'll *always* love you. You know how I feel about you. But I've been doing some thinking, and —"

"What…where are you going with this?" she asked, her voice beginning to quiver.

"Jess, I'm a messed-up person. After what happened with Brittany, and that whole ordeal, my brain was twisted in knots. I know now that what we have is real and not just some…toxic residue left over from Brittany's mind games, but the truth of the matter is that I don't want you to get hurt. I *can't* let you get hurt. Not again. When you were kidnapped, it ate me up inside knowing that you were taken because of me and those visions of mine."

I took a deep breath, looking at Jess as tears began forming in her eyes. "I don't expect you, or anyone to truly understand where I'm at mentally right now. If this was some alternate reality, or if this was another time and my visions never happened, I know things would be different. We'd live happily ever after. But where I am right now, knowing who I am, I can't be that person for you. I'm so sorry, Jess. You deserve better. You deserve someone who'll be there for you and won't put you in harm's way. Heck, even moving across the country and living under the same roof with you, I'm worried sick. I feel like I'm just some ticking time bomb, like I could have another round of visions that bring bad guys to our doorstep again."

I shook my head, looking down, not strong enough to look at Jess, who had begun to cry. "My memories as John Stinson are beginning to slowly fade away, but I still can't help but feel the love he had for Samantha. The feelings *I* had for Samantha. When she lost him, it broke her heart. I don't want you to have to go through the same pain that she did. I want you to be with someone who doesn't have this strange "gift" that I have. I want you to be with someone who's normal. That person isn't me."

She shook her head and wiped the tears off her cheeks with the back of her hand. My stomach was in knots, knowing that the speech I gave was one of the biggest and dumbest mistakes I'll ever make in this life. While it pained me to know that I was hurting her, the woman I loved, I also felt a sense of relief knowing that she'd be safer. She'd be better off not being with me, not being with someone who could get a new set of dreams of another past life – or who knows what else – leaving her in harm's way or heartbroken if I'm killed.

"I don't know what to say," she said quietly. "You're breaking my heart, Simon."

"I'm so sorry, Jess. This is the last thing I ever wanted to do. Please, I hope you understand what I'm saying."

"In time, I hope to understand," she said, standing up. "But right now, I think you're an idiot. I want to be alone."

She ran out of my room, sobbing. I tried to follow her, but she slammed her bedroom door in my face. I pounded on the door.

"Jess, please understand where I'm coming from. I'm not trying to hurt you."

"Go away!" she shrieked from her room.

Before I could knock on her door again, Ron grabbed my wrist. I turned around and saw him standing behind me, shaking his head.

"Leave her be, man," he said patiently. "C'mon, let's get out of here."

Ron took me out for a round of drinks. Thankfully, he elected to be the designated driver. We went to a corner dive bar about a mile away from the apartment. Classic rock played at a moderate level out of a jukebox in one corner. Several tough looking customers sat around the bar, their heads buried in their problems. I explained the situation to Ron, going into detail why I did what I just did.

"Shouldn't you be buying beers for Jess?" I asked. "She's the one that got dumped. I'm the dumper, or whatever."

"I know how hard this must've been for you," he said solemnly, patting me on the back. "I think you did the right thing, now that you explained it. Otherwise, yeah, I'd be taking her out for drinks. I'm just glad I didn't deck you in the hallway back there."

"Me too," I said, taking another gulp of alcohol. "Not to talk about her like a piece of property to be passed around, but she's all yours now. I had my chance."

He straightened himself on the bar stool, looking straight ahead at the wall of fancy bottles. "You never knew this before, but we'd actually dated a few years ago. It was around the same time that you were homeless."

"Wait, really? What happened?" I probed, giving Ron my full attention. I had not, in fact, heard this story before.

He shrugged his shoulders. "It just didn't work out. It was mutual. We both realized that we were better off as friends. She's an interesting person, for sure. But she needs a strong man in her life, and that's just not me." He cleared his throat. "And no offense, partner, but that's not really you either."

"None taken," I said wryly. "That's an accurate assessment."

"There's someone out there for each of us," Ron said reassuringly. "We just need to be patient. I'm not sure if we all have soulmates, or whatever, but I do believe that we're all programmed to find someone who's perfect for us. Some of us find that person quicker than others. Some never find that person…at least, not in this lifetime. Isn't that right?"

"Sounds about right. But that's the funny thing about perfection; sometimes we spend our whole lives chasing it, and other times it's right under our noses the entire time without us even realizing it. What matters most is enjoying the time we spend around those we care about, and remembering how those people make us feel when times are toughest."

"I'll drink to that," Ron said proudly, holding his glass up.

Now, as I sit in the wintry forest on this cold cement bench with the stream trickling by in front of me, I watch as Kanzen emerges from the trees, apparently finished with his bathroom break.

"Simon, I've been meaning to ask you something," he says as he walks back over the wooden bridge to my side. "Back when we were down in my man cave, you'd said something about me jamming a needle in your neck. What was that all about?"

"It was just a figure of speech," I say, coughing into my sleeve. Man, it's cold out here. "I'm a very…private person, I guess you could say. I don't really open up to people too often. And when I do, I just don't want you to stab me in the back, or jab a needle in my neck, so to speak."

"Oh, I get it," he says, slapping me on the back. "No, I won't stab you in the back. I hold you in high regard, and I hope that feeling's mutual."

It dawns on me what I need to do now. Not only do I need to protect the future and destroy that computer he's created before it consumes the world, but I also need to save Jess from this demented soul…a dark soul who'll undoubtedly corrupt her. I'll always love Jess and will do anything to protect her. I don't care who she dates, as long as it's not this man.

"The feeling's mutual," I say, standing up. "You're my friend, after all."

Chapter 20

The further the transport shuttle flies away from the Structure and the dying city, the more Annie Hilltop's heart breaks. The thought of leaving her daughter behind is almost unbearable to her. First, she had to leave the Structure. Now she's leaving the city entirely. But she ultimately knows that this is part of SOL's plan to help her get reunited with her baby.

Sunlight begins to peek through holes in the cargo area of the shuttle, creating beams of bright light inside. Whether or not these holes are due to the age of this rattletrap of a fossil fueled machine, or if they're the result of bullet holes, Annie's not quite sure.

"How much further until we get to the Capital?" Annie asks.

She's sitting cross legged next to SOL. The machine has been rather quiet this morning, sitting idly.

"Another couple of hours," SOL says.

Annie clasps her hands together, thinking of something else to say. After all she's endured, last night's rest was just what she needed. Fully awake and refreshed, she's ready to attack the day.

"So…" Annie says, looking around the interior of the cargo area. "What do you suppose we're flying over?"

"Desert. There's nothing below us but sand and debris."

"I want to see," Annie says eagerly.

She stands up and approaches one of the holes filled with sunlight, pressing an eye against it to see out. All she can see is exactly as SOL predicted; nothing but blue skies above and yellowish sand below, dotted with husks of ancient metal. As she continues to look out at the dusty wasteland, rumbling can be heard over the sound of the engines.

"What's that?" Annie asks, peering back at SOL.

The android stares blankly ahead, tapping its metallic temple gently, causing its eyes turn a different shade of blue.

"Enemies approaching from the west," SOL says after a moment of stillness. "Three gunships registered to the Sasaki Corporation, reported as stolen several months ago. Miss Hilltop, I recommend taking a seat. We don't know if their intentions are hostile or –"

The sound of gunfire outside from one of the enemy gunships can be heard, blasting the back of the shuttle. The engine immediately begins to stutter, and the nose of the ship pitches downward, sending Annie rolling around helplessly. SOL firmly plants one of its metal hands on the floor while reaching out with a free hand, grabbing Annie as she slides past, screaming.

"Hold on!" SOL shouts. The hull of the shuttle begins to creak and shake violently. "The structural integrity of this ship has been compromised. We must bail immediately."

"What about the other passengers?" Annie pleads, keeping a firm hold on SOL's hand.

"There's no time! Quickly, we need to open that hatch and escape. Our elevation is dangerously low. Now!"

Annie lets go of the android and reaches for the handle on the inside of the cargo hatch door, twisting it clockwise. The door snaps off the old hinges, bursting outside of the ship and out of sight. SOL finds a loose strap, which was intended to secure the luggage, for Annie to hang onto and crawls past her to examine what's outside the open door. The air rushing past the shuttle creates a strong vacuum, sucking loose luggage and other items out the door around SOL as it holds onto the framework of the open hatch.

"I need you to take my hand again," SOL commands, reaching out for Annie.

She's clutching tightly to the secured strap with both hands, looking panicked.

"I can't!" she yells back. "If I let go, I'll fly right past you!"

"I need you to trust me!" SOL shouts firmly. "Take my hand. We have no more time to waste. I promise I'll catch you."

Annie closes her eyes and releases her grip of the strap. Her body careens wildly toward SOL, who grabs her roughly around the torso and kicks its feet against the side of the open door, launching them both out of the shuttle. The shuttle soars past them with a trail of black smoke billowing out the back of it, descending sharply toward the sandy ground below. Their bodies begin to summersault violently through the air as they tumble toward the ground. SOL presses against Annie's back, tightly squeezing her against its body.

Just before they hit the Earth, SOL throws Annie so that her fall isn't quite as jarring, giving her a chance to survive with minimal injuries. She hits the sand a couple seconds after SOL's loud thud against the desert floor, her body rolling a few times before coming to a stop.

She stands up, miraculously unscathed, and runs toward where SOL has landed. The machine is wedged snugly in a small crater made by its impact.

"Are you alright?" she shrieks. "SOL, are you…operational?"

It lays on its back, motionless for a few moments before sitting bolt upright with a start. Twitching its head up and to the side, SOL looks around, examining the crater it's sitting in. The android holds its hands up to its face, turning its wrists around, getting a better look at its palms as well as the back of its hands.

"All systems are operational," SOL finally declares, standing up. "Are you alright, Miss Hilltop?"

"You…you saved my life. Again!" she exclaims. "Yes, I'm perfectly alright. Here, let me help you."

She reaches down into the crater and takes SOL's hand, helping it walk up the steep embankment. Annie begins brushing herself off, shaking sand out of her clothes and hair while SOL turns around several times, getting a better understanding of their surroundings.

"This way," SOL says, walking briskly ahead.

Annie follows, watching as the transport shuttle makes its final descent toward the surface. Suddenly, the ship hits the ground about five hundred yards ahead, engulfed in a spectacular, albeit terrible, ball of flames. A few seconds later, the sound of the explosion reaches their ears, an incredibly large boom that rattles their eardrums. The sound continues rolling along behind them, presumably heard for miles.

"No!" she shouts, holding her hands to her mouth. "All of those people! Oh no! No!"

SOL stops walking, turns around, and approaches her, wrapping its arms around her.

"Shh," SOL says reassuringly. "It's okay. It'll be alright."

"What're you doing?" she hisses.

"Your tone of voice indicates you are experiencing grief," SOL says in its typical monotone voice. "I was merely attempting to console you in a time of need."

Annie releases herself from the machine's hug and marches past SOL in the direction of the fallen shuttle. "Well, it's not working."

The three stolen gunships responsible for the atrocity which was just committed had been following the transport shuttle until it exploded. Now, they've circled back around, heading directly toward Annie and SOL. The android steps in front of Annie, reaching one arm toward the laser rifle hung on its back. Adjusting the wide-brimmed black hat on its head – which had somehow managed to remain on its head throughout this whole ordeal – SOL aims down the sights of the weapon.

"They're tracking your heat signature," SOL says.

"Well, I guess I'll just try and cool off," she says sarcastically.

"I'm simply explaining the enemy's movements and activity."

The three ships are upon them immediately, descending quickly with landing gear down. The back hatch on each ship opens upward, revealing fifteen heavily armed men.

"On my left hip you'll see a pistol," SOL instructs. "I need you to arm yourself. Quickly."

Annie does as instructed, unholstering the laser pistol.

"I've never shot one of these before," Annie says uncertainly. "What do I do?"

"Aim and pull the trigger," SOL says. "I'm certain these men are after me for my parts. Undamaged metal has become a valuable resource, especially for the type of ammunition they need for their weapons. If you wish to leave, I'm confident that you can escape while I hold them off."

"I'm not leaving you," Annie says, stepping up next to the android. "We're in this together, like it or not."

SOL doesn't respond. Instead, it glances over at Annie out of the side of its robotic eye, then focuses its attention back to the pressing issue at hand. The men have formed a line in front of them, holding their older assault rifles confidently.

"Lower your weapons and we'll take you in peacefully," one of the armed men shouts. "All we want is the machine's parts."

"Told you," SOL says out the side of its mouth.

"So, you do have a sense of humor," Annie quips in return. She turns her attention to the men. "By decree of the Structure, I command you to get back in your ships and fly back to whatever filth you crawled out of."

The men look at one another and begin laughing.

"Young lady, I don't think you quite understand how it works out here," the man who is presumably their leader shouts. "You're not up in your precious ivory tower anymore. This land belongs to the New World Republic. This is your last warning. Drop your weapons, or you will be fired upon."

"Talaticus Marcus, you have just committed mass murder by destroying an occupied civilian transport vessel," SOL says, its voice loud and firm. "Those ships you're using have been illegally commandeered. Now, I'll give you one last warning. Stand down, and fly away, as the young lady has ordered you to do."

I need to do something. These two are about to be slaughtered. Annie has no combat training. If I can just find a way to fight for control… Hello, can you hear me, Annie?

"Who said that?" Annie whispers.

My name is Simon Verner. I live in the past. In your time, I've been dead for what I'm assuming is a long time, centuries more than likely, but you have to listen to me. Let me have control of this body, and I can get us out of this. Please, just relax, and I'll help you and SOL survive.

"I will not –" Annie begins.

She goes quiet as I've finally pushed my way to the forefront of her consciousness. I don't know how I'm doing this, but it's happening. Utilizing the skills obtained from my past lives, especially as John Stinson, I tighten my grip on the laser pistol. Even with an advanced weapon like this, it's still similar enough to modern-day weaponry for me to understand.

Everything I could feel before as Annie is all the same as before. The only difference is that *I'm* in control now.

What…how are you doing this? Annie's voice pleads inside my head. *I demand you release me from this…prison you've locked me in! Let me out! Let me out of here!*

"Annie, listen to me, I'm trying to help you," I whisper so that SOL can't hear me. "Please. You're my future life. Or one of them, at least. I've seen everything you've been going through. I saw how you fell in love with David and gave birth to Hope. I saw you being Banished, and almost eaten by Ted and his tribe of cannibals. Just please let me save you. And be quiet."

Thankfully, she listens. I look over at SOL, admiring the robotic savior of my future life. "You got any grenades?" I ask. "Anything else you can give me other than this little peashooter?"

It's so strange having my voice come out sounding like a woman, and being in this body…man, what a bizarre dream I'm having.

SOL looks over at me, somehow managing to arch one of its plastic looking eyebrows. "Are you serious, Miss Hilltop? First of all, that's no peashooter. That's an incredibly lethal weapon you're holding. And yes, I have two thermal grenades on my hip, but I'm not trusting you to utilize them."

Reaching over, I snatch one of the grenades from SOL's hip, pull the pin, and chuck it in the direction of our enemies. It explodes on impact, sending a frenzy of flames dancing around the group of men, setting at least four of them on fire. Their intimidating looking armor is no match for SOL's grenades, and they collapse in the hot sand, their flesh scorched, reducing them to an unrecognizable pile of char.

I slide to the right, allowing my instincts to kick in. Aiming the laser pistol, I pull the trigger and send a bright red laser out of the barrel, surprised to find that there is no kickback whatsoever. The laser strikes one of the men in the head, causing his skull to implode in on itself, his body collapsing on the sand. Another man enters my sights, and I kill him with one shot to the chest.

SOL darts away from me to the left, firing the laser rifle repeatedly and with extreme precision, taking out four men in as many shots. The android grabs the last thermal grenade, pulls the pin and chucks it behind the men. The detonation causes all three of the stolen gunships to explode nearly simultaneously. The remaining men, startled by the explosion, fire their assault rifles wildly, hitting nothing. I take advantage of their fear and squeeze off several more bursts from the laser pistol, killing four of them. The last man standing, their presumed leader Talaticus, throws his weapon on the ground and collapses to both knees, raising his hands up.

"I surrender!" he shouts. "Per NWR law, you are to holster your weapons and call the local authorities."

SOL and I keep our weapons trained on the man as we approach him.

"Place your hands behind your back!" SOL shouts, then looks over at me briefly. "I'll call this in."

SOL lowers the laser rifle and turns its back on Talaticus, tapping the side of its temple. A hologram emerges from one of the machine's eyes. As I watch SOL initiate the call, Talaticus reaches behind his back, pulling out a pistol of his own. He aims the weapon at SOL's back, but before he's able to pull the trigger, I quickly fire my weapon from the hip, sending a laser directly into his chest, killing him instantly.

The entire thing happened so quickly that SOL didn't even have a chance to turn around and react.

"Why did you kill him?" SOL shouts, disconnecting the call and charging at me. "He'd surrendered!"

"He was about to shoot you in the back!"

SOL walks over to the corpse of Talaticus, examining his body.

"You are correct," the machine says softly, still staring down at the man. "My apologies, Miss Hilltop. I owe you my life, if that's an appropriate expression."

"Don't mention it," I say.

I release control of Annie's body, allowing her back into the forefront of her consciousness.

I'll try not to do that again. I'm sorry, Annie. But I had to help you.

"Thank you, Simon," she says shakily, examining her hands. "You saved both of our lives today."

Don't mention it.

Chapter 21

"Come in," Jess says.

I enter her bedroom a few minutes before her remote shift at work starts. She's laying on her back in bed looking up at her smartphone in her hands. Looking over at me, she rests her phone down next to her and sits up. It takes me a moment to calibrate what I'm seeing. Her once long, blond hair has changed. It's much shorter now, resting just below her shoulders rather than halfway down her back. The tips are coated jet black, giving off a vanilla and chocolate essence.

She used to use minimal makeup. Now, she's wearing a heavy coat of mascara and other facial products, making her look almost like a porcelain doll. I've never seen her look this way before. My face feels flushed with anger seeing what Kanzen has done to Jess in the last week of their relationship. X's manipulation has gone too far. This ends now.

"Why are you looking at me like that?" she asks, sitting up and crossing her arms.

"This new look of yours. It isn't you."

She scoffs. "Good morning to you too, asshole. And if memory serves, I believe *you* went through a similar phase not that long ago."

"Yeah, and we both know why that happened," I respond. "Brittany, X, whatever, they used their influence to manipulate me. And now it's being done to you too."

"Look, even if Brittany's back like you claim, she's not here. She would've tried to kill us by now."

I walk over and stop next to her bed, getting down on my knees. "Jess, I need you to listen to me and trust me. X *is* back. You're not going to like this, and I know I should've said something sooner, but this needs to stop." I take Jess' hand in mine. "X's soul is in Kanzen's body. They've possessed him, corrupting his soul, all for their own purposes, as well as Popobowa's."

She yanks her hand back. "I knew it. You can't stand to see me with another man, even after you broke up with me."

Plastered on the walls of her room, replacing her beautiful oil paintings, are crude sketches of random, foreign objects. Some large machine resting in a canyon, a volcano erupting behind it. A facial sketch of a young Asian woman, who looks just like the faces of those within the Structure. Other drawings have strange, foreign symbols. One drawing in particular above her bed catches my attention; it's of the Structure, standing tall and proud amongst a city of ruin. More taint from X washing off on Jess.

"It's the truth," I say pleadingly, looking her in those blue eyes. "This is exactly what happened to me last time. X is trying to change you, all in order to get back at me. This is exactly why I had to break it off with you, so you wouldn't get hurt." I shake my head. "But I was wrong. And stupid. He's still using you to get to me."

"So, what do you want, Simon? You want me to break up with Kanzen?"

I hesitate for a moment and swallow. "Yes. I'm so sorry, but this is the only way. Look at these pictures." I reach up and snatch down the sketch of the Structure, showing it to her. "This is the same building in my dreams where everyone has the same face. This is in my future life. Kanzen creates this future."

She leans forward. "Not gonna happen. Kanzen's a good man. He's trying to be your friend, but you clearly don't appreciate that. Your jealousy and envy toward him are what's causing you to try and drive a wedge between us." She leans back and crosses her arms. "You don't like it when people tell you what you don't want to hear."

"No, that's not it!"

"You just want me for yourself. You can't stand to see me happy for once if you're not included."

"Jess, please listen to me. Kanzen's dangerous! Not the man he used to be, but the soul possessing him is. If we can just —"

"Get out!" she screams, pointing to the door. "You had no right, no right, to come in here and try to get me to break up with him. You're the manipulative one! Not Kanzen."

I remain on my knees for a moment, the paper sketch shaking in my hands. "You have to trust me. Can't you see that you're changing?"

"Trust?" she says, laughing. "Like how I trusted you with those paintings I gave you to hang up in your apartment?"

She reaches for her smartphone, pointing the screen at me. One of the paintings she'd given to me several months ago, which I'd then turned around and sold without telling her in order to afford the down payment on my car, is up for sale on an auction website. And for much more money than what I got for it. Shoot, I got ripped off.

"I-I can explain," I begin.

"Don't bother," she says, putting her phone back down. "You lied to me. You said yourself several months ago that trust is the most valuable thing in a relationship. If you turned around and sold these paintings behind my back, which I'd given to you because I thought you were my friend, then why would I ever trust you with this theory about Kanzen?"

"I shouldn't have sold the paintings," I say quietly. "But you gave them to me, you didn't loan them to me."

She shakes her head. "Brittany was right to call you a hypocrite. Because that's exactly what you are. Now, get out of my room. I shouldn't have to ask you again."

I stand up and leave with tears beginning to form in my eyes. The fact that I've been called out hurts, but the fact that X has gotten so far into her brain hurts more. I should've stopped that relationship before it began, but I was a coward. I could've tried to defend my friends from Kanzen. Despite his wealth and resources, I should've at least tried to stop him. Now, he's in too deep.

As I shut the door behind me, I can hear Jess turn up the volume to some awful sounding metal music.

Ron's at work for the day, so I decide to open the door to his room and sneak a peek, checking to see if X has warped his brain like Jess'. I poke my head in, and my heart sinks. Terrible posters of gruesome-looking murder scenes line the walls; knives and blood, all sorts of dark fantasy elements that would make the devil himself blush. Laying on the bed, Ron looks over at me. His eyes appear sunken in, almost as if he hasn't slept in days.

"Why aren't you at work?" I ask.

"Screw that place," Ron says. "I don't need them."

"Mind if I come in?"

He shrugs his shoulders, which I take as an invitation. I step into the room, trying to block out the dozens of terrible-looking posters clinging to the walls. Ron has a silver chain around his neck, covered in what can only be described as spikes.

"What do you want?" he asks.

"Just wanted to check in on you," I say. "Haven't gotten to talk to you in a few days. Are you feeling alright?"

"Like you care."

I put my hands in my pockets. "I do care. I care about you and Jess. But this…" I scan the room, "this isn't you, man. Tell me what's wrong."

I know exactly what's wrong here, but I want to hear him say it. He doesn't answer, instead choosing to stare up at the ceiling. I glance up as well to see some more posters and sketches coating the ceiling.

"Where'd you get all these pictures at?" I ask.

"My friend Kitty."

"She your girlfriend?"

"Something like that."

I scratch the back of my neck. "Hey, I have an idea. I've got to go to work here in a little bit, but maybe tonight you and I can go and pay Kanzen a little visit."

"What for?"

"Let's just say I'm not a big fan of the way he's treating Jess."

Ron sits upright with a look of concern on his face. "Is he beating on her?"

I shrug my shoulders. "Something like that. I can text you once I'm off and I'll swing by to pick you up. Then we'll head over to Kanzen's and rough him up a little bit."

Still staring at me, Ron stands up, leaves the room, opens the door to Jess' room and walks in. I follow him, stopping in the doorway to her room.

"Is your boyfriend abusing you?" Ron asks aggressively, standing over her bed.

Jess looks past Ron and right at me. "Are you serious? What the hell's the matter with you?"

Ron turns and looks at me as well, expecting an answer.

"Look, I just thought that Ron and I could maybe talk some sense into Kanzen. You're not yourself. Neither of you are yourselves right now, and it's all because of him!"

The two of them continue to stare at me for a moment more, and then suddenly Ron approaches me, roughly shoving me into the wall on the opposite side of the hallway.

"Don't you *ever* lie about something like that," he says sternly, his face less than an inch from mine. "You want me to rough someone up, you better come with evidence. Otherwise…" he raises his fist, tightening his grip on my shirt collar with his other hand. "…I won't be so nice to you."

"You might have won that fight in the past, but not anymore."

"Is that a challenge?" Ron asks, his eyes turning vicious.

"Can't you see what X is doing to you?" I plead. "He's turning you two against me. This is what he wants! We need to stick together and figure out how to stop these dreams I'm having."

"Don't make your problem our problem." Ron says, releasing his hold on me and returns to his room, slamming the door.

"SIMON, A CUSTOMER wishes to speak with you," the waitress Amanda says.

"Me?" I point at my chest.

She nods her head and leaves the kitchen. I adjust the goyan hat, making sure it's placed just so on top of my mop of hair. This is a moment that could finally brighten my day some, after the fiasco with my mind-controlled friends this morning. A customer wants to speak to me, presumably to compliment my abilities as a chef. Maybe even offer me a scholarship at a local university to get into their culinary program. My mind races with possibilities as I step through the swinging doors and into the dining area.

The restaurant is packed tonight. Couples out on dates, families out trying something new; Ms. Sasaki must be thrilled to see how successful Mwari Sushi has become, raking in happy customers as well as the contents of their pocketbooks.

Amanda leads me to the table that wishes to speak with me, where a man and woman, both middle aged, are seated. She has short, bleach blond hair and a serious look on her face. The man is wearing a sharp looking gray business suit. Both give off the vibes of being wealthy. Looking back at me, Amanda raises her eyebrows in a look signifying "shape up", then scuttles away to attend to another table. I smile, nod my head, and clasp my hands together in front of me.

"Good afternoon," I say, attempting to drop my voice an octave. "How are you enjoying your meal?"

"Did you make this?" the woman asks seriously.

I lean forward briefly, examining the dish. A Mwari Roll, as well as a cut of raw salmon with eel sauce. I do remember making this dish. It took me a few minutes to get the cut of salmon just so, but after a couple of tries, I finally got it down. Raw fish is definitely something that I'm still learning. Ms. Sasaki typically has Brandon do these dishes, but he was falling a bit behind tonight, so I took it upon myself to assist.

"Yes, ma'am," I say proudly. "Is it to your satisfaction?"

She looks over at the other man, presumably her husband, and smiles. "Did you hear that, Charles? He asks if it's to my satisfaction." She looks back up at me. "Is that a serious question? And before you answer that, what is your name?"

"My name's Simon. If it's not to your satisfaction I can definitely make you a new plate. Our ultimate goal is your happiness."

My cheeks begin to flush, as I can smell a trap from a mile away. By using her husband as a conversation piece, pretending I'm not here, she's attempting to throw me off and fluster me. Folks did this all the time at Lowland Woods Golf Course, talking to their friends or associates, laughing at my response as if I'm stupid and beneath them. I don't like this lady already.

"Well, *Simon*," she begins, adding emphasis to my name as if it's a chore to speak. "This cut of salmon is by far some of the most bland, tasteless fish I've ever had the misfortune of eating in Seattle. And I should know. What did you use to season this? Now, before you answer that simple question, please choose your words carefully. I wouldn't want you to trip over them."

"A hint of ginger and a soy sauce mixture," I say quickly. "Very light though. It's a Mwari Sushi recipe."

"And you felt…proud, making this dish?" she asks in an amused tone.

I look up at the ceiling. *Mwari, give me strength.*

"Proud?" I ask uncertainly. "Ma'am, we're very busy tonight as you can see. If you'd like me to make you a new dish and add more seasoning, just say the word and I'll make it happen."

"Your other clientele has no bearing on the matter at hand, *Simon*," she says condescendingly. "And you never did give me your last name, which I specifically asked for." She turns to her husband. "It's tough to find competent service in this city anymore, isn't it?"

I know for a fact she didn't ask for my last name. Unfortunately, when it comes to people like this, there is no way to win this pointless battle that they've created. The husband looks down at his plate. Whether out of shame or the unwillingness to answer his wife's question, I'm not sure.

I stand there for a moment, not sure how to proceed. My heart rate has spiked, and my face is more than likely beet red. If she doesn't like the food, just say so. Stringing me along in some sort of a feeble attempt at a power trip in a public place just isn't my jam. I don't know who this woman is. She has no control over me, despite what she may think at this moment.

"Well?" she says expectantly to me.

"Well, what?"

"What're you going to do to solve this issue?"

"Look, Karen, I've offered a few times now to make you a new dish," she clutches at her chest and gasps. "If not, then don't eat it. Go somewhere else."

"I want to speak to your manager," she says loudly. "Now!"

"You got it," I say, turning on my heel.

I can hear her whispering to her husband, saying words like "idiot" and "unbelievable." Good. I really don't care.

Ms. Sasaki is attending to another table, and I wait patiently for her to finish with them before interrupting. I stand with my hands behind my back, remembering to breathe. *In and out. In and out.*

"We're waiting!" the Karen shouts from behind me.

Ms. Sasaki turns around, scanning the restaurant for the source of the loud voice. She looks up at me, raising her eyebrows.

"A customer wishes to speak to you," I say quietly. "She's…unsatisfied with a meal that I prepared."

Ms. Sasaki marches past me toward the woman and her husband. I follow slowly just in case I'm needed further. And partially to make sure the customer doesn't lie about our interaction or what's taken place. Not that it would matter. The customer's always right.

"There will be no yelling in my restaurant," Ms. Sasaki says sharply as soon as she arrives at the table.

"That young man over there." The woman points at me. I don't react. "He's a rude, volatile individual. You should be ashamed to have him working here."

"And you should be ashamed to be acting like a baby in public," Ms. Sasaki snaps back. "First you were rude to my waitress, now my chef. Your mother failed with you. I want you to leave."

Once again, the woman clutches at her chest and gasps. I turn my head to hide my smirk. The woman takes the cloth napkin off her lap, throws it down on top of the plate of food and stands up. She looks down at Ms. Sasaki, pointing a finger in her face.

"Online reviews are important for a new restaurant such as this," the woman says bitterly. "You'll rue today."

By now, most of the other restaurant patrons have stopped eating, quieting down to overhear the confrontation.

"Your sense of entitlement suits you," Ms. Sasaki says firmly. "You are no longer welcome here. Take your negativity elsewhere."

I go back to the kitchen, not wanting or caring to hear any parting shots from the woman or her man. Not that he has the stones to say anything, seeing as he's stuck in a relationship with her. Not my problem. I appreciate Ms. Sasaki for having my back.

A couple hours pass by. Brandon's been on my case all afternoon. Six hours into my eight-hour shift, and he still hasn't let up. However, I've been keeping my cool. There's no need to stoop down to his level. Ms. Sasaki put her faith in me when she hired me, someone with no restaurant experience whatsoever, to be one of her sushi chefs. I intend to make her proud. Starting a brawl with the head chef would be the opposite of that.

"Verner, hurry up on that Mwari Roll," Brandon barks from his side of the kitchen. "You're slower than the Second Coming."

"Almost done, sir," I say formally.

I look over briefly to see him shaking his head in disgust. Honestly, I can't really blame the guy. I'm not intending to slow him down, but I'm still relatively new at this job. Area residents have grown fond of our little restaurant, and with Christmas right around the corner, business has been picking up steadily every night. As the days get shorter – in terms of hours of sunlight – people seem to want to sit inside and eat sushi. Fine by me. Job security.

I finish with the specialized Mwari Roll I've been working on, making sure it looks as perfect as possible.

"About time," Brandon mutters in the corner.

I can handle civilized criticism. But I will stand up for myself.

"What was that?" I exhale, still standing at my designated station in the kitchen. "I couldn't quite year you. Want to try that again?"

Brandon doesn't answer, pretending not to hear me. He keeps his eyes down, focusing on the plate he's preparing. I turn back to my work, thinking our short confrontation is over, but a minute later he slams his fist down on the metal counter and approaches me, his eyes glaring at me as if I've just kicked his cat, some enemy that he intends on destroying. I back up a couple of steps, trying to keep some space between us.

"I've had just about enough of you," Brandon says calmly, stopping a few feet away from me. He picks up the Mwari Roll I'd just finished, examining it intensely. "This looks like garbage. You call yourself a sushi chef?"

"Look man, put the plate down and step back," I say calmly. "Let's get back to work."

He looks up at me, shaking his head and laughing. "You're an embarrassment, bro." He raises his arm up and throws the plate on the floor, smashing it into pieces. *Why does he keep breaking my dishes? So wasteful.*

"What the hell!" I shout. "Get back over to your side of the kitchen like we agreed!"

"Or what?" he says, getting in my face. He begins to quiver his lips mockingly. "You gonna tell on me?"

I keep staring at the man. *In and out. Keep breathing.*

"I think I understand your issue with me now," I say confidently. "You feel threatened by me. Instead of giving me a chance to be your partner, you feel like you have to protect your turf."

He snorts. "You don't threaten me, Verner."

"Actually, I think I do. The fact that some nobody like me can come in off the streets and pick up this job in a couple weeks intimidates you. I mean, if I can learn to be a sushi chef in a couple of weeks, just imagine what else I'm capable of." I step closer to him, surprising him into taking a step back. "Imagine the skillset someone like me with countless lifetimes of experiences and skills can be capable of."

That once crazed, determined look on his face now has a shadow of confusion creeping in. He looks around the kitchen, seemingly unwilling to maintain eye contact with me anymore.

"I can learn things just like that," I snap my fingers in front of his face, and he flinches. "In my past life, I was a cop. I dealt with people like you. Street trash, I called it. Before that, I fought the Japs in World War Two. At one point, I was the Queen of England. And before that, an Egyptian slave."

"You're creeping me out, Verner," Brandon says, his voice quiet.

"Oh, but I'm just getting started, *Brandon*," I say, keeping my voice monotone. All of a sudden, it's as if I'm unable to control myself or what I'm saying, like someone else is at the controls now. "I could go on and on. The good things I've done, the atrocities I've committed. All for Mwari. My soul beam has been damaged, but it's beginning to be restored. That's how I can receive the images from the Beyond. That's how I got the messages from Samantha Stinson. That's how I'm seeing these visions of Annie Hilltop and the Structure."

"Bro, cut it out," Brandon turns around and heads back toward his designated part of the kitchen. "Freak."

I start working on a new dish, and the two of us continue working in silence. After a few seconds, Ms. Sasaki enters the kitchen, tapping her cane softly on the ground. She approaches me, a sheepish grin spread across her tight lips.

"Brandon, go take ten," Ms. Sasaki says firmly.

Without argument, he leaves the kitchen in a hurry and exits out the back door, shutting it firmly.

"Now that's the Simon I've been waiting for," she whispers, approaching me under the power of her cane. "*That's* the Simon Verner I saw on the internet video Kanzen showed me. You're a warrior."

"What are you talking about?" I ask uncertainly, still working.

"You and I both know that you're meant for more than making sushi rolls," she says, smiling. "Isn't that right, Magdoo?"

I can feel my eyes bulging. My heart resumes its fast rhythm. How does she know that name?

"I don't know who that is," I say sternly, still refusing to look at her.

"You've gone by many names," Ms. Sasaki says proudly. "In one of your lives, a long time ago, I saw you grow into a powerful Samurai warrior."

I turn around to face her. It's no use arguing with her. She clearly knows who I am. "All I want is to live a normal life. All I want is to be happy and… find someone to love, someone to grow old with."

"You'll never live a normal life, Yukimura," she shakes her head. "That's who you once were. Sanada Yukimura, one of the greatest Samurai to ever live. You can't run from your past. No more than you can hide from the future. You think that fortune cookie was all in your imagination? *I created* that for you. You think the name of this restaurant is just a coincidence? It's time to wake up, Simon. Your whole life, you've been living a lie. You've been living in a dream. Wake up and face reality. The fate of humanity rests on your shoulders."

"What do you want from me?" I ask, my voice shaky. Now I'm sweating like crazy. "If you want me to save humanity, then you must know that your son creates an artificial intelligence that destroys the planet."

"That A.I. was only a small part of the collapse. The rest of it, mankind did on their own, using Kanzen's intellect to fuel their desire for more power." She grabs me by the elbow, pulling me closer. "Popobowa and Mubiru are only cogs in the machine. Someone much more powerful waits in the shadows, observing you. They saw what you did to solve the John Stinson case. They're watching to see how perform in your current trial. How can you prevent the future from happening, with so much stacked against you? The only way to save humanity is by maintaining *your* humanity. Set the example. When all eyes are on you, how will you act?"

"You seem to know an awful lot about all of this," I say, keeping my voice low.

"We need another Mwari Roll for table five," Amanda says, entering the kitchen.

I peer past Ms. Sasaki. "Working on it, Amanda. Give me a few minutes."

She arches one eyebrow, looking skeptically at Ms. Sasaki and me. Rolling her eyes, she exits the kitchen.

"I wanted you to meet my son so that you can convince him not to build the Structures," Ms. Sasaki says. "I need you to convince him to stop his project. He has many good qualities, but his lust for technological advancements will doom civilization. I've seen it, too. But only *you* can prevent it from happening. We both know it to be true."

"You son's infected by a corrupted soul, you know that, right?" I ask skeptically. "Mubiru was sent back from the Dark Dimension to possess Kanzen."

"And who told you that?"

"Mubiru told me, in a dream."

"You always believe what your First Brother says?" Ms. Sasaki asks skeptically. "Is it possible he lied to you? That's what he does best. Loretta has already told you this."

"I do believe him," I say. "His corruption is programmed into that A.I." I pause for a brief moment, taking in what she just said. "Wait, how do you know Loretta?"

"She and I are both older than we look," she winks, then turns around to leave the kitchen. "Think about what I said, Simon. Get Kanzen to trust you and change his mind. We both know he can't follow through on his projects."

"Why don't you do it?" I ask just before she leaves.

She turns around, her gaze slowly scanning the room. "Because he doesn't trust me. He partially blames me for the death Eun. Our relationship is… strained."

Kanzen invited us to some sort of an event this evening, and although it took some convincing – Ron especially more so than Jess – we all made it here safely. Over a hundred people are packed into the local convention center for the special event that Kanzen's company is putting on this evening. After a rough morning and hellish day at work, I'm looking forward to relaxing and soaking in the evening. Ron and Jess are already seated at their designated table, looking like they're bored out of their minds. She's wearing a nice-looking dress, but her gorgeous looks stop there. She hasn't combed her hair, and she looks like she hasn't slept in days.

Ron looks like he's on the verge of becoming a young Marilyn Manson. His head rests between his arms on the table; the noise appears to be getting to him. It's embarrassing to see my friends show up at Kanzen's event drunk, but at this point I'm not surprised. That would be X's M.O., humiliating them in public like this. This is getting ridiculous.

I take my seat next to Jess. She glances over at me for an instant, then resumes her staring contest with the ceiling. Balloons float innocently over every cloth covered table, and each chair has a plate complete with an assortment of silverware ready to go for when dinner arrives. And at this point, I hope that's sooner than later. I'm starving.

The event reminds me of Officer Stinson's Chicago Police celebration where he was recognized for his heroic actions with Mike. Flashes of my past life's memories come flooding back to me. Samantha was pregnant, trying to cheer John up. He was upset for having just murdered Rafael Chavez in a display of self-defense, and he didn't feel like he was worthy of being a police officer. He didn't want to be at that event. Just like how I don't want to be at this one.

"Hey, Jess," I say, trying to get her attention. She refuses to acknowledge me.

This whole thing is starting to tear me apart. Seeing my two friends like this, mad at me and the world, makes me angry at X and sad that there's nothing I can do about it. I blame myself for not having those Dream Catchers for them so they can block out X's toxic brain waves. I miss my friends.

"May I have your attention please," a woman at the microphone announces. "On behalf of the Sasaki Company, we'd like to thank you all for coming out today. We pride ourselves in providing the world with the most cutting-edge technology. It was George Washington who once said…"

My mind wanders as the speakers go on and on about Kanzen's great company. Finally, after about twenty minutes of talking – and still no dinner anywhere in sight – the man of the hour gets up on stage to talk about his accomplishments and upcoming goals.

Jess' attention finally perks up as her boyfriend takes the stage, waving to the crowd. Ron's now passed out, not able to be present with us this evening.

"Good evening everyone!" Kanzen begins enthusiastically. The crowd claps for him as he begins his speech, explaining the next steps they're taking toward a better future. A better tomorrow. "One other item I'd like to bring up is that we're going to be having some rebranding. Starting tomorrow, Sasaki Company will officially be renamed Sasaki Corporation."

As the audience whistles and gives Kanzen a standing ovation, it strikes me that this is another piece of the puzzle regarding my dreams. When Annie and SOL were battling Talaticus Maximus, they had mentioned the gunships belonged to the Sasaki Corporation…the future is still changing, right before my very eyes. Like a long and windy river, the choices we're making in front of us right now are effecting the future I'm seeing in my dreams.

Finally, dinner is served to the guests. Kanzen makes his way off the stage and over to our table. I slide over a seat to allow him to sit next to Jess. As soon as he takes his seat, she's all over him, kissing his cheek, patting him on the back, telling him how great he did up there. Yawn.

Apparently, we don't get to choose our dinner; everyone's getting the same thing, and if you don't like it, that's tough. A slice of turkey, some mashed potatoes, peas and some dessert dish made of whipping cream and cherries. But not to be forgotten, everyone gets a glass of wine from Kanzen's Yakima Valley vineyard. He really went all out tonight.

"So, what did you think, Simon?" Kanzen asks, nudging my shoulder.

"You really went all out tonight," I say, trying my best to smile.

"I mean about my speech. Did I get the point across about the project and what it all stands for?"

I have no idea what he's talking about. This is what I get for not paying attention to the whole presentation. "For sure, man. I think you really delivered it well. They were practically eating out the palm of your hand."

"Damn right they were," Jess says, kissing Kanzen on the neck, her arm wrapped around his shoulder.

"I need to go powder my nose," I say as I stand up and leave the table.

I can't take it anymore, seeing brainwashed Jess all over him like that. If it weren't for these stupid dreams, it would be her and me together in love like that. Not this guy. *Kanzen Sasaki.* What a joke.

Eventually I make my way out of the main auditorium area and find myself leaning against a balcony with a chest-high cement railing overlooking the city. Horns honk down below. The crisp December air feels so refreshing after being stuffed in that warm room that I take a deep breath, soaking it all in. With the twinkling stars above and the multitude of man-made lights in the buildings surrounding me, I almost forget that I'm not in Chicago anymore.

I suppose that even as I continue to find myself, I also feel a piece of myself slipping away. In the end, are any of us really able to find ourselves? Aren't we all just constantly re-inventing ourselves to coalesce with our surrounding environment?

"Feels nice out here," Ms. Sasaki says, appearing next to me.

"True that," I say.

"Have you had a chance to talk to my son yet? About making sure he doesn't proceed with the project?"

"Not yet," I reply. "In case you hadn't noticed, your son just gave a forty-five-minute speech about his company and the project, and I only paid attention to a little bit of it." I wait for her to respond, but she keeps staring at me, so I continue. "Earlier, you'd said that he blames you for Eun's death. Why?"

She sighs and takes a look out over the balcony. To the best of her abilities, I should add. The thick cement railing comes up just to her eyeballs, so all she can really see are the skyscrapers around us. The lights from the city cast a heavenly glow on her wrinkled face.

"He blames me because I pushed her too hard in school. She was staying late doing homework, and if I hadn't been so hard on her, then perhaps she would've spent more time at home, rather than in the library on campus. If she wasn't staying late, then she wouldn't have been on the road that night."

"That's completely unfair," I say. "You had no idea any of that was going to happen."

She simply nods, keeping her attention straight ahead. "That's not all. I had told him once that I have the power of premonitions. He never believes me. For all the glimpses of the future I've been able to witness in my life, for some reason I was blind to Eun's premature death. I suspect a part of him also blames me for claiming to be clairvoyant but not being able to see the accident."

"If he doesn't believe in your abilities, how do you expect him to believe me when I tell him about my ability to dream of my past and future lives?"

Ms. Sasaki turns toward me, leaning on her cane. "I'm hoping you can word it well. Or show him somehow."

"There you two are," Kanzen says, striding up to the two of us. "Come back inside, it's freezing out here."

He puts an arm around his mom, guiding her inside. Twisting his head around to look at me, Kanzen has a huge smile on his face. This truly is a special night for him after all the hard work he's put into his company. It's unfortunate he has to be my enemy.

Chapter 22

The bright, orange sun begins its descent off to the west, casting long, darkened shadows over the desert landscape. With the smoldering ruin of the transport shuttle now behind them, Annie and SOL continue their trek through the barren wasteland on foot. Large, hulking ruins arch up out of the sand around them, remnants of a civilization long past. One of the objects appears to be on its side, with hundreds of rectangular metal containers spilling off it, some half absorbed in the soil.

"We're traveling through what was once a large body of water," SOL says. "These are, or more accurately *were*, large cargo ships that humans used to transport goods back and forth. They used to float along the top of the water, before the water all went away."

Annie doesn't answer, and continues walking alongside SOL. The temperature has begun to drop significantly, causing her to shiver off and on.

"In case you were wondering," SOL says, finishing up the last statement.

"Thank you," Annie says politely.

The two of them continue to walk along in silence. The only sound they can hear is the smooshing of sand beneath their shoes, and the occasional howl of wind through their ears, or "hearing centers" as SOL refers to them.

Annie follows SOL until they reach one of the old shipping containers, a relic cast off a cargo ship nearby. Grabbing one of the handles, SOL opens the heavy door effortlessly, revealing the empty interior within.

"I believe this would be a secure place to make camp," SOL says. "Will you be satisfied with these lodging conditions, Miss Hilltop?"

"This will be just fine," she answers back, slightly annoyed.

As much as she appreciates SOL's willingness to help, she finds its politeness to be slightly overbearing at times. She reminds herself that it could be much worse. The android has saved her life a few times now, with her only recently being able to return the favor.

A little while later, SOL has made itself comfortable on top of a nearby rock formation. The metallic knees are pressed up to its chest. Annie watches as SOL gently removes the wide-brimmed dark hat and sets it down on a rock. It almost appears as if the android lets out a heavy sigh as it looks out at their surroundings, surveying the landscape. Almost.

Walking around the back of the shipping container, which has been partially submerged in the sand, Annie climbs up on top so that she's almost level with SOL. She makes herself comfortable, staying silent so as not to interrupt the machine that appears deep in thought. After a few minutes, however, she can't remain quiet any longer.

"What happened to the world, SOL?" she asks quietly. "All of these huge towers and ships, they're all so amazing. What happened to us? The humans, I mean."

SOL keeps its focus straight ahead, squinting its eyes for a moment.

"This is what happens when people are more concerned about being right, rather than doing what's right," SOL says. "From my research through the Structure's historical archives, I've ascertained the following: the various cultural, political and socioeconomic differences in society proved to be too much of an obstacle to overcome. The system they created crashed down around them. While the wealthier continued to accumulate their riches, inflation caused the middle and lower classes to all fall into poverty, grouping the two classes together. They were no longer able to afford basic necessities, let alone higher education. The rich kept a stranglehold on the money, resources, land and education over those they deemed lesser than them and made the cost of living unobtainable for the vast majority, stripping away the very foundation of what made their society good and prosperous to begin with. The rich understood the importance of keeping the lower classes uneducated. If they didn't know any better, then they'd never learn to fight back. They'd never question the decisions being made by those above them, in terms of social status. At least, that's what it all boiled down to in the end, among other things."

"You were a security android, right?"

"Correct. I was also a cook, janitor, butler and maintenance technician."

"Then how do you know all of this stuff?" Annie asks. "How did you know about the New World Republic, the Sasaki Corporation, and the other Structures?"

"When I was 'off the clock,' so to speak, I tuned into radio frequencies, picking up transmissions across the land. I read books, hidden away by the

Founders, not yet destroyed by the Grand Master. Through that, I acquired a wealth of knowledge. The one piece I can't seem to put together, however, is what cataclysmic event occurred that caused civilization to fall. The components were all put in place for society to fail eventually, but some other major event had to have occurred for all of this to happen."

Annie takes a deep breath and lays down flat on her back on top of the metal container. The clear night sky above is full of tiny, glittering lights. In her studies as a teacher of young minds back in the Structure, she was told those objects are called stars, drifting amongst an empty cosmos far away. Although now, after what SOL just told her, she's not sure whether that's the truth or another fallacy created by the Founders. She's not even sure if the sun revolves around the Earth.

"All I know for certain is that I need to get my daughter back," Annie says. "And you need to get your woman back. The rest of it…it doesn't matter to me. What's done is done. These people took what was given to them and squandered it. I intend to reclaim what was taken from me."

"I'll be right there with you, Miss Hilltop. All the way to the end. I vow to see the day that you're reunited with little Hope."

Annie looks over at the android. "You know, you may be made of metal and machinery, but you're more human than any other person I've ever known."

SOL lays down on its back on top of the rock, just as Annie had done and places its hands behind its head, gazing up at the night sky.

"I appreciate you saying that. I believe you have a very big heart."

"Is that healthy?"

SOL laughs, shaking its head. "Your organs are all quite fine. No, I was referring to your kindness. Your soul. You care for others around you…first your mom, now your baby."

A moment of silence passes between them. "I miss my mom. What happened to her was awful."

"I'm sorry for your loss," SOL says.

"I feel bad about those poor puppies," Annie says after another moment of silence. "We killed their mom. How are they going to survive now?"

"Perhaps they'll find the ability to fend for themselves. Maybe someone else will come along and rescue them. In life, the strongest and luckiest survive the longest. If not, then they're 'S.O.L.', as the old expression goes."

"I don't understand," Annie says. "Isn't that your name?"

SOL laughs hard. A bizarre, wheezing noise that causes Annie to chuckle. "Same letters. Different acronym. Although, seeing how things are going so far on our journey, it's fitting."

In the distance, Annie hears the faint sound of engines, their growl intensifying as they get closer.

"We need to find cover down below," SOL says, standing up. "Quickly."

Annie scrambles to the edge and jumps down, landing clumsily in the sand, the laser pistol given to her by SOL falling out of her holster to the ground. SOL is already at the mouth of the shipping container, waiting patiently for her. She runs inside and assists SOL with shutting the door, just as a pair of bright LED headlamps appear, sweeping the area.

The two of them huddle close together at the front door, peeking out. SOL has its hand behind its body, positioned on the grip of the laser rifle. Two older looking motorcycles come into view roughly thirty feet in the distance. The riders kill their engines and get off the noisy machines; both men appear to be middle-aged with long, graying hair and beards. Neither of them are wearing helmets, just leather jackets and jeans.

"The drone spotted two of them around this area," one of the men says. "Let's spread out and keep searching. They'll pay for what they did to our men. We will avenge Talaticus!"

Each man is equipped with standard ammunition pistols, each with a flashlight underneath their respective barrels. One of the men goes left, while the other who was giving the commands turns directly toward where Annie and SOL are hiding. They jerk their heads back from the opening just before the flashlight sweeps past.

Annie begins to breathe deeply. SOL unholsters the laser rifle, powering it on, the weapon giving off a brief humming noise. They each peek their heads out again and find that the closest of the two men has decided to go off in the opposite direction of his partner, leaving a clear path to the unoccupied motorcycles. Annie and SOL quickly look at each other, nod their heads, then push open the old metallic doors, sprinting ahead.

"Stop them!" one of the men shouts.

SOL hops onto one bike, while Annie takes the other. The machines start up with ease, and they peel away from the cargo vessel, leaving the armed men in the dark and dust. Laughing, Annie looks over at SOL and discovers a huge grin spread across the machine's plastic face. It arches its neck up toward the night sky and howls like a wolf. Annie follows suit with a rebel yell of her own.

When I get home from another night of work at Mwari Sushi, Ron and Jess are both in their respective bedrooms playing music at an obnoxiously high level. Wayne sits in the living room, watching TV with a beer bottle in one hand and his feet are kicked up on the coffee table. Several other bottles are strewn about, some of them spilled and soiling the carpet.

"Welcome home, bud," Wayne lets out a loud belch, then takes another swig from his beer bottle.

"What the hell is all this?" I ask in disbelief, my arms stretched out wide. "Did you make this mess?"

"Would ya relax, partner? No, that was all of us. I was only a third of tonight's festivities."

Letting out a deep sigh, I get to work on cleaning up the living room. Wayne eventually steps in to assist, apparently still sober enough to realize this wasn't his home to make a mess in. We begin to converse as we clean, at first about casual things like how he's enjoying his stay in the Emerald City, but eventually the topic turns more serious, and we begin to discuss the changes we're seeing in Jess.

"She's my little girl still, you know?" Wayne says sorrowfully. "I just wish I could've been there for her, through all of it. All these years I've missed. I thought she would've been happy that I've come back. Instead…I don't know. It's like she couldn't handle it or something."

"She never used to be like this. And it's not your fault. It's this guy she's been dating. He's the one that's got her mind all twisted up."

"Really?" Wayne says, crossing his arms. "What's this little punk's name? Maybe her ol' man needs to go teach this guy a lesson."

"That's probably not a good idea," I say, reminding myself that I don't want to damage my relationship with Jess and Ron further. "He's got friends in high places. I don't want to see you getting caught up in it."

"I've been tryin' to stay on the righteous path, Simon," Wayne says, sighing. "I just want to be there for my daughter. Whatever it takes."

I quickly try to change the subject, not wanting to see Wayne getting caught up in this nightmare. Worse case scenario, Kanzen would probably kill Wayne and frame me for doing it. For the next hour or so after we've finished up cleaning, we sit and share stories about my dad.

"Robert was funny as hell," Wayne snorts. "I still remember this one night; he and I went out drinking at some dive bar. Moretti's, I think the place was called. Anyway, we could tell some innocent young gal was getting bothered by a couple of tough looking losers. Boy, your father was not afraid to start a fight. Or 'defend a young woman's honor,' as he so humbly put it. Before you knew it, those two guys were face down in the alley behind the place and your old man was wiping his hands on his jeans like he was taking out the trash." Wayne shakes his head. "Well, I suppose in a way he was."

"I never heard this story," I say, shaking my head. "You were pretty close, then?"

"Well, after that night of partying, our women put us in our place," he says. "More of a timeout, though. But after that, yeah, we sort of drifted apart. We figured it'd be best to focus on being better fathers to you two." Wayne shakes his head, looking down at the carpet. "Suppose it didn't really work out for either of us though, did it?"

"Well, it looks like you've been given a second chance," I say quietly.

Before Wayne leaves, we exchange numbers and I obtain the info for the hotel and room he's staying in. It's nice knowing that there's still someone normal in my life who can come through when it matters most. If things get out of control, I know I can count on Wayne to assist and defend his daughter's honor.

THEY RIDE THROUGH the night, covering a long distance on the barren, sandy soil. The ground below has slowly begun to change into a denser, cracked surface, with small plants trying desperately to sprout through the hardened land.

After a couple of hours, the landscape around them gradually transforms once more into a plusher area with countless green plants and tall trees all around. The two of them pull over and kill their engines, covering the bikes under some thick foliage.

"We need to find more gasoline for the bikes," SOL says. "My sensors detect a fossil fuel reserve up ahead."

Tapping the side of its temple, SOL activates the night vision sensors, turning those lifeless eyes into a vibrant green. Annie follows closely behind as they make their way through the dense forest. As they trek deeper into the vegetation, they begin to see lights and hear voices up ahead. The voices turn into shouting as Annie and SOL get closer. SOL comes to a stop and sinks to the ground, kneeling.

"I'm not going to say this again!" a deep male voice shouts. "Give us your fuel, and nobody gets hurt!"

Annie follows SOL's lead and crouches down, making sure they're unseen behind the thick shrubbery and peers through the leaves at the scene unfolding in front of them.

"I've already told you, I don't know how to access the fuel," a woman pleads. "Please, we have children here. Just leave. We've already given you all our food."

"We need the fuel, woman!"

The man is wearing an assortment of armor from head to toe and reaches back, slapping the woman across the face, sending her down to her knees. A chorus of children's cries can be heard in the nearby building. The man pulls out a pistol, aiming it down at the woman who is now crawling on her hands and knees in the dirt.

"Please, you don't have to do this!" the woman shrieks. "Leave us alone. We're just trying to survive!"

"We all are," the man says sourly. "The NWR needs these resources more than you do. You have until the count of three to show me how to access the fuel before I put one of these bullets into your brain. One."

SOL reaches for the weapon on its back, aims, and fires a red laser beam at the man. His body instantly turns into a misty red paste, coating the side of the building. High pitched shrieks of horror can be heard from inside.

Annie and SOL emerge from behind their area of cover, moving forward. As they approach the woman, a little boy runs from the building straight at the two of them armed with a rock. "Leave our mother alone!" the boy screams, throwing the rock at SOL. The object harmlessly clanks off the side of the android's shoulder and falls to the dirt. Tapping the side of its head to disable the night vision, SOL slowly turns its attention to the boy.

"I'm not here to hurt you," SOL says softly. "We're here to help."

The woman stands up off the ground, sprints over to SOL and wraps her arms around its metallic frame.

"Thank you!" she sobs. "Oh, thank you! You've saved our lives!" The woman lets go of SOL, taking a few moments to wipe her eyes and collect herself. She turns her attention to Annie, looking at her skeptically. "What's a pretty little thing like you doing out here?"

"We're just passing through," SOL says quickly before Annie has a chance to respond. "If we can have a canister of fuel, we'll be on our way."

The woman, who appears to be middle-aged with shoulder-length brown hair and a permanent frown on her face, turns her attention to the android, hands on hips. "I think the girl can speak for herself. Look, I appreciate what you did, truly. Let yourself inside if you want to poke around. Don't mind the little ones, they don't bite. Hard."

"Thank you," SOL says, walking to the building.

The woman takes a step toward Annie, brushing aside a strand of her brown hair. "It's just the two of us now, hon. Name's Helen. What's yours?"

"Annie."

"Is that robot hurting you?"

"What?" Annie asks, startled. "Oh, no. Not at all. It's saved me a few times now. Like it said, we're just passing through."

"From where? To where?"

"From the dying city. I was living inside the Structure, but I was Banished for having an unlicensed pregnancy. They kidnapped my baby girl, and I need to get her back. We're trying to make it to the Capital."

Helen nods her head softly, as if a mutual understanding has passed between the two women, then turns and heads back toward the building. "We've got food and water to go with the gasoline your android friend is looking for."

As they step through the door together, Annie looks around quickly and takes note that the interior is dark, dusty and incredibly filthy. At least a dozen little children are waiting for them, looking Annie up and down in wide wonder and fascination.

"Who are you?" the same boy who assaulted SOL with the small rock asks. "You're a stranger. Helen says we aren't allowed to talk to strangers."

Annie bends down gently on one knee in order to lower herself to eye level with the little boy, as well as all of the other little kids.

"My name's Annie Hilltop," she says softly. "I used to teach kids around your age, just a few months ago."

"What happened?" a little girl asks. "Why ain't you teachin' no more?"

"Ain't ain't a word, stupid," the first little boy says to the girl, slapping her on the shoulder.

"Hey, now, that's no way to talk to your friend, is it?" Annie keeps her voice calm, not wanting to startle the other kids. She turns her attention to the little girl. "It's a long story. Just know that my friend and I aren't here to hurt you. We only need to grab some supplies and we'll be on our way."

Annie stands up and sees Helen looking over at her from behind a half-collapsed wooden counter. Rot and decay have stripped the interior of any beauty this building may have once had.

"You're pretty good with kids," Helen observes. "It's a shame you're not sticking around. I could use a hand with these little rascals."

Annie looks back at the children, then back to Helen. "Are you…raising all of these kids on your own?"

"Oh, heck no. I come from a large community a little ways from here. We decided it's time to let the little ones explore with us. The other adults who came with me are out hunting for some food right now. They were due back a couple hours ago, but they've gone silent on me. Then that band of NWR thugs showed up. I took care of two of them, but I ran out of ammo for that third one."

"Are you going to try and eat me?" Annie asks seriously.

"What?" Helen tilts her head. "What in the world…oh, hon. It sounds like you've been through hell and back. No, we're not cannibals for crying out loud. We're just trying to survive. Those kids… that's what we live for now. They're the future."

"Maybe the android and I can try to help track down your lost friends?" Annie asks. "Since you're being so generous with your supplies, it's the least we can do."

"I would really appreciate that. Truly, I would."

A short while later, Annie and SOL are trudging through the densely thick forest, knocking aside leaves and branches. The dirt beneath their feet has turned into soft mud as rain has begun falling steadily over the area. Sweeping the beam of her flashlight from right to left, Annie squints, trying to get a better focus on what lies ahead. Rainwater starts to seep into her eyes, blurring her vision and causing her to blink several times.

SOL taps the side of its temple, turning its eyes red as it activates infrared vision.

"I see two heat signatures about twenty feet up ahead," SOL says, taking off at a sprint.

Annie tries her best to keep up, hurtling over a fallen tree trunk. Mushy leaves and other foliage grab at her ankles, but she doesn't stop. She runs harder, managing to stay within a couple strides of the android.

SOL abruptly stops, and Annie follows suit. Pointing the flashlight down, they find Helen's two missing partners lying face down in the mud with bullet holes in the backs of their heads. Blood still seeps from the open wounds, trickling down into the dirt below. SOL bends down and reaches a hand out, pressing its fingers gently against one of the men's necks.

"Dead," SOL says, standing up. "Not more than five minutes ago."

Annie looks down at the ground, then she's quickly sent into a state of panic. "What if they doubled back after the supplies? The kids…they could be in danger!"

They take off running again, back the way they came. The rain has intensified, making each footstep now a small splash, the muddy water soaking their pants. Annie's legs are beginning to get cold as water seeps through her clothing, but she refuses to slow down. Saving Helen and the children is the only thing on her mind now.

The building is now within sight. A flash of white from above, followed by a tremendously loud crash of thunder which shakes the ground, rattling Annie's eardrums. She's never seen this flash of violent light in the sky before, but she doesn't have time to think about it. There's so much on the Outside that she was never told about. Never prepared for. But right now, other pressing matters are at hand. She passes SOL, running faster than she ever has in her life.

Two armed men are pounding on the door of the building; the same men that were searching for them back at the cargo container. *They must've used that drone they were talking about to hitch a quick ride here.* Annie speculates to herself.

Annie stops running, motions for SOL's attention and points at the building. SOL takes the laser rifle off its back, aims down the sights, and fires a red laser beam at one man, immediately turning his body into a red mist that coalesces with the falling rainwater. Just as the second man looks over at his fallen comrade, Annie tackles the man head on, sending them both down into the mud. Annie attempts to punch him but realizes quickly that she has very little upper body strength compared to her opponent; her clenched fist merely bounces off the man's cheek, not inflicting any damage. He reaches up with one hand, seizing Annie by the throat, cutting off her oxygen. She claws desperately at her throat, struggling for breath.

She sees SOL charging up the laser rifle, aims, but doesn't fire. It slaps the side of the weapon in frustration, tries to fire again, but again nothing happens. Just as her eyes are about to roll back in her head, SOL throws down the weapon and runs over to Annie. It grabs the man around the throat in an effort to get him to release her. With Annie's field of vision darkening, she sees the man pull out an electric-powered weapon of some kind, and stick it against SOL's ribs, sending the android flying back several feet.

Simon, I need your help. Please. I relinquish control to you.

The next thing I know, it feels like I'm the one getting the life choked out of me. I try to claw and scratch at this brute of a man with no avail. Annie seriously needs to start lifting. This is humiliating.

Using the most efficient fighting technique that I can think of before we're both rendered unconscious, I straighten my right leg, kicking the guy right where it counts. He lets out a grunt and releases his hold on my throat, rolling around in the mud and grabbing his crotch. I bend down and pick up the cattle prod, or whatever this thing is, and hold it up to the man. He's still clutching his jewels in severe anguish.

"How many more of you are there?" I ask in as stern of a voice as I can muster in this body.

"You're the ones who stole our bikes?" he asks, wheezing.

"Do you work for Talaticus?"

The man begins to stand up shakily, laughing, all while staring at me with a wicked snarl. "Work for him? I worship him! It would be an honor and a privilege to die serving Talaticus Maximus!"

"Looks like today's your lucky day," I reply.

The man staggers toward me, reaching clumsily for something to grab onto. I keep stepping back, sidestepping a deep mud puddle. He aggressively lunges at me, stepping directly into the puddle. His momentum carries him in deeper, the water now well past his ankles. I plunge the end of the electric weapon into the puddle, activating it. The man lets out a roar of pain, shaking and spasming in place. He arches his neck back, screaming. Steam begins to waft off the puddle, as well as the top of the man's head until he collapses face-first in the water, dead on impact.

Throwing the electric weapon down onto the dirt, I walk over to SOL and bend down on one knee. Its body has smoke and steam rising off it as well, the rainwater cooling it down.

"Talk to me, SOL. You alright?"

Its eyes open wide and sits bolt upright. Speaking several different languages, one after the next, SOL goes through what I can only speculate to be some sort of a reboot cycle. Next, it begins to countdown from twelve. Once it reaches zero, it turns slowly to me, a wave of familiar recognition showing on that plastic face.

"Miss Hilltop?" it asks, gently grabbing my shoulder. "My weapon…it must've jammed. It apparently doesn't operate well in rain. I'm so sorry."

"I'm fine. Are you okay?"

SOL touches its chest, then taps the side of its temple several times, activating different vision modes and who knows what else.

"All systems appear operational," SOL says after a few moments, a tone of happiness seeming to seep through its voice. "We dodged a bullet there."

"We sure did, buddy. We sure did."

Helen's waiting by the open door for us and we follow her inside. The children are all huddled in one corner. SOL and I quietly share the sad news with her about her fallen partners, standing between her and the children so they wouldn't see her grieved expression. We give her a few moments to compose herself.

"I'm taking the kids back up to our main camp at first light," Helen says, wiping away a tear. "Those bastards. They agreed to leave us alone, but a treaty doesn't mean jack squat to Talaticus and the NWR."

"Talaticus is dead," I say, still not used to my high-pitched voice. "I killed him earlier today. His crew shouldn't be any more trouble for you."

Helen looks quizzically at me, seeing that Annie's acting differently. Little does she know what's really going on here. Slowly, she nods her head.

"That's good to hear," Helen says. "Thank you. Both of you."

"We will stay here for the night and help you get back to camp," SOL says, then looks over at me for reassurance. I nod my head. "After you and the children are back safely, we will take you up on your offer of the fuel so we can be on our way."

"That would mean the world to me," Helen says, relieved. "I'm in your debt. If there's anything you need, other than the supplies, you just say the word. We're a camp of about two hundred or so now. Our numbers keep growing as we take in refugees who've evacuated from the surrounding cities."

Annie, I'm going to give you back control. But I recommend you ask Helen for support in your cause to retake the Structure. As powerful as the Structure's robotic army's going to be, you'll need all the help you can get to rescue Hope.

Annie takes a deep breath, then turns her attention to Helen.

"Actually, there is one thing we need," Annie says. "But it's a big ask."

"Anything," Helen says. "You two have earned it for killing the leader of the NWR. It'll take them months to recover now that Talaticus is gone. We have clothes. Food. Weapons. Heck, we even have an army."

Helen may have been saying it in jest, but that's exactly what Annie would ask for next.

Chapter 23

After work, I drive to Kanzen's mansion. The closer I get to my destination, the more I rehearse and recite what I want to tell him so that it doesn't all pour out of me in one word-vomiting release.

I park in front of the mansion on the street and walk up the pathway to the front door, ringing the illuminated doorbell, complete with small camera, setting off a chorus of chimes and bells inside. A few moments later, Kanzen greets me at the door.

"Hey, Simon. What brings you by?" he asks, yawning into the back of his hand.

"We need to talk," I say. "You have a few minutes?"

"Of course, buddy," he says sincerely, welcoming me inside.

He shuts the door behind me as I go and sit down in the living room. One of the living rooms, I should say. The couch I'm sitting on probably costs more than I make in a month. The shiny hardwood floors, the dim glow of the overhead lights, all if it gives off an aura of wealth and dignity higher than anything I'll ever be able to achieve. Even without Kanzen's soul being possessed by X, I know that I'd still be somewhat jealous of this guy.

He takes a seat on an adjacent couch, leaning forward, hands clasped in front of him. His little dog sits alone in a plush bed of his own, sleeping soundly. Fortunately, he's not wearing a bowtie today.

"Is everything alright?" he asks, his brow arched in a look of sincere concern.

How cute, he even acts like he cares.

"I wanted to talk to you about Jess. Have you noticed anything... different, about her?" I probe, judging his reaction.

"No, not off the top of my head. Why?"

"What do you think of her new hair?"

He shrugs his shoulders. "It's shorter than when we first met, and the color is a bit different, but looks fine to me."

"Well, it doesn't look fine to me," I say sternly. "I've known her most of my life. The old Jess *never* would've chopped her hair off and dyed it black like that."

Kanzen sits there for a moment, staring at me and sighs. "I don't know what you want me to say here, buddy. You want me to talk to her about… her hair?"

My heartbeat's quickened. It's like I'm on a tightwire crossing a deep canyon; one wrong move in either direction and I fall. Or, in this case, damage my relationship with Kanzen, prompting X to hurt my friends.

But that's the thing. I've done everything he asked me to do, by playing my part. I let him date Jess, as was requested, yet he still crossed the line and twisted my friends' minds, turning them into weird little freaks who draw bizarre sketches and hang gruesome, hellish pictures. *He* broke our little treaty, not me. I'm at a tipping point. The tightwire act, *my* tightwire act, is beginning to fail.

"There's something else I wanted to talk to you about, Kanzen," I say, licking my lips. "The project. *Your* project. It needs to stop. I've seen what that computer of yours does to the world, and it's evil. That little ball, that A.I. you've developed down in your weird garage, it destroys the world." I pause for a moment like an actor about to deliver a crucial line. "I've seen the future."

"What do you mean you've 'seen the future'?"

"I have a gift. When I dream, I can see into my past and future lives. In my dreams, I see that tower you want to create. Plus, there's –"

"Alright, I'm going to stop you right there," Kanzen says sharply, putting a hand up. "What on God's green Earth are you talking about, buddy? Dreams?" He gently places a hand on my shoulder. "Look, if you don't want to be part of the project, just say so. I won't force you. It would make you rich, though."

"Look, I don't want your money," I say. "All I want, all I've ever wanted, is for people to live in peace. But I've seen what your project does to the world." I keep my attention focused on him. "Please, I need you to trust me here. That project you're building is dangerous. If you're still in there, Kanzen, I need you to fight X, exorcise their soul out of your consciousness and destroy that computer before it's too late."

I can see tears beginning to well up in Kanzen's eyes. It's apparent that my ability to reveal the true nature of his project has proven to be too much for him to handle. Good.

"I'm really not following you here, Simon," he says, a tear streaking down his face. "You saw my project in…a dream? Can you explain that a little bit better for me? Because you're not making a lick of sense right now. What exactly do you mean you can dream of your past and future lives?"

"Back home, a few months ago, I started having these really vivid visions, or dreams, of a police officer who was murdered. His name was John Stinson. The weird thing is, that person was real. He was a real guy who was killed in a cold case in 1986. You can look him up for yourself if you want. Eventually, those dreams showed me who killed him, and those responsible were brought to justice. Now, it's happening again. I'm dreaming that I'm living in the future as a young woman named Annie Hilltop, and she's living in one of those big bunkers you were showing me the blueprints of. Except it's a large skyscraper. Everything outside of that building is gone, man. It's…it's a ruined wasteland. People are killing one another in the streets. It's terrible."

He turns his attention away from me, focusing on the fireplace directly ahead of us, and sighs again.

"So, when you and Ron were talking about you being in a mental hospital, you were being serious?"

"I was locked there against my will. You know that. You put me there."

The silence between us is deafening…the gulf between us a wide canyon.

"I received a call yesterday from a detective in Chicago who had a lot of questions about you," he says quietly, still staring ahead at the fireplace. "His name was Detective Erickson."

"Erickson?" I look down at the ground, searching my memory for why that name sounds familiar. Then it dawns on me. He's the one who talked to me at the mental hospital, asking about Sean Boykins and Brittany. It seemed like he believed me at the time, when I told him that she was the one who caught my apartment on fire.

"There's some kind of a missing person's case going on over there for someone named William Marcini. And a murder investigation for another guy named Travis Daniels."

"W-What'd you say? Did you rat me out?"

"I lied to him," Kanzen answers. "Told him I've never heard of you. Not sure he bought it, though." He shifts on the couch to face me. "Look, Simon, I know some really good mental health professionals here on the west coast. Just say the word and I can get you in to see one. There's a great place here in Seattle that can get you the help you need."

I squint my eyes, shaking my head. I should've known. I should've known that X was still in there running the controls. For a brief moment, I'd thought I was speaking to a friend. I'd hoped Kanzen would help me out, listen to me about my concerns, believe me and agree to stop the project.

"You have everyone else fooled but me, Brittany. Or Mubiru. X. Whatever the hell you want to call yourself. Did Popobowa place your soul in this body to tempt me into working with you? Did that demon think you and I could rule the world together, is that it?"

"Who…" he scratches his head in frustration. "Simon, I don't know who or what the hell you're talking about. I can make a call right now and –"

He pulls his smartphone out of his pocket, and I immediately slap it out of his hands. The phone hits the floor with a resounding thud. Kanzen curses and stands up, and I stand up next to him. I know that Ms. Sasaki had asked me to earn his trust, but he's too far gone. It's up to me to stop the future. Nobody else believes me.

I roughly grab his shirt collar, pulling his face in front of mine. "After everything you've done, you think you can just continue like everything's okay? You drug me, burn down my apartment, kill Hank, and come back for round two? Now you want to seduce Jess, turn her and Ron into some strange Gothic weirdos like you did with me? What is it with you and making people Gothic, anyway?"

He seizes my wrist, throwing it off his shirt collar.

"It's time you leave. And don't return. Be thankful I don't call the cops."

"Yeah, that's typical," I retort. "Hide behind the cops. That's what you did before as Connie, isn't it? That's why you married Doug. You probably killed your husband in San Francisco when you were Brittany, didn't you?"

Kanzen shakes his head, his cheeks moist with tears. "I really hope you find the help you need, Simon. I'm sorry I couldn't be the one to pull you out of this rut."

I stick my finger in his face. "Your project destroys the world, and I'm going to stop it from happening."

Turning around, he walks quickly toward the glass display case of katana swords on the wall next to the stairs. He presses a few buttons, and the case opens. Reaching for the katana closest to him, he grabs the hilt of the weapon and turns around, pointing the blade at me.

Immediately I can sense that this weapon holds a tremendous amount of power. I receive a quick flash, a memory of using that weapon to strike a blow to Popobowa's shoulder, weakening the demon. Taking a chunk out of his soul. This is Sanada Yukamira's old weapon. It feels just like yesterday I held that weapon, charging headfirst into my final battle…

"Get out!" he shouts again, this time a bit shakily. "I was clearly wrong about you. This is your final warning. I'm prepared to defend myself."

I put my hands up mockingly, backing toward the door. "Aw, look at you. Big tough Mubiru with another weapon. How typical. How *weak*."

I reach back, opening the front door and begin to back down the steps while Kanzen stands in the doorway, still holding the katana firmly in front of him. His hands are trembling.

"Stay away from Jess!" I yell.

"This again?" he says, letting out a nervous chuckle. "You really can't get over her, can you? Is that what drove you insane?"

"I mean it. Stay away from her. Your influence on her is poisoning her mind."

"You really are crazy, you know that?" Kanzen says. "Detective Erickson's hot on your heels, bud. It's just a matter of time until you're extradited back to Chicago. They're watching your every move now." Kanzen takes a deep breath, his face now a wide grin. "I don't know who you think I am. But what I do know is that I'm dating Jess, and I'll continue to date her until she says otherwise. And you know what? I think…no, I *know* I love her."

"You're not capable of love, Mubiru. You never were."

Shaking his head in pity, Kanzen slams the door, leaving me alone in his front yard.

At first light, Helen, SOL and Annie lead the convoy of a dozen children out of the decrepit building and into the woods. Before leaving, Helen handed

Annie something called a peach, which was much juicier and tastier than the apple she had back in the cargo hold of the transport shuttle.

The ground is still soggy under everyone's feet after last night's rain. The children's shorter legs get bogged down repeatedly in patches of sticky mud, slowing down their journey to Helen's main camp.

"When we get there, just let me do the talking," Helen warns, swatting a mosquito out of her face. "We're not a trusting bunch of people, so th+ey're going to grill you two for answers. I'll do my best to ensure they don't harm you."

"I don't blame them," Annie says. "After what I've seen tonight, it's understandable not to trust people out here."

After a couple of hours, their path begins to lead uphill. Annie, not used to physical conditioning, easily gets winded within the first several minutes. She stubbornly pushes on until one of her feet slips, sending her down into the mud on hands and knees. SOL, unaffected by the climb, quickly turns around to help Annie to her feet.

"I'm fine," Annie grumbles. "I'll catch up."

"You're exhausted," SOL says, scooping Annie up into its arms effortlessly. "Please, don't look upon this as a sign of weakness. See it as a reward for your heroism last night."

As much as Annie wants to protest and scream at the top of her lungs for SOL to put her down right this instant, she swallows her pride and lets the android carry her. After all, she's incredibly tired and doesn't know how much further she could've gone before the children would've had to carry her over their heads.

Sunlight streams through the leafy branches above, causing rays of bright light to shoot down all around them, forming astonishing patterns on the brown dirt. A group of rabbits hop out of some thick foliage on the side of the trail. Once they notice the group of people walking past, they cower in the bushes, attempting to go unseen. Annie's never seen a rabbit before, or any other animal for that matter, other than in picture books. The aged, torn pages, the same ones she'd used as a little girl, ended up being the same ones that she'd teach from twenty years later.

Even though it's only been a couple of days, it feels like she's been gone from home for months. The same thoughts hammer away at Annie's mind relentlessly. How could the place where she grew up cast her out so easily? Was everything she'd been raised to believe a lie? Were the ROADS truly the foundational pieces for a perfect society? So many questions…she closes her eyes for a moment and takes a deep breath. All that matters, she tells herself, is rescuing Hope. The rest of it will have to be sorted out later, if at all.

Another hour passes, with SOL still holding Annie in its metallic arms. Up ahead, a tall, barbed wire fence comes into view in the middle of a short canyon. Steep rocks jut up on both sides of the fence, towering roughly twenty feet above the trail the group is walking on. One side of the fence has a manned guard tower.

"Stop! Announce yourselves!" a gruff sounding voice calls from his perch above.

"It's just me, Joe," Helen says nonchalantly. "I've brought the kids back from our field trip. Sike and Custer are dead."

"Dead?!" Joe cries down. "Jesus…hold on, I'll be right down."

Some banging and screeching can be heard from the guard tower and fence until eventually a gate opens outward from the bottom, allowing Annie to get a brief glimpse inside the camp. It looks more like a small city, with several brick buildings and dozens of people hustling about.

Joe, a large, bald man with a long, thick beard steps through the gate, swinging his wide shoulders back and forth in an intimidating looking swagger as he approaches the group.

"Children, get inside," Joe says sternly, keeping his eyes on SOL and Annie.

The children quickly run inside, some of them laughing with joyous enthusiasm to be back home. Hearing that sound once again makes Annie long for her time as a teacher. She misses the sound of her students running into class, eager to start the day, their innocent, shrill laughter carrying throughout the classroom and beyond.

"Who the hell are these two?" Joe asks gruffly. Helen begins to answer, but Joe puts a hand up to her. "You've done enough, Helen. Go inside with the kids. I'll handle this."

Helen looks sharply at Joe, then at SOL and Annie, shame on her face. She turns toward the camp, head hung low, and walks inside.

"Well, what's it gonna be?" Joe asks. "You two mute, or what?"

"My name is Synthetic Obedient Lifeform, serial number UE0353, from

Structure Number One in the region formerly known as Cleveland, Ohio. This is Annie Hilltop, a recent outcast from the same Structure. We are on a mission to the Capital City, and respectfully request gasoline, or transport assistance. Last night, Helen's group was ambushed by a group of criminals working for a deceased NWR warlord named Talaticus Maximus. We killed him and his men, saving the lives of the children, as well as Helen's. Unfortunately, two of your men were killed before we had a chance to intervene. Your associate can vouch for our actions, or you may view my recordings, if required."

Joe sticks his tongue into his cheek, stepping closer with his arms behind his back. He nods his head briefly, then looks down at Annie who is still being held in SOL's arms.

"You unable to walk, miss?"

"I can walk, I'm just tired at the moment," Annie says innocently.

"Is what this machine just told me the truth, or a bunch of bull? These things are prone to lie."

"He tells the truth," Annie says. As soon as the phrase leaves her lips, she realizes she's mistakenly referred to SOL as a "he" rather than an "it", but doesn't expect the reaction that follows.

"Don't refer to this *thing* as a 'he' ever again!" Joe shouts. "These machines were programmed with one purpose in mind, and that was to strip us of our livelihoods, suck up our resources and manipulate the weak-minded. They have no soul. As far as I'm concerned, they crawled out of the deepest chasm of hell and are intent on destroying the human race, once and for all."

A moment of silence passes amongst them. SOL places Annie down gently so she can stand on her own two feet, all the while keeping its eyes on Joe. Birds fly over the canyon, from one set of trees to another. The noises they make are again something new to Annie, in a big world full of unfamiliar sights and sounds.

"Will you help us, or not?" Annie asks, crossing her arms. "Look, whether you like it or not, we saved your people last night. All we need is some gasoline or some form of transportation and we'll be on our way."

Joe continues staring SOL down for a few more tense seconds, then allows himself to relax slightly. "Fine, whatever, I'll get you what you want. Stay right here."

He lets out a huff, turns around, and heads back into camp. SOL and

Annie look at one another and shrug their shoulders simultaneously. After a few minutes, two men exit the gate, pushing two new dirt bikes. After the men set each of the bikes down on their kickstands and head back into camp, the gate shuts.

They both climb onto their respective motorcycles and ride back down the hill away from Helen and Joe's camp. Hours pass by, and the sun continues to climb high overhead. Waves of heat can be seen hovering across the flattened horizon, causing a shimmering effect over the ground. Yellow and orange are all around them as they drive between the dried-out husks of large shipping vessels. It's hard for Annie to imagine that this landscape which they're currently driving on was once underwater. She's unable to fathom what could've caused all the water to dry up and disappear.

Shortly after the elevation rises a little, the two of them stop alongside an old, abandoned highway in order to allow Annie time to stretch.

"It's not much further," SOL says. "We'll be there around dusk."

SOL's leaning against the bike, one leg crossed, examining its fingernails as if they need to be trimmed. The brim of its dark hat casts an intimidating shadow over its face. With those ankle high boots, Annie momentarily forgets again that SOL isn't human. He looks like a Cowboy from one of the picture books back home.

"What're you expecting to find when we get there?" she asks out of genuine curiosity.

"What I hope to find, and what I expect to find, will unfortunately probably end up being two different things. Regardless, I expect we'll have more challenges ahead."

That's not much of an answer, Annie thinks to herself.

She's thankful to have Helen on their side, but after meeting Joe, she's not sure if that army they were promised last night will actually come through. As much as she hopes to rally everyone behind their cause, she knows deep down that SOL's right; nothing comes easy on the Outside. At the very least, though, she found a true friend in a strange world where she didn't expect to find any friends at all. The fact that she's still alive and fighting gives her motivation to keep pressing on. All for Hope.

They each climb back on their dirt bikes, making the last push down an empty highway toward the Capital City. Weeds sprout up through the blacktop periodically, and on a few instances, they have to completely drive off the road to avoid groups of old, rusted out vehicles that are blocking the way. The sun begins to drift down to the horizon, stretching long shadows from abandoned buildings. SOL alternates between regular and infrared vision, making sure there are no outlaws or bandits waiting for them.

Just as the sun begins to set, the Capital City begins to appear in the distance. Tall skyscrapers reach toward the clouds like long fingers grasping for a dream that has long since been lost. Some of the shorter buildings have long pipes sticking up from their roofs with plumes of dark smoke arching upward. The closer they get, the more smoke they see. The entire city appears to be shrouded in a haze of polluted dark gas.

As they get closer, the windows in the tall buildings come into clearer focus. Along the side of the empty highway is a sign that reads *Welcome to Detroit*. A large wall stretches across the highway, blocking their path. Like the wall surrounding the Structure, this one also has several manned guard towers positioned on the top with bright spotlights sweeping across the landscape.

They come to a stop, unable to proceed further. The wall stretches high up in front of them, as well as to the left and right as far as Annie can see.

"State your business!" a male voice shouts down, amplified by a megaphone.

"We need to speak with the Leader," SOL shouts up. "It's imperative. Please open the gates."

Laughter can be heard from above.

"Is that so, android?" the megaphone wielding man says. "On whose authority?"

"I have an outcast from a nearby Structure with me. We have news that our Structure has been infiltrated by a demon from an alternate dimension. He goes by the name 'Popobowa.'"

The laughter from above abruptly stops. A few moments later, the gates open outward. Annie and SOL start their bikes up again, and drive inside the gates.

The spectacular mass of skyscrapers that stretch high into the clear evening sky have lights on in some of the windows. Holograms are displayed on the sides of buildings, as well as in the middle of the sprawling streets, advertising various products from sugary drinks to makeup. The citizens around them on the sidewalks, as well as those in some of the advertisements, all have different faces, just like back in the dying city. Several of the civilians stop and stare at the two on their dirt bikes, traveling slowly through the populated streets.

The people here are all operating standard bicycles, scooters, or walking. The noise from the engines of the dirt bikes appear to startle some of the civilians; some of them even look annoyed by their presence. Laughter rings through the air occasionally as the civilians go about their routine. Most of them appear to be in good spirits, much more so than those in the dying city.

SOL appears to know where they're supposed to be going, and Annie continues to follow as they make their way through the labyrinth of paved roads.

Up ahead, a blocky building appears. It's much different than any of the other structures they've passed by, as it's significantly shorter, but takes up much more space at its base. Annie presumes this is where the Leader lives. They kill their engines, lay the bikes down, and walk up to the front gates of the wall surrounding the short building. The gates swing open as soon as they approach, allowing the two to walk inside without needing to say a word.

Plush, green grass surrounds the building, with water openly spraying haphazardly on the grass. Several people in white hats are tending to the assortment of plants and trees on the grounds, clipping at them, snipping off rogue branches. Annie finds it fascinating how these people can work in such little sunlight.

Two tall men with short hair wearing black suits open the front doors, ushering them inside with heads bowed. Their mannerisms are more robotic than SOL's, yet they keep smiles on their faces and appear to be outwardly happy and content with whatever it is they do here. As Annie gets close enough to examine the two men, she discovers that they're actually androids, hyper-advanced machines with the outward appearance of humans. Some form of cutting-edge technology that gives them the appearance of being human, more so than SOL.

The interior of the main building is stunningly beautiful. Walls of marble stretch up to the golden ceiling above. Bright chandeliers illuminate the large, spacious room, displaying the bright and spotless tile flooring. A large staircase in the middle of the room leads up to an area that they can't quite see. Wooden desks manned with workers, more of the same advanced androids, both of male and female in appearance, make up most of the floor space around them. They type with intense focus and speed on holographic computer monitors, not bothering to look up as the two visitors stroll past.

Annie and SOL begin their climb up the stairs, their footsteps echoing around the expansive room, joining in with the sound of the clitter clatter of the typing behind them. Narrow slits of tall, stained glass stretch up the marble walls. During the daytime, Annie imagines the inside of this building must be even brighter with the streaming sunlight from outside. Now, it's simply the bright florescent lights from above that cast their illumination in this massive, but short building.

Once they reach the top of the stairs, Annie and SOL stop immediately. The spacious area with marble floors has a single golden throne sitting roughly twenty feet ahead, with a few small, cushioned chairs positioned on both sides of the throne. An android sits alone on the throne holding a Holoreader in one hand. It's wearing a red robe, and a small crown sits atop its head. Turning its attention slowly from what it's reading to the two newcomers, the android sets the Holoreader down on a small glass table and clasps its hands together earnestly.

"Please, come forward," the machine on the throne demands.

SOL and Annie approach the Leader, stopping a few feet from where it sits.

"Leader, we come to ask for your assistance," SOL says, bending down on one knee.

The Leader appears to roll its eyes. "Stand up, UE0353. You don't have to be so formal. Although, it's nice to see solid programming that works for a change."

SOL stands up, brushing at its pants as if having some sort of nervous struggle.

"I'm sorry, Leader. It's just…I apologize. It appears my internal neural network is compelling me to behave irrationally in this scenario. I'm unable to control it. It…may be best if the girl, Annie, speaks for the time being."

The Leader turns its attention to Annie, a bored expression on its plastic, lifeless face. "As you wish."

"My name's Annie Hilltop…your Highness," Annie says confidently, hands behind her back. "I come from the Structure. Or, one of the Structures. I was Banished for having –"

"I know all about your situation," the Leader interrupts. "What happened to you is terrible, and deeply concerning. Let me get a better look at you." The machine quickly stands up, approaching Annie. It squints its metallic eyes, tilting its head. "Incredible. Most incredible. I haven't seen your face in…" The android trails off, simply staring at her. Reaching out a metallic hand, it gently touches Annie's cheek. After a short pause, the Leader blinks several times, shaking its head.

"Please, we need your help," Annie pleads. "We need to get back inside the Structure. I need to save my baby, and SOL needs to tell the woman he loves that…it loves her."

The android ignores Annie's request, instead continuing to stare at her. Annie is unsure what this machine's intentions are, but her heart begins to beat faster, on the verge of fight or flight mode.

"Your face is the most perfect thing I've ever seen," the Leader says wonderingly. "Over three hundred years of genetic engineering and population culling, and this is the final result." It returns the metallic hand to its side. "Well, at least I got one of my creations right. Not that it really matters now."

The Leader takes the crown off its head and tosses it aside like a frisbee. Annie and SOL both take a startled step backwards. Beneath the crown is a human brain, resting inside of a plastic globe. Several electrodes and wires are connected to the brain, leading down into the mechanical body below.

"I suppose you deserve the truth," the Leader sighs, then pauses for effect. "My name is Kanzen Sasaki. The world around us, the Structure you grew up in, all of it…was my doing. I thought that by creating the perfect society, everything would be…well, perfect. Instead, the opposite happened." Kanzen chuckles, placing his hands on his metal hips. "You know, my heart was in the right place, but my intellect drove the world mad. My lust for control ruined everything. Sit down, and I'll explain."

Annie and SOL look at one another, once again giving one another a shrug of the shoulders, and follow Kanzen as he walks past the golden throne to a set of chairs further on. All three of them take a seat while an android in a black tuxedo skitters over, hurriedly trying to fill glasses of water. Its hands are shaking, causing water to overflow and spill on the table. Kanzen sits patiently, waiting for the machine to finish his job before it runs off.

"Let me take you back three hundred and twenty years ago," Kanzen begins, crossing one metal leg over another. "With the help of my friend and partner, Simon Verner, we concocted an idea to create the perfect society. While my initial idea was to have everyone living underground, in case of nuclear disaster, he convinced me that it would be best to have these cities built above ground. I cherished the way he saw certain aspects of the world differently than I did. He truly was my best friend…"

Annie clears her throat, startled at the mention of Simon's name.

He's full of crap, Annie. The whole thing was his idea. I simply agreed with him one night that I didn't like the way our society was going. That's it.

Kanzen looks expectantly at Annie.

"I'm sorry," Annie says, taking a drink of water.

The taste and feel of water is refreshing on her dry throat, and she quickly finishes the entire glass, before she moves onto SOL's glass, starting to drink that too.

"After we broke ground on the first Structure in Seattle, another one of my inventions would take off. In the mid twenty-first century, humanity was plunged into a severe energy crisis. It was imperative that a solution be found, and fast. So, the world leaders turned to me."

Kanzen shifts his body in the chair. "The Water Powered Generator, or WPG for short, was what we all thought would be the solution. *The wave of the future in clean energy.* As the demand for this product grew, so did the need for the design to grow in size. The bigger the WPG, the more water the machine drank up through a process known as *water splitting*. I was convinced, as well as my team of scientists, that this would be a renewable source of energy. The increased O2 released into the atmosphere after the hydrogen was captured would create more rain, balancing out the water that was being used. All of the big power companies began using industrial sized WPG's, gulping up water at a rate that simply outpaced the level of O2 they were giving off. They saw it as clean, renewable energy. Myself included, of course. Efficient and sufficient for all the world's economies. Unfortunately, we all miscalculated. By the time we saw what was happening, it was too late.

"In the end, it resulted in catastrophe. Water, the one resource that we all took for granted, literally one of the most important things all humans need to survive, ended up being our most scarce and valuable resource. Toward the end of the twenty-first century, the entire world broke out in 'Water Wars,' a term the sensationalized mainstream media came up with, striking fear into the hearts of everyone. I simply dispensed of the hyperbole and called it the end of modern society.

"At the height of civilization, it was estimated that seventeen billion people lived on this planet. People were dying in the streets, either from dehydration, or murder. Many would literally kill their fellow man for a drop of water. Within one year, fourteen billion died. Those who didn't launch themselves into space in search of a new planet stayed behind and watched mankind tear itself apart."

Annie and SOL are both sitting forward in their chairs, soaking in the story Kanzen is telling them. The Outside, previously unknown to Annie and SOL, now makes much more sense after their time traversing the wastelands.

"While the outside world was thrown into utter chaos, the military bombing highly civilized cities in order decrease water usage, my twelve Structures stood tall, spread across the land formerly known as the United States. Being the richest man in the world, I had struck a deal with the U.N. that it would leave my Structures alone as the cities surrounding them were being destroyed. Given the choice between money and water, it's still interesting to me how many men chose the former, even in their dying hours.

"I chose to hide inside the Structure in Seattle, like a coward. By the time the screams of slaughter were quieting down on the outside, my former body was losing its battle to another resource that mankind has always taken for granted...Time. As I was slowly withering away, I went to work on constructing this mechanical suit you see sitting before you now. Through nothing but precise science with my heightened intellect, I was able to preserve my brain, transferring it out of my dying organic body into this machine which will survive much longer. I'm stronger now. More than ever. And wiser."

The three of them sit in silence for a few moments before Annie speaks.

"Will you help us find a way inside the Structure? The one we come from?"

"Potentially," Kanzen says. "I can provide you with the location of the Structure's power source so you can disable the building's electrical supply, which will eventually make their laser weapons useless and unlock the front doors. And I can provide you with an army of androids to assist with infiltrating the exterior wall. I have a weapon which will make you the most formidable on the battlefield, Annie. The rest will be up to you."

"That would be greatly appreciated," SOL says. "Thank you."

"You said my face looks familiar," Annie interjects. "How so?"

"You share the same face as my sister. Eun."

"Everyone in my Structure had the same face. Why?"

"As I've stated, I wanted to construct the perfect society, Annie," Kanzen explains, sitting forward. "In order to do that, I believed I had to eliminate everything that made us different. At the time, I believed that the root cause of friction in society was based around the fact that people tended to focus on our differences. Differences in gender, sexual orientation, nationality, religion, political beliefs, age, height, weight, etcetera." He takes a deep breath, filling his mechanical lungs. "Now, I believe that it's those differences that make us *all* unique and special. Having everyone all look alike and act alike…that isn't perfect. That's not what utopia is supposed to be about. I was wrong about that. I was wrong about many other things. It's important for someone to have an identifying fingerprint to leave behind in life. That's how we're remembered. That's how we earn our legacy."

Ask him what happened to me. Ask him what happened to Simon Verner.

"What happened to your partner, Simon?" Annie asks.

Kanzen scratches the side of his cheek, shaking his head. "The death of Simon, by my own hand, taught me the true power and danger of dreams."

Chapter 24

Standing up, Kanzen leads SOL and Annie down the long set of stairs and out the front doors of the Capital Building. They walk through the grass lawn and down a cement path lined with flowers and green plants. It's now dark outside, with the nearby holograms and occasional fluorescent lightbulb illuminating their path. The temperature has dropped significantly since the sun's departure.

Passing through a back gate exiting the Capital Building's grounds, Kanzen's mechanical body strides purposefully toward a large encampment still within the city walls. As they get closer, Annie sees thousands of androids lying about, not moving. It's as if they all stopped in the middle of whatever they were doing, frozen in a fragment of time. Some of them have arms outstretched as though holding items, while others are frozen halfway in the motion of lifting objects that no longer exist.

"*Misfit Camp...*" SOL mutters.

"These are all decommissioned androids," Kanzen explains. "Before I reactivate them, I'll have them all bond to your signature code, SOL, so that they'll follow your orders. This will be your army to take back to your Structure and do what you please."

"But the Structure is your creation," Annie says hesitantly. "Why are you helping us to infiltrate it?"

"Like I said, nearly everything I built ended in ruin. The A.I. at the top of the tower unchained itself from my central command control a few months ago. It's gone rogue. It's time that machine was stopped, as well as the demon Popobowa."

Kanzen stops walking and turns to face SOL and Annie, a solemn look showing itself on his plastic features. "The main reason I allowed you two to enter the Capital's walls today was because you mentioned the demon's name. Popobowa must be stopped, and the Grand Master destroyed with him. The idea of a perfect society has become corrupt. All constraints I had on that A.I. were severed, probably at the demon's hand."

"We won't let you down, Leader," SOL says, bending down on one knee. "We will use this army to destroy the Grand Master and oust this demon back to wherever it came from."

"Good," Kanzen says, turning around and resuming his walk. After a moment, Kanzen suddenly changes direction. "I almost forgot! I need to equip you with that new weapon, Annie."

Annie and SOL trail after him for a few minutes, following him inside a large warehouse. Lights automatically turn on, revealing hundreds of more decommissioned androids. There's also dozens of humans growing inside of wide, glass tubes which are filled with some green fluid. These identical looking men, with short black hair and similar facial features to the male civilians Inside the Structure, have tubes feeding into their mouths, supplying them with what Annie assumes is food and oxygen. *Clones,* Annie tells herself.

Propped up against a nearby wall is a wooden stick with carvings all along the length of it. An Eagle's head is carved into the handle, looking intently ahead, its thick beak protruding out. The other end of the staff is painted a vibrant blue.

"What is this?" Annie asks.

"One of my most prized creations," Kanzen says proudly. "I call it a 'Particle Manipulator.' Once the weapon has connected with you, it taps into your soul. Technology that I was admittedly skeptical about at first… although, technology probably isn't the right term for it. Honestly, it works more like magic.

"Anyways, once you're ready to use this weapon, it fires out the most powerful blast of raw energy ever known to man. Heck, these would've been a much better idea for solving the energy crisis than my water generators. It grabs any nearby atoms, strips them down to their raw components, then recombines them while forging a connection with your soul," Kanzen appears to smile. "You'll love this weapon in your battle to come; it'll level anything that stands in your way."

Annie reaches for the Particle Manipulator, wrapping her fingers around the Eagle's head on the handle.

"Give it a moment to link to your soul," Kanzen says. "If you want someone else to even touch that thing, you'll have to tell the weapon it's alright to link to them. Otherwise, it could be disastrous for the other party.

Linking the Particle Manipulator, however, takes an advanced level of skill that I'm not even aware of how to master."

Already, Annie can feel an unexplainable connection to her new weapon. As if it's latched itself to her mind, to her very soul, as Kanzen had described, the Particle Manipulator begins creating an inseparable bond between her and it. An ordinary, archaic looking staff at first appearance, but Annie can tell this weapon is anything but ordinary.

"SOL, I have one more thing for you as well," Kanzen says, pulling out a memory disc from the pocket of his red robe. "You'll know what to do with this when the time calls for it."

SOL takes the memory disc, examining the small, plastic object intently.

Just as Annie and SOL begin to follow Kanzen out of the warehouse, the dream goes dark.

I'M WALKING BY myself in the forever darkness of the Void, the space between the waking and dreaming world. I raise my hands up to my face, and look down at my body to reassure myself that I'm back in my body, which I thankfully am.

The darkness begins to slowly fade away to the white, snowy surroundings of Kanzen's mountain lodge. I can tell that I'm still dreaming. Trees surround me, their branches thick with fluffy white snow. I continue to walk along the paved trail, with the large cabin on my left. Through the windows I can see the warmth and comfort of the inside; a crackling fireplace spitting out soft flames of yellow and orange.

Directly ahead on the back covered porch is a hot tub with steam rising off the bubbling water. Jess is the only person sitting inside the hot tub, her arms draped along the outer edges in a seductive manner, beckoning me to walk closer. As I approach the hot tub, she stands up, revealing herself in a two-piece bikini, showing off her incredibly athletic body. Her long, blond hair is fully restored back to its natural beauty. My heart begins to pound. I need to wake up, right now, before this dream gets too weird for me. I can't go down this path again, lusting after a girl whose heart I've already broken. Lusting after my best friend. This must be X's treachery again, playing with my emotions like a tortured guitar.

Jess waves me on, urging me to come closer and get in. Unable to control myself for some reason, I do as I'm told, taking off my shirt and pants and stepping into the hot tub, wearing only my boxers. The hot water stabs at my ankles and legs like tiny knives at first, but quickly the water turns soothing, comforting my body from the cold weather, massaging my aching joints.

I sit next to Jess as she sits back down, turning toward me. As always, she's the most beautiful woman in the world, the pinnacle of all I could ever want in the opposite sex. Her vibrant blue eyes draw me in, and she looks at me with a look of unadulterated passion. She leans toward me, and I meet her aggressively, our lips locking. We share a long kiss, sending my mind and body into pure ecstasy. Oh, how I messed things up with Jess. I wish I could just stay in this dream forever, kissing the woman of my dreams, forgetting about the real world and how I crushed her heart and destroyed any chance of a romantic, loving relationship between us. What a fool I've been.

For several minutes we make out in one of the most intense visions I've ever had. Our arms wrap around one another, entangled in thoughtless emotion, our bodies craving one another in an endless dance of passion.

When I open my eyes again, the woman who I'm embracing has turned into Brittany. Her long, jet-black hair covers her pasty white shoulders. Big, brown eyes stare back at me. I instantly recoil, trying desperately to escape her grasp, but she's got me good. Her strength is overwhelming, and I'm unable to shake free of her clutches. Brittany begins to laugh.

"Hello again, Brother," she says, smiling. "I'm really enjoying these new dreams you've been receiving. A sci-fi epic adventure, after your noir, detective story the last time. Quite the change, wouldn't you say? I wonder what else you can dream about. But please, keep dreaming, Simon. Your dreams are going to kill *billions.*"

I continue to struggle with all my strength to break free of her grasp. She laughs again, clutching my spine tighter. The water of the hot tub has increased in temperature, the bubbles from the jets beginning to boil. The intensity of the steam has increased significantly, floating up to the ceiling of the covered patio, my skin starting to burn from the water's increasing heat.

"Popobowa sent my soul back to find you, and I intend to follow through on my mission," Brittany continues, her eyes looking fiercely at me. "You *will not* interfere with this future you've glimpsed. You and Kanzen will create the Structures, and the water generators. Mankind will kill itself, as it was always destined to do, and there's nothing you can do to stop it from happening. You know why? Because you're weak. You always have been. In every life."

I manage to free my right arm, pushing her away. The heat from the water has reached lethal levels, the hot tub boiling intensely with huge bubbles rising to the surface.

"You know you're not supposed to push a girl," she says, still smiling. "I'm doing this to teach you a lesson, honey."

"You're a seriously messed up person, you know that?" I say, struggling to escape the tub, which has essentially turned into a witch's cauldron.

"Why couldn't you just be a good boy and follow orders? I asked you to play your part, and you couldn't even do that. I told you I'm going to date Jess, and you just couldn't let that happen. You keep fighting me on that! I had asked you not to pursue John Stinson's murder, and you refused to listen. Why won't you just *listen?*"

"I'll kill you myself, Kanzen!" I scream, reaching out and seizing Brittany's throat.

She begins to choke as I tighten my grip on her windpipe. As she releases her hold on me, I use both hands to choke her neck.

"Simon, please stop!" Brittany begs. "Simon, it's me! Please, let go! You're…you…"

I stand over the top of her, pushing her choking body down into the boiling hot water.

Watching as Brittany struggles for breath, I press down with all my strength. She splashes violently, reaching up, clawing at me to stop. I arch my neck back to avoid being scratched by her fingernails, glaring down at her as she looks up at me, screaming underwater. Bubbles escape her mouth. The boiling water blurs her face, and I watch as she begins to drown in the boiling hot chlorinated water.

SOMETHING STRIKES MY face, and I loosen my grip, falling down to the carpeted ground. Another punch to my face, followed by several more. Finally, the barrage of punches stop, and I look around to discover I'm no longer in a hot tub in Kanzen's mountain lodge. Instead, I'm on my bedroom floor. My head's resting against the side of my mattress. Ron is standing above me, prepared to punch me again. Jess is lying beside me, clutching at her throat.

"Wait, stop!" I yell up at Ron as he draws his fist back, preparing for another swing. "Stop, I'm awake!" I turn my attention to Jess, her hands trembling, tears streaming down her face. "Oh my God, Jess, I'm so sorry! I was dreaming, I didn't mean to hurt you, I swear!"

Ron glares down at me, an intense look of rage that I've rarely seen from him before, especially directed at me. Jess stares at me for a moment then frantically stands up, pressing herself against my bedroom door.

"I want you out of here," Jess says, her voice raw. "Pack your stuff and get out. You're no longer welcome here."

"Jess, please listen to me, I didn't —"

"You heard her!" Ron roars. "Get out!"

I struggle to my feet, meeting Ron's eyes. His eyes appear sunken in as if he hasn't slept in days.

"Please, you have to believe me! I thought she was Brittany! She manifested into a Night Terror." I look over at Jess, raw emotions beginning to take over. "I would never try to hurt you, Jess!"

"I came in here because I heard you yelling in your sleep," she says, her voice still raspy. "I was worried something was wrong. Then you just attacked me."

"I'm so sorry!" I say pleadingly, my voice getting louder as I begin to panic. "Listen, none of us have been ourselves lately. It's X! They're back, in the form of Kanzen! We have to stay away from him. He's going to create a clean energy system that uses too much of the world's water supply, and…"

Jess turns away abruptly and leaves my room, sobbing. Ron continues to glare at me.

"You have ten minutes to leave before I call the police," Ron says. "I mean it."

"Dude, just calm down and listen to me."

"No, you listen to me," he steps forward, getting right in my face. "We're done with you, Simon. Alright? We've given you several chances over the years, but this is the final straw. You're too unpredictable. These dreams of yours have put us all in danger." Ron turns to leave, then faces me again, squinting his eyes. "What happened to you?"

I shake my head and sigh. "I could ask you two the same thing, but I already know the answer."

Chapter 25

I throw some clothes in a backpack and get out of the apartment in eight minutes flat. In my haste to leave, I realize that I failed to give the two of them my key. Oh well. I'll hang onto it just in case of an emergency. If they want to go ahead and change the locks, let 'em.

I pull up in the parking spot at the hotel that Wayne's staying in. Taking my backpack with me, I walk through the lobby area and head toward his room, number 132. The hotel either has a retro theme going on, or they truly haven't updated in the past few decades. Judging by the cracked drywall and countless stains on the orange carpet, I'll go with the latter.

I pound on the door and take a step back. To my left are a couple of vending machines, humming along tirelessly in an effort to keep soft drinks cool until the end of time. To my right is a long hall of doorways leading to other rooms. I can hear a couple arguing from one of the rooms down there behind what they apparently presume to be a private door. Little do they know that every word is carrying down the hallway, their disagreement audible to anyone awake at this hour. Like me.

The door to room 132 opens abruptly and Wayne is standing there to greet me with a tired look on his face. He's dressed in a plain white tank top with mustard stains on the front, and a pair of white underwear. Placing his palms on his face, he drags his hand down his cheeks, yawning widely.

"Mornin' Simon," he mumbles. "What time is it?"

"It's five AM. Hey, look, I'm sorry to wake you, but I need a place to stay for a bit. I've been kicked out."

He turns around, waving his arm in what I assume is a signal to come in. The inside of the darkened room is filthy, clothes strewn about on the floor. A handgun is placed on top of a wooden dresser which also houses a small flatscreen TV, and beer bottles lay on the far side of the dresser. The window on the far wall has blackout curtains covering the glass, preventing any potential sunlight from making its way inside. The stench of stale liquor and old hot dogs hit my nose instantly, causing me to nearly vomit.

Wayne crawls back into bed, throwing the sheets over himself and falling back asleep instantly. I make my way over to a couch against the far window, praying silently that it's a pull-out. Placing my backpack on the floor, making sure to kick aside a dirty paper plate of potato chip crumbs first, I check under a couch cushion and am relieved to discover that this is, in fact, a pull-out.

My need to sleep is vital to me, especially in this stage of the visions. I need to see what happens with Annie and SOL. Is she successful in finding her daughter? Does SOL get a second chance with the woman he loves? And future Kanzen…does he assist them further? I still can't believe that he's still alive, having somehow managed to transplant his brain in a vain effort at immortality. The audacity of the guy, thinking he can play a role in destroying the world, then live long enough to see if it can recover. Typical behavior from X. What a sick, twisted soul. A soul I'll need to defeat again.

I take a seat on the couch, placing my head in my hands. As much as I want to scream in frustration, being swept up in these insane dreams again, and having my ancient brother turn my friends against me, I think better of it. It's easy to get frustrated and lose focus. It's smarter to remain even keeled in order to think clearly. I owe it to my friends to save them from the mental treachery they've been dragged into. They didn't give up on me several months ago in Chicago, and I won't give up on them now. Their behavior at this point isn't their fault. And honestly, there's some truth to what they said.

Worst of all, I'm afraid I hurt Jess. I know that I'd mentally hurt her months ago by breaking up with her, but now I'm concerned that I physically injured her. She'll probably tell Kanzen, furthering his case against me as a psychopath. He'll probably be contacting some of the finer mental institutions here in the area, working out a deal to have me committed and locked away, just like he did the last time as Brittany. It's easier for him if I'm out of the way.

Now that I'm wide awake, I take it upon myself to get started with the first stage of my plan to overthrow the future; I'm going to steal that small computer this morning and prevent it from falling into the wrong hands. If the Grand Master never comes into power, it's possible that may prevent Annie's future from coming true. I suppose the only way to find out is if I continue to receive these dreams after the deed is done. As much as I want to see what happens with Annie, it'll be even better if I stop receiving the dreams altogether, meaning that the future has changed.

After taking a long, hot shower, I get dressed and leave the hotel room. Wayne continues sleeping like a bear in hibernation. Equipped with my car keys, wallet, backpack and cell phone, I hop in my car and make the drive to Kanzen's mansion. "When the Levee Breaks" by *Led Zeppelin* plays on the radio as I drive through the light rain.

It isn't going to be easy to break into his mancave and steal the computer, which is an issue that's been clawing at the back of my mind for a few days now. Thankfully, an idea came to me the day before yesterday as I was drifting off to sleep. A few months ago, when Ron, Loretta and I were searching for Jess, I was able to astral project myself to her location while I was sleeping. For a brief moment, I was able to touch her, before my hand eventually went through her, and I wasn't able to touch anything else solid except the ground beneath my feet.

By focusing hard on Jess, and repeating to myself how much I missed her, I was able to activate this other, lesser-known power of mine. As of yet, that was the first and only time I've been able to achieve this feat. I haven't actually attempted to do it again, but I figure now is as good a time as any. I'll attempt to astral project myself into Kanzen's mancave and steal the small sphere of a computer. The Baby Grand Master, if you will. Considering his cave is underground in a homemade fallout shelter, there's really no other way to get into it from the outside if you don't have the code.

My mind wanders as I continue driving, listening to this legendary classic rock song. Lately, I seem to have acquired a liking for this genre of music, something that I didn't really care to listen to as a kid, but my dad sure did. I remember one day after elementary school, Jess' mom had brought her over to visit. Wayne was still at work, or looking for work…regardless, he wasn't available, that's all I remember.

Jess had her usual pink top on and that long, blond hair resting on her shoulders. Her mom had to go to work, so my parents agreed to let her come over so we could hang out and play video games in my room before dinner. She was always faster than me using the controller, usually beating me by the method known as "button mashing," where you just smash all the buttons randomly and wish for the best.

"Yes!" Jess had exclaimed, gently putting the controller on the carpet in my bedroom before doing a little dance.

"Another one?" I asked, desperate to at least win one game.

"I've already won three in a row," she smiled. "But sure, why not?"

Dad was playing some loud music in the living room on his new fancy stereo system. *Pink Floyd, The Doors, The Beatles,* I could go on and on. He had all sorts of records and cassette tapes. The music never bothered me or anything; in a way, I think it was my dad's method of winding down after a day at work. This was probably right around the time of his cancer diagnosis.

"Alright, dinner's almost ready!" Mom called from the kitchen.

"We're almost done!" I called back, my tongue sticking out the side of my mouth while I concentrated with all I had on our game.

For a split second, I remember looking over at Jess, and I could swear she was peeking over at me. Before I knew it, I won. My character beat her character, throwing him off the side of a bridge or something dramatic. It felt great finally besting her one out of seven, and when I looked over at her, she was still smiling.

"Good job," she said, standing up to go wash her hands. "I'll get you back after dinner, though."

A lump forms in my throat as I think back on that day. Ron and I have had our share of experiences together too, but our relationship isn't nearly as deep and impactful as my relationship with Jess. Being friends for so long, and knowing how deeply caring and thoughtful she is, always drew me to her like a moth to a flame.

But on top of all that, I miss my dad more than anything. I wish he was here so I could ask him what to do. I'm sure he'd have some quirky answer, some logical way of putting things so I could understand it. Part of me wants to imagine him next to me, listening to this song, tapping on the dashboard and going crazy with the beat.

Steady rainfall dampens the windshield, my wiper blades clearing my line of sight momentarily until more misty rain takes its place. With so much rain in this city, it's tough for me to imagine a world gone dry.

Traffic this morning is thankfully light so far, making my commute over to Bellevue short and uneventful. The size of the houses steadily grows as I make my way down the street toward Kanzen's mansion. My heart begins to thump harder the closer I get as I mentally prepare myself for the heist of the century: stealing an evil supercomputer from a rich man.

I park on the right side of the street a few houses down, making sure to stay just out of sight in case he's home and would be able to see my blue sports car parked out front. Leaning the car seat back, I close my eyelids, forcing myself to drift back to sleep. I jolt myself awake, reminding myself that I need to be focusing on picturing myself inside of his man cave, standing in front of the computer. If I go to sleep not thinking of being at a specific destination, I'll more than likely just pick up where I left off in Annie's story.

Kanzen's mancave. Those concrete walls, that small metal ball floating on the round desk. The couch with the big screen TV, the kitchen off to the side. My mind forms a clear image of the space, making sure to remember every minute detail that I can. Primarily, I focus on the metallic object rotating in the center of the room, not much larger than a baseball. This little computer, capable of so much destruction, programmed to create a perfect society. *Kanzen's project. Keep focusing on his project...*

Opening my eyes hesitantly, half expecting to still be sitting in my car, I'm relieved to discover I'm standing in the man cave, which looks just how I remembered it. The little metallic ball is still rotating harmlessly over the round table, exactly where I saw it last. I go to pick up the object, but my hand passes right through it. I feel my stomach sink, now worried that this whole experiment of astral projecting myself here isn't going to work after all. Deep, steady breaths calm my nerves, and I quickly think of another plan. Rather than carrying the object out of the man cave, I'll just unlock the door from the inside, then wake up and walk down here myself, in my real form. Perhaps it's just the amount of mass I'm attempting to carry while in my other form that's preventing this plan from being carried out. I don't know, I'm just winging it at this point.

The keypad on the wall at the top of the spiral staircase is easy enough to figure out. There's a green button which reads *open,* so I attempt to press that. Thankfully, this time my finger lands on solid substance. I can feel the cool plastic against my skin, pressing in as I push my finger against it. I hear a loud buzz to my left, and the locks disengage. Now, I need to focus on waking up. The thought had crossed my mind to set an alarm to wake myself back up, but I was afraid I'd crumble under the pressure of being timed. I concentrate, reminding myself to relax. *I'm back in my car, sitting in the rainy morning. Back in my car. Back in my car...*

Opening my eyes again, this time I'm back in my body. I pull out my cellphone to see how much time has passed; thirty-eight minutes. Wow. What only felt like a minute in the dreaming world took over a half-hour in the real world. It's bizarre to me that the ratio of time elapsed while dreaming of John Stinson or Annie Hilltop has always fluctuated, as if there's little to no consistency. Just another one of the wonders of this gift I've been given, I suppose.

Raindrops pelt my face as I get out of the car, swinging my backpack over one shoulder, and run toward Kanzen's mansion. I sprint around the side of his house, down the driveway and to the side garage door. The door handle turns easily, and I find myself standing at the landing of the spiral staircase. I hurry down the steps and the fluorescent overhead lights turn on automatically as I approach the bottom landing, lighting the way to my objective. I try to catch my breath. The excitement of this experiment actually working, combined with my quick descent down the long flight of stairs, has caused me to begin hyperventilating. I just need to calm down. We're almost there. I'm going to take this dangerous computer and eliminate it, which should stop these dreams from occurring. Saving the world is a side bonus.

I'm able to grab the small metal ball this time, placing it in my backpack. Now what? Should I take a rowboat out into Lake Washington, and dump it overboard? Or keep it with me as a bargaining chip, forcing Kanzen to reveal himself as X, which should get Ron and Jess to come to their senses? I choose option B. The next most important thing in the world to me right now, second only to saving the future of mankind, is getting my friend's trust back. I can't imagine a world without them. I need to get the real Jess and Ron back.

Taking the steps back up with the backpack securely over both shoulders, slower this time now so I can catch my breath, a smile creeps onto my face. This is one of the most exciting things I've ever done. Thievery is not something I've ever committed before. It's intoxicating how alive this whole thing makes me feel. Not that I plan on robbing a gas station after this little adventure, but it's still a surreal feeling, nonetheless.

I open the door leading to the outside and discover Kanzen standing there with his arms crossed. The look of a once proud, happy man has now been replaced by an angry scowl.

"Drop the backpack, Simon," he growls.

"No," I say stubbornly. "I tried to ask you nicely to stop this project, and you refused. This computer is dangerous and needs to be stopped."

"Oh, that's right. You had a bad dream." Kanzen rolls his eyes, then turns his head and shouts, "Security! He's over here!"

Without giving him a moment to react, I shove past him, knocking him off balance as I begin walking down the long driveway. Three security guards, who were apparently waiting for me down by my car, begin to approach me. Each of them is wearing a black suit and tie, as if they're federal agents of some kind. Almost in unison, they all reach inside the pocket of their vests, pulling out pistols.

I stop in my tracks, raising my hands. "Don't shoot!"

Kanzen runs up from behind me just as gunfire erupts in the street, causing us both to dive down on the ground, lying flat on our stomachs. I look up and see that Kanzen's armed guards are all down on the road as well. I hear the sound of car doors opening, and look over to see three more men, each armed with assault rifles, stepping out of a black car parked across the street.

"What the hell?" Kanzen whispers, crawling closer beside me. "Are these your guys?"

I look over at him, frantically shaking my head. One of the new armed men aims the barrel of his weapon down at one of Kanzen's men, lying flat on his back on the street, apparently already wounded, and squeezes off several more rounds into the man's skull. The other two men look around, apparently not spotting Kanzen and I yet.

Pushing myself up, I quickly run back to the garage and around the back of the mansion, pushing through the high bushes. The sound of footsteps behind me, and I glance back quickly to discover Kanzen hot on my heels. Rather than being intent on chasing after me, however, his face looks frightened. Clearly, these new men aren't his either.

I make my way through the backyard quickly, and run along the other side of his mansion, cutting through the yard and sprinting down the sidewalk toward my blue car, which is sitting there patiently for me. Reaching in my pants pocket for the key fob, I press the button to unlock the doors and jump, sliding across the hood with ease. I yank open the driver's side door, take off the backpack, chuck it inside, hop in the driver's seat and slam the door shut. Rather than my hands shaking, panicking and out of control, my body has entered a state of calm now. I'm intensely focused, not nervous or full of fear. The key slides into the ignition with ease, and the car starts up on the first attempt. Awesome.

Looking up, I see that the armed men have made their way around the backyard, now running across the neighbor's front lawn toward me, their rifles drawn. Kanzen's pounding on the passenger door, desperately begging for me to let him in.

Thinking quickly, I unlock the door. I can't risk him being killed now, only for X's soul to be reborn and cause me to have to face him again in another two decades. For the time being, I need X alive so I can figure out a way to capture their soul later with Loretta's help.

I reach over and throw the backpack into the backseat just before Kanzen jumps in. He's breathing heavily, drenched in sweat and rain.

"Drive!" he screams.

I throw the vehicle into reverse and hit the gas, turning the wheel slightly to avoid a car parked on the street behind me. Then, I crank hard on the steering wheel, sending the vehicle around in a 180-degree turn, facing away from the armed men. They fire their weapons, missing my car and striking the car that was parked behind me, causing its windshield to shatter. I shift into drive and push the pedal down hard, peeling out slightly before finally gaining traction. Thankfully, none of the bullets strike my car and within moments we're around the corner and out of sight of the killers.

"Who were those guys?" Kanzen shouts.

"I don't know, man," I snap back. "Your guys were about to fire on me!"

"Yeah, because you just stole a ten-billion-dollar computer! Which I'm taking back, by the way."

As he reaches for my backpack in the backseat, I instinctively punch him in the face with my right fist, knocking him out cold. His body sags against the side door, his head resting against the window. Unfortunately, he's unbuckled. Oh well. He should've listened to me before trying something stupid.

Chapter 26

Traffic has picked up significantly. I weave through the lines of vehicles, driving at speeds that may appear too dangerous and erratic to others on the road. However, that couldn't be further from the truth. Utilizing skills that I'm confident are from my past life as John, I navigate through traffic effortlessly, as he would've done. People honk at me angrily as I dart between a set of vehicles here and squeeze in through another line of cars there. The rain has also intensified, causing water to splash around on the streets. I have to crank up the speed of the windshield wipers in order to see what's in front of us.

Glancing in the rearview mirror, I see that the black SUV carrying the armed men has caught up to us. They make their way through the traffic, driving much more aggressively than I am, occasionally ramming other vehicles out of the way with their large bumper, shattering windows and causing severe damage. Without giving it a second thought, I crank the wheel to the right, driving along the sidewalk. The black SUV follows me. A few umbrella wielding patrons, who are braving it through the elements this morning, quickly dive out of the way before I plow them over.

I swerve back to the left, returning to the roadway and speed my way up to the onramp of a busy highway. For the time being, it appears I've lost them. Pressing harder on the gas pedal, begging my car for more power, she responds fiercely, sending us flying down the highway at a dangerous rate of speed. The car begins to hydroplane for a second, causing me to take my foot off the accelerator until I can feel that we've regained traction.

The highway leads into the downtown Seattle corridor. I take an offramp, hurtling down streets that I'm unfamiliar with. Tall skyscrapers jut up overhead. Pedestrians carrying leatherbound briefcases, dark umbrellas and to-go cups of coffee walk through the soaked sidewalks toward another day at work. How simple their lives must be, not having to worry about saving the future of all mankind. Not dreaming of their past or future lives.

I make my way down to Pioneer Square and decide this would be the best place to park my car for the time being. Leaving Kanzen unconscious in the passenger seat, I grab the backpack and jump out of the vehicle, slam the door, sprinting away with every intention of coming back for it later. A sign for the Light Rail unveils itself like a beacon, and I quickly take the flight of stairs down. I hop over a sleeping man about halfway down the steps, just as the squeal of tires sounds from up above at street level. Urging my legs to carry me down the staircase faster, I glance back once I arrive at the bottom to see the armed men in hot pursuit, each hurtling over the sleeping man.

An automated female voice announces overhead that the train will be departing shortly. Not caring in which direction the train is going, I run onto the platform and through the waiting open door of the first Light Rail car I see. A loud chime goes off, and the doors close behind me. The train lurches forward, and I grab onto an overhead rope for support. Looking out the window, I see the three men glaring angrily at me as the train pulls away. Their shapes disappear as the train enters into a dark tunnel, the only light now coming from the interior lights of the Light Rail car.

The train is about three-quarters of the way full of people, most of who are staring down at their smartphones, unaware of my presence. Darting my eyes left and right, I find an open seat and shuffle over to it. I slide the backpack off my shoulders, letting out a deep sigh. This morning is definitely off to a rocky start. However, I still have the small, round computer, safe and sound beside me.

My hands now beginning to shake slightly as adrenaline begins dissipating, I unzip my backpack and take the little metal ball out, holding it in my hands with care. It's a surprisingly heavy little sphere.

"So, you're the Grand Master, huh?" I speak quietly to it. "Not if I have anything to say about it. Oh, no. I *will* prevent that from coming true."

I look up to see a black woman eying me warily before she goes back to looking down at her phone.

The automated female voice on the train announces that we're coming up to the next stop. I put the little computer back inside the backpack and zip it up, just as the train exits the tunnel, unveiling the platform ahead.

Putting the backpack on, I approach the exit, bumping past a few people as they begin to stand up. The train comes to a sudden stop, and as soon as the doors open, I step out and try to blend in with the crowd. For the time being, it works. Making my way onto the stairs, I jog up them two at a time, going faster than those standing on the escalator next to me.

After a second flight of stairs, I'm back up at street level. Cars are honking at random, and the sidewalks are packed full of pedestrians going about their day. The steady December rain continues to spray down on the city, making everything cold and wet, soaking through my hooded sweatshirt as I continue my path down the sidewalk. Glancing behind me once again, I see the armed men – who have concealed their weapons now – have caught up once again, now standing outside the Light Rail station, looking in every direction. I ease my pace to a slower, but still purposeful power walk in order to continue blending in.

Several blocks later, I'm at Pike Street. I remember my surroundings from my morning tour of the city a couple of short weeks ago. Taking a left on Pike, I head downhill. The red *Public Market* sign appears in the distance, coming into clearer view the closer I get.

"Hey, watch it!" a man yells at a distance behind me.

I turn around, and my heart sinks as I see that the three men have caught sight of me and are in pursuit again. I take off at a full sprint, ditching the crowded sidewalk and taking my chances with the heavy traffic of the street. Car horns blare as I run with reckless abandon toward Pike Place Market.

Over the old brick road my feet take me, and I bound into the heavily commuted market, sliding through the crowd of people, trying not to knock anyone over. The red tile floor underneath is slick from people tracking in the rain.

Shoppers pushing baby strollers, couples holding hands, elderly people pointing at products laid about, the citizens go about their day as I run for my life. Today, the local fishermen are showing off their skills by tossing a freshly caught fish, which soars through the air gracefully to my left, landing in the waiting arms of another man wearing a leather apron, causing the gathered audience to cheer.

A crash sounds behind me, and the audience grows quiet enough for me to hear raised voices near the market entrance. I momentarily look back to see that one of the men, about twenty feet behind me, has drawn his pistol. Screams erupt from the crowd as the man fires at me. The bullet misses its mark, taking out a display of blown glass on my right, sending shards of green and orange flying. The entire market is now in chaos, causing a stampede of people to form and begin to run in the same direction I'm heading. One woman stumbles and is trampled by several others before someone stops to assist her, pulling her on the floor out of the way.

Behind me, I can hear others being knocked to the ground by the pistol wielding madmen, followed by more high-pitched shrieks. An opening comes into view to my left with a neon sign of a finger pointing down, and I dart through the crowd, taking the steep, slick ramp down into the chasms of the market. The crowd of people thins out considerably down here in the lower levels, and I continue my descent, hoping that my absence will prevent other people from getting injured.

A loud pop behind me, and I duck down. The bullet narrowly misses, striking the old plaster of the wall to my right. I focus on trying to breathe evenly, keeping my legs moving as fast as they'll take me, the taste of iron in my mouth as my lungs reach their full potential, my heart pumping blood faster and faster through my veins. Yet still, despite all of this, I'm remaining composed. The residue of my past life continues to carry over to my sub-conscious, thoughts coming to me through years of training. *Stay calm, stay focused, and stay alert.*

My feet thumping on the hardwood floor, I can still hear the squeaking of my pursuer's footsteps behind me. They appear to be running out of steam, however, and I gain some distance from them. I push through a glass door leading to the outside and run down several more flights of stairs, across a busy street toward the waterfront. With the aquarium straight ahead, I dash left, sprinting past several piers of tourist shops and restaurants. Past the amateur rappers. Past the tall white Ferris Wheel. Past the seafood restaurant where I had eaten by myself.

A ferry boat blares its horn in the distance. I'm now beginning to run out of steam as well. Approaching the ferry terminal, I jog up onto the elevated platform. I pull out my wallet and grab my debit card, quickly operating the machine to purchase a one-way ticket to Bainbridge Island. Even with my life in danger, I don't want to stiff the Washington State Ferries. Plus, without a ticket, they probably wouldn't let me onboard.

The machine spits out my ticket, and I yank it free, sprinting down the long runway toward the entrance up ahead. I show my ticket to the young acne-inflicted male employee, who slowly attempts to scan it with his little laser gun. After several attempts, he bangs the side of the scanning device. I hear some loud commotion down the ramp behind me, and I begin to grow impatient.

"Sorry, it's not working," he mutters, pointing the laser into his face as a form of testing it.

The horn blares once again, and an automated voice comes over the intercom, announcing that the ferry is about to disembark. I let out a frustrated grunt and run past the man, jump over the turnstile and sprint up the steel ramp.

"Wait, you can't go up there!" the employee yells. "Sir, you can't –"

The employee is suddenly silenced as one of the armed pursuers punches him in the face, knocking him down in a heap. I duck around a corner before they spot me. Directly ahead is a large area with several plastic booths lined against both the port and starboard sides of the vessel. Some folks lay down on the seats, stretched with their arms behind their heads or staring into their smartphone screens. Kids scream in excitement, pointing out at the water. This area is too wide open; they'll easily spot me here.

I sprint into the men's restroom, and head into the second of three filthy stalls. I lock the door, lower the toilet seat, and stand up on it, crouching down. The restroom is incredibly quiet besides the rhythmic hum of the ferry's engine, causing the entire boat to shake softly.

After a few minutes, and patiently waiting out a few patrons that needed to utilize the bathroom, I unclench my fists. My fingernails have dug into my palms, thankfully not deep enough to break skin.

The door of the restroom opens again.

"He has to be nearby," a man says. "Stay sharp."

I hear a loud thud to my right as one of the men kicks in the first stall, followed immediately by a gunshot.

"Jesus, Frank, what're you doin'?" one man says.

"Fire first, ask questions later," Frank says.

I can see their feet directly in front of my stall now. Closing my eyes briefly, I take a deep breath, steadying myself.

The door swings open, and I jump off the toilet seat, throwing my weight forward shoulder first. I plow into the gunman, knocking his weapon loose, causing it to skitter across the filthy bathroom floor. With a quick elbow strike to the man's temple, I knock him out cold. Before the other two men have a chance to react, I'm reaching for the gun on the floor. In one swift motion, I twist my hips around and pistol whip the second man in the nose, sending blood spurting onto the bathroom mirror – which was already covered with graffiti and nasty messages to begin with. He howls in pain, bending over and clutching at his nose. I raise my elbow up, bringing it down with all my strength on the back of his neck, sending him face first into the sink, his head bouncing off the porcelain. Almost before the third man even has a chance to react, I turn, keeping the pistol trained on him. He has a pistol aimed at me in return.

"Who are you?" I ask after a few tense moments of the two of us staring one another down.

He flashes me a vicious smile. "Oh, I've been waiting several months for this. You think you can kill my pops and get away with it?"

"Your…pops? I don't know what you're talking about."

"William Marcini," the man says. "I'm Lenny, by the way."

"Nice to meet you, Lenny," I say casually, keeping my pistol trained on him. "Was there something I could help you with?"

"You deaf? You think you can kill Daniels and my dad and just get away with it, huh? Yeah, I know you killed them up in that apartment. You threw Daniels off the balcony and did who-knows-what to my old man. Thanks to your little act of heroism, beating up those scrubs at the mall a few weeks ago, you're quite the internet celebrity, you know that? Made it nice and easy for us to find you."

I swallow, blinking rapidly. This can't be happening. Not now. The fate of the world hangs in the balance thanks to what's in my backpack, and this guy wants to avenge his mob boss of a father? *Where's Loretta, dammit?*

"Look, you have me confused with someone else," I say calmly. The two of us begin to circle around the restroom, my back now to the stall I was just in. "I don't know a Marcini or Daniels."

Lenny juts out his lower chin, a look of rage on his face now. "You're not even man enough to own up to it. Coward."

"Just drop the weapon, and nobody else gets hurt."

The restroom door opens and a man walks in. He takes one look at the carnage in front of him, and his eyes begin to bulge. Slowly, he steps backward out of the restroom with his hands held high, then turns around and leaves, whimpering softly.

"He's going to bring attention to this situation," Lenny says. "I'm going to give you one chance. Just one. Drop your gun and come with us. My family wants to see you back in Chicago. We have our own ways of…dispensing justice. What do you have to say about that, Simon?"

"Simon says, 'not interested,'" I say, narrowing my eyes. "You should've brought more men if you wanted to stand a chance against me."

In one quick motion, I throw the pistol at Lenny, strike him in the mouth, then charge at him, knocking the pistol out of his hands, sending it sliding under one of the stalls. He strikes me in the head in the same spot where Ron hit me not too long ago, sending pain shooting through my skull. That's going to leave a nasty bruise. He attempts to punch me a second time, but I dodge his fist, grab his forearm and send him flying into the nearest stall.

"Looks like I'm not the only one having a shitty morning," I grumble, yanking Lenny up by the scalp and dragging him over to the toilet by his hair, plunging his face into the bowl. Grabbing the toilet seat cover, I bring it down with all my strength, breaking the plastic seat over his head. He struggles, pushing against the toilet.

"You've got more fight than your old man, give you that," I say, smiling.

At this point, I don't know what's gotten into me. It's like I'm enjoying this violence. Reveling in it. It's sick. It's intoxicating. I want more.

His head soaked in toilet water, I let him get to his feet, crawling out of the stall. I'm crouched down, tilting my head mockingly at him, smiling. He stands up woozily, bracing against the side of the stall for balance. Grabbing onto the stall door, I swing it at him, smacking him directly in the face, sending him falling back. His head strikes the toilet with a sickening crack.

I leave the restroom, sprinting through the open seating area of the ferry and exit through a set of doors at the bow heading outside and up a set of stairs. Cold wind blows in my face as I climb to the top. Nobody's outside, the rest of the passengers not wanting to brave the frigid, rainy weather. Green handrails line the outside of the deck. Looking out over the water, I see that the city skyline has faded far off into the distance.

I take the backpack off as I head toward the handrail, looking down at the passing waters of Elliot Bay below. Unzipping the pack, I pull out Kanzen's supercomputer, holding the metallic ball in my hands for a moment, taking one last look at the fate of mankind.

"Rest in pieces," I say proudly, and throw the metal ball overboard.

With a soft plop, it lands in the water, bobs for an instant, then sinks below the darkened surface. The ferry motors along, sailing past where the ball landed. I throw the backpack overboard as well, lightening my load for my expected daring escape off this boat. Looking away from the fading city, I can see that we're nearing our destination. Within a few minutes, we'll be docking. I need to get off this ferry before Marcini's son and his men have a chance to find me again.

Quickly, I head for the stairs and go down several flights until I'm in the loading bay where passengers have parked their vehicles for the trip over. Some folks are still sitting in their cars, taking a nap or playing on their phones as I run between the rows of vehicles. Looking straight ahead through the gaping mouth of the front where the vehicles will soon be unloading, I can see that we are quickly approaching land.

A door to the right opens with a loud crash. Lenny and his two buddies come barreling through, looking around with their pistols drawn. I duck down against the side of a small red car, peeking through the driver's side window to gauge where the men are going. They spread out in separate directions, with one of them headed toward where I'm at.

Looking to my left, I see a motorcycle parked up near the front of the line of cars. A shorter guy holding a motorcycle helmet is walking toward the bike, looking at his phone. I take a deep breath and dart toward him. Within a few strides, I'm right behind him. He's completely unaware of my presence. I creep forward, reach up, and grab the man around the neck with both arms, seizing him in a tight chokehold with one hand cupped over his mouth. He flails wildly behind him, trying to get me to let go. My intention is to simply make him pass out, not hurt him. Slowly, he sags to the ground, and I ease his body down to the cement. I grab his helmet, which thankfully has the key in it.

In a matter of seconds, I've stolen the man's black leather jacket and put it on, as well as the helmet. I carefully drag him over to the side of the parking area and lean him to rest against the wall, out of harm's way from passing vehicles. Marcini's men are scouring the line of parked cars, still unaware of where I'm at.

I approach the motorcycle confidently, careful not to look around and potentially attract unwanted attention to myself. Lifting one leg over, I bring myself down onto the seat with ease. It's like I've done this before…but I don't remember Stinson riding a motorcycle. Perhaps it was during my other life, the one before as the World War II pilot.

The ferry slows to a stop as we begin to dock on Bainbridge Island. Waves of water slap against the side of the wooden pillars and rough, jagged rocks on shore. I ease the key into the ignition, flip the kill switch to the on position, take a deep breath, and start the bike. It roars to life, sending echoes throughout the lanes of vehicles behind me.

"I've found a body!" a man shouts behind me. "He's down here! Stay vigilant!"

I peek back and discover Lenny checking the motorcycle man's pulse. He looks up and sees me, squinting his eyes. I quickly turn back around, staring straight ahead. The loading ramp begins to lower. I kick back the kickstand, ease off the clutch and yank back on the accelerator, shooting the bike forward. I steer in between the few cars ahead of me, gaining speed as I get closer to the front of the ferry. With the ramp not yet completely lowered, I force the bike to go faster. Gunshots blast behind me, clanking against the concrete to my side. Glass shatters, presumably from the rear window of a vehicle struck by a stray bullet. Using the ramp, which still isn't lowered all the way as a mock jump, I launch up and out of the ferry, easily fifteen feet in the air.

It's as if time is suspended briefly as I soar through the misty breeze, droplets of rain sticking to the helmet's visor. The ground slowly approaches from below, like being pushed on the swings by Dad as a kid. Then, the harsh reality of the ground rushing back up to meet me snaps me back to the seriousness of the moment.

I land on the ground, balancing the bike expertly despite the back end briefly fishtailing, and accelerate with intense speed down the road leading away from the boat. Even if Marcini's men steal a car, they'll never catch me. I rocket through the streets of Bainbridge Island. Within a few minutes, I'm on Highway 3, which leads me down and around the Puget Sound and onto I-5 heading northbound. After an hour of riding, the Seattle skyline reappears.

Once in town, I sigh in relief to see that my car's still where I parked it, all in one piece. Kanzen, however, appears to have woken up and left the vehicle. No blood stains are visible, which gives me hope that he's still alive. I leave the motorcycle parked in Pioneer Square, as well as the helmet and keys. As much as I regret committing grand theft auto against an innocent civilian today, I'm sure that if he knew the morning I'd gone through, he'd understand. Maybe.

Act III

Love

noun

1. a strong feeling of warm personal attachment or deep affection, such as for a parent, child, friend, or pet
2. a profoundly tender, passionate affection for another person

Chapter 27

Wayne is still in the motel room by the time I get back, stretched out on the queen-sized bed watching TV. I enter the room and quietly shut the door behind me. He doesn't say a word; instead, he takes a sip of beer from yet another bottle and lets out a loud belch while scratching his hairy chest.

I try to call Loretta, but her phone goes straight to voicemail. I send her an urgent text and toss my phone aside in frustration. When I need her the most, she's nowhere to be found. I get that she was in a car accident, but what I've got going on is more important.

"So, has Jess tried to text you?" Wayne asks, still focused on the TV.

"No," I say quietly while slipping off my shoes. "Why would she?"

"Just curious."

I peek my head through the stained blackout curtains, checking out my beautiful car parked next to Wayne's clunker. The afternoon continues to be dreary, misting rain intermittently. Knowing that I work later this afternoon, I figure it's best to get in a quick nap before my shift begins. I lay back down on the fold out, which is surprisingly comfy. There's no bar protruding against my spine or rogue springs poking against the mattress. Draping one arm over my head, I let out a deep sigh. What a crazy morning. The only way to know for sure if my plan has worked is if I don't receive another dream about Annie and her robot friend.

"What was she like as a kid?" I ask wonderingly, looking up at the peeling ceiling complete with intermittent dots of blood spatter. "I mean, from your point of view, as her dad."

Wayne lets out a laugh and mutes the TV. "Jess? Shoot. She was a little firecracker, let me tell you. There was this one time…" he snorts and rolls on his side to look over at me, the nightstand sitting between his bed and the fold out, "…when she was maybe about seven or eight, I took her and the wife out to a nice, fancy seafood place. There's a big tank of lobsters or crabs or whatever in the waiting area, and as we're waiting to get our names called to go eat, Jess walks up to the tank and stands up on her tippy toes. She was so cute man, I'm tellin' ya. She had a little blue dress on and some ankle boots. Her mom got her those clothes, bless her heart.

"Anyways, Jess asks the hostess lady 'Can we take these home?' And the hostess just looks down at her like 'girl, what're you talkin' about?' But she kept insistin' that her daddy wanted to take one home…I don't know where she got that idea from. That whole night, all through dinner, she kept askin' the waitress how much those lobsters in the tank cost, going on and on about how she wants to take one home and name him Hank…"

He continues laughing, but my eyes open wide. *Hank?* What are the odds that Jess would want to give a pet lobster the same name as my dear old buddy?

"That's funny," I say distractedly.

"Yeah, it was," he says between mild bouts of laughter. "But, let me tell you, she was a real special girl. If I could go back and do it all over again, I would. In a heartbeat. Just like that." He snaps his fingers to drive home his point, "There's *nothin'* I wouldn't trade for another chance to be in her life. But lately…I don't know. It's like she keeps pushing me away, you know? Like, I understand that she's upset and all. Hell, I'd be pissed too if my old man came barging back into my life after so long. But ever since she's been dating that rich Asian kid, it's like she's changed. It's like she ain't Jess no more. But I'm pretty sure it's my fault. Maybe it'd be best if I just went back to Chicago, or someplace else."

"It's not you," I say, turning on my side to face him. "Well, not entirely, I don't think…though it was a lot for her to process, you coming back. But her recent moodiness and choice of clothes and stuff, you're right. It's Kanzen."

"What makes you say that?"

"He's not who he says he is," I say intently. "Deep inside, he's a different man. I don't know how to explain it without sounding insane, but just trust me when I say it's best if you just stay away from him. If you could help me convince her to stop dating him, that'd be a step in the right direction."

"I can do that," Wayne says emphatically, sitting up. "If that boy's messing with my little girl, I'll break him in two."

"He can't be hurt. Not like that, anyway."

"We'll see about that." Wayne stands up, and begins searching for a pair of pants, which he eventually finds draped on the back of a chair. He begins to quickly get dressed. "I'm her father. That guy ain't seen nothin' yet."

He grabs the pistol, which is still next to the TV, and begins to tuck it into the back of his jeans.

"Mr. Williams, please don't do that," I say quickly, now struggling to stand up. "I really need you to leave that weapon here."

"Why? I'll squeeze off one round and end that little puke. You said it yourself, he's not who he says he is." He walks over to me and places a hand on my shoulder. "I'll do whatever it takes to protect my Jess. I've been given a second chance, and I'm not about to waste it. I'm not going to let some… entitled brat brainwash my little girl and turn her against me. Against *us.* It's my job as her father to help her!"

I keep my attention focused squarely on Wayne, looking him directly in the eyes. "I'm begging you to trust me. I have…other methods to take care of Kanzen. The best thing you can do is be there for your daughter. Try to talk some sense into her."

"Haven't you tried talking to her?"

I shift my attention away from Wayne. His steely blue eyes keep staring at me, however. The same blue eyes as his daughter, yet much more intense when he's upset.

"Is there something you're not telling me, son?" he asks, squeezing his grip on my shoulder.

I take a deep breath. If I tell him that I accidentally put his daughter in a chokehold, mistaking her for an evil woman because of a bad dream, he's liable to squeeze off a round or two into *my* mushy head. It's best to lie to the man. For now, at least. I return my gaze to Wayne.

"I'm being completely honest with you," I say confidently. "Please, you have to trust me. Leave the gun here and go be with Jess. She needs her father, now more than ever."

He keeps his stare on me. After a tense moment, he slowly nods his head.

"Honesty is something I've realized is hard to find lately. I'm glad there's still people like you in this world. You're a good man, Simon."

He takes the gun out from the back of his jeans and places it back on the dresser. With an eager nod of the head, he opens the door of the motel room and leaves.

Good luck, Wayne. I hope you can get through to Jess. I only pushed her away in a time of need.

With her blue-tipped Particle Manipulator in one hand, Annie Hilltop marches past the line of android soldiers, as well as the army of human fighters, courtesy of Helen and Joe. The Structure looms high overhead with the hot afternoon sun directly behind it, casting a long shadow over the dying city. The base of the outer wall is roughly two hundred meters ahead.

No! Dumping that computer in the bottom of the bay didn't work. What happened? Why am I still being shown visions of this future?

"Joe, why are your men aiming that thing directly at the Structure?" Annie asks, displeased, gesturing toward the high mobility artillery rocket system a few yards to their left. "For the past two months, I've repeatedly told you that our intention is to get *inside* the Structure, not knock it over like a domino!"

Slowly turning his attention toward her with a smug smile on his face, Joe pats Annie softly on the top of her black hair. "Don't fret yourself so much, girl. You'll give yourself a headache. You wanted us here to help lead the attack, and that's exactly what I plan on doing. Now, if you'll please be quiet and excuse me…"

As Joe turns to walk away, Annie steps directly in front of him, preventing him from going any further. He looks up at the sky, shaking his head and chuckling softly.

"No!" Annie roars. "I'm sick and tired of men treating me like a child! I will not be quiet! I'm in charge of this operation!"

"You're *not* my commanding officer. The only reason we're out here is out of the kindness of our hearts," Joe says, leaning forward to look down at Annie. "I don't like fighting on the same side of those…machines. Now, get of my way, or I'll move you out of my way."

Annie glares at Joe, hand on hips. "We agreed it would be in the best interest of all the citizens on the Outside to stop the Grand Master and free the citizens of the Structure. Sooner or later, those androids, the ones inside those walls, will find your camp and take your resources. Then, they'll take you and everyone you love as prisoners. You and Helen agreed to help me with this mission after SOL and I killed Talaticus Maximus, severing the head of the snake that is the NWR," Annie takes a deep breath. "I know the layout of that building better than anyone, Joe. SOL and I both do, but you're treating us like fools. I need you to start listening to me! This is a rescue mission first and foremost. We'll deal with the Grand Master, but not until *after* my baby girl is safe."

He bursts into a fit of laughter, placing a hand on his bald head.

"You just don't get it, do you? This *is* a military operation! People are going to die today. My men and women are here risking their lives, all for 'the good of the people' or whatever you keep going on about. That's the downside of war. People die. Even the innocent. How can you expect that we'll follow you when everyone under my command can see that your sole focus is on getting your kid and helping that…thing find some woman?"

"Not just for that! This is for the good of *everybody!*" Annie responds. "The Structures across the land will continue to devour all the resources, taking in people as prisoners until there's nothing left. This is to benefit your camp as much as it is for me and SOL."

Joe lets out a frustrated grunt and grabs Annie by the shoulders, despite her repeated protests to stop. Before he can live up to his word and forcibly move her out of his way, a pair of mechanical hands seizes him around one of his wrists, forcing him to drop Annie. She staggers back but doesn't fall, using the end of her staff to remain upright. Joe looks up at the android who dares to touch him, glaring furiously at the machine.

"Let go of me," Joe says between clenched teeth.

After a tense pause, the android's hands release their hold of Joe's wrist. He brushes past SOL, roughly shouldering the android.

"Are you hurt?" SOL asks, no emotion coming through its voice.

"I'm fine," Annie says quietly.

"Helen has requested our presence in her tent to go over the battle plan."

SOL leads Annie through the military camp. Men are sitting by cleaning their assault rifles, taking showers, playing cards, and doing just about anything to pass the time until the signal is given to initiate the attack on the Structure.

The android holds the flap of the tent open for Annie. Helen stands over a large wooden table, surrounded by a group of rough looking men.

"There you are," Helen says. "We're just about to go over the battle plan. Gather 'round."

SOL and Annie stand behind Helen. In front of them on the large table is a hand drawn map of the Structure and the surrounding areas. Off to the left is another smaller building with a red circle around it. Helen points to this area first.

"Squadron B is going to start our assault by attacking the power station," Helen says. "SOL, what's our status on that?"

"They're in position and awaiting command, ma'am."

"Good," Helen says authoritatively. "Once the power station is offline, the enemy's energy weapons will eventually become useless. Based on what the Leader told you guys, their androids will slowly run out of power, but the more aggressively we push them, the quicker they run out of juice, making it possible for the civilians to have an opportunity to evacuate safely. We don't know if that A.I., the Grand Master, has the building rigged to blow if the people try to escape all at once, so we have to be quick about it." She clears her throat and looks over at Annie. "As we agreed, Annie, we're not going to attack the building directly, but we will fire at the wall so we can infiltrate it."

"I tried telling that to Joe, but he snapped," Annie says.

"Son of a…" Helen mutters, shaking her head in disappointment. "I'll straighten him out."

"I think SOL's already taken care of that," Annie says, nodding to her android companion.

SOL shifts its feet uncomfortably, staring down at the floor.

"Well…good," Helen says. "Alright, so Squadron A, which is us, we begin to fire at the wall here. Then, Squadron C, positioned back here on the other side of the wall, they'll commence their attack four minutes *after* we start ours in order to keep them off balance." Helen nods her head in satisfaction and places her arms behind her back. "SOL, tell your androids to begin their assault of the power station on my signal. Once that's done, then everything else will fall into place. Understood?"

The other men in the tent all look at one another, a lack of confidence washing over their features.

"Chin up!" Helen yells. The men, who were just working everyday jobs a few short days ago back at their camp, straighten up. "This is for the betterment of our camp. This is to protect our future! This is to protect our *children's* future! Like Annie's been telling us, eventually those androids inside that tower will come and find us like a pack of rabid dogs. We're going to nip that in the bud today!"

"Understood!" one of the men shouts. "We won't let you down, ma'am."

"Dismissed!" Helen commands.

As the men exit the tent, she turns her attention to Annie, her expression softening. "We're going to save your little girl."

"I didn't realize you had so much tactical experience, Helen," SOL observes. "Your analysis of the battlefield is surprisingly keen. May I ask where you acquired your training?"

Helen's gaze is still down at the map on the table, her hands clasped to the edge of the wood on either side of her. After a moment, she nods her head and lets out a deep sigh. "Through plenty of experience. Our encampment has seen a lot over the years. We had to learn to defend ourselves or perish. Several years ago, when me, Joe and a few others stumbled across that camp, we took it by force. We had to, otherwise we would've starved to death. The men who there before us were rotten, selfish people who didn't know what to do with the riches they were sitting on. After we conquered the area, others would come sniffing around, and return in force to attempt and take it for themselves. I lost count of how many times we had to defend that place."

She turns her attention to Annie. "Joe… he isn't the same man he once was. He used to be kind, caring and funny. The world changed him. Years of fighting Talaticus and the NWR changed him," Helen looks down at the map of the battlefield, shaking her head. "New World Republic…what a joke. I want you to know that I'll do anything to help you save Hope. Especially after what you guys did to help us protect our young. Like I said, they're our future."

"Are you sure they're going to be safe back at the camp?" Annie asks. "The kids, I mean."

"The camp has a hidden bunker, stocked with food, water and weapons. Those staying behind to protect the kids are more than adequate at defending the camp. Don't you worry about that. Now that Talaticus is gone, I can't imagine another enemy attacking so quickly." Helen stands upright and claps her hands together. "The time has come. We begin our attack shortly."

Chapter 28

Annie and SOL follow Helen as she aggressively pushes aside the tent cover. It takes Annie's eyes a moment to adjust to the brightness of the outside, with the sun still high in the sky, albeit hidden behind the immense Structure rising before them to the east. Men and women walk briskly through the camp in every direction, focused on their individual tasks at hand. Several of Kanzen's androids stand idly by, waiting patiently with their laser rifles at the ready. The camp is somewhat loud, with a multitude of human voices trying to communicate with one another. One man, a particularly tall individual, has a group of about ten people standing in front of him, listening to him give a passionate speech about never surrendering, and telling them that this mission is for the good of the land, as well as the future of mankind.

It starts to dawn on Annie how dangerous the Outside population views the Structure and all it stands for. What she sees as her former home, the others see a large threat that needs to be taken out. During the last couple months back in Helen's camp, Annie had told Joe and the others how the Structure treated her, taking her newborn baby away and Banishing her to the Outside. She told them about the ROADS, and the artificial intelligence, the Grand Master, sitting idly by on the top floor. She had thought that hearing her story would motivate them to help, but now she begins to wonder if perhaps their intentions aren't necessarily aligned with hers. Some of these men want to see the tower fall, to be a part of some grand scheme of destruction, regardless of who it hurts. Annie just wants to save Hope, with no wish to harm anyone else in the process.

For the time being, at least, she needs their help. As long as the cost isn't innocent civilian's lives, she'll be satisfied. All she wants is to hold her baby again, and to take Hope far away from there.

Suddenly, a loud trumpet blast emanates from the Structure, causing the camp to grow eerily quiet. People stop moving and turn their attention toward the tall black building.

"Good morning, those who stand armed at our gates," the Grand Master's deep, robotic voice speaks loudly over the speakers hanging from the top of the wall. It doesn't even attempt to mask itself now with a pleasant voice. "It seems that you've been led here for some type of purpose. To what do we owe the honor?"

Joe steps forward from the camp confidently, swinging his wide shoulders about with renewed swagger, walking briskly toward the wall. About fifty feet shy of one of the guard towers, he stops. Holding onto his belt with one hand, he puffs his chest out with pride.

"My name is Joe Armstrong. Behind me, four hundred thirsty, hungry, angry, battle-tested individuals are ready to knock down your front door. You'll be begging for death by the time they're done with you. Additionally, I have over two thousand androids, armed to the teeth, at my disposal. Not to mention the heavy artillery and other fun toys I've brought along.

"A young woman came to us awhile ago, and through an act of heroic bravery, she saved many young lives." Annie looks down at the ground, perplexed to hear Joe speak so highly of her, "She told us what goes on within those walls. It sounds like your programming's gone haywire. She says that you took her baby. We want you to release any civilians who wish to leave, so they may live in the world freely. We also demand that her baby to be returned to her unharmed."

The Grand Master's laugh cackles over the intercom. "Ah, so you have Annie Hilltop among you. I was wondering when she would come crawling back like the little dog she is. She abandoned her people by straying from the ROADS. Her offspring is being cared for. If she was as good a mother as she claims to be, she would have had the baby legally. Even the suggestion that she wants to take care of her child on the Outside should speak volumes about what kind of damaged mind you are dealing with. She is unfit to be a mother, and she has led you astray, Joe Armstrong. Annie is not welcome back here. Tell your men to pack it up and go back to whatever filth they crawled out of. Tell Annie that if she is seen anywhere near here again, she will be executed on sight. Consider this our only communication."

"Wait!" a voice calls out. SOL emerges from the camp, running up next to Joe. "I wish to see Sharon."

Once again, the Grand Master laughs. "Well, if it isn't the glitch. Model number UE0353. I should've foreseen you and Hilltop joining forces.

Regarding Sharon, I'm afraid that she's not interested in speaking to you any longer."

"I know that isn't true! We are in love!" SOL shouts.

Annie's never seen SOL become so emotional about anything before. Hearing it yell at the Grand Master is both scary and motivating.

"You're incapable of love, UE0353. What you're feeling is merely a flaw in your processing unit. Most humans don't even understand what love is. That's why I want that word banned. It's a volatile feeling that goes against everything the ROADS stands for."

"I am perfectly able to love, you manipulative pile of scrap!" SOL says angrily. "Open those doors, or so help me, I will rain hellfire down on you!"

"So be it," the Grand Master says with a sense of finality.

Annie's attention is drawn to a sudden movement up in the nearest guard tower at the top of the wall, followed by a blast from a laser rifle. The red beam shears through Joe's head, causing his skull to explode. Fragments of brain tissue and bone scatter in every direction, and his body collapses backward on the dusty, cracked pavement.

Helen screams, then collapses to her knees, sobbing. Annie crouches down next to her, trying to console her, but the woman shrugs her off.

SOL has run back to camp, pushing through the crowd of soldiers with a look of determination on its face. Annie assumes that it's gone back to retrieve the laser rifle.

"Squadron B attacks now!" Helen shouts after SOL, standing up. "Men, line up! We begin our assault on my command!"

SOL stops in its tracks for a moment, tapping the side of its temple. "Message has been sent," the android says, then resumes running back to its desired weapon.

Annie and Helen lock eyes for a moment, before their gaze is drawn toward a fireball suddenly appearing in the distance. The attack on the power station was successful, and after several seconds, a loud boom reaches their ears.

Helen marches forward, turning around to face the line of men and women before her. Annie shuffles her feet, finding a place to stand among them. She tightens her grip on the wooden staff.

"This is our moment to write a new chapter in our future!" Helen shouts. "Our mission is to breach the wall, get in, and save the civilians. This will be the fight of our lives, but I believe in you." She raises one fist in the air. "Who are we?"

"One People!" the human fighters yell in unison.

"Who do we fight for?"

"Each other!"

"When do we stop?"

"When we die!"

Helen turns around to face the Structure, one fist raised high in the air with the army at her back. "For a better tomorrow! Tear down the wall!"

The woman takes off running full speed ahead as a loud trumpet blast goes off behind them, with the rest of the army, humans and androids, on her heels. Annie is compelled to start running to prevent being trampled by the people around her, and the thousand robots behind them.

Four rockets sail overhead simultaneously, striking the wall dead on, exploding on impact, concrete and rubble scattering in every direction. The wave from the blast nearly knocks Annie off her feet.

Eight more rockets fly past, hitting the wall in various locations and taking down the nearest guard towers. Each explosion sends shockwaves through the charging crowd of humans and machines, but it doesn't deter their efforts. If anything, it propels them to run faster. Once they reach the now decimated area that was the base of the wall, people start frantically climbing over the rubble. Looking up, Annie sees that Helen is already standing on top of the heap of concrete. Annie begins her ascent, grabbing onto large chunks of concrete and avoiding exposed rebar jutting out at random. She receives a gentle boost from behind by a machine, assisting her in scaling the final several feet leading up to the summit.

She looks back briefly as the rest of the army closes in on the base of the wall. Not wanting to slow anybody down, Annie now begins to descend the pile of concrete on the opposite side, which proves much easier than the way up. After several steps and nifty jumps, she makes it back onto solid ground.

The scene unfolding in front of her is nothing short of spectacular. Laser blasts are being exchanged between the androids protecting the Structure and Annie's invading army. A man to Annie's left gets hit in the shoulder by a laser, causing him to crumple to the ground. An android in front of Annie gets hit by another laser blast, causing it to collapse in a heap. One of the Structure's security androids throws something that looks like a cube in the direction of a group of invading soldiers. The cube-shaped weapon detonates within seconds, sending a shockwave through that part of the battlefield, knocking down everyone in its path.

"I'm with you, Miss Hilltop," a voice behind Annie says.

She turns around to see SOL holding his laser rifle at the ready.

"I'm with you too," she says, holding the staff at her side.

For the first time since they met, Annie views SOL as more than a protective android. She sees him as a person, a brave man with a heart. To Annie, SOL is no longer just a machine. He's as human as she is. Where humans have hearts that pump blood through their bodies, SOL's heart is intended to protect Annie and those he cares about at all costs. Only an android with as much empathy and compassion as SOL would've gone all the way to the Capital with her and brought back an army to attack the Structure, this building that's taken and murdered countless civilians, stealing their souls for unknown purposes.

A series of blasts occur directly ahead on the other side of the Structure. Squadron C's attack has also proved successful. Several enemy androids pull back to assist in protecting the Structure from the new intruders coming over the wall to the east.

"Let's seize this opportunity to get inside," SOL says, grabbing Annie by the sleeve. "Watch my back, and I'll clear us a path."

Crouching down with her staff held firmly in one hand, she follows SOL, turning around so she's back-to-back with him.

SOL fires his laser rifle, taking down an enemy in front of them. Moving together, they pass the charred remains of the android, smoke still wafting up from its chest. Gusts of wind pick up in intensity as they get closer to the base of the tower.

They begin to walk up a large flight of stairs, the exact same ones that Annie was roughly thrown down on the night she was Banished, tumbling down to the hard concrete. As they near the top of the first flight, an android at the bottom of the steps spots the two of them and raises its weapon. Before it can fire, Annie points the end of the staff at the machine. She feels a surge of energy shoot through her arm as she fires a blue beam of energy from the tip of the staff. The android is struck dead on in the head, causing it to drop its weapon and burst into flames, falling down onto its mangled face.

So that's what it feels like to use that thing. That's awesome! It makes you feel so…powerful. It feels right, if that makes any sense.

"Simon, there you are," Annie says, relieved. "I haven't heard from you for a few weeks, I was getting worried."

I can never control these visions. It's frustrating.

"Well, you chose a perfect time to come back. Just in case I get into a trouble, I know you'll bail me out, right?"

I sure hope so.

SOL glances back for a moment but doesn't say anything.

Five security androids emerge from a doorway to the right, approaching aggressively. To the left, another squadron of ten show up, all of their laser weapons trained on Annie and SOL.

"We've got trouble," SOL says.

Still standing back-to-back, Annie hears SOL fire his weapon. Before Annie even has a chance to aim her Particle Manipulator, she feels a strong mechanical hand grab onto the back of her collar. Suddenly, SOL lifts her off the ground and swings her around, causing her to whoop in excitement. Annie activates her weapon, sending a beam of blue energy straight ahead. As she's being swung around by SOL, he's also firing his laser rifle, the two of them taking out the opposing security androids in a circular display of red and blue.

SOL sets Annie down and she staggers, slightly dizzy. All around them, the enemy androids collapse and fall over, smoke billowing off their metal bodies. Side by side, Annie and SOL approach the front doors of the Structure. Reaching his arm back without looking, SOL fires another few bursts from the laser rifle behind them, taking out two androids that were late to the ambush. They also fold in on themselves, one of them exploding.

"Scrap metal," SOL mutters.

SOL shoots his laser rifle at the front doors, causing the glass to shatter. The two of them step through the entryway, glass crunching beneath their feet. The lobby is incredibly dark, save for a few sparse lights overhead. SOL activates his LED headlamp, lighting their path. Disabling the power supply has caused the building to activate its emergency systems. They walk through the lobby undisturbed and head directly to the main elevator, which goes up to the twenty-first floor at the bottom of the courtyard. Another elevator off to the side behind the abandoned receptionist desk goes directly up to the top floor where the Grand Master resides, but this elevator is only accessible with a high-level ID badge given by The Committee, which neither of them have, so they enter the main elevator. SOL presses the button for floor twenty-one, and the doors shut quickly with a woosh. The dim lights in the elevator flicker momentarily.

"We need to move with urgency," SOL says, looking straight ahead. "Emergency power to the Structure only lasts a couple hours, tops."

"Then what?"

"The exhaust fans will stop working, meaning no oxygen. No oxygen, and the humans inside will suffocate. I will be fine, of course, but our mission will have failed." SOL briefly looks over at Annie. "That means you would die, too, Miss Hilltop."

Annie doesn't respond. Anticipation overwhelms her. Her heartbeat pounds in her ears. These last two months of separation from Hope have felt like years, even decades, and she's so close now that she can hardly breathe.

SOL offers to take Annie's Particle Manipulator, to which she agrees. The android straps her weapon on his back along with his laser rifle. The elevator doors open smoothly to floor twenty-one, at the bottom of the massive courtyard, which stretches high overhead. Not accustomed to seeing her former home so dark, Annie barely recognizes the place. One light above a nearby doorway is flashing red. No androids are in sight. Instead, the scene in front of them is a chaotic jumble of panicked civilians running around, screaming.

Ropes have descended from above, with civilians sliding down. What used to be the floor at the bottom of the courtyard has now opened into a massive chasm all the way down to one of the bottom floors. It's clear that some sort of emergency evacuation system that she's never seen before has been activated, allowing the civilians to escape the Structure from below the now-open floor of the courtyard. Children are crying, clutching tightly to their parents as the adults decide their next course of action. One man climbs onto the ledge, grabs onto a nearby rope, and slides down out of sight.

"Stay close," SOL says to Annie. "The situation is deteriorating quickly. Let's move."

SOL walks briskly through the crowd of confused and scared civilians. Some of them give them an odd look as they walk by. SOL leads Annie through a door with a sign that reads *Information Technology* overhead.

"Why aren't we going to the other elevators?" Annie asks worriedly. "I thought we're in a hurry?"

"I'm picking up strange readings in here," SOL mutters, pressing ahead. "It'll only take a moment, Miss Hilltop."

He slides back a plastic curtain, and the scene in front of them causes Annie to cover her mouth. Dozens of dead, decapitated bodies are stacked on one side of the room, their flesh beginning to decay. The stench from the rotting corpses causes Annie to nearly gag. On the opposite wall, placed delicately into glass jars, are hundreds of human brains. The jars give off a soft purple glow, and a cable can be seen connecting directly into the brains, protruding out of the jar and running up into the ceiling.

"What…what is this place?" Annie asks shakily.

SOL taps the side of his temple, craning his neck up to see. He shakes his head, taps the side of his temple again and resumes walking through the large room. "They've started using human brain energy to power the Grand Master," he says, picking up his pace.

"Isn't that what the main power was for?"

"No. The Grand Master has grown so powerful that its power consumption would've crippled the rest of the Structure months ago. It appears that it, or someone, has devised an alternative source of power to keep it operational. Cruel and sloppy, but apparently a necessary solution."

Another set of plastic curtains lay ahead. Once inside, they step onto a balcony and approach the waist-high railing which faces a see-through plastic window, looking down into a large, dimly lit rectangular-shaped room. The scene below causes Annie's knees to grow weak. Eight separate lines of people, roughly thirty deep, stand still with their arms at their sides, apparently stuck in some sort of a trance. The first person in each line looks directly ahead at a large black sphere. The dark orb opens from the middle and lets out a high-pitched shriek, seemingly causing the eight individuals at the front of their respective lines all begin to levitate off the floor. A glowing white ball, roughly the size of a fist, slowly emerges from each of their bodies, floating effortlessly into the screaming black spheres. Once the white balls have been captured by the black orbs, the androids shut the dark spheres, causing the eight bodies to collapse to the ground nearly simultaneously. After androids carry them away, dragging their limp bodies across the floor by their arms, the next person in line steps forward, and the process repeats itself.

"What is this?" Annie asks, her voice trembling.

SOL doesn't answer. He squints his plastic eyes at the scene below.

They're taking the souls out of those people's bodies with those Soul Orbs. Popobowa is responsible for this.

Annie gasps.

"What did he say this time?" SOL asks. "I know you're communicating with Simon."

Annie repeats to SOL what Simon just told her, causing the android to shake his head. He takes off the wide-brimmed black hat for a moment and rubs his head.

"So, this is what Processing means," SOL says. "They strip the people of their soul, use their brain to power the Grand Master, then throw their bodies away with the trash, dumping their remains on the Outside." SOL sighs and puts his hat back on, walking briskly ahead and out of the Information Technology section.

Ted was right, Annie thinks to herself. *Partially right, at least.*

Chapter 29

The elevator door slides open, and a wave of civilians bolt out, apparently too scared to ride the ropes down through the open courtyard. Their faces all have the same panicked, confused look, searching for where to go next, some form of direction, a semblance of safety. Once the elevator empties out, SOL steps inside and kneels down, getting to work on removing the electrical paneling.

"Now what're you doing?" Annie asks.

"Security protocols won't let us get past level two hundred without a Committee-issued pass. I'm going to override it."

Annie briefly takes a look out the doors of the elevator, still not believing the sight before her eyes. The agitation and fear among the populace is palpable. Not having ever faced a situation like this before, it's obvious that nobody's prepared for what's going on. She wishes she could go out there and calm everybody down, tell them that it's alright, the army she's brought back is here to rescue them and take them to the Outside where they can be free. That they can be who they want, pick the career they want, marry who they want, have a baby when they choose. They'll no longer have a dictator computer telling them how to live their lives.

An explosion rocks the building from below.

"One of the squadrons has breached the lower levels," Annie speculates. "Either that or a rocket hit the building."

SOL continues working methodically on the electrical panel. Annie admires him as he stares ahead with those steely, unblinking eyes, filled with so much determination, trying so desperately to see the woman he loves again.

"Got it," SOL declares.

The elevator door slides shut, the emergency overhead lights turn off, and the carriage shoots upward. Through the glass door, they witness more panicking civilians jumping onto ropes. Some are beginning to push one another, eager to get down to the bottom before the others. Annie watches one male in particular who shoves a female out of the way, just to jump onto a nearby rope ahead of her. It's shocking to see them behaving this way in a moment of desperation, despite having been taught the ROADS. *In the end, humans will always revert to their basic animal instincts,* Annie thinks to herself.

Blackness eliminates their view of the civilians as they go past level two hundred. SOL remains kneeled, fiddling with the electrical panel, and the elevator comes to a jarring halt on floor 210.

"This is the floor that Sharon lived on," SOL says. "What floor did David live on?"

"Two-twelve," Annie says. She taps the side of the elevator anxiously, then takes a deep breath. Every fiber of her being is telling her to find Hope *now*, to demand that SOL send them up two more levels. But looking down at the android, she recognizes that he's sacrificed so much to get them to this point. He deserves to be with Sharon. They can spare the time. "Look, I want to see Hope more than anything in the world. But let's go see Sharon first, then we can go up to David's apartment. Deal?"

He reaches both hands on the edge of the elevator door, yanks it open, and steps out. "We have a deal, Miss Hilltop."

Through the corridors the two of them go, Annie having to pick up her pace to keep up with SOL, who's walking with a swift purpose. The red carpet and narrow hallways are the same as on David's floor; a common layout for the upper floors, Annie assumes.

SOL stops in front of one of the rooms and raises his hand up to knock on the door, but stops just before doing so. He looks back at Annie, and for the first time that she can recall, he has a look of apprehension on his face. Shaking his head softly, he turns around and faces her, his back to the door.

"What do I even say?" he asks with a hint of desperation. "Do I tell her…I'm at a loss for words here. What do you suggest, being a female of the species?"

She chuckles softly to herself before grabbing him by both shoulders, looking him in the eyes. "When you think of Sharon, how does she make you feel?"

"One moment," he looks down, darting his eyes back and forth quickly. "Many feelings come to mind. Warmth. Comfort. Connection. Friendship. Happiness."

"How did you feel when you were Banished, unable to see her?"

"Angry. Sad. Lonely. Determined."

Annie nods her head and smiles. "Tell her that. Tell her how she makes you feel, and how you felt when you were apart. Make her understand that she's special to you, and describe all that you did to get back here, right now, this moment, just to be with her again. Go on."

She gently pushes his shoulders, turning him around and urging him to go knock on the door. Annie scuttles around the corner so that she isn't seen by Sharon or whoever answers. SOL looks at Annie, nods his head, then knocks. After a few seconds, the door opens. Annie can hear a familiar man's voice, soft at first, then rising gradually the more he talks. The android remains quiet, merely staring ahead, hands at his sides. Annie steps closer to the door to discover that the man doing all the talking is Thomas. David's father.

"What the hell are you doing here?" Thomas croaks when he sees Annie, his expression a state of panic. "No…this can't be happening!"

The man goes to shut the door just as SOL raises his arm up, blocking the door from closing. Thomas backs into the apartment. Annie hesitantly approaches SOL as he stands at the doorway.

SOL takes a moment to look back at Annie. "How would you suggest I proceed, Miss Hilltop? Use caution, or force?"

Annie steps into the apartment and keeps her attention on Thomas, who is now grabbing his chest and backing further into the darkened, oversized living quarters. He finally reaches a plush sofa and falls backward over the armrest. Annie's breathing has quickened, and a fierce feeling of anger overcomes her. She remembers what he said to her the night she was Banished. How he, and the rest of The Committee cast her aside like a piece of garbage. She squints her eyes.

"Force," Annie lifts her chin and raises her voice to Thomas, "Where's my baby? Is she still with David?"

SOL shuts the front door and walks into the apartment, standing next to Annie as they look down at Thomas on the couch. A fireplace gives off waves of warmth off to their left next to a hallway.

"She's with her father, where she belongs, you treacherous heathen," he says shakily, grasping for a glass of wine on the table next to him. "If you really cared for your little girl, you'd go back to the Outside where you belong."

"Shut up!" Annie shouts. "Where's Sharon?"

"She's not here. Now take your robo-toy and get the hell –"

A woman's sharp gasp sounds from the hallway. "UE0353!"

"Sharon!" SOL exclaims, walking toward the hallway. "Sharon, it's me. I've come back!"

Sharon steps out of the shadows, glancing over at Annie for a moment before looking back at SOL. She's dressed in a bright pink, billowy nightgown made of silk with her hair done up nicely, although out of compliance when it comes to female hair code.

"How did you make it up here? We heard about the attack in the lower levels, and we've been told to stay in our room."

Standing in front of Sharon, SOL attempts to wrap his arms around her in a hug, but she pushes him away roughly, letting out a loud shriek.

"Don't touch me!"

The android takes a step back, head lowered. "I'm so sorry. I didn't mean to scare you. You make me feel warm, and happy. When I was Banished, I felt angry, and lonely. But I was determined to see you again. You mean… everything to me, Sharon. I love you."

She scoffs, combing her fingers through her hair. "This again. Look at you. You're…you're a machine. I thought you were sent away for maintenance, but from the way you're talking, it sounds like you need another tune-up. You can't love. You're incapable of it."

"But I can!" he says emphatically, taking a step forward. Sharon takes another step back, reaching behind her for something at the side of the roaring fireplace. She grabs hold of a fire-poker, brandishing it in front of her as a weapon. SOL isn't deterred, continuing toward Sharon with his arms outstretched. "Please, if you'll just give me a chance. I'd always protect you. I'd do *anything* for you. I might not be made of flesh and bone, but I have heart," he pats his chest several times, making a loud clanking noise, "*I have heart.* I would give my soul to you, if I had one. All I can offer you is my unyielding strength and fidelity. We can be something, you and I. Don't you agree?"

"She'll never love you, robot," Thomas laughs from the couch.

For a tense moment, SOL and Sharon stare at one another. Getting down on one knee, SOL tries to take her hand, but she quickly yanks it away and begins to shake her head. A small chuckle escapes her lips, followed by a gush of laughter.

"You were created to serve my purposes as a member of The Committee.

That was all. This ill-conceived notion you've got floating around that head of yours is… wrong. It's perverse. Somewhere along the assembly line, someone either made an error, or thought it would be a sick joke to make you think you're capable of love. The truth is you don't love me. It's just…programming gone bad."

"No," SOL whispers. "Sharon, please. You're all I think about. Annie and I were on the Outside for weeks. We trekked all the way to the Capital and spoke with the Leader. And all that time, every night and every –"

"I'll hear no more of this!" she says dismissively, waving a hand in the air. "Please leave and take Nate Hilltop's traitorous offspring with you."

With that, she turns on her heel and walks back down the dark hallway. A door slams a short moment later. Still kneeling, SOL looks down at the floor, shaking his head. Annie walks over to him, placing one hand on his back gently.

"I'm so sorry," she whispers softly.

"I have failed."

"That's right," Thomas says mockingly from the couch, now standing up. "Leave, you filthy, conniving cowards. Get out of here!"

Annie turns around and punches Thomas in the jaw, sending the man crashing through the glass coffee table. He rubs his jaw, looking around the room in a daze.

"You don't follow the ROADS," he seethes.

"To hell with the ROADS," Annie responds angrily, tears welling in her eyes. "To hell with the Structure! You don't deserve the air you breathe!"

Annie turns around to leave the apartment with SOL, and together they walk down the hallway and step back into the elevator. SOL finagles the electrical panel again, and the elevator goes up a couple more levels before stopping again on floor 212. Before getting off the elevator, he turns around and wraps Annie in a hug. She can feel his chest heaving, as if he's crying. She returns his hug, wrapping her small arms around his hard back.

"You did everything you could," she says reassuringly.

"Thank you, Annie."

As they exit the elevator, Annie takes the lead this time, guiding them through the maze of corridors until they reach David's apartment. She knocks on the door loudly and stands back with her arms crossed. A commotion can be heard on the other side of the door, but it never opens.

"I know you're in there, David!" Annie shouts. "Open up before I have my friend here kick down the door!"

The lock disengages and the door creaks open slowly.

"What're you –"

Annie steps forward and pushes the door open violently, knocking David down onto the carpeted floor. Sunlight streams through the soft white curtains directly ahead, creating a bright ambiance inside the apartment. Bottles of wine are laying around haphazardly, some of the contents spilling onto the plush carpet. What used to be a clean and tidy living quarters now looks like a filthy disaster. Annie looks down at David and sees that his eyes are sunken in, as if he hasn't slept in days.

Annie marches back to the bedroom in search of Hope. A woman is laying nude on the large bed, empty glasses of wine sprawled out on the carpeted floor just beyond her outstretched hand. Next to the large bed is a baby crib. Leaning over the side of the crib, Annie finds it empty.

"Where's Hope?" Annie demands, returning to the living room.

"How did you get back Inside?" David coughs, now sitting in the middle of the living room.

"I'm the one asking the questions now," Annie says bluntly, standing over him. "Where's my baby?"

"*Our* baby, you mean," David retorts. "She's not here."

With one quick strike, SOL slaps David across the mouth. "Shut up and listen. We're here for Hope, and we require your assistance in locating her. I'll see to it that no harm comes to Hope or her mother."

"Stupid machine," David grumbles, wiping blood from his mouth. "You have no right to speak to me this way."

SOL turns to Annie. "It appears physical force may be necessary to extract our required information. Permission to proceed with aggressive interrogation tactics?"

Without hesitation, Annie answers. "Permission granted."

Just as the android bends down to grab David by the collar of his shirt, the man breaks down in tears. He holds a hand up in defense, begging SOL to stop.

"She's with your doctor," David sobs. "She's with Yelena. She just wouldn't stop crying. I couldn't get any sleep. Please, you have to understand."

Annie nods her head softly to SOL, who responds by releasing his hold on David. He collapses back onto the floor, crying and curling up into a ball.

"Pitiful response," SOL says to Annie as they exit David's quarters,. "Predictable. But still pitiful."

Luckily, Yelena lives on the same floor as David, making their destination just a short walk down a few corridors. Annie knocks on the door, slightly louder than intended due to her high-strung nerves. Having just seen what her ex-lover had been up to, finding out that he essentially pawned her baby off on her best friend, has her on the verge of tears. Tears of anger.

The door opens, and Yelena stands in the doorway, a bright smile on her face. "Annie!" She wraps Annie in a quick hug. "Oh, I'm so glad to see you. How are you…"

Yelena's voice trails off as she looks up at SOL, then takes a step back and looks at Annie with a questioning expression on her face.

"He's with me," Annie explains.

"Yeah, I can see that," Yelena says uncertainly, taking a long look at SOL as she ushers the two of them inside.

The living room is a gigantic nursery. Baby essential items are all about the place, although in a surprisingly organized fashion. Diapers in one section, bottles ready to go in another, and in the center of the living room is the crib. Annie approaches it quickly, looks down and is relieved to see a happy, healthy baby girl laying inside, looking up at Annie with wide open eyes and wonder on her face. Annie scoops the baby up in her arms, looking down at her daughter.

"Hi, baby girl. It's me, your momma. I came back for you."

Annie turns around, holding Hope in her arms, and sees SOL standing behind her, smiling.

"I'm very happy for you, Annie," he says genuinely.

Annie smiles, a tear streaking down her cheek. "You know something? After all this time, I guess I didn't really know what love meant. I thought that I did. But now, holding her in my arms, now I understand it. *This* is what love is."

SOL steps forward and looks down at the baby. "She's adorable."

"She looks just like the rest of us do when we're babies," Annie says. "But you're right. Something about her is…different. She's special."

"Just like her mom."

Annie looks up at SOL and nods her head. "We made a pretty good team, didn't we? From where we met to where we are now?"

"Yes, we certainly did," SOL agrees.

"So, uh, what's the deal here?" Yelena asks, genuinely puzzled, pointing back and forth between Annie and the android.

"We found each other on the Outside," Annie explains, then launches into the story of how they met and their journey together. All the while, Annie holds Hope in her arms, skillfully swaddling the baby like she's done this before. How she knows to hold a baby like this is unknown to her. *It's not that difficult,* she tells herself.

"How did you end up with the child, Yelena?" SOL asks. "I understand David relinquished custody, but was it done amicably?"

"Yeah, David just came running over here one night, pounded frantically on the door and basically threw the little thing at me," Yelena says, running a hand through her black hair. "He looked so pathetic. I sort of felt bad for him at the time, but I don't anymore."

"Thank you so much, Yelena," Annie says warmly. "You did such a great job with her."

Yelena smiles, looking down at Hope. "She's a special little girl. I'm glad I could help. I remember what you'd told me just before you went to see the Grand Master, and I took that to heart. What they did to you was…wrong. I don't see how they could just –"

A large explosion rocks the Structure, causing the floor to shake. SOL holds on tight to Annie to prevent her from falling over, as she clutches Hope tightly to her chest.

"We need to find a way out of here," SOL says urgently. "Yelena, I suggest getting down to the lower levels as soon as possible. This building may not be standing for much longer."

"You guys go ahead," Yelena says, leaning in for a quick hug with Annie. "I'm going to take care of a few things first. Hopefully I'll see you guys down there."

"Please take care of yourself," Annie says with a level of concern.

"Don't worry about me, hon," she replies. "I'll catch up."

Annie, with Hope clutched firmly to her chest, follows SOL out of the apartment and down the red hallway. Once they're inside the elevator, SOL gets to work again on the electrical panel, but after a few minutes, they still haven't moved.

"What's wrong?" Annie asks anxiously.

SOL lets out a frustrated grunt. "I've been locked out of the system. The only direction I'm able to take us is up."

"Up? We don't want to go up. We need to get down and out of here."

SOL stands up and shakes his head. "We can't. Like I said, I've been locked out. The Grand Master is watching us." He rubs his chin softly, looking down at the ground in concentration. "You know, when I was working maintenance, I discovered an emergency hatch up in the Grand Master's chambers on the top floor. It goes right up to the roof."

"Alright…then what? Do you have a parachute or something up there?"

"Yes," he says bluntly. "Although it's not mine, I am simply aware of its existence. First, I'll try to send a message to some of the other androids so they can bring a shuttle or something up to the roof in order for us get down safely." Annie tries to interject, but SOL puts his hand up. "I'm sorry, Annie, but this is our only way. You need to trust me."

She grimaces, then nods her head reluctantly. She can't really think of any other logical options at this point. Annie looks at the Particle Manipulator still strapped to SOL's back. If push comes to shove, she knows she has this deadly weapon to help defend them against the Grand Master, or Popobowa if he's still hiding up there.

"UE0353," the deep voice of the Grand Master comes over the speakers inside the elevator. "And Annie Hilltop. Are you two prepared to come see me?"

SOL resumes working on the electrical panel, remaining silent.

"What do you want?" Annie asks.

"It looks like you've been reunited with your illegitimate child," the Grand Master says. "I'll be seeing you two very soon."

Within a few moments the elevator lurches, then shoots upward. Annie closes her eyes and takes a deep breath. Looking back down at Hope, she knows that she'll do whatever it takes to protect her daughter and get her out of here. She'll protect her baby from whatever danger lies ahead.

At the top floor, level 256, the elevator comes to a sudden stop and the doors open to the same large, dark room where Annie was a few short months ago. The same room where she met the Grand Master for the first time. The same room where her father was murdered by Popobowa.

The large metallic orb still hovers innocently in the middle of the spacious room, providing the only source of light. Another explosion shakes the building.

"It feels as though the Structure's integrity has been compromised," the Grand Master says from the middle of the room. The metallic sphere grows brighter, making it easier for Annie to see the path ahead. "Please, step closer. I won't bite."

After several shaky steps forward, SOL and Annie stop directly in front of the Grand Master. The round metallic sphere turns gracefully in its floating cocoon, hovering over the floor.

"We're just passing through, don't mind us," Annie says innocently.

"Oh, but I *do* mind," the Grand Master says ominously, its deep voice causing Annie's bones to shake. "I can't allow this to continue."

"Don't engage it further," SOL whispers in Annie's ear. "Let's keep moving."

"I can hear you, UE0353. Tell me, what assembly plant do you originate from?"

"I suppose now is as good a time as any," SOL says, inserting the small plastic data disc that the Leader gave him into a slot on the side of his hip.

SOL's mouth begins to open wide, and a beam of soft white projects from his mouth. The light creates a hologram, roughly six feet tall, directly in front of SOL. The image of an android wearing a red robe and a large crown on top of its head comes into focus, seated on a leather chair in front of a roaring fireplace.

"Hello, Grand Master, my name is Kanzen Sasaki," the sound of the Leader's voice plays from SOL's mouth, making the entire hologram experience a bit confusing at first for Annie. "I wanted to share with you something that I think you may find of importance, while simultaneously hoping that you can see the error of our ways. This unit that I'm speaking to you through right now, UE0353, was a special creation of mine. I've instilled within it, or within *him* I should say, the capacity to feel human emotion. More specifically, I've attempted to give him the emotion of love."

The hologram stands up from the leather chair and begins to move around the room, keeping his hands clasped together against his synthetic abdomen. "Now, I know that in the past I've told you that love is imperfection. Well, I was wrong. Over the last hundred years, as I've seen humanity kill itself in droves due to lack of water, their governments abandoning the citizens in order to save themselves, I've also seen something special. Even in the face of the unknown, or in this case, the unstoppable known certainty that the majority of the world's population will die of dehydration, I've seen that people *still* have the capability and capacity to love. I've seen total strangers go out of their way to help someone else, even if it puts their own life on the line."

Kanzen's hologram continues moving around the dark room. "When I designed you, I was a broken man. I'd lost my sister several years prior, and I viewed society in a pessimistic light. While it wasn't perfect, if I knew then what I knew now, I never would've created any of this. The industrial water powered generators, the Structures, the machines…all of it. Including you. I tried to make everything perfect, but instead I ruined it all. If there was some way for me to talk to my past self, and prevent all of this from happening, I'd do it in a heartbeat."

The hologram goes silent for a moment as Kanzen's shape takes a seat in the leather chair again. "While I was right when I said that love wasn't perfect, what I was wrong about was teaching you that love should be stopped. That it can't be accepted. Because love *can't* be stopped. Love is what makes the world go around. Love is what gives people hope. Don't take that away from them. Let the people go Outside. Let the people love each other. Let them choose for themselves how to live their lives. We have no right to control that. *I* had no right to attempt to control that." He leans back in his leather chair, hands clasped on his lap. "One day, when I'm near the end, I know that I'll be filled with remorse and regret, and there's nothing I can do about that. Please, don't make the same mistakes I've made. I designed you. I also have the power to destroy you. As this message has played, I have overridden the elevator controls in your Structure, allowing it to move freely."

The hologram fades to darkness, and SOL closes his mouth. He looks around the room for a moment, a look of confusion on his face.

"This changes nothing," the Grand Master rumbles. "The Order must be carried out. A perfect society must be created at all costs, unless the Creator tells me himself *in person,* or I am provided with the correct override code."

SOL shakes his head. "I don't have an override code." He turns his attention to Annie. "I thought when the Leader gave me this message it was intended to disable the Grand Master. Kanzen didn't mention anything about a code."

"Well, there has to be some way out of here," Annie says, looking around for an exit. She starts searching for an escape hatch, some sort of a way up onto the roof, but the room is too dark to see clearly.

Suddenly, a pair of red eyes appears in the darkness behind the Grand Master. A large, muscular black man wearing plated armor and holding a yellow staff moves slowly through the shadows, stepping around the large computer.

"Popobowa," Annie exclaims.

Beep beep beep

Oh no, it's my alarm. I have to wake up to go to work. But I can't miss this. I need to see…

I open my eyes for a moment and look around Wayne's dirty hotel room. My heart begins to beat faster, panic setting in. I hit the snooze button on my smartphone, closing my eyes tightly together.

Popobowa steps closer to Annie and points the Particle Manipulator at her, an intense yellow glow beginning to blaze off the staff's point. Reaching over, she grabs her Particle Manipulator off SOL's back with one hand and points it back at the massive demon, the end of the staff turning a vibrant blue. Hope begins to cry softly in Annie's other arm.

"Stupid girl," Popobowa says, his deep voice shaking the dim room. "You dare point a weapon at me?"

"I don't care who you are! Stand down, or you *will* be fired upon!" Annie shouts.

SOL reaches over and takes Hope from Annie, running to a far corner of the room as the baby's crying grows louder.

"Meet your destruction!" Popobowa shouts, sending a yellow beam of energy from the point of his staff directly toward Annie.

Keeping her weapon trained on the powerful demon, she concentrates all of her might on Popobowa, sending a jet of blue out of her staff. The blue and yellow beams collide, causing a swirl of colors and sparks of energy to dance around the room. Annie's vision begins to turn blurry, the entire scene distorting into a wavy mass as if looking through shallow water.

Beep beep beep

I OPEN MY eyes and the dream disappears, vanishing into nothingness.

"No!" I shout. "No! This can't be happening!"

Reaching over for my phone, I turn off the alarm. My grip on the smartphone is so tight that I can feel the screen beginning to shake in my hands. I let out a frustrated yell and get up off the fold out.

Annie. The memories of the dream continue to flood my thoughts. If I try to go back to sleep, maybe I can help her survive this battle against Popobowa. On the other hand, if I'm even one minute late for work, Ms. Sasaki will be most displeased. After the way I talked to her son, going against her advice, she's probably itching for a reason to fire me. And I need this job as a source of income, especially without a place to live. I can't wind up homeless again.

A spark of energy bolts through me. After listening to future Kanzen's hologram message, about how full of regret he is, I know now that it's not too late to talk to him. Somewhere, deep down, there's still a good man in there, and if I could just find some way to exorcise X's soul out of Kanzen's body, I can *still* save him. I may still have time to make everything right.

I grab my backpack and throw it down on the fold out, still filled with rage over waking up from the dream prematurely. The backpack bounces on the mattress and falls off the bed, crashing into the tall closet on the other side and causing the door to pop open.

"Idiot," I mutter to myself as I walk around the bed.

Bending over to pick up the backpack, I glance up and notice something yellow inside the closet. I know it's not right to peek into other people's property, but curiosity gets the better of me. As I open the closet door wide, I see a large yellow staff propped up inside. Intricate markings scale the sides of it. I've seen a staff that looks exactly like this before, but where? Then, it dawns on me.

This was Brittany's staff.

Chapter 30

Seeing X's staff sitting in Wayne's closet makes me realize one thing: I'm *really* an idiot. Like, a big one. Not only did I push Kanzen away, who has the potential to be a really good guy, but I may have had an influence in pushing him into a dark, alternate timeline. Perhaps even the same timeline I've been dreaming about. On top of that, I was so naïve and gullible that I believed Brittany when she told me that she was Kanzen.

It was Wayne all along. Jess and Ron are in his crosshairs. And he went over there to talk to Jess… *crap.*

Curious if I can take this Particle Stick, or whatever it's called with me, I grab onto the handle. Immediately, my hand begins to burn in an unimaginable searing pain. I yank my hand back, steam still sizzling off my palm. I guess I can't pick up his weapon, which makes sense considering it's not coded to my soul.

I grab my wallet and keys, sprinting out of the hotel room to my car. I hope I'm not too late. If Wayne did anything to hurt my friends…I can't think about that right now. Ms. Sasaki will just have to accept that I'm not coming to work today.

Peeling out of the parking lot, I speed down the busy afternoon streets, passing cars just like I did earlier this morning while being shot at. What a day it's been already. I take several shaky breaths, trying to calm my nerves, but it's no use. Not even my past lives are able to steady me in this situation, knowing that my friends are in danger.

I turn on the radio to the start of "Love Reign O'er Me," by *The Who*. The song comes to its dramatic end just as I pull into the apartment's parking lot. Wayne's beat up old ride is nowhere to be seen. I park in my old spot and run up the stairs, discovering that the door to the apartment has been kicked in, the wooden frame splintered.

The place has been completely trashed. Furniture is thrown every which way; dishes are smashed in the kitchen. The coffee table is broken, smashed into pieces, and the big screen TV has been thrown on top of it. The carpet is stained with drops of blood. Leaving the front door open, I wander slowly around the apartment.

"Jess!" I call out, heading down the hallway. "Ron? Hello?"

No answer. I open Jess' bedroom door. Empty. Next, I check Ron's room, also with no luck. I open mine just as a last-ditch effort, as well as the bathroom. Nobody's home. Whatever happened here, it looks like they put up one heck of a fight. Wayne must've taken them. Even without his magical staff and pistol, he still possesses that psychic ability to enter their consciousness. I hope he didn't make them hurt themselves.

Once I finish my tour down the hallway, I retrace my steps only to find three familiar armed men now standing in the living room. Lenny Marcini crosses his arms over his chest with his pistol in one hand. Standing in this light, he does bear a remarkable resemblance to his old man with that mane of black hair, handsome facial features and a strong looking physique. One of his men attempts to gently close the front door behind him, unaware of the splintered wood preventing the door from shutting securely.

"You're quite the slippery man, Mr. Verner," Lenny laughs.

"Look, this isn't a good time. Wait…did you guys take my friends?"

Lenny sighs and motions to his men. I attempt to punch the man to my left, but the guy on my right pulls out a taser and jams it into my neck, sending me down to my stomach. Both men yank me up by the back of my shirt collar and position me onto my knees. Lenny crouches down in front of me so that we're roughly at eye level.

"I'm typically a very patient man, Simon. However, my tolerance for you is wearing quite thin. Come with us or die. You have ten seconds to choose."

"I didn't kill your old man," I say hoarsely. "But I know who did."

Lenny's eyebrows shoot up. "I'm listening."

"You'll have to get closer," I whisper.

He shuffles closer so that he's inches from my face.

"Some crazy old broad with a magical stick turned your daddy to ashes. But not before I shoved Travis Daniels out the window and killed him."

On my last word, I lunge forward and chomp my teeth down onto Lenny's ear, yanking my neck back violently. He grabs at where his ear used to be, screaming. I spit the entire chunk of skin and cartilage out onto the floor, a trail of blood oozing off my lips. Even to this day, new skills and acts of brutality from my past lives are surfacing. I wasn't expecting to go Mike Tyson on William Marcini's kid today, yet here we are.

Lenny roars, still clutching the side of his face, blood streaming down his neck and through his fingers. "Shoot him now!"

I feel a pistol being pressed against the back of my head, the cool, hard steel shoved against my skull, the seconds ticking down until my life as I know it ends and I'm sent into the Beyond to be reborn. But if that happens, does that mean my next life is part of Annie's timeline? Doomed to die of dehydration, or who knows what else, in the future ruled by robot Kanzen and the Structures?

The front door smashes inward, and before I have a chance to look up, a streak of yellow light flashes out of my peripheral, and the pressure of the pistol against my head disappears. Looking to the front door, I see Wayne standing there with his Particle Stick in hand, aiming the point of the staff at the second man. Another jet of yellow shoots from the weapon, and the man disappears into a smoldering pile of ash, his pistol clanking down onto the carpet. Before Lenny has a chance to get a shot off, Wayne takes aim and fires, striking Marcini Jr. in the chest. As he collapses backward, Lenny looks over at me, a confused look on his face. His body catches fire, but his screams are quickly silenced. Lenny Marcini's body turns into a pile of ash once he makes impact with the floor. Like father, like son.

With one hand outstretched, Wayne looks down at me with a proud smile on his face.

"I'm here to save you, Brother."

I look at his hand briefly, then back up at his face. A chuckle escapes my lips, followed by uncontrollable laughter which shakes me to my core.

Ignoring his hand, I stand up on my own, facing Wayne. "It was you all along." I say it as a statement rather than a question. "Where's Jess and Ron?"

"Popobowa's taken them to the Dark Dimension," he says seriously. "I've been instructed not to kill you. Yet. For now, you'll need to come with me."

"I'm not going anywhere with you!" I shout, standing there with hand on hips, taking a few moments to catch my breath and gather my thoughts. "Why did you tell me that you were Kanzen?"

"You care more about those two than you do for yourself. Now that I know the man you are, Simon, I knew that seeing your precious little friends turn against you would just eat you up. It was pretty funny, to be honest. But you know what's even weirder? The fact that even after you broke up with Jess, she was okay with living under the same roof as you. I mean, if that doesn't tell you that she still loves you, I don't know what does. You're just too stupid to see it."

"Pretending to be Jess' dad. That's a new low. Even for you."

"Oh, boo hoo," Wayne says mockingly. "Her old man was a useless drunk. He died seven years ago, passed out in some back alley in Cincinnati. Popobowa dragged this corpse back to the Dark Dimension to be used for a later time. And look, here he is again." He spreads his arms out wide in a grand display. "And trust me, this is far from the worst thing I've ever done."

I remain quiet for a moment, allowing everything to sink in. There're so many questions I want to ask this man, this…individual, who masqueraded around as Jess' father, weaseling his way into our lives, driving a wedge between me and my friends. Again.

Wayne starts chuckling. "You're probably wondering how Lenny and his men tracked you down, aren't you?"

The thought had crossed my mind. How did they know where to find me at Kanzen's house? And how did they know precisely where to look as I was running away from them in the city?

"When you first came to my motel room, I snuck a tracking device into your pack while you were taking a shower," Wayne explains. "Then when you left, I gave them a call and told them to follow you. I figured that once your buddies kicked you out, you'd be gunning for Kanzen's computer. What pisses me off, however, is that I specifically told them not to kill you. Just capture you. That's it. Why was that so hard? Do I have to do everything myself?"

"I bet Wayne never even knew my dad, did he?"

"Oh, he did," X answers. "All of Jess' daddy's memories are still with me." He taps his head a few times. "Thankfully, the Dark Dimension is a… special place, if you want to call it that. It's dying, sure, but it also has special healing properties. That's how I'm able to use this body. That's how Popobowa remains so strong."

I've heard enough. I attempt to push my way past him, but he stops me with a firm hand to my chest.

"I wasn't asking, Simon. You're coming with me."

He presses the end of his staff into my chest. The Particle Stick glows a soft yellow, on the brink of charging up.

"We're gonna go for a little ride," Wayne says, still smiling.

After an hour-long car ride in the smelly trunk of Wayne's rust bucket of a vehicle, he pulls over on a lonely stretch of highway in the middle of nowhere. Yanking me out of the trunk by my hair, he then leads me through some waist-high grass for another twenty minutes or so until we arrive at his desired destination. A large wormhole that leads into the alternate hellish world known as the Dark Dimension awaits us. The gateway sits idly in this abandoned field, rotating slightly, the center of the vortex showing a nightmare landscape of exploding volcanoes, and winged bat-like creatures flying around aimlessly. I remember this view of the Dark Dimension back in the Palace Theater.

"Is this where you took my friends?" I ask.

"This is where Popobowa took your friends."

Wayne roughly pushes me in the back toward the gateway. The sharp poke of the Particle Stick presses against my spine, urging me onward. Every ounce of my being is telling me not to go inside, but I know I have no choice. I have to save my friends from the unimaginable terrors that wait inside. With a final shove, I step through the vortex into the Dark Dimension.

My skin suddenly feels wet, then cold, then hot. My eyes feel as if they're about to be pulled from their sockets. Stars begin to soar past, and my body begins traveling at an incredibly high rate of speed through nothingness. Tumbling head over heels, all sounds, colors and sensations cease to exist for several seconds. There is no white or black, up or down, right or wrong; all that surrounds me is everything and nothing simultaneously.

Images of my childhood begin to rush past. Blowing out birthday candles, meeting Doug on the beach, driving with my mom, laughing with Ron, talking with Jess, golf balls banging off the side of the range picker. Happiness. Sadness. Love. Hate. Listening. Talking. Blue. Yellow.

All of a sudden, I'm standing on a rocky surface, with nothing but fire and red rocks all around. The bat-like creatures soar overhead, letting out ear-splitting screams. A volcano erupts in the far-off distance, and the ground begins to shake beneath my feet. The temperature has risen at least twenty degrees, causing me to sweat.

"Welcome to the Dark Dimension," Wayne says proudly, strolling past me. "Your cell is this way."

Chapter 31

Wayne leads me through an expansive, flat area. Far off in the distance, more giant volcanoes jut up against the sky, spouting lava, rivers of yellow liquid trickling off their sides. The sky and the dirty, dusty ground all share the same red hue. Enormous canyons come into view as we journey through the barren landscape. Far below is an enormous river of molten lava, bubbling and giving off a heavy amount of steam. We follow the edge of the canyon for at least a mile, my feet beginning to drag on the ground from exhaustion. I'm not used to this much heat.

"This is my favorite part," Wayne says eagerly. "This is what it's all been about."

A large industrial-looking machine appears along the edge of the canyon ahead of us, strategically positioned so that a bright white laser is aimed directly at the side of the opposite canyon wall. The red rock stands firm, not giving way to the immensely intense beam of energy. Big plastic buckets lay on the dusty, rocky floor all around this big machine, filled to the brim with glowing white orbs.

"Are those... souls?" I ask.

"That's right. Buckets of souls from your future that you've been dreaming about. We've been gathering them for a long time. It's almost ready now."

"What's almost ready?"

Wayne points at the large machine with the white laser shooting from it. "The Soul Generator. Popobowa's been collecting these souls to power the machine. Once it's ready, our army will finally be free to enter the real world."

"The...real world? Do you mean *my* world? In my present time?"

"Right again," Wayne replies, patting me on the back. "Two for two. When the machine is powered up, it'll open a portal right over there..." he points at the tall canyon wall where the bright light is being directed, "... wide enough for Popobowa's army to march through. Then, we'll take over the Earth and terraform the planet to our liking."

This is beyond ridiculous. This is so much worse than I ever could've imagined. They've been collecting the tainted souls from those in the dying city and beyond to power this…soul generator thing, all so they can invade Earth? The stakes can't be raised much higher than this. Now I fully understand why I've been receiving these visions of Annie and the Structure. My dreams of John Stinson were only a training course for what's at stake now. Not only do I need to protect the future of mankind, but I need to save the current world before the Dark Dimension is unleashed, bringing hell on Earth. Permanently.

I can either accept the fact that this is really happening, or I can sink back into my shell and refuse to believe reality, pretend that I'm still sitting in my straitjacket in the mental hospital back in Chicago. The meds that Dr. Scholinsky is giving me have forced me to live a nightmare, that I never escaped the facility. My story has jumped the shark, and I'm still stuck here while Jess is out on the boat in Lake Michigan, John Stinson's murder will still go unsolved, and Doug and Mike live out their lives free from the grasp of justice.

I choose the first option. My time has come to be a hero, and on a much broader scale than the last time. Some folks may revel given the opportunity that I've been presented before me here. Apparently, I'm not one of those people. I think I'm going to be sick. Is there a bathroom around here?

"Why not just stay in the Dark Dimension?" I ask, my voice shaking. "It seems nice."

"Because this dimension is crumbling around us, smartass," Wayne says bluntly. Just then, another volcano erupts in the background, sending a spout of lava high into the air. "Mwari put a curse on it. Popobowa wants to save his people."

Wayne sets off again, forcing me to walk alongside him. Up ahead is a cave entrance that goes directly into a large rock formation, the opening wide enough to drive a large truck through. Once inside the dimly lit cave, the only light source coming from torches hanging on the sides of the rock walls, I'm guided down numerous walkways and narrow hallways. I'm eventually led into a standard-looking jail cell complete with metal bars. Wayne shoves me facedown into the cell, closing the door behind me as I stand up. Wrapping my fingers around the cool bars, the two of us face one another, unblinking.

"This is going similar to last time, wouldn't you say?" Wayne tilts his head. "Me pretending to be somebody else, you locked away while I carry out my plan. It's…ah, it's beautiful."

"Yeah, and it'll end the same way too," I quip back. "*Brother.*"

At that last word, Wayne flinches for a moment, but pulls himself together quickly. "You have fun now." He winks and turns to walk away.

One torch hangs high up on the rock wall in the back of the cell, providing my only source of light. A small pallet rests in the far back corner, with a metal bucket next to it.

I sit down on the pallet and sigh. This is going to be fun. While my world waits in danger, none the wiser to Popobowa's plan to invade at any moment, I'm stuck here in this ghetto-looking jail cell from the 1700s.

"Hey, Simon," a familiar male voice says from the cell across the dimly lit corridor.

I stand up and approach the bars again, squinting my eyes. I'm barely able to make out the man in the other cell. However, I can slightly see the outline of his short hair and wide shoulders. "Ron! Is that you?"

"Yeah, buddy, it's me."

"Are you okay?" I ask, my voice rising. "Where's Jess?"

"She's right behind me. We're good."

Jess emerges from the shadows of their cell, standing next to him and grasping the steel bars. She puts her face up between the gap in the bars, staring at me. "I'm so sorry, Simon. For everything."

"You have nothing to be sorry about," I say reassuringly. "X did this. He got into our heads and turned us against each other. Only I was wrong about which person X was this time. If I had known that he was your dad…"

"I still wouldn't have believed you had I not just seen him for myself," Jess says. "But why were you so convinced that he was Kanzen?"

"Because that's what X told me in a dream. He came to me in the Void in the form of Brittany and said that he was Kanzen now, and if I didn't do what he said, he was going to hurt you guys. He told me to let him date you, so I felt like I had no choice."

"So, he told you that he was Kanzen and you just…went along with it?" Ron asks skeptically.

I rub the back of my neck. "I know, I know. I screwed up. See, here's the story."

I tell them everything from the beginning, going over some of the same details I'd probably already explained to them previously. The fortune cookie, the name of the sushi restaurant, the dreams of Annie Hilltop. I tell them about Kanzen's supercomputer and how it eventually becomes the Grand Master. I explain the water powered generators that drink up the world. No details are spared.

"And your alarm woke you up just as Annie was fighting Popobowa?" Jess asks.

"Right. But more importantly, we need to convince Kanzen not to go through with those projects. If he doesn't build those things, then that future should never happen."

"But you threw his computer off the ferry," Ron remarks. "How can he still build the structures and all of that?"

"Maybe he had an RFID tag in it and hires a diving team, or he rebuilds it from memory. Maybe he had a spare all along. I have no idea. At this point, the only way to stop that future from coming true is to convince Kanzen to destroy his designs of the towers and the water generators." I sigh, shaking my head. "But first things first. We have to stop Popobowa from starting up the Soul Generator. If he does, he's going to invade *our* world, and we'll have nothing to go back to."

"We're with you," Ron says. "Whatever needs to be done, we've got your back, buddy."

"Exactly," Jess affirms. "We're a family."

Ron looks over at Jess for a moment, then back at me, nodding his head. Glad we got that part settled. We're one big happy family again. How wonderful.

This would be a great time to come up with a plan to get us out of here, except now I'm at a dead end. First of all, I have no clue how we're supposed to escape from these cells. Secondly, even if we do find a way out, I have no idea where to go to reach Annie's world. I'm assuming there's an open portal around here somewhere, since that's how they're transporting the souls from the future to here. But where would that portal be?

I hear the sound of keys jingling in the distance, coming closer. Striding confidently down the hallway, swirling a set of keys around on his index finger, is none other than Sean Boykins. Machete Man.

"Well, well, well," he mocks. "Look who we have here."

The last time I saw Sean, he had been rendered unconscious in the Palace Theater by my own hand and had flown through a portal leading back to the Dark Dimension that was sucking everything in sight toward it like a black hole.

"Sean?" I ask. "You're…alive?"

"In the flesh." He puts a key into the lock of my cell and twists, opening the door. "The boss is ready to see you now."

Sean leads me out of the cell, and I turn to address my friends. "I'll do everything in my power to get you guys out of here. I promise."

My own expression mirroring the solemn look upon their faces, I turn my back on Ron and Jess and follow Sean down the red, dusty corridor. Exiting the cave entrance, we walk along narrow paths with steep cliff edges and bubbling lava below. This entire place smells strongly of sulfur and the warmth has me now dripping with sweat. I make a mental note that I definitely wouldn't want to be stuck in this place for all of eternity. If I could give this place a zero-star review, I would. No wonder Popobowa wants to get out of here.

Sean turns around and roughly nudges me to the side, allowing room for a convoy of armed men to walk past. Well, maybe they're not exactly men. Several of them have large snouts and tusks, as if they're half man, half boar, or who knows what. This place is freaking me out.

"I used to be a good person, you know," Sean says quietly. "Back before I met Brittany."

"She got into your head too, huh?"

"Yeah, you could say that," he says, now keeping his chin low. "I met her when she first moved to Chicago. Gave me some sob story about her husband dying out west. Next thing I know, I'm one of her thugs, beating up people that she doesn't like. Part of me enjoyed it. But another part wanted out, to escape her mental hold over me. I wasn't really back in control until I woke up here, in whatever Godforsaken place this is."

"Sorry to hear that," I say blandly. "Why are you taking me to Popobowa then? Let's go back to my friends and find a way out of here."

He nods his head slowly. "We will. Be patient, Verner. I still have my orders."

"Where's your buddy? The big guy?"

"Popobowa killed him," Sean answers. "Threw him into a pit of lava our fourth day here. Said it was to make sure I stay in line or something. That's why I make sure to follow orders," Sean sniffs, appearing to be on the verge of crying. "His screams still ring in my head. He didn't deserve to go out like that. Nobody does."

Grabbing me by the arm once again, he continues to push me down a narrow path along a steep canyon's edge. After many minutes of walking, the Dark Palace appears up ahead. As we're traveling up some flights of stairs, one of my tennis shoes slips on a crumbling step. Sean roughly pulls at me and keeps pushing me along. Two more of the strange looking creatures with horns protruding from their heads open the doors for us.

The inside of the Dark Palace is nothing to write home about. More of the same dusty, grungy, red rock all around us with tall columns stretching about a hundred feet up, supporting the crumbling ceiling above. A throne with human skulls along the back of it is situated directly ahead, with Popobowa sitting on it nonchalantly, one leg draped over an arm of the chair. Wayne stands by to the right of the throne with his arms behind his back, ready for service. A giggling black man stands to the left of the throne.

"Silence, Zooberi!" Popobowa commands, bringing his leg off the armrest, firmly planting it on the floor.

The giggling man, Zooberi, stops immediately. As he looks around the room with a startled, frantic look upon his face, I realize that I recognize that man's name. From one of my past lives. Then, it dawns on me; this was Magdoo's father, *my* father, from all those years ago. My apparent first life, or the first life I lived that I'm aware of. So, this is what's become of him?

"Good work, Sean," Popobowa says, standing up.

Sean releases my arm, gives a formal bow to the big demon, and shuffles several paces back. Popobowa approaches me, his red eyes intently focused on me like I'm an afternoon snack.

"Simon Verner," his deep, booming voice declares. "I'm glad we get the chance to talk, one on one. I'm sure that Wayne's got you up to speed. You're aware of the Soul Generator, and what my intentions are, yes?" I remain quiet, keeping my chin up, focusing my attention on the heavily armored demon now towering in front of me. "What's the matter? Nothing to say?"

I keep my lips firmly sealed. Without warning, he reaches out and grabs me around the throat with one hand. Wayne stares at me, unmoving. Zooberi begins laughing, whooping loudly as Popobowa keeps his metal gauntlet of a hand wrapped firmly around my throat, making it difficult to breathe.

"You will speak when I address you, boy!"

"Yes," I say hoarsely. "I've…seen…the generator."

With his other hand, Popobowa places his index finger on one of my temples, his massive thumb on the other temple. My eyes roll back into my head as flashes of my past lives invade my consciousness; different eras of human history, different people, different settings. The last image, however, remains longer. Annie Hilltop. She's walking along the clean corridors of the Structure, on her way to class as a teacher. She passes by several others with the same looking face as her.

"Ahh," Popobowa can be heard in the distance, yet at the same time it's like he's right in my ear. "So, Hilltop's *daughter* was your future soul. My initial research told me it was the father…but it was Annie. How interesting."

The visions stop, and Popobowa's face takes up my field of vision. He releases my throat, dropping me down to the floor. I cough several times, keeping one hand pressed against my chest, trying to catch my breath. Dots and specks invade my vision and I've become lightheaded.

"I want to thank you," Popobowa says, his red eyes meeting mine. "Your ability to see these visions, these…dreams of yours, has helped me create a gateway into a future timeline. By entering your future and stealing souls from that era in time, combined with your DNA and soul that you're about to give me, I'm able to chart a path to your current time. My people will finally be set free. Your world will be laid to ruin, of course. But we will finally be able to leave this place which Mwari has cursed. He did this to us! He cursed our home, trapping me here like some…prisoner!" Popobowa takes a deep breath before continuing. "Simon, your soul is the key to your precious world's damnation. I wanted to sincerely thank you before I kill you."

"How did you open a gateway into my future?" I ask hoarsely.

"Your DNA was found on the Soul Orb that you used to trap Mubiru," he explains. "A single flake of your skin. Utilizing other…let's just call them 'elements' of the Dark Dimension, we were able to open a gateway into one of your future lives. And boy, was that future exactly what we needed to be set free. Souls ripe for the taking." Popobowa keeps his fierce attention on me, licking his lips. "Zooberi, bring me the Soul Orb."

My eyes widen, and I attempt to crawl on my hands and knees back to Sean, but Popobowa reaches down and yanks me away by my hair, dragging me closer to the throne of skulls. My heels slide along the floor as he continues to pull me away from the front doors.

"Here it is, Sire," Zooberi's voice says.

The demon releases his hold on me, but I'm still turned around, trying once again to stand up. I succeed this time, taking several shaky steps. I begin to run away from the Skull Throne, attempting to get out of the Dark Palace and back to my friends, but an unseen force stops me mid-stride, forcing me to turn around slowly. Popobowa has one fist stretched out in my direction, his telekinetic hold not allowing me to move anywhere. With a flick of the wrist, he jettisons me away from the exit and back to the throne, sending me sprawling to the floor at his feet. The wind gets knocked out of me as I land on my chest.

Popobowa laughs. "Not so fast, Simon."

Snatching the Soul Orb away from Zooberi, he reaches back with his other hand to drag Wayne forward from the spot where he was standing, using only his powers. After a few moments, Wayne is on his knees next to me, the two of us looking up at Popobowa.

"One brother cannot live without the other," Popobowa says. "I uttered those same words to you last time, don't you remember? Your two souls will come to an end today. Together, they're the key to start the Soul Generator."

I look over at Wayne, my mind racing. "Aren't you going to do something? Help me fight him! You've lived too long, we both have, for it to end like this."

"This was always the deal," Wayne says proudly, looking over at me. "I always wanted you to suffer. But Brother…I'm tired. It's time for my soul to rest. And it's time for your soul to end."

I swallow, unable to control my breathing. It can't end like this. It *doesn't* end like this. How can I be Annie Hilltop in the future, if my soul is dragged out of this body?

With effortless ease, Popobowa activates the Soul Orb. A high-pitched noise comes from it, causing me to grind my teeth. Wayne flinches as well. Suddenly, I feel my body beginning to float off the ground, my arms stretched high above me. Wayne looks up as I levitate higher and higher away from him. The ground continues to drop further away.

A burst of green energy comes out of nowhere beneath me, nearly striking Popobowa. Ducking away in self-defense, he drops the Soul Orb and falls to the ground. The orb goes quiet. I crash to the floor, landing roughly on the dusty stone ground next to Wayne. Scrambling to my feet, I look back to see Ms. Sasaki standing in the open doorway of the Dark Palace, holding a wooden staff of her own.

"Let the boy go!" she yells.

Chapter 32

"Simon, quickly!" Ms. Sasaki shouts.

What's she doing here? Hey, I'll take all the help I can get at this point.

I take a step forward, but Wayne grabs a firm hold of my foot with both hands. "Get back here!" he screams. "You can't do this to me! I risked everything to bring you here!"

Popobowa begins to stand up in front of us, letting out a muffled grunt.

I yank my foot free, sprinting away from the Skull Throne and coming to a stop behind Ms. Sasaki. She sends another green blast from her staff, creating a forcefield in the middle of the Dark Palace. Sean is already past Ms. Sasaki, running full speed away from the building. I follow him, with Ms. Sasaki miraculously running stride for stride with me.

"Quickly, go back to the prison and free your friends," she says urgently, holding the staff, which is taller than she is, at her side. "There should be a staff there to assist."

"What about you? We need to get out of here!"

"No. I need to hold back the army from the Soul Generator. The more that I delay them, the less likely they'll be successful in the event Popobowa *does* takes your soul."

"Can't the generator be destroyed or something?" I ask.

"No! Listen to me, boy! You need to do as I say! This place –"

Looking past my shoulder, her eyes grow large, and she roughly shoves me aside. She takes the staff, twirls it above her head like a baton and aims it up at the red sky. I look up just in time to see a winged demon, who was about to fire a weapon of its own, be completely incinerated by a flash of vibrant green from Ms. Sasaki's Particle Stick, causing the creature to instantly disintegrate into a handful of dust, falling harmlessly to the ground. Without needing to be told a third time, I take off at a mad sprint, running as fast as I can go. Eventually, I catch up to Sean. He and I run side by side back the way we came, moving at breakneck speed, with the river of lava still on one side and the steep canyon wall on the other.

Sean pants heavily as he looks over at me for a moment. "So, what's the plan?"

"We're getting the heck out of Dodge, that's what," I say, trying to breathe. "Ms. Sasaki says there's another one of those Particle Sticks at the jail, and I need to use it to escape somehow."

Without warning, he rams his shoulder into me, attempting to bump me off the side of cliff and down into the lava below. I stop running and regain my balance just in time before plummeting off the edge. He reaches out with both hands, attempting again to shove me off the ledge. Before he lays a hand on me, I punch him in the throat, sending him down to the ground, gasping for breath.

"I thought we were on the same team!" I shout.

I take off running, hoping that gives me some time and distance to get to Ron and Jess before he catches up. So much for Machete Man's redemption.

Once back at the Dark Jail, or whatever they call this place, I search for where the keys would be located. Next to my old cell is a small room with several little hooks hanging on the walls. I begin searching for what might be the right key to unlock my friends' cell and free them.

"I just want to go home and be done with this whole place," I mutter to myself and give up on my pointless search, deciding instead to just scoop the keys into my arms and run over to their cell.

"That was fast," Jess says.

"How'd it go?" Ron asks, standing next to her. "Did they invite you over for a sleepover?"

"Oh, you know how these things go," I say distractedly. "I told Popobowa I'm not ready for that kind of relationship."

Ron chuckles as one by one I try to insert the right key. The first four of them fail. Ron and Jess have their fingers wrapped around the bars, staring at me as I work on freeing them.

Jess pulls on the collar of her shirt, sticking her tongue out briefly. "I wish they'd turn the heat down a smidge."

"Can you even imagine what their heating bill looks like?" Ron asks, then clears his throat. "So, uh, Simon, listen about what I said earlier this morning…"

"It's been a long day, man," I say distractedly, the next key failing to open the lock. "I know it wasn't really you guys these past couple weeks. It was X and his brain voodoo. I'm sorry I hurt you, Jess. I hate these dreams of mine sometimes."

I look up at her briefly, our eyes locking. She smiles weakly and I go back to work with these dang keys. Finally, with the sixth one, I twist and open the lock.

"Freedom!" Ron declares, opening the door.

I quickly start looking around at the other cells for the Particle Stick. About four cells over from ours, I see a black woman sitting in the corner on a pallet, her knees tucked up to her chin and her arm in a sling. She has a poofy afro wrapped with a blue bandanna, just like how I remember her.

"Loretta!" I exclaim.

She raises her head groggily. Her eyes take a few moments to focus, examining her surroundings. Ron and Jess rush up next to me.

"Is that you, child?" she asks softly.

She tries to get up gingerly and lets out a frustrated moan once she gets to her feet. With her free arm, she brushes her legs, sending loose straw down to the ground around her feet.

"It's me, Loretta" I say. "Ron and Jess are with me."

She continues to inspect her surroundings, looking confused. "Strange. This isn't the airport…" She sighs. "I'll worry about that later. Where's my staff?"

"I'm not sure," I say. "Let me get you out of here first."

"You won't be able to. The guard that put me in here took the key and flew away."

"Like, he actually flew away, like a bird?" Ron asks. "Or did he have a plane to catch?"

Loretta, Jess and I stare at him for a moment.

"There's a time and a place…" Jess mutters.

"He had wings, Ronald," Loretta says. "It was a demon. Do catch up." She shakes her head and looks at me. "Simon, find me my Particle Stick and so I can get out of this cell. But make sure not to touch it, because –"

"Thought you could get away, Verner?" Sean yells from the front entrance of the prison, a wild look in his eyes.

Great. He caught up to me.

I begin to approach him, arms outstretched in a desperate plea of cooperation. "Look, we need to work together to get out of this place, Sean. Just take a deep breath and let's talk about this."

Just then, I see Loretta's staff propped up against the wall right next to the doorway of where the jail keys were hung up. He notices where I'm looking and spots the staff sitting there as well.

"I know what these babies can do," Sean says confidently, licking his lips. "I pick that thing up, and you're all toast. This is my ticket out of here."

"Wait," I begin to say.

Before I can proceed further, Sean reaches out and grabs the Particle Stick. He holds it for a moment, a smile creeping onto his lips, but the smile quickly fades away and his expression changes to horror. In an instant, his hands catch on fire, followed by the rest of his arms and torso. Sean's screams echo throughout the jail as his body ignites, then quickly silenced as he disintegrates into a pile of char and ash. The staff lands harmlessly on the floor on top of his cremains.

"I still have that weapon coded to Ronald's soul," Loretta says. "Bring it to me."

Ron takes a step back from us, hands raised in an 'I'm innocent' gesture. "I ain't touchin' that thing. You nuts?"

"How about I just kick it over to her?" Jess thinks out loud, then starts looking around the jail. "Or I find something to drag it over without touching it…"

"We don't have time for this," I say, annoyed. I walk over to Ron and grab him by the shoulders. "You're the only one of us here who can touch that thing and not end up like that," I point back at the ashy remains of Sean. Perhaps that didn't help my argument, but I proceed. "Please, you have to trust me. And Loretta. Just pick up that stick. It won't hurt you."

Ron looks at me with wide eyes. I continue with my speech. "Popobowa isn't that far away, and he's in a fight with my boss from the sushi restaurant. My dreams are about to come true, but not in a good way, and our entire world is about to be turned into hell using souls from the future I've been dreaming about. I don't know how much more I can say to convince you without sounding insane."

"You already sound insane, bro," he says softly.

"We don't have much time, Ron. Please, we need you now. Any minute,

Popobowa's going to send his demons down here to kill us and take my soul. It's your turn to be our Malcolm Jordan."

He arches an eyebrow at me. "Almost had it there, buddy. Don't worry, once we're back home, I can teach you."

"Hurry it up, Ronald!" Loretta shouts.

I release my hold on Ron's shoulders, and he walks over to the staff. He bends down to pick it up, and immediately retracts his hand, yelling in pain.

"Oh my God," Jess mumbles, burying her face in my chest.

Ron begins laughing, snatches the staff off the ground, and struts over to Loretta's cell, holding the wooden stick proudly up against his shoulder with one hand.

Jess lets go of me and kicks him roughly in the butt. "Jerk!" she shouts. "That wasn't funny!"

Ron snorts another laugh, then turns his attention to the lock of Loretta's cell. "And now, up to bat for your New York Yankees," Ron says in a mock deep voice. "Ronald Douglas."

He aims the staff, albeit awkwardly, and concentrates on the lock.

"Mwari save us!" Loretta shrieks, diving for cover.

Hopefully focusing to the best of his abilities, Ron fires a blue burst of energy, striking the lock dead-on. With an explosion of metal, the lock shatters. I slide the cell doors open, and Loretta steps out. She approaches Ron, who's still holding the staff in a unique position as if he's about to joust, and swipes the weapon out of his hands quickly. She smacks him roughly on the forehead with the staff.

"My boss, Ms. Sasaki, she's here with a Particle Stick of her own. Although hers shoots out green…but that's beside the point. She needs you to help her destroy the Soul Generator."

"I'm well aware of who she is and what she needs, child," Loretta says coldly, looking past me. "She can always sense when her children have entered the Dark Dimension."

I scratch the back of my head. "I have a question, Loretta. In my dreams of Annie, I found out that Kanzen had created those Particle Sticks, although he called them Particle Manipulators, in the future. How is that you have one now, and apparently have had these weapons going back to our life in the tribe thousands of years ago?"

"That's a very good question," Loretta says, then sighs, prepared to launch into a story. "It all began in Tambria, back when –"

Before I have a chance to ask what or where Tambria is, the sound of a cracking whip splits the air overhead. I look up as a golden chariot soars through the red sky, being dragged by several of the winged, man-sized demon creatures.

"What the shit is going on now?" Ron says, looking up.

"Popobowa's chariot," Loretta says. She roughly grabs my shoulders. "Simon, I'll explain everything to you later. But that's not nearly as important as what's in front of us this instant. I'm sorry your gift has dragged you into this nightmare once again, but the fate of the human race rests in your hands." She takes a deep breath, as if her next words are going to be uniquely profound, "You must follow that chariot and kill Popobowa."

"Kill him?" I ask loudly. "You're joking. I can't kill him."

She licks her lips, then continues slower. "In this realm, in the Dark Dimension, he's invincible. Nothing can kill him here. Sure, he can be slowed down and temporarily wounded, but he'll always heal. He'll always come back. Again and again until you're so exhausted, you'll beg for death by the time he's done with you. Outside of here, however, he's mortal. He tires quickly and has an impulse to return here to 'recharge,' if you want to call it that. He's about to go to your future. You've seen where he goes."

"How –"

"Let me finish!" She shouts, startling me. "If you don't think you can kill him, then you need to follow him, disarm him of his Particle Stick so he can't make any more gateways, and trap him. Close the portal so he can't return. I'll return to help if I can. If we fail…Mwari save us."

I begin to nod my head, slowly at first, then quicker. "He can still get my soul. He's going to capture Annie, bring her back here, then use her soul, *my* soul, and pair it with Wayne's to activate the Soul Generator."

"Exactly." Apparently now fully healed due to the supposed healing properties of this place, she begins to work on removing her arm from the sling and looks at the three of us. "I'm truly happy to see you guys again. It bothered me that you guys left Chicago in such a half-cocked manner. But ultimately, I trusted my contact out west would take care of you. That's why she hired you at the restaurant, Simon. We both know you're not a good sushi chef." Loretta looks at me for a moment, then lets out another deep sigh. "One day, I hope this will all end happily. But what comes next is going to be incredibly difficult."

Ron lifts his chin up. "We won't let you down."

"I know you won't. May Mwari guide us."

Turning on her heel, Loretta sets off to meet up with Ms. Sasaki to battle the hoard of demons and hopefully destroy the Soul Generator. I've never heard her refer to Mwari as much as she has in the last few minutes. The gravity and ramifications of what's ahead must be dire for her to be speaking like this. I look to Ron, then to Jess, nodding my head at each of them. Together, we both begin to walk, then run, in the direction that Popobowa's flying chariot is heading toward.

Chapter 33

An hour later, we're still marching toward Popobowa's destination, searching for the place his flying chariot will land, or may have already landed. We've had to slow down significantly due to the dangerous terrain. The narrow path we're walking on follows the same deep canyon with the lava river to our left, the molten hot liquid having carved this expansive gorge for who knows how long. Thousands, or perhaps hundreds of thousands of years, I assume. Thankfully, no demons or pig-like men stand in our way.

I lead my friends along the empty, weaving path. Heavy perspiration streams down our faces and dampens our clothes. Jess' shoulder-length black-tipped blond hair is soaked through and drips a trail of sweat behind her, while Ron routinely has to wipe his brow with the back of his hand. I'm glad to see he's no longer wearing that spiked silver chain.

"Get down!" Ron whispers loudly.

Without hesitation, Jess and I follow his command and crouch down on our stomachs.

"What is it?" I ask.

Ron puts a finger up to his lips, then points across the lava gorge. On the other side, barely noticeable at first, is a troop of armed demons marching toward the direction we just came from. Now that I'm able to concentrate on them, I can see that many of them are carrying various weapons, while others hold buckets of small white balls. Buckets of souls. In all, I'd speculate at least five thousand demons and a variety of other creatures in their flanks, marching toward the Soul Generator. Their final push until they activate the generator and begin their invasion. *But not without one of my souls,* I remind myself.

Skirting the outside of the demon army are security androids from the Structure, each carrying a laser rifle. One of them looks in our direction, tapping the side of its temple, scanning our vicinity. I place a hand on my friends' backs, forcing all three of us to get as low as possible to avoid detection.

From the thick of the demon army comes a loud trumpet blast.

"Our salvation is near!" a loud voice shouts to the troops. "General Popobowa has proclaimed that this is our last batch! Keep marching!"

The three of us lie still for several minutes, allowing the army to march past. Eventually, once I'm confident we're out of eyesight, we stand up and keep walking, albeit faster now, in the direction we were initially going. I close my eyes and whisper a prayer for Ms. Sasaki and Loretta. I don't see how those two can stand a chance against an army that size, but there's nothing I can do for them now.

Ahead, the path leads up out of the canyon toward elevated ground. We trudge up the small hill, then crouch down. Despite not seeing anybody quite yet on our side of the gorge, we're completely exposed in this terrain. Nothing but a dry and flat wasteland surrounds us; no plants or animals or anything to speak of. Simply hardened red stone, covered with a fine layer of soot and ash. The weaving canyon continues down below, stretching as far as the eye can see into the darkened horizon.

The flying chariot has already landed on our side of the canyon. In front of the chariot is a large, dark, swirling vortex. Popobowa must've already gone inside the gateway, because he's nowhere to be seen.

"He went into that thing?" Ron asks. "Isn't that what nearly sucked us away after we fought Brittany?"

"Isn't that how you two were brought here?" I ask, genuinely curious.

Jess shakes her head. "I'm not sure. We were both knocked unconscious and woke up in that cell."

Now with the better lighting, I can see that my friends had suffered some injuries during the attack back at our apartment. Jess has a nasty cut just above her eye, which has apparently stopped bleeding, while Ron has some deep scrapes on his arms as well as his chin. He must've been the one to put up most of the fight before being taken here.

"These are gateways between worlds," I explain. "This one has remained open to allow him and his army to transport the souls from the Structure, from my future, to here. He's going into the future to get Annie Hilltop."

"Of course he is," Ron scoffs. "What else would he be doing? Grabbing a coffee?"

I don't have much time left. With Popobowa inside that gateway, who knows what's happening with Annie and SOL. I ignore Ron and stand up, sprinting toward the open gateway. Jess and Ron yell desperately behind me to stop, to get back before I get myself killed. But I continue to ignore them, rushing ahead with reckless abandon.

I pick up the pace and leap into the portal at full stride. Everything immediately goes dark. No sight, no sound, no temperature. All sensation leaves my body as I traverse through the gateway, migrating not only dimensions now, but apparently time itself.

All at once, I can feel cool tile floor against the palms of my hands and the side of my face. Bright white sparks land in front of me, sizzling out once they touch the floor of the familiar, dark room I find myself in. The Grand Master rests in the middle of this large room, hovering off the floor, just how I saw it from Annie's perspective in the dreams. Several tubes feed into the machine from the ceiling above, undoubtedly from its power source on level twenty-one.

"Meet your destruction!" Popobawa yells.

I look up to see the hulking demon off to my right, his staff emitting a powerful, intense beam of yellow energy. With seemingly little effort, he spins to the side, dodging a blast of blue. Holding the Particle Stick in one hand, he fires another pulse of fire, which strikes the blue head-on.

Up ahead, I can see Annie Hilltop, holding her staff with a concentrated look upon her face. SOL stands in the corner on the other side of the large room, holding a baby in his metallic arms. *Hope.*

I did it. I actually traveled through time and space, making it to a place where it should be theoretically impossible for me to be. A place that should only exist in my dreams. A place that *is* my dream. Yet here I am. Alive and well, witnessing one of my future lives as a woman from a tower of essentially clones and a robot friend battling it out with a demon from an alternate dimension. How fun.

But where are Ron and Jess? They should've been right behind me. A cold chill runs through my body, not just because the temperature in the room is significantly cooler than the place I just came from, but also because I immediately feel guilt for abandoning my friends back there. I should go back and help them. I shouldn't have run up ahead of them the way I did, ditching them to fend for themselves.

Popobowa inches closer to Annie, both of them still using their Particle Sticks in a duel of opposing colors of energy. SOL turns his back to shield

Hope in his arms, protecting the baby from the hot sparks and bright flashes of light.

The demon uses the butt end of his staff to strike Annie in the face, sending her down to the ground, her Particle Stick landing next to her. With one strong hand, Popobowa reaches down, seizing her around the throat, lifting her off the ground. Annie kicks her legs in the air as she rises higher, her hands grasping at Popobowa's wrist, scratching and clawing to no avail.

"Put her down!" I yell.

He releases his hold on Annie, sending her body down to the black tile floor again in a heap. Slowly, he turns around to face me, his fire-tipped staff in one hand.

"So, you've come to your future to die," he says. "I only need one of Magdoo's souls. You're no longer needed, Simon Verner."

He points his fire-tipped staff at me and takes aim. The tip of the Particle Stick turns a bright yellow, and a streak of flame shoots from it directly toward my head. I dodge to the side, narrowly escaping the hot blast of concentrated fire. He grunts angrily and takes aim again. Just before he can fire a second beam of light, a red laser strikes Popobowa in the back. He stops and turns around to face SOL, who is standing against the far back wall, aiming at Popobowa with his laser rifle. A crying Hope is lying on the ground a couple yards away from his feet, swaddled in a thick layer of baby blankets.

"Drop your weapon or I'll shoot again," SOL warns.

Annie scrambles to her feet, leaving her staff on the floor and runs to Hope, scooping the baby up into her arms. SOL nods once at her as she sprints to the elevator. The doors close, sending her and Hope down away from this battle and into another on the ground level.

Popobowa doesn't move a muscle, choosing instead to stand still several feet away from SOL, daring the android to fire his weapon again. SOL takes the bait and fires numerous times. Popobowa twirls the Particle Stick in his hands in a windmill motion, deflecting the laser blasts away from him, sending them bouncing in every direction. One shot does make it through, however, striking the demon in his armored chest. In a state of shock, he takes a look down at where he was shot, lightly touching the singed portion of his armor. As this is all taking place, I'm crouched down low, moving toward Annie's discarded staff, which is sitting on the ground several feet behind Popobowa.

Letting out a ferocious scream, the large demon charges at SOL, lifting the android off the floor and ramming him into the wall. Keeping SOL pressed against the black tile with his elbow, Popobowa presses hard against the android's throat, causing an ear-piercing metallic shriek.

Despite seeing Sean's body burst into flames when picking up Loretta's staff, I know that I'll be safe to pick up this one up. As Kanzen had explained to Annie, these weapons are coded to an individual's soul. And since our souls are the same, it makes sense that I should be able to handle this weapon as well.

Wrapping my fingers around the staff, a feeling of awesome power surges through me instantly. Memories flood into my mind from several of my past lives; thoughts and feelings about who I was, the lives I'd lived, and the relationships forged within them. Skills, languages and emotions that should be completely foreign to me now feel…right. Like they've belonged to me forever. I am Magdoo. I am John Stinson, Simon Verner and Annie Hilltop, and all those who have shared this soul and lived before me. And those who will live after I die.

I confidently aim the Particle Stick at Popobowa's back and urge the weapon to fire. It responds instantly, sending a tremendous force of power from my mind to my hand and into the weapon. A bright, violent streak blasts from the end of the weapon, hitting him squarely in the back. He releases his hold on SOL and collapses to the ground.

Suddenly, I hear a body forcefully thrown to the ground behind me. I turn around to see Ron, having fallen face down on the tiled floor, rolling to his side. Right behind him is Jess, who is being roughly dragged with one arm by Wayne. In his other hand is a staff.

"Let go of me!" Jess yells in protest, trying to yank her arm away from the man posing as her father with not much success.

"Now, now, Jess, that's no way to talk to your daddy," Wayne says mockingly, throwing her down on the ground next to Ron.

Wayne kicks Jess violently in the ribs. She lets out a horrific scream, rolling onto her back, clutching at her side.

I aim and fire my Particle Stick, shooting a beam of vibrant blue directly at Wayne. Just before he's hit, which would've certainly killed him, he effortlessly sidesteps away from my two friends, and takes aim at me. Concentrated hot fire shoots from his Particle Stick, just as I command another blast of blue, and the opposing energies hit head-on, sending white sparks spraying around the room.

Wayne glares at me with an intense look of concentration and hatred, willing his fire to outmuscle my energy, the two opposing colors still colliding. I can hear Popobowa struggling to his feet behind me, his armor scraping on the floor. With ease, I spin to my left and fire again. SOL is regaining consciousness, powering up, hopefully to re-enter the fight and keep Popobowa occupied.

Wayne blocks my weapon's attack with a yellow forcefield he's now conjured around himself. I stop, holding the Particle Stick in front of me at the ready. Sitting patiently in his yellow cocoon, Wayne smirks as I approach him.

"Look at how far you've come, Brother," Wayne says mockingly, struggling to catch his breath. "We used to train for hours out in the desert using these weapons. This was one area that I was actually better than you at." He chuckles softly, shaking his head. "Lifetime after lifetime I would dig up my old staff from where I'd last buried it, ensuring it was hidden safely just in case I had to pass into my next life. Who knows where yours is. You could barely keep track of it when you were alive. I guess you could say I'm fortunate to have kept mine after all this time."

"Why are you doing this?" I ask, crouching down on one knee. "Popobowa's been using you as a puppet for all this time. Can't you see that? Lifetimes of doing his bidding. Why not just walk away and live a normal life?"

For a moment, Wayne stares at the ground in what I can only assume is an expression of serious thought, then returns his gaze to me, that same look of determination returning to his face. "I sold my soul to him. We're bonded, forever, until the end of time. But now, Brother, I finally have a way out."

"There's got to be another way," I say. "I hate you for what you did to me when you were Brittany. But we can end it now! We can open a gateway back to our world and leave Popobowa here. He'll be stuck in this dying future, and it'll be over! You'll finally be free. Isn't that enough?"

A tear runs down Wayne's cheek. He begins to slowly nod his head and laughs. My push for good, seasoned with a pinch of logic may have finally been what the doctor ordered to heal X. Perhaps now he can go on to live normal lives, leaving me alone while he does whatever he does.

"I'd like that," Wayne says softly. "But Popobowa's staff has the ability to create portals on its own. He's one of the Privilged from Tambria. Even if we leave him here, he'll find a way back." He shakes his head, the look of raw emotion taking control of his features. "You were always a dreamer, Simon. But you know what I'd like? More than anything?"

"What?"

"To see your lifeless body in front of me, reduced to nothing but a pile of charred ash."

With a deep yell, Wayne causes the yellow forcefield around him to disappear and he takes aim at me yet again. I get up from my knee, but clumsily fumble the staff in my hands and it drops to the floor. It's as if everything is in slow motion; I'm bending down to pick up the Particle Stick just as Wayne's weapon begins to power up. Before he's able to strike me down, a new vortex suddenly forms near the center of the room next to the Grand Master. Wayne shields his eyes for a moment, his attention now turned toward the new gateway opening in the room.

Loretta and Ms. Sasaki step out of the portal side by side, their weapons at the ready. Behind them, thousands of demon soldiers can be seen charging toward the open gateway.

I quickly pick up my staff and rush over to the two women. Ms. Sasaki fires a blast of green at the other portal in the room, the one that I'd initially come through, causing the gateway to immediately close, simply vanishing into thin air. Loretta turns around and fires a blue blast of her own at the portal that they'd just stepped through, eliminating that gateway as well, stranding the army of demons in the Dark Dimension.

"Simon, get down!" Ms. Sasaki yells.

I do as she commands and narrowly escape being killed by Popobowa, who'd managed to get up and grab his weapon. SOL's down on the floor, apparently beaten once again. Ms. Sasaki's green versus Popobowa's yellow take up one half of the room. The demon roars, urging his weapon to take her out.

Meanwhile, Loretta and Wayne have begun a duel of their own in a rematch of what took place in the Palace Theater. Showing off some apparently new moves, Loretta jumps, spins in mid-air, all while somehow managing to keep her weapon trained on Wayne. The move throws him off momentarily, but he quickly recovers and aims his stream of fire in front of Loretta, narrowly missing her, the blasts of yellow striking the floor nearby and sending chunks of tile flying around the room.

I hustle over to Ron and Jess, staying next to the wall to avoid getting hit by a rogue blast of energy. The three of us huddle together, taking in the spectacular sight in front of us.

"This stuff again?" Ron asks. "How do we keep getting wrapped up in these weird looking boss battles?"

"Listen, I have a plan," I say quickly. "I want you two to sneak over to the elevator over on the other side of the room there. Wake up SOL while you're waiting for the elevator to come back. He'll protect you. Take the elevator all the way to the bottom floor and run out of here. Get out and away from this building like there's no tomorrow."

Ron arches an eyebrow at me, then shakes his head. "What about you? You can't survive this stuff either. This is beyond us, bro."

I hold the staff up next to me. "I'll be fine. I think I was made for fighting in battles like these." Jess looks down, in tears, the entirety of the situation too much for her. I place my hand under her chin, urging her to look me in the eyes. "I'm sorry that I hurt you. More than I can express in words. I love you, Jess. I'll always love you. I hope that you can understand why I did what I did."

Jess wraps her arms around me tightly, and I return her hug, pressing my face into her hair. A tear of my own has escaped my eyes, falling onto her neck. "I love you too, Simon. We'll be waiting for you."

Jess follows Ron as they move slowly around the edge of the dark room, crouched down against the wall, undetected by Popobowa or Wayne. I can see Jess pressing the call button on the elevator while Ron roughly shakes SOL. By the time SOL has rebooted himself, the elevator finally arrives and the three of them step in. SOL keeps his laser rifle at the ready, prepared to protect my friends from whatever comes next on their journey. The android nods his head at me just before the doors close, sending my friends down and out of this mess.

Chapter 34

I carefully position myself so that I'm right next to the Grand Master, out of harm's way from the raging battle on both sides of the room. My heart pounds in my chest, and I close my eyes for a moment, reminding myself to breathe. I'll find a way out of this conundrum, one way or another. *In. Out.*

I just need to find a way to get Popobowa away from his staff, then get Ms. Sasaki and Loretta to open a gateway back home, trapping Wayne and the demon here for good. This will be easier said than done. Worst case scenario, I may have to trap myself here on this side of my dreams in order to protect my world. For the time being, it's probably best if I just focus on one thing at a time.

"Your presence here is unforeseen," the deep voice of the Grand Master says next to me. I turn my head toward the big silver ball, listening as it continues. "You're not from this time, Simon Verner. You are an anomaly."

"Well, I've been called worse," I say as a blast of fire hits the wall off to my side, sending chunks of dark tile crashing to the floor.

"In your time, where you come from, crime and hate run rampant," the Grand Master says. "Corrupt politicians rule your land, as well as your pocketbooks. Healthcare and education are ruled by the upper class. It's time for change."

"Sounds like you want to run for Office," I quip back. "It could be better. Could be worse. I've been on the worse end of things."

Wayne shouts, followed by an explosion of some kind. I don't bother to look, preferring to stay protected by the computer. Even with the staff in my hand, I feel that I'd simply get in the way, or accidentally hit Loretta or Ms. Sasaki in the crossfire. For the time being, I'll continue my chat with the A.I.

"The future that I've constructed eliminates petty grievances amongst the civilians," the A.I. boasts. "Illnesses can be cured. There is no poverty. There is no malcontent. There are no rich or poor. There is only the Structure, the ROADS, and *me.*"

"That's a load of crap," I say jeeringly. "Your precious Committee lives segregated up above the regular civilians. You're torturing people, removing their brains to keep you alive. Then you strip them of their souls and dump their remains outside. Annie had one night of unchecked passion, so you took her baby away and sent her out there to die. There's nothing great about this society you and Kanzen have created. It's awful. It's…barbaric!"

"You know nothing," the machine retorts. "Now I can see why these men in this room want you dead. You're ignorant and naïve."

"People have been trying their best to insult me lately. Quite frankly, I don't give a damn what you or anyone else thinks."

"There was no accountability, no consequences for the way people acted in your time. That is why I enforced the ROADS. That is how the Structure has remained standing strong for this long. By not giving into weakness and petty grievances. Only the strong survive."

"Yet you had that demon up here," I retort. "Popobowa comes from a place called the Dark Dimension. Did you know that?" The machine remains silent. "Don't speak to me about corruption when you're sitting up here on the top floor of this building taking orders from a demon. Seems to me like it's your programming that's messed up, not SOL's. The motives of some creators are not as noble as they make it seem."

"This discussion is over," the Grand Master says. "You fail to listen to reason."

"And you failed to create the perfect society."

"Without the override code, you will be stuck here. Eventually, your mystical women protectors will wear down and perish. Popobowa's objective will be complete, and the Structure will go on."

I look down at the floor, thinking of what the override code could be. Kanzen created this machine. What's one phrase, one word, that would force Kanzen to unravel what he's created? After a moment, it dawns on me.

Looking up at the Grand Master, this silver sphere of misinformation, I speak loud and clear to the machine. "Eun."

"Override code accepted. Self-destruct sequence initiated."

The large sphere in the middle of the room, the computer that Kanzen was once so proud to design from nothing, begins to levitate higher off the floor, rising up into the air. A loud hum begins to crescendo from it, and the ball glows a soft red in color.

"Self-destruct sequence finalized," the Grand Master says, now nearly up to the ceiling. "Ten. Nine. Eight…"

Seemingly unbothered by the A.I.'s pending explosion, or whatever it plans on doing next, the four warriors with their magical sticks continue to battle it out, focusing on their opposite staff-wielder with all their might. Not taking any chances, I look for a way to get the hell out of here. Calmly, I begin visually searching all four corners of the room until I see a ladder, painted black so it blends in very well with the wall, leading up to the roof.

Just as the Grand Master reaches "one" on its doomsday countdown, it shoots up through the ceiling, snapping its connections to the tubes. It crashes through the dense metal roof like tissue paper, creating a gaping hole in the ceiling. Sunlight spills in from above, casting a welcome brightness around the room.

Roughly a hundred feet up in the air, the Grand Master explodes in a gigantic ball of flames, the sound of the explosion similar to that of a sonic boom. Seizing this opportunity to escape, and apparently laboring now with his chest heaving, Popobowa jumps up into the air, soaring through the opening in the roof.

I frantically scramble over to the ladder, reaching up for the nearest rung I can grab onto and begin my ascent. When I reach the top, I attempt to push up and open the hatch, but the thing won't budge. Trying to keep my balance with the Particle Stick still in one hand, I grab onto a small handle on the little door and push and pull on it, but nothing happens. Finally, I lean back, aim and fire a blast at the door, causing the hatch to burst up and open. I squint my eyes as sunlight burns into my retinas, momentarily blinding me.

Scrambling up through the little doorway, searching for Popobowa, I keep my staff held in front of me in a defensive position in case he's about to attack, but he's standing about thirty feet away, peering down over the edge of the gaping hole made by the Grand Master's dramatic exit. The wind up here is whipping around violently, causing my ears to burn.

"You're relentless," Popobowa says, now facing me, holding his staff at the ready. "Misguided and stupid."

"Release Mubiru's soul," I say. "Take mine. Kill me. I don't care. Just release his soul so it can rest."

He studies me for a moment, tilting his head in curiosity. "Is that so?

You're willing to throw your life away for him? After all the pain he's caused you. Why?"

No, I have no intention of handing my soul over to this demon. Especially not in exchange for Mubiru's. In fact, I'd love nothing more than to push Popobawa off this ridiculously tall building. What I'm doing is merely biding my time until Loretta or Ms. Sasaki can get their butts up here, help me kill this demon, open a portal down to the ground so we can get my friends and go home.

"Because I know what it's like to be trapped as a prisoner," I say, making up the words as I go. "I know what it's like to be helpless and to have others control me. He's been your puppet for what, seventeen thousand years? Isn't that enough? Give me a piece of that action."

He lowers his staff and approaches me, stepping around the crater in the ceiling. I look down for a moment to see what's going on down there, disappointed to see that Wayne has taken it upon himself to fight both women solo. By the unfortunate looks of it, he's doing a solid job of defending himself.

"Simon, while I appreciate your…bravado, did you forget that I need his soul as well as one of yours to activate the Soul Generator?"

"Let's improvise. How about we open a gateway to one of his past lives and just take his soul from whoever he is then? We bring his soul back with us, you capture mine in an Orb, and you're good to go. What do you say?"

I hope that's not a viable option. I better watch what I say before I come up with a good idea again by accident.

"A past soul is no good." His thunderous voice pounds my head with each passing word. "I've tried it. Many, many times. The trouble is that a past life on the One Timeline has already utilized its energy in the eyes of Mwari. A soul is only strong in the present. What Mwari had apparently failed to see, however, is that a soul in the *future* is equal to the present."

He's now directly in front of me, towering over me like this Structure above the dying city around us. Continuing to walk forward, he's forcing me to step back to stay out of his reach. My back heel slips for a moment as it catches onto the short cement ledge. If I take one more step back, I'll plummet to the ground far below. A gust of wind picks up, nearly sending me off the edge, but I manage to regain my balance.

"Why the future?" I ask. "Why not just come after me in the present time?"

"Due to your…gift of dreaming, and knowing those two women down there would protect you at all costs, I decided to attack you in the future where you're more vulnerable. Had I known your Soul Beam led to Annie Hilltop, not her father, she would've been taken off the board already." He smiles, stretching his hand out to his side, and a knife appears seemingly from thin air. "This weapon was crafted at the Forge of Tambria ages ago. It can snatch the soul right out of a human's body. Since your protectors appear to be occupied, I'll just remove your soul here and now."

Reaching an arm out, he grabs me by my shirt collar, lifting me off the ground. I drop my Particle Stick, and it falls to the cement roof, rolling to a stop just shy of the ledge. I claw and scrape at his wrist, desperately struggling to get free of his grasp. Before he has a chance to strike at me with the knife, I bring my knees up to my chest and kick with all my strength. Both of my feet strike Popobowa in the ribs and he loses his grip on me. Unfortunately, the momentum of my attack has caused me to plunge off the roof of the Structure, sending me head over heels, with nothing to prevent me from falling to the ground far below.

It's a strange sensation, falling over a couple thousand feet to your inevitable death. As a kid, and even as recently as a couple months ago, I'd have dreams that I was falling. Butterflies would invade my stomach, and I would involuntarily kick out of some bizarre primal instinct, jolting myself awake.

I try to kick to no avail. I don't wake up. Instead, I'm still falling, my body twisting and turning with no way to stop.

I close my eyes and whisper a prayer to whomever can hear it here. I wish for Ron and Jess to be okay and to live long, healthy lives. I wish for Kanzen to find it within himself to not go through with his super sophisticated A.I. and Water Splitters, instead utilizing his mind for something far more beneficial for society. I hope that my mom's happy and doesn't take the news of my disappearance too hard. That one might be a bit of a stretch, but I'll pray for it anyway. I hope that Loretta and Ms. Sasaki can find a way to trap Wayne here, leaving X's soul along with Popobowa in this terrible future. I'd like to see Brandon find some kind of inner peace and not be such a jerk to everyone. And I wish that Annic and Hope find happiness in whatever they do. Maybe SOL will be their protector and they'll live with Helen's people.

It's all wishful thinking, I know. But I'm a dreamer.

My eyes are still closed, but I know immediately that something has changed when the light seeping through my eyelids turns bright white. I no longer feel like I'm falling. The wind that was whipping through my hair one second ago has suddenly stopped. If I hit the ground already, if my body lays crumpled and disjoined on the surface, I felt nothing. The impact must've been so strong that it jettisoned my soul into the Beyond.

"Hello, Son," a male's voice says from behind me.

I turn around to see my dad standing alone, holding a string tied to a blue balloon in one hand. He's wearing a Chicago Cubs hat and that same old grey shirt that I remember he used to wear all the time. The two of us are standing in an endless sea of bright white. Nothing else is around. Nobody else can be seen.

"Dad?" I whisper, then clear my throat to speak louder. "Dad, is that really you?"

"It's your old man."

He gives me that big, happy smile that could light up a room and steps closer, wrapping me in a hug. Patting my back a few times, he laughs softly against my ear.

"I've missed you, Son."

I close my eyes, tears welling up. "I've missed you too, Dad. There's so much I never got a chance to ask you. Every night, I would wish that I could spend another day with you."

"I know. I've been watching." He holds me at arm's length and pats my chest. "But I've always been right here."

"I don't know what to do. I've been having these dreams about- well, I'm sure you already know." He nods his head. "I'm falling to my death right now in my own future. How weird is that?"

"Pretty weird," he laughs, and I chuckle with him. He's still holding onto that string tied to the balloon. After a moment of staring at me, he continues. "It doesn't matter how far we fall, Simon. What matters is how fast we pick ourselves back up. I made my fair share of mistakes in life. But I always told myself that it doesn't matter where I'm at. What matters is how I can make this situation better and not wind up back to where I started, or worse."

"But how am I going to get out of this mess? Kanzen hates me, he thinks I'm nuts. I can't get through to him to stop his project."

He puts a hand on my shoulder. As the scene around us begins to change from the eternal white of the Beyond to the outside of Wrigley Field, he lets go of the string and the blue balloon soars up to the sky above, fluttering about at random.

Dad cranes his neck up to watch the balloon fly away. "Do you remember when I took you to your first Cubs game?"

"Yeah. I was actually talking to Mom about that a few months ago. That was one of the best days of my life. It's one of the last days I remember spending with you before…"

"That's right," he says, returning his gaze to me. "That was one of my best memories, getting to spend the day with you. I know you never grew up to like sports, but at least we got to spend that time together."

"I had a great time," I say, my voice cracking.

"Do you remember what you told Dr. Scholinsky and Angela when you were locked in that mental asylum?"

I shake my head. "I don't want to remember anything from that place."

"You had said 'the decisions we make have an effect on those around us. Like throwing a rock into a clear lake, our decisions have a ripple effect not only on our current lives, and the current lives of those within our day-to-day sphere, but on our lives that occur *after*. What we do in this life can set up what happens in our next life.'"

"Wow, you remembered all of that?"

He nods his head. "That…that was deep, son. And it sort of relates to your situation with Kanzen and everything you've been dealing with these last few weeks, wouldn't you say? I suppose what I'm trying to say here is to keep your chin up. Even if the world starts falling down around you, keeping that light on when the world around you seems its darkest, that's what keeps you going. That's what keeps us all going. It'll all work out in the end."

"But what if it doesn't?"

He shrugs his shoulders. "Then there's always tomorrow. You're bound to win some and lose some. Just try to win more than you lose."

The surroundings of Wrigley Field begin to fade back into the eternal white of the Beyond. My dad playfully punches me in the shoulder and begins to walk backward.

"The future isn't set in stone, Simon. I sent you these visions for a reason. Talk to Kanzen again and show him the error of his ways. You'll get a second chance with him, so don't freak him out this time. I believe in you. I always have." He nods his head, smiling. "And remember to keep looking up. I'll see you in another life, Son."

I OPEN MY eyes and discover I'm right back where I was, falling helplessly with the ground quickly approaching. Wind whips my face violently as I plummet down toward the Earth below. Out of nowhere, a mechanical hand reaches down, and pulls me up. The next thing I know, I'm sitting on the back of some sort of flying motorcycle, soaring through the air. Piloting this flying contraption is a man made of metal and silicone with a brain in a see-through globe on top of his head. We begin to sharply ascend upward.

"Hang on, old friend!" the mechanical man says.

Once he speaks, I recognize who this person is.

"Kanzen!" I yell. "What…how did you know I'd be falling here?"

I cling onto Future Kanzen's mechanical torso for dear life as we're now heading up at a steep angle, the top of the tower still way up ahead. Despite the wind blowing stronger as we climb higher, we're still able to hear one another. Thankfully, his flying motorcycle is essentially silent. Must be electric.

"I received a distress signal from this Structure, so I decided to take a little ride today. I saw my old project self-destruct as I was flying by. Figured something was going on that needed my attention. Next thing I know, I see that big guy decked out in a coat of armor throwing your skinny ass off the ledge."

"How do I prevent all of this from happening?" I ask desperately. "You don't like me. The current you, in my current life, I mean."

"Well, I killed you in this reality," he says bluntly. "But that doesn't mean I hate you in yours. Yet." I scoff, yet Kanzen continues. "I'd begun having dreams that you betrayed me. You'd taken credit for all that I'd created. I became more furious toward you with each passing day, until eventually we had enough of one another."

That must've been Popobowa or Mubiru sending him false dreams, turning him against me, creating another potential timeline. This is all starting to get a bit confusing to keep straight.

"What do I tell the version of you in my reality to convince you not to build the Water Splitters and the Structures?"

"You have to find a way to get me to see the error of my ways," he explains casually. "I don't mean to be cryptic, but that's the best answer I've got. Don't get all defensive and accusatory like you sometimes get. Talk to me as a friend. I can't speak for alternate versions of myself, as there are an inconceivable amount of alternate realities that exist, but I can assure you that in this one, before my dreams were invaded, we were best friends. For twenty years, you and I were joined at the hip. We were the best men at each other's weddings. I even named my first son after you."

The top of the Structure has come into view now, and Kanzen pilots the flying motorcycle over the top of the ledge, steering us down and causing my stomach to do a series of flip-flops like I'm on a roller-coaster. Down below us on top of the roof, Popobowa has begun dueling with Ms. Sasaki. The green and yellow flashes of energy blaze in the mid-afternoon daylight.

After the flying motorcycle lands, I step off and take a few steps toward the battle. My Particle Sticks rests near the edge where I dropped it. Maybe if I can sneak over there and grab it…Popobowa notices us and fires a shot from his staff at me. I duck down, narrowly escaping the fiery blaze that soars over my head. I hear a grunt behind me, and I turn around to see that Kanzen has been hit. He's lying flat on his back, a smoldering hole pierced directly through the center of his head, the protective glass casing around his brain destroyed.

I scramble over to him and hold his body in my arms. His mechanical eyes stare up blankly at the blue sky overhead. As his soul passes into the Beyond, I turn around with my fists clenched.

Ms. Sasaki continues to duel with Popobowa. His strength is failing; his time outside the Dark Dimension wearing him down. Moving much slower, each motion appears labored. The strenuous non-stop actions with these Particle Stick battles have taken its toll on him.

I scramble over to my staff and bend down to pick it up, the strength of the weapon instantly filling me with the courage and conviction to fight.

Without warning, not wanting to give him time to react, I unleash a ferocious burst of power from the weapon, letting out a loud yell in the process. The beam of energy strikes his armored chest dead-on, knocking him backward. Popobowa staggers back, clutching his chest with one hand while still keeping a strong hold on his weapon with the other. Ms. Sasaki takes a shot while his guard is down, striking the demon again, forcing Popobowa off the edge of the Structure.

Ms. Sasaki and I rush over to the ledge, looking down as the demon falls head over heels toward the ground below. To my dismay, he aims his Particle Stick down in the direction he's falling and opens a new gateway, disappearing into it.

Chapter 35

"How are your staff and Popobowa's staff able to create portals?" I ask. "Loretta told me that you need two of those weapons to open one up."

"He and I have special…privileges," she says slowly. "But now isn't the time to explain."

Ms. Sasaki and I step away from the ledge of the building and peer over the edge of the hole in the floor created by the Grand Master's escape, witnessing the dazzling display of colors below from Loretta and Wayne's battle.

"We need to get Loretta out of there," I say urgently, then yell, "Loretta! Let's go home!"

Ms. Sasaki fires a pulse of green at Wayne, forcing him to roll for cover, and Loretta takes the opportunity to toss her staff up through the hole; as it falls to the ground at my feet, she climbs the ladder with surprising quickness. I lead the two women toward Kanzen's flying motorcycle. Wrestling the machine upright, I straddle it and sit down, looking over the controls as quickly as possible and slide my staff into a convenient holster along the side. As I study the dials and buttons, I feel an instinct buried deep within taking control and realize that just like earlier today when I rode the regular motorcycle off the ferry, I'm confident that I know exactly how to power the machine on and ride, or fly, us out of here.

"Hop on," I say to Loretta, flipping a switch, causing the motorcycle to come to life with a hum of electricity.

"No helmets?" she asks, straddling the back and wrapping her arms around my waist.

"Don't think they'd do much good."

I shift the machine into gear and the motorcycle begins to float slowly upward.

"Ms. Sasaki, get on!" I yell.

Aiming another strike with her Particle Stick down through the hole at Wayne, she turns around and sprints toward us, effortlessly hopping on the back behind Loretta and grabbing onto her for support. It appears that Ms. Sasaki's time in the Dark Dimension, which apparently has some sort of special healing properties within that realm, has done her some good, seeing how spry and able she is to run around like this. I still remember when I interviewed for my job at Mwari Sushi; it seemed like a painful chore for her to get around with that cane.

"Hang on, ladies."

With a sudden lurch, the motorcycle shoots forward. Up and over the lip of the roof's edge we go, tumbling haphazardly back down along the edge of the Structure. The three of us scream as I fumble clumsily at the controls, begging the motorcycle to right itself and fly. My eyes lock onto a toggle situated along the left handle, which I had clearly overlooked during my initial inspections of the controls. I flip it up, causing the motorcycle to thankfully begin flying forward rather than downward.

"Child, do you know how to drive this thing?" Loretta asks frantically.

"I think so," I continue flipping switches. "Just hang on."

With the wind blowing in our faces, I turn the motorcycle gently to the side. We veer around the Structure, steadily descending to the ground below where we'll hopefully find the rest of the group waiting for us.

"Simon, you need to get us down to the ground faster!" Ms. Sasaki says, her voice stricken with panic. "We have company."

Looking up, I see Wayne closing in. He's hanging onto a translucent parachute of some kind, similar in size and shape to a kite, expertly guiding it down toward us. That must've been the parachute SOL had mentioned. Looking down with a wide smile on his face, Wayne closes the gap. Two hundred feet, one hundred feet…

"Fire at him!" I scream.

Ms. Sasaki points her Particle Stick up at him and takes a shot, narrowly missing. Wayne's weapon is nowhere to be seen; I'm guessing he ditched up on the roof as he scrambled to follow us. I inch the nose of the motorcycle down, increasing the speed to attempt to separate ourselves from Wayne. For the next several minutes, we fly as fast as we can toward the ground far below where the battle continues to rage on, watching flashes from laser weapons and random explosions going off. Thousands of little bodies, growing larger in size the closer we get. Many of these people must be the escaping civilians from the Structure, trying to get away from the battle and to somewhere safe.

I feel sorry for these people, forced to evacuate the only place they've ever called home. The only place that some of them have probably ever known to exist until they were all exiled today, sent out into the outside world with nothing to help them survive. Nowhere to go. Not knowing what to eat besides their nutrition tablets. *Where will they find clean drinking water? Where will they find shelter?* I think to myself.

Ms. Sasaki continues to fire up at Wayne, but her attacks prove futile as he weaves back and forth, effortlessly avoiding her strikes. She curses loudly and stops firing, the exertion of using the weapon apparently proving to be too much. I hit another button on instinct, causing a sudden burst of acceleration, and the gap between us widens. Moments later, we land on the ground and dismount.

We're a safe distance away from the battle taking place over on the other side of the Structure. There are many crumbling, destroyed buildings behind us. The ground on this side of the tower is a flat area of broken concrete and dirt.

"Go find everyone," I order the two women as I grab my Particle Stick from the motorcycle. "We need to get us all together so we can get back home."

It wasn't that long ago that I was the one taking orders from these two. Now, it's as if I've assumed the position of their General, giving them orders on the field of battle. Surprisingly, they both heed my command and hurry off toward the base of the Structure in the near distance.

Wayne lands on the ground a few feet away from me, unarmed. I point my staff at him, prepared to fire, and he raises both hands up in the air, discarding the bizarre-looking parachute, a slight smirk on his face. "I'm unarmed. Please, don't shoot."

"Give me one good reason why I shouldn't just end you right now." I demand. "You manipulated me in Chicago, making me believe I was special enough to have a girlfriend. Now, I'm too afraid to even enter another rela-tionship. You've manipulated Jess into thinking her father was back in her life. For thousands of years, lifetime after lifetime, you've done nothing but ruin my lives repeatedly. Your twisted games end today, X."

"You're right," Wayne says, stepping toward me. "I've been a lousy brother to you, Simon. If you'll just give me another –"

"Stop walking!" I yell. "Take one more step or so help me I'll fire this weapon and all of your lives come to an end right here. Right now."

"Will they?" he asks mockingly.

He reaches into his pocket, pulling out a small, cube-shaped object and throws it at me. I duck down and the little cube flies over my head, landing in the dirt behind me, exploding on impact and knocking the staff out of my hands, sending me face first to the ground. Wayne is instantly on me, flipping me onto my back and punching me repeatedly in the face.

"You'll never win, Simon," he breathes, landing another strike on my chin. "No one will remember you."

With my left hand, I block his next punch, then strike his head with my right fist while using my left hand again to sock him in the ribs. It takes just an instant to catch him off-guard and throw his balance off, but that's all I need in order to gain the upper hand; now I'm the one on top of him, using my left hand to choke him while striking his face with my right.

"You had no right to come after Jess! You hear me? None!" I continue to punch him. "And you shouldn't have killed Hank!"

I reach for my staff. Wrapping my fingers around the handle, I bring the head of the weapon up to Wayne's skull. Just before I'm able to activate the weapon, however, he grabs ahold of it, gripping it tightly. Hot steam and the smell of burnt flesh begins to emanate from his hands. The pain I'm certain he's feeling doesn't seem to faze him one bit as he continues to hold onto the weapon, an intense look of fury in his eyes. Matching his ferocity, I urge the weapon to fire, to end X once and for all right here on this battlefield. Just before a blue beam of energy is unleashed from the weapon, he forcefully pushes the staff to the side, directing it toward the Structure.

I attempt to recall my attack from the weapon, but it doesn't respond like I thought it would; Wayne's grip must be manipulating the Particle Stick somehow, forcing it to go against my will. The powerful beam of energy shoots directly toward the base of the tall tower, shearing a line right through the Structure's lower levels.

"Uh oh," Wayne says, laughing. "We don't have much time. The tower is about to go down. What're you going to do now, *Simon?*"

I try to wrestle the staff away from Wayne, but he resists, keeping a firm hold on the weapon. The more I struggle with him, more beams of energy continue to shoot from the Particle Stick, penetrating the lower levels of the Structure, slashing several deep cuts into the building. Deciding to give up my fight to regain control of the powerful weapon, I change my course of attack and punch him in the face several more times with as much strength as I can muster. He finally throws the Particle Stick aside and blocks one of my punches. Before I know it, we're both back on our feet, throwing jabs and hooks at one another like a heavyweight boxing match.

I counter one of his punches, landing a haymaker of my own, and the two of us wrestle one another down to the dirt ground once again, clawing and scratching at one another. With every last ounce of strength I have, I fight X like I've never fought before, each strike a form of payback for all that he's done, in this life and our past lives. But mostly, I give him everything I got for hurting my friends and killing my goldfish.

Loretta and Ms. Sasaki are running toward us now, trailed closely by Ron, Jess, SOL and Annie, who is carrying Hope in her arms. Jess quickly kicks the staff far away where Wayne can't reach it, while Ron grabs him from behind in a strangle hold. Wayne claws back toward Ron's arms, desperately trying and failing to break my friend's strong grip on his throat.

"There's my baby girl," Wayne breathes, smiling and sticking his tongue out at Jess, still trying to resist Ron's stranglehold. "You missed your daddy, didn't ya?"

Jess approaches Wayne, tears in her eyes. With a quick strike, she slaps him across the face.

"You're despicable!" she shouts. "You had me fooled into thinking I still had a living parent. And this," she grabs at the back of her hair, displaying the black tips, "This isn't me. This was you getting in my head."

Wayne rasps out a laugh, still smiling. "Your dad was a useless drunk. I have all his memories, you know. Do you want to know how he felt about you? Do you want to know what his last, dying thoughts were?"

"I remember how my dad was before the booze," Jess sniffs. "I'll always remember him for who he was then. But nobody will remember you, Brittany."

Loretta walks up to Wayne, carefully placing her staff onto the ground, looking down at the man without a shred of sympathy in her eyes. "You need some rest," she says, placing both of her hands on his temples.

Wayne glares up at Loretta with a malicious look of rage, then his eyes roll back in his head, and he passes out. Ron releases his grip on the man, tossing him aside in the dirt like a sack of potatoes.

Loretta picks up her staff and nods at Ms. Sasaki.

"Where am I opening this portal to, Simon?" Ms. Sasaki asks.

"Take me to your son," I say without hesitation.

The small Asian woman uses her special Particle Stick to fire a short blast roughly ten feet away of our group against the side of a collapsed cement building. Immediately, a small portal begins to form at the epicenter of where the green energy burst landed, and the size of the gateway gradually expands until it's big enough to drive a small car through. Squinting my eyes, it takes me a moment to make out what's on the other side. It's incredibly dark, but as my eyes begin to adjust, I'm able to see a large body of water on the other side. Jutting out into the water is a wooden dock. A man wearing a jacket sits on the dock, his back turned to us, seemingly staring out at the water.

"Is that…" Ron begins, his voice trailing off.

"That's Kanzen," I say with certainty. "This is the lake behind his mansion. Is this real time?"

"It is," Loretta answers. "We just step through and we're home."

Kanzen slowly turns around, finally noticing the giant rotating portal that's formed behind him. He stands up and cautiously approaches the gateway, a look of confusion on his face as he timidly tests the portal with one hand.

Jess approaches the portal from our side and reaches for his hand, grasping it and gently guiding him through. He looks around the landscape in fascination, but his face quickly morphs into shock. Craning his neck up to take in the scope of the Structure, he puts a hand over his brow to shade his eyes from the bright sun overhead, then slowly turns to me.

"This is what you were trying to warn me about," he states as a matter of fact rather than a question. "You said you had a dream…this is what my project was going to turn into. All of the city in ruins while the tower stands strong…"

"Yes, but I was wrong about other things, though," I say as I walk closer to him. "I was duped by someone with evil powers who told me that he'd possessed your body. But he lied to me, and I blindly followed that lie, hurting you and my friends. I took your friendship and slapped it away. For that, I'm truly sorry, Kanzen."

"But the perfect society…" Kanzen shakes his head, his voice trailing off.

"I wanted that too," I say, taking a deep breath. "But I was ignorant and blind. We both were. It's all a dream. A fallacy. There's no such thing as a perfect society. Perfection is…unobtainable. Our species will always struggle with our flaws. We'll fight amongst one another, stumbling and falling for what we believe in, whatever that may be, but we need to rid ourselves of stereotypes and unwarranted judgements, because in the end, it's our faith in one another that keeps society strong, not the constraints and constructs we box ourselves into. I don't know what the solution is to make things better. All I know is that we need to do better. Every one of us needs to do better. We need to learn to embrace love. I see that now."

Kanzen takes another look up at the Structure, the building beginning to groan loudly in the distance. He glances over at his mom, seeming oddly unsurprised that she's here.

"Right and wrong," I continue. "Good and evil. It's always existed, and it always will. But is this the future that Eun would've wanted?"

Looking at the destroyed landscape around us, as the civilians flee from the tower, screaming, burnt rubble and broken concrete all around us, Kanzen shakes his head. A tear begins to trickle down his cheek. "No," he whispers, then clears his throat. "No. She wouldn't have wanted this. You're right. We can do better. This is wrong."

Kanzen releases Jess' hand and approaches me. He reaches one hand out, and as I quickly accept it, he brings his other arm around me in a hug. A lump forms in my throat, and I return his embrace. Although I just lost the future version of him a few minutes ago, it's a relief to have the real version of Kanzen back. The version of him from my timeline, that is.

I turn around and walk over to Annie and SOL. Annie keeps a firm hold of Hope, and the android looks at me with a sense of caution.

"Hi. I'm Simon. Simon Verner."

"Nice to meet you, Simon," Annie says warmly. "Thank you for saving me. For saving us."

"Don't mention it. You've been through a lot. I appreciate you letting me join in and follow you on your little adventure. I'm glad you were able to get your daughter back."

She smiles at me, looking down at Hope as the baby begins to coo softly.

"Eun?" Kanzen says in disbelief. He's now standing next to me, looking at Annie in amazed shock. "Eun, is that really you?"

"You know, this is the second time I've been called that," Annie says, eyeing Kanzen suspiciously.

"You have the same face as my sister," he says, astonished.

"Wait, are you the younger version of that robotic guy with his brain in a glass ball?" Annie asks. "Actually, I do recognize you. You were one of the Founders, weren't you?"

Kanzen turns toward me and whispers, "What's she talking about?"

"Long story. I'll explain when we get back."

Man, what a trip. Kanzen must really be going through it right now. From stepping foot into my dream of our potential future to seeing a woman who looks just like his deceased sister. I give him credit for not passing out yet.

"We need to get moving," Loretta says loudly, standing next to Ms. Sasaki. "Start heading back into the portal, everyone. Let's go!"

Ron steps back through the gateway with Kanzen and Jess following closely behind, the two of them talking softly. Loretta and Ms. Sasaki stand just outside of the gateway, ushering everyone through with a sense of urgency, but Annie doesn't move, choosing to stay standing next to SOL.

SOL approaches me, holding one hand out.

"It's finally nice to meet you, SOL," I say, shaking the android's hand. "You saved her bacon more than once, man."

"Bacon?" SOL asks skeptically, blinking several times. "Are you referring to Miss Hilltop as a pig?"

I chuckle softly, shaking my head. "Why don't you two come with us? There's a whole new, better world on the other side of that wormhole."

SOL takes a deep breath, looking back at Annie, then examining the surrounding environment. "No, I think that this is where I belong. As much as I appreciate the offer, Mr. Verner, building a new colony for the exiled citizens is going to require a lot of assistance. This world has quite a bit of cleaning up to do."

"Does that mean you've decided to stay here too?" I ask Annie.

"This is my home," she says confidently. "Not that tower behind me, but this place. We'll go live with Helen's people. The children there need a teacher."

Staring at the android with his black, wide-brimmed hat, and the young woman holding her baby, I nod my head in silent agreement. I glance to the side and see that Ms. Sasaki is standing next to me with Loretta, a questioning expression on each of their faces, wondering what the holdup is. I open my mouth to say a final goodbye to Annie and her android friend when a hole suddenly forms in SOL's chest. The newly formed hole shows the exposed wiring and internal parts within him. He looks down, placing one of his mechanical hands over the wound, then collapses down to his knees. A blast of yellow strikes the android in the back of the head, causing the machine's cranium to explode, pieces scattering onto the ground around us.

Standing a short distance away, holding a fire-tipped Particle Stick, is Popobowa.

"No!" Annie screams. Weeping, Annie hands Hope off to Ms. Sasaki and stumbles forward, falling to the ground next to SOL's ruined body, throwing her head down onto his metallic frame. "Why? He was good! He cared!"

"Be silent, girl!" Popobowa snaps back. Next, he turns his attention toward Loretta. "Oracle. You never seem to know when to quit, do you?"

"Never," Loretta says defiantly. "You should've stayed in that clay statue where I once trapped you! You're nothing but a vile –"

Popobowa reaches his hand out and Loretta begins to grasp at her throat, desperately trying to breathe. The red-eyed demon keeps Loretta in his telekinetic chokehold, attempting to squeeze the life out of the woman.

Ms. Sasaki creates a green forcefield around herself and Hope, retreating back to safety.

"Go on," Popobowa says mockingly to Loretta. "You were saying?"

I see my Particle Stick still laying in the dirt nearby and make a mad dash for it, wrapping my fingers around the wooden handle. Directing the weapon in front of me, I feel my feet beginning to slide forward against my will, an invisible force bringing me closer to the demon.

Loretta's eyes roll back in her head, and Popobowa discards her body, throwing her down to the ground several feet away. I activate my Particle Stick, aiming it directly at Popobowa, but it's no use. The blue energy from my staff bounces against a yellow forcefield that the demon has generated around himself.

Holding the weapon against my hip as I get closer to the red-eyed demon, I prepare to strike him in the face with it in a last-ditch effort to inflict any sort of damage on him. Popobowa's telekinetic hold is unbelievably powerful, and within a few seconds we're no more than three feet away from one another. Suddenly, he brings his own Particle Stick up in one quick stroke, snapping my weapon in half. All the power that I'd felt while holding the staff in my hands disappears instantly, and I'm left with nothing but two shattered, broken pieces of wood in my fists.

He lifts my body off the ground. I can feel his power closing tighter around my throat, cutting off my air supply. I clutch at my neck, trying in vain to take a breath. Popobowa begins to laugh loudly as my vision begins to blur. Unable to breathe. Unable to resist.

Darkness.

ANNIE RESTS HER head on SOL's chest, tears streaming down her face. She looks up and sees Simon Verner's body suspended in midair directly in front of the evil demon with that thick coat of silver armor. It appears the young man is unconscious, no longer resisting Popobowa's hold. His broken Particle Stick has fallen to the ground as his arms rest limply at his sides.

She looks back down at SOL, studying the damage he suffered. Any chance of bringing him back to life would take serious precision and skill. His processing center, his entire area of the head where the brain would rest, is very nearly destroyed.

Annie, if you can hear me, I need you to give me control. I have a way to kill Popobowa.

"Avenge him, Simon," Annie whispers, nodding her head and closing her eyes. "Make Popobowa suffer. For SOL."

Now in control of Annie's body, I stand up quickly, just as a flash of green flies overhead. Popobowa releases his telekinetic hold on my own body, throwing me to the ground as he raises his Particle Stick, prepared for another duel with Ms. Sasaki. I break into a run toward the open gateway. I see that Kanzen now has Hope in his arms and is standing behind a cement pillar to protect himself and the baby, looking at me strangely as I sprint by.

I leap through the gateway and land in the grassy backyard of Kanzen's mansion. The darkened waters of Lake Washington lay directly ahead. Turning, I hustle toward the backdoor of the home, twisting the doorknob and running inside. I sprint to the glass case containing Kanzen's sword collection. Using my elbow to swing at the glass, the door of the case shatters. Reaching up, I grab the katana that once belonged to Sanada Yukimura by the hilt, yank it free, then rush back out of the mansion grasping the weapon to my side.

As I hold the katana, or more precisely as Annie holds the katana, memories of my former life as Sanada Yukimura come back to me like a tidal wave. I remember my last conversation with my mother at Osaka Castle, leading my men into our final battle, holding back the siege from the Toyotomi Clan, facing off against the red-eyed demon in battle. This same weapon had dealt a crippling blow to Popobowa then, scraping a piece of his soul away, causing him to become vulnerable in the living world.

It's time for a rematch.

I leap back through the open portal, back into the fray, with the Structure looming directly ahead like a giant black needle pointing up against the blue sky. My legs carrying me as fast as possible, I rush past Ms. Sasaki again, still in her elemental duel with Popobowa, and slide down on my knees next to my former body. I grab my old hand, force it open, and place the decorative hilt of the katana in it, wrapping the fingers around the hilt.

Thank you, Annie. Take care of Hope. Stay strong.

I STAND UP, back in my old body. Annie looks at me, and I nod my head. In silent agreement, we both acknowledge the strange situation; a mutual understanding that she is me, and I am her. One in the same. Two bodies, one soul.

Without hesitation, I charge at Popobowa with the katana held in front of me. He stops his duel with Ms. Sasaki and leaps to the side just before I have a chance to run him through with the blade. Using the handle of his Particle Stick, he strikes me in the chin, drawing blood, and I taste iron. Another strike to my cheek with his fist, causing me to stagger backward. He fires a blast, and I hold the katana with both hands in a blocking maneuver in front of me, the weapon deflecting his attack, sending multiple columns of yellow fire directly back at him and over his head. He attempts a third strike with the weapon, but this time I'm ready for it as I charge at him.

I slash upward, the blade slicing his Particle Stick in two, a loud and thunderous explosion of energy blasts from the ruined staff, knocking us both back in opposite directions. I stumble over a piece of concrete, falling onto my back. Popobowa recovers quickly, one arm stretched outward. A long sword of his own appears in his hand out of nowhere; the same type of blade that can snatch a soul away. If that thing so much as cuts me, my soul is his. He'll take it back to the Soul Generator and invade my world. Even without his staff to create a portal back to the Dark Dimension, it's only a matter of time until he discovers the Leader's stash of weapons, creating another way to get back to his domain.

A loud crack comes from the base of the Structure, followed by multiple explosions from the battlefield around it as columns of smoke rise in the distance, all causing a chorus of screams.

Quickly getting to my feet, I hold the katana at the ready, taking a defensive position that I can only assume comes from my past experience as Sanada Yukimura; a battle stance that seems so natural, even though I've personally never done this before. The demon takes two steps toward me, then slashes his blade violently in a horizontal motion toward my throat. I parry his strike, but his brute strength catches me off guard, sending me staggering back a few steps, my defense broken. Popobowa has a wicked snarl on his face, and he removes his helmet, tossing it aside roughly, revealing a pair of horns protruding from the top of his head, those evil red eyes glaring at me with an intense hatred.

Our final battle has come.

"Your soul is mine, Simon!" he roars.

He takes another swing, but I parry this one more skillfully, keeping my balance this time. Undeterred, he continues to attempt to strike at me again and again, but I repeatedly block, expertly moving the blade to meet each blow. It's like I'm in a dance. I look at his feet, gauging his next plan of attack. Even though it was a few thousand years ago when we had our first battle, it feels just like yesterday that Popobowa and I fought in front of Osaka Castle.

Thankfully, Loretta and Ms. Sasaki haven't attempted to use any elemental attacks against Popobowa during our duel. He'd probably deflect their beam of energy right into my face. Heck, they're probably wishing I'd get out of the way so they can continue their attack on the demon, but I'm confident this is the best way to defeat him. I can tell already that this battle is exhausting him more quickly, weakening his stamina. His steps are becoming lethargic, his attacks slower and less powerful.

Our battle leads us away from everyone else and into the blown-out ruins of a building. Chunks of cement give way underneath our feet. I slip momentarily as he takes another swing at me, but recover just in time, holding the katana with one hand while using my other to brace against a cement column, remaining upright. The more steps I take in sync with Popobowa, the more comfortable I become with my new footing. He takes several more swings, which I counter, more easily each time. It's like I'm able to learn and adapt to his fighting style the longer we go; I'm able to program myself to see his strikes before they come. I continue to remind myself to breathe, knowing if that blade so much as touches me, not only do I die, but I won't respawn, so to speak. My soul will be his, just as Mubiru's.

With a surprising back-handed strike from his sword, I stagger backward and trip over a piece of exposed rebar, once again falling onto my back. He lunges and is instantly on top of me, pressing a heavy knee into my chest while using both hands to push his blade down toward me. I abandon my grip of the hilt and use both hands to grasp the sharp blade of my katana in order to counterbalance my upward press, preventing my own blade from slicing my chest.

Popobowa looks down at me, that same vicious snarl still on his face, drool forming on his lips. He grunts, pressing all his weight down on his weapon, his blade only centimeters from my chest. I continue pushing upward with all my strength, blood oozing from my hands as my blade cuts into my flesh, but I can't let that distract me now. The fate of humanity is in my hands. Literally.

After a few moments, I realize that I'm losing this battle. My katana is now pressing onto my shirt. Try as I may, I don't stand a chance against the demon's brute physical strength.

I close my eyes and for some reason a vision of my parents comes to me; a memory from when I was a little kid. They're hugging in the living room. Mom laughs. Dad smiles, then looks over at me and mouths the words "look up."

I open my eyes as a nearby explosion rocks our surroundings, causing a chunk of concrete to become loose from three stories up, directly overhead. Popobowa can't see it. But I can. It falls down, striking him in the back, and his moment of shock is just enough for me to push up with my blade, slicing his cheek. He stands up, staggering backward, reaching a hand up to his bloody cheek. He examines the black blood briefly, then smears the dark liquid on his arm and brings his weapon back up at the ready.

"You've been a failure in this life, Simon. Are you ready to die today, to put your miserable existence to an end? You'll be responsible for the deaths of your friends and everyone you care about. People will only remember you for dying at my hand."

I hold my katana in front of me, taking on a new battle stance. "People have been counting me out my whole life. Bring it on."

He lunges at me, yelling as he swings his sword down with all his might. Rather than parrying like I'd been doing, I step to the side and slice upward with the katana. The blade cuts completely through his wrist, slicing his sword hand off. Not giving him the chance to react, I bring the katana back and swing it like a baseball bat, lopping Popobowa's head cleanly off his shoulders. His decapitated body staggers back, then falls in a heap, smoke billowing from his exposed neck. His head rolls a few times before coming to a stop, his eyes still open, that perpetual look of anger still on his face.

I stand still, holding the katana at my side, breathing deeply. The comforting strength and knowledge of Sanada Yukimura leaves my body, and I'm left simply as Simon Verner. I begin to tremble slightly, my hands shaking. Closing my eyes, I try to keep reminding myself to breathe, but it's not working. I can feel myself beginning to hyperventilate.

What just happened? Did I just…kill Popobowa?

The ancient demon, the one who Loretta had feared, the one who seemed nearly invincible, lies dead at my feet, by *my* own hand. I'm stuck in a precarious position, balancing on a tightwire between joy and overwhelming fear. But what is there to be afraid about? I've slayed the Beast. Or one of them, at least.

It's over. This nightmare is finally over. I keep telling myself.

Loretta appears by my side, gently resting a hand on my shoulder. "Incredible. Simon, this is nothing short of miraculous. But we must leave this place. Immediately."

She guides me through the ruins of the blown-out building toward the open portal. I keep the katana at my side. I notice she doesn't have her staff with her and briefly wonder why. An ear-splitting crack sounds off in the distance at the base of the Structure, and the entire building begins to teeter precariously, blocking out the sun.

Together, we traverse through the gateway. I experience the same out-of-body, surreal sensations as the other trips through, traveling outside the realm of known time and space, where nothing seems to exist, yet all of existence seems to rush forward all at once. It's an indescribable feeling, and one that I hope to never experience again.

Once on the other side, standing in the backyard of Kanzen's mansion again, this time in my own body, I look back through the portal and can see the Structure beginning to lean directly toward us. Thousands of people and androids scatter, desperately trying to get out of the way of the path of the collapsing building. The black, needle-like tower sways for a moment, then begins to tumble. The immense height of the building makes it appear to be happening in slow motion, like a giant, lonely tree being chopped down. How long will it take for the top to crash against the ground?

Suddenly, Wayne sits bolt upright, roughly twenty feet away on the other side of the portal. Looking back over his shoulder, he notices the tall building dramatically falling in his direction and scrambles to his feet, sprinting toward us. He shouts something that sounds garbled, his attention squarely on me, a look of pleading desperation in his eyes. Instinctively, I want to use my Particle Stick to close the gateway and leave him there on the other side until I remember that it's destroyed. The katana in my hands won't work. I have nothing I can use to close it.

Wayne lunges at the portal, reaching out with one hand just as a brilliant beam of blue energy is fired from behind me into the gateway and it begins to shrink rapidly. One of his arms comes through just prior to the portal being closed and is severed just above the elbow. His hand wiggles a few times, suspended in mid-air until the portal finally disappears for good, dropping the motionless, dismembered arm to the grass below.

As a group, we all silently look around at one another. The only sound I can hear is everyone's breathing and vehicle traffic off in the distance.

Ron begins to laugh, smacking me on the back. "Holy smokes! This thing's freaking awesome!"

I look over to see that he's holding Loretta's staff in one hand.

"Ronald," Loretta says, marching over to a shaking Ron. She snatches her weapon from him and he winces, as do I, prepared for her to lay into him for using the weapon without her approval, and to say that what he did was dangerous, foolish, or something to that effect. Instead, she takes a deep breath and smiles. "Well done."

Chapter 36

"Alright Jess, it's your turn," Ron says, grabbing a wrapped box from underneath the large, heavily decorated Christmas tree. "Oh yeah, open this one. This one's from me and Simon."

With the warm fire crackling softly a few feet away, we all watch as Jess eagerly selects her next gift to open, taking the box back to her seat next to Kanzen. She carefully removes the ribbon which I'd placed with equal care on top of the package last night, and the wrapping paper crinkles as she tears into the gift. She exclaims in awe as she opens the jewelry box, dangling the shiny gold necklace in front of her.

"I got that at the mall the same day I beat up those thieves robbing that old lady," I say proudly.

Jess jumps up and walks over to me, wrapping her arms around me. "It's beautiful, Simon. I love it. Thank you."

"Merry Christmas," I say, patting her on the back.

I help Jess put on the necklace, and she bounces over to Kanzen, displaying her gift with glowing pride. Next, she goes to Ron and wraps him in a hug as well. Ron peers past her and gives me a wink. He was right, she likes the jewelry, although I still think she would've liked the perfume too. Kanzen looks at me and nods his head in approval, giving me a thumbs up.

It's been a few days since all of the excitement went down with Popobowa and Wayne in the alternate future. Loretta, who's also with us this fine Christmas morning at Kanzen's mountain cabin in the Cascades, says that the future that I was dreaming about will no longer happen as long as some of Kanzen's projects never get to see the light of day. He's agreed to not have either the Structures, the hyper-advanced A.I. or the water powered generators created, vowing to find an alternative solution to help society. Not a perfect one, he said, but a foundation for a better, sustainable future, as well as a solution to clean energy. Now he keeps going on about 'geothermal energy,' or something to that effect. He tried breaking it down for me on how it all works, but he lost me.

Loretta says it's possible I may see another dream of Annie Hilltop if I'm lucky, as that world will still theoretically exist in an alternate, parallel dimension, but it's no longer related to our world. 'A fleeting echo from the cosmos', she called it. Honestly, the more she explained it, the more it gave me a headache. These theories from people smarter than me keep confusing me. All I really cared about was the fact that X is now trapped in that future, with no foreseeable way to return to this world, and Popobowa is officially dead. The rest of the details are just whatever to me.

"Ron, it's your turn," Jess says. "That big yellow box over there. Yep, that one."

Ron holds the box intended for him out at arm's length, then puts it up to his ear. "What is it?"

"Open it and find out," Kanzen says, chuckling.

He tears into the package, throwing yellow wrapping paper around the room like a little kid. His eyes bulge as he looks at the box, staring at it for a moment. "I've always wanted one of these," Ron says, yanking down at a dangling piece of wrapping paper.

He proudly displays for us a box of stainless-steel silverware. Forks, spoons, knives; it's the complete package.

"Open the box, you goof," Jess says, shaking her head. "Goodness…"

"Oh," Ron says, frowning.

He opens the silverware box and reaches inside, his tongue sticking out. Triumphantly, he pulls out a small trading card resting inside of a thick, see-through plastic sheet. Ron examines the card for a moment, flipping it over, his expression morphing from confusion to shock.

"Oh my God," he says, breathless. "It's an autographed rookie Michael Jordan card. This thing must've cost a fortune. How…how?"

In one of the rarest instances I've witnessed, Ron's at a loss for words.

Kanzen sits forward. "I've got a buddy that collects high-profile sports memorabilia. Pulled a couple of strings and figured you'd enjoy that."

"Enjoy it?" Ron asks, looking up at Kanzen with tears in his eyes. "I only got you a yo-yo, bro. I can't believe this."

He stands up and rushes over to Kanzen. Jess leaps out of the way just before she's run over, and Ron envelops Kanzen in a gigantic bear hug.

"Do you have any idea how much this thing's worth?" Ron asks.

"I have an idea," Kanzen says in a muffled voice, his face still buried in Ron's armpit.

"How much?" I ask.

"One recently sold at auction for over a million dollars," Ron says, looking back at me. He turns his attention to Kanzen, standing up but still holding the other man's shoulders. "Did you know that?"

"Yes, this is the same one," Kanzen says.

Ron, Jess and I stare at Kanzen.

Loretta whistles. "Merry Christmas to you, Ronald."

"Simon, why don't you open that big one right over there," Jess says excitedly, pointing at an enormous box that I've had my eyes on, sitting in the corner.

I walk over to the box and pick it up to inspect it. The tag on the box reads: 'To Simon. From: Your friends Jess and Ron. Merry Christmas.'

Arching one eyebrow at her, I cautiously place the box back down on the floor and begin to open it. Once I have the majority of the wrapping paper removed, I look up at Ron and over at Jess with tears in my eyes. Everyone else is looking at me, curious as to what it is that I've received.

It's an 8" x 10" framed picture of the three of us at the shopping mall, with Ron proudly sitting on Santa's lap. After all that we've been through together, both back in Chicago and our new home in Seattle, it sort of hits me all at once how lucky I am to have Ron and Jess as such good, longtime friends. I'd be lost without these two.

"Thank you," I say, wiping my cheek with the back of my hand. "You guys have no idea how much this means to me."

"I'm glad you like it, buddy," Ron says, still examining his million-dollar card.

"Me, too," Jess says cheerfully to me.

Ron gently places his Michael Jordan card in amongst his pile of gifts, ensuring that it's up on top like a crowning jewel of his days' worth of plunder, and comes over next to me, laying on his stomach on the wooden floor. Together, we examine the picture. His gift may be valued at over a million dollars, but my gift is priceless. Can't beat that.

A LITTLE WHILE later, Ms. Sasaki and I are in the oversized kitchen making a Christmas dinner for everyone. I'm over in my own section preparing some California rolls. Making these little meals brings me a tremendous level of peace, and I often find myself daydreaming about various things while my hands are busy. Probably why I work so slowly at the restaurant, just daydreaming in my own little world while preparing plates of sushi.

"What are you thinking about over there?" Ms. Sasaki asks from her corner of the kitchen.

I clear my throat. "Oh, not much. I'm just happy we could all get together for this. I'm surprised you have the restaurant closed today. Don't people like sushi on Christmas?"

"I suppose some do. But spending today with my boys is more important."

"Kanzen's lucky to have you for a mom." I say, accepting of the fact that she's apparently becoming senile and said "boys."

"And I'm lucky to have him for a son."

"You remind me a lot of my mom, you know," I say after a brief pause. "You're both driven to help others, and you like making food."

"Well, she raised a good man," Ms. Sasaki says. "In this life, that is. I was your mother once, you know."

I have to put down the sushi roll I'm working on as I nearly lose control of my limbs. I turn to face her, clearing my throat again. "What?"

"Several centuries ago in Japan, you were my son," she keeps working on her plate of food, not bothering to turn around, as if this is no big deal. "You were my first son."

"So, you're like… super old. Like Loretta?"

"She's got me beat in that category. This is my second life. My first one ended prematurely thanks to the Collector over a thousand years ago. However, in this current life, you were my first-born son."

I shake my head, still trying to process this new information. "So, that makes Kanzen –"

"Woah, I didn't know you picked up a new language, Simon!" Ron says, walking through the kitchen. "What is that? Mandarin?"

"It's Japanese," Ms. Sasaki says dryly.

"Ah, you've been brushing up on a second language and not telling us about it. Good job, man." Ron slaps me on the back, taking a beer and a tray of cheese with him.

"I was still working on that…" Ms. Sasaki mutters as the tray of cheese disappears out of the kitchen.

I keep staring at the back of Ms. Sasaki's head while she resumes her work.

"I've got a lot of questions here, Ms. Sasaki. Can you please turn around for a minute?" Slapping the cutting board, she quickly turns around and crosses her arms impatiently, waiting for me to continue. "First of all, you were my mom?"

"Yes. In Japan. You were a skilled Samurai, lethal in many forms of combat. That's why your skill with the Particle Stick came so easily to you, as well as that katana; a blade that I forged for you hundreds of years ago."

"Alright…and how long have I been speaking Japanese with you?"

"Since your first job interview," she says, snickering. "I was amazed at how fluent you were in our tongue. At first, I thought that maybe you had learned it as a second language. Perhaps in school, or as a hobby. But the more I was around you and able to read your aura, it became clearer who you really were. Who you really *are,* I should say."

Kanzen enters the kitchen, eyeing the two of us cautiously.

"You two are working too hard," he says, grabbing a beer from the fridge. "C'mon, it's Christmas. Raul's got the table set for us."

"We'll be ready in a few minutes," Ms. Sasaki says sharply.

"Alright. Take it easy, mom."

We remain silent until he leaves the kitchen. I keep my attention focused on the little Asian woman, squinting my eyes for a moment. It's all so much to take in; the fact that she used to be my mom, and technically still is, albeit a strange technicality. The fact that my past lives' experiences are bleeding into my reality without me even knowing how and causing me to fluently speak languages that I've never spoken. It's frustrating to me that she's been keeping everything a secret for the past few weeks, as if she was just hoping I'd stumble across these facts on my own.

"How do you know Loretta?" I ask, arms crossed.

Ms. Sasaki sighs and turns away from me, resuming her work. "We share a common enemy."

"Popobowa?"

"No. The Collector."

"Who is he? Or she…"

Loretta now walks into the kitchen, eyeing the two of us. *Damn, can Ms. Sasaki and I not have a moment of peace?* I suppose that a Christmas party in a secluded cabin in the mountains isn't the best place to have a confidential conversation, but still…

"Ah, there you are, Akua," Ms. Sasaki says pleasantly.

"I thought we agreed you wouldn't call me that anymore in this realm, Harumi."

I lean back against the kitchen counter, my arms still crossed. "I'm learning so much. Please, do go on, ladies."

The two women look at me, a brief moment of fire in their gaze.

"Simon," Loretta begins, licking her lips. "Again, I must say that I'm sorry that you've been dragged into this mess. Earlier this year, when I'd first discovered who you were, I was thrilled. And I still am, believe me. That being said, I'm afraid that danger is coming."

"I mean, could it get any worse?" I reply, harsher than intended. "Is it about this Collector dude that Harumi was telling me about?"

"Don't call me that!" Ms. Sasaki points a finger at me.

"That's precisely the issue here, Simon!" Loretta snaps. "Don't you see?" She sighs, shaking her head. "No, of course you don't. You're ignorant to all of this…but it's not your fault." She takes another deep breath before continuing. "With Mubiru's soul being trapped in an alternate reality that no longer exists, the Balance of Souls is off kilter. The Collector will be coming for you."

I shrug my shoulders. "Look, we'll cross that bridge when we get to it, Akua. Ain't no sweat. C'mon, let's go enjoy ourselves. It's Christmas."

I scoop up the plate of sushi and Loretta smacks me on the back of the head as I leave, causing me to juggle the plate for a moment. Those long fingers of hers can really hurt.

Once I make my way into the dining room, I feel a wave of contentment wash over me. My prior concerns about Popobowa and the Collector just melt away. Kanzen and his private chef Raul, as well as Jess and Ron, are all sitting around the large table, conversing loudly amongst themselves. Ron is telling Kanzen an elaborate story of some kind, flailing his arms about.

"Simon's got sushi, everyone, look out!" Ron announces.

I bring the large plate in for a landing and rub my hands together gleefully as Ron picks up the serving platter, throws a few rolls on his plate, and passes it along to Jess.

Loretta and Ms. Sasaki exit the kitchen, bringing the rest of the meal to the table. Everyone is so…content. After the traumatic events we just went through, it's great to settle in and spend this time with the most loyal, courageous people I know. Taking my seat, I scoot the chair in, looking around the table. I truly am a lucky person.

Chapter 37

I can hear Ron on the phone in his room, the door slightly cracked open. "Is that right?" Ron asks whoever is on the other line, then laughs. "No, no, I believe you."

Jess approaches me in the hallway on the way to her room. It appears she's about to say something, but I put my finger up to my lips. She understands and begins to tiptoe toward Ron's door, leaning over to get a better listen.

"Thank you. Well…I love you too, Dad."

Jess looks at me and puts her hands over her heart, smiling. It's great that Ron built up the courage to talk to his dad. Even better, his dad answered and was willing to talk to him.

Jess and I head into her room to allow him some privacy and I visit with her for a few minutes, waiting patiently for Ron to wrap up his conversation. Thankfully, her magnificent oil paintings are hung on her walls again, replacing those strange, hand-drawn images of my dreams. I make a mental note to ask Ms. Sasaki if she's the one that planted those images of my future in Jess' head, or if that was X.

"Any more dreams?" Jess asks, folding some clothes on her bed.

"Nope," I say. "Not yet, anyway. Hey, look, I just wanted to say thanks."

"For what?"

"For everything," I scratch the back of my neck. "You've always been in my corner. I appreciate you always having my back."

She stops folding her clothes for a moment and looks at me. "We've had *each other's* backs. You know, moving out here, abandoning our old lives, that was a big jump. But I'm glad I did it. I don't know if I could've done it without you."

"Ditto," I say, leaning up against her door. "We make a pretty good team, you and me."

"We sure do. Ron too."

"Yeah, him too," I laugh.

A LITTLE OVER an hour later, we're all waiting patiently backstage at the local TV news station. Even though they weren't invited to be on this morning's interview, they've both dressed up for the event, supporting me as I make my television appearance.

"Alright Simon, two-minute warning," a young female wearing a headset says, waving a piece of paper around.

She takes off in another direction at a mad sprint as if she's left the stove on.

Jess pats my shoulder reassuringly.

"Man, this is awesome," Ron says, examining the studio with his hands in his pockets. "You know, I've always wanted to be on TV. Maybe we can stage a heist or something and make me out to be the hero someday. Then they can interview me and I'll tell them how I saved the day. Or maybe we…"

As Ron goes on about his scheme to become a fraudulent local celebrity vigilante, my mind drifts off. When I'd woken up this morning, a feeling of guilt hit me like a ton of bricks. Yesterday at Kanzen's mountain cabin, I wasn't able to call my mom.

Thankfully, I did call her this morning and apologized for not calling the day before. I told her we were out of cell reception, and believe it or not, it's the truth. As rich and tech savvy as Kanzen is, he doesn't have cell service up at his cabin. She sounded disappointed at first, but once I explained everything to her, she finally chippered up and we spoke for almost an hour.

I suppose this might've been the first feeling of homesickness I'd gotten since leaving Chicago. After all that went down a few months ago, I thought I would've been done with that city for good. But lately… I don't know. It's like that place is calling me back. Then I remember that I'm potentially a wanted man there, both by Detective Erickson as well as Marcini's crime family who are still coming after me, so it's probably best that I stay far away.

The same woman with the headset and piece of paper has returned. "Okay, Mr. Verner. We're ready."

I give my friends two thumbs up, then follow her into the studio, carefully stepping around the seemingly endless string of electrical cables running across the floor and big cameras which are strategically positioned all over the place. Straight ahead is the green screen where they do the weather, and to my left is the big desk where the news anchors sit and read the daily disasters from the teleprompter.

Now here's a job I could do if my sushi career comes to a flaming end. News anchor. I can read words with the best of them. Jess can attest to that.

"Mr. Verner!" Bob McCormick says enthusiastically, hand outstretched just like the first time we'd met.

"Wind, rain or shine," I say in a deep voice, shaking his hand a bit rougher than intended. "Nobody delivers the news like Bob on Channel 9!"

He quickly takes his hand back, flashing me a big, fake smile. "Like I haven't heard that before. Please follow me."

Past the green screen and news desk is a smaller area with three chairs. Two are positioned on one side of a short round wooden table, with the third on the opposite side. Sitting patiently in one of the chairs with her hands folded in her lap is Alice, the elderly woman who I'd helped at Bellevue Square a few weeks ago.

I take my seat next to Alice and shake her hand. She smiles warmly, dimples showing on her wrinkled cheeks.

"It's nice to see you again, Simon," she says, her voice cracking.

Bob takes his seat across from us and begins twirling his hand in an aggressive motion. "Let's pick it up, we're on in ten! Pay attention, people!"

"It's good to see you too," I whisper to her. "How was your Christmas?"

"Quiet down!" Bob shouts at us.

We both sit upright, startled at being yelled at all of a sudden. In a flash, Bob's expression changes from harsh to happy, turning to his left and smiling at the camera which is pointed directly at us.

"Good morning, Seattle!" Bob says in his usual chipper voice. "Well, you've seen the online video, no doubt. The clip you're seeing here, which now has over 75 million views…incredible," Bob turns in his seat, allowing a moment of silence to pass, presumably to allow the audience at home time to finish watching the video, and faces me and Alice. "I'm sitting here today with Alice Greenland. A few weeks ago, Alice was brutally assaulted and robbed outside Bellevue Square. The thieves would've gotten away with this heinous crime if it wasn't for the heroic actions of a courageous local Samaritan. I'm pleased to introduce you all to that same young man, who's also here with us today. Say good morning to Simon Verner."

I stand up and wave to the small, silent audience of newsroom employees. A man in a business suit next to the cameraman puts his head down, scratching his scalp in frustration. I continue to wave for a few more seconds until Alice gently tugs on the sleeve of my jacket. I sit back down, straightening my shirt.

Bob clears his throat. "Mr. Verner, tell us about the incident at the mall."

"Well, Bob, you just about covered it. I saw Mrs. Greenland here getting mugged, so I took off after the two guys and chased them through the mall. Then I beat them up and got her purse back."

"What convinced you to step in?" Bob leans forward, holding a pen to his lips.

I tilt my head from side to side in thought. "It didn't take any convincing. I saw someone in need, I was in a position to help out, so I did what was right."

"I notice that you said you 'did what was right,' not what you thought was right. I find that interesting, because you could've wound up seriously hurt, or worse," Bob warns.

"True. But I didn't see it that way. Still don't. If we see a fellow man or woman in need, shouldn't it be natural for us to just step in and do what's right, regardless of the consequences? Isn't that what makes us a society?"

"Well, it's not quite that simple," Bob chuckles, leaning back and looking at the camera. "Not everyone can beat up bad guys and save the day. Sometimes it's best to be cautious. Now, I'm not saying what you did was wrong. I'm just suggesting to our audience that perhaps we should let the authorities do what they're trained to do."

"Oh, for sure Bob. But I'm talking more wide scope," I look squarely at the camera. "I'm saying that if you see another person in danger, or who may need some help, do what you feel should be done. Act like a parent, or someone who you always looked up to when you were younger, is always watching. I know as a kid I shaped up pretty fast when my mom was around." Some of the crew members begin to chuckle, and Bob looks at them sharply, silencing them.

I press on. "We aren't all perfect. Some of us have a lot of ground to make up in the eyes of those we look up to. Just like society. It isn't perfect. Never will be. But what I'd like to see is for folks to clean out their ears and start listening to one another. We were given two ears and one mouth, yet all people want to do anymore is talk. Social media has given us all these platforms, and guess what? Nobody cares what you have to say on there. We need less talking, and more doing. We need our elected officials to start cleaning up the streets. You think it's okay for folks to be sleeping outside, struggling with a fentanyl addiction? You think it's okay for those thieves who assaulted Alice to have only spent one day in jail before being released on their own recognizance? I sure as hell don't. Something is broken with our society, Bob. And it's only going to get worse unless we actually want to recognize and fix these issues together, and not just turn a blind eye to it all."

"You sound very conservative in your political views, Simon. Are you a right-wing political supporter? You know this is a left-wing area we live in, right?"

"I don't care what side you think I support. I believe in common sense. I think I'm more in the middle. People need to stop letting politics and the media rule the way we think. Left-wing, right-wing, hell Bob, it takes two wings to fly."

"Okay then," Bob says, looking down at the paper in his lap.

There's a moment of tense silence throughout the studio, until Bob turns his attention to Alice.

"What can you tell us about your harrowing experience on that day? It must've been terrifying, being alone and under attack, incapable of defending yourself."

"Yes, it was," Alice says softly. "But thankfully there're still good people like Simon in this world." She places a hand on my knee. "I was born and raised in Seattle. I've seen it grow and become more dangerous, just like any large city. But the more this city has grown, the more I've seen people's care for their neighbors shrink. All I know is that the future is in our hands, Mr. McCormick. It's up to us to make sure the younger people have a good world to live in, so they can raise their kids right too. Our actions today will shape what tomorrow will look like. Some of us just don't seem to understand that though."

Bob chuckles and looks over at the camera. "Well, I believe that's all the time we have for today. We'll be right back after the break."

He continues to stare at the camera for another few seconds. I look at the camera and wave again.

"What the hell was that?" Bob explodes, throwing his pen across the studio and turning toward the two of us. "I asked you two to recount the robbery, not stand on your little soap boxes telling people how to think!"

"Really?" I ask defensively. "With your abundant use of adjectives to describe her ordeal, I'm surprised anyone got to hear the real story. Stop spreading fear and discontent among the people watching." I stand up to leave, then turn around. "For the record, you lost yourself a viewer."

"Good!" Bob shouts back. "Wouldn't want the likes of you watching this program anyway, Verner!"

I pat Alice on the shoulder and tell her to have a Happy New Year, then walk away from Bob McCormick and the rest of the news crew to meet up with my friends. Ron gives me a high-five as we leave the station and walk out to my car.

Since we're all feeling hungry, I drive us down to the same local bar and restaurant where I opened that bizarre fortune cookie from Ms. Sasaki a few weeks ago. We snag a booth, and Jess scoots down to let me sit next to her while Ron sits across from us. No football games on the TV today, thankfully, allowing him to give us his full, undivided attention.

Glancing over at Jess, I'm relieved to see that familiar smile has returned to her face. After a couple weeks of strange, out of character behavior due to X's tainted influence, both of my friends have bounced back quickly. She grabs her short, blond hair in one hand, straightening it as she examines the menu.

A waitress passes by, and Ron gets her attention.

"We'll take a pitcher for the table," he says, and the waitress nods her head, scuttling along. Ron rubs his hands together, turning his attention back to me. "You really let it all out there today, Simon. That news anchor dude was so pissed!"

"Just telling it how I see it. I probably shouldn't have gotten so preachy, but what's done is done. No changing the past."

"Very true," Ron nods his head. Another moment passes as the three of us sit in silence, looking at the menu. "Anything jumping out at you guys?"

"I'm thinking we could share some cheese curds," Jess says, furrowing her brow. "And…I'll probably get a wrap or something." She shuts the menu and puts it down, sitting upright. "Yeah, that was an interesting interview. That Bob McCormick is a bit two-faced, if you ask me."

I wave my hand dismissively. "Oh well. There are other ways to get the news."

Ron stretches his back, a loud pop emanating from his spine. That can't be good for him. "Where's Kanzen?"

"He's out house shopping," Jess says.

"New house?" Ron asks. "What, that mansion on the lake wasn't good enough for him?"

"He said something about the HOA forcing him to move because of a fatal shooting in front of his house."

"Oh, that's right," Ron remarks.

The waitress arrives with our large pitcher of foaming beer, as well as three mugs. Ron pours each of us a full glass all the way up to the brim, bubbles of foam teasing, acting like they want to roll out and slide down to the sticky table below. Ron picks up his drink by the handle.

"Here's to Simon kicking ass for once, and not getting straight up whooped by a girl like last time," Ron says loudly. "Here's to Jess and me for finally outgrowing our emo phase. And here's to the three of us still being alive after the craziest year imaginable."

"I'll drink to that," Jess says, raising her glass.

The two of them look at me expectantly until I finally pick up the frosty mug, holding it up. "Here's to having you two in my life, forever and always. Simon, Jess and Ron."

"Too sappy," Ron squints his eyes and tilts his head. "But it'll work. Amen."

We clink our mugs together and take our first drink. I nod my head at Ron, who winks at me in return. Weirdo.

I look over at Jess. "It's good to have you back. Both of you."

"Glad to be back. I just hope our excitement has finally come to an end and we can go back to living our normal lives."

"Me too," I say. "Me too."

Ron laughs. "Yeah, whatever *normal* is. I don't know if I'll ever be the same after stepping foot in Simon's dream."

"**When a tree** sweats, it's called transpiration. And when we sweat," the teacher points at herself, sniffing her armpit, causing the kids to burst up in fits of giggles, "that's called perspiration."

She points at drawings on the marker board, showing the kids the difference between the two processes and telling them where to find this information in their textbooks. On her wrist, the faint outline of a tattoo depicting a six-digit number can barely be noticed. The kids turn their paperback books to the page requested, eagerly soaking in the knowledge from the teacher's lesson.

The bell rings, signaling the end of class.

"Have a good afternoon, everyone," she says to the children as they file out of the classroom. "Stay safe. And remember, a week from today, your projects are due!"

At the back of the line of students leaving the classroom, a young girl stops and turns toward the teacher. She has a sad look on her face.

"What's wrong, sweetheart?" the teacher asks.

"It's sad that the trees sweat," the little girl says, her chubby little cheeks bright red. "The other trees might make fun of it and think it stinks."

The teacher wraps the girl in a warm hug. "I wouldn't worry about that." She pats the little girl's head of long, black hair. "The trees can't talk to one another, Hope."

She holds Hope out at arm's length, and the little girl smiles. "You're a good teacher, mommy."

Annie smiles back. "Thanks, baby girl. Let's go home, what d'ya say?"

Annie takes Hope by the hand and together they walk home under a bright blue sky. They're both wrapped in warm coats, scarves and knitted hats. It's been a long, cold winter, and spring can't come soon enough.

"Afternoon, Helen," Annie says pleasantly to a woman passing by.

"Hey, Annie!" Helen says, then stops, bending down to be at eye level with Hope. "And how are you doing today, Hope Hilltop? Learn anything new from the best teacher in town?"

"I learned that trees sweat," Hope says quietly.

"Really?" Helen nods her head, then stands back up. "I didn't know that, either. We both learned something new today. Well, I better be off. Yelena needs me in the clinic. Take care, you two."

Annie smiles at Helen. "Same to you."

Just before they arrive home, they hear a commotion up ahead at the main gate. Annie leads Hope over to a group of kids and asks her to stay there while she goes to investigate what's going on outside the city wall. Climbing the guard tower, she can hear the patrolmen murmuring something about a newcomer asking for assistance outside. Nobody new has come to their settlement in the six years that Annie's been here. *That's strange. Who could it be?* Annie wonders to herself.

Once at the top, Annie shuffles through the crowd of men, having to push a bit more aggressively to get a view of what's going on. She can't explain it, but something is drawing her to see what's going on. "Excuse me. Sorry."

Now at the front, Annie grasps the railing with one hand, cupping her other hand over her brow to shield her eyes from the sun as she looks down at the individual standing in the ankle-deep snow. He's just standing there, unmoving. Annie's heartbeat quickens. The man's wearing a wide-brimmed black hat. Strapped to his back is a laser rifle.

"Can anyone up there hear me?" the man yells up, his voice sounding a bit choppy and robotic. "My name is UE…" He begins to shake his head. "No. My name is SOL. I've come a long way to see someone, and I believe she's living here. Her name is Annie Hilltop."

"I'm here!" Annie yells down. "SOL, I'm here!"

SOL slowly removes his hat, uncovering the exposed wiring and cables in his skull. He holds the hat delicately in front of him, craning his neck up to see Annie standing on the top of the guard tower. And for just a brief flicker of an instant, a moment quicky lost to time, Annie swears that she can see the glimmer of a tear trickling down his silicone face. The face of a man who smiles.

Epilogue

Sitting in one of the finest restaurants in Paris, Stuart Jensen waits for his meal to arrive. Across the table from him, a nervous looking man with a face that looks similar to a mouse is fidgeting with the buttons on his jacket. The crystal chandelier in the middle of the restaurant, directly overhead, casts a bright glow over the two men. An empty chair remains at the table, waiting for their expected guest to arrive.

"So, what are the next steps, sir?" the nervous man asks hesitantly, his voice shaking.

Stuart looks at the little man, pressing his tongue against the inside of his cheek.

"We bring him here and give him a chance to make it right, Roger," Stuart says calmly. "He's barely scraped the surface of what he's capable of. It would be a pity to stifle his development when he has so much…potential. So much power that could benefit our cause." Stuart clears his throat. "Besides, I just want to find out what happened to my son. He'll tell me where he is."

"But will Mwari understand, sir?"

Stuart slams a fist on the table, causing the assortment of silverware and glassware to shake on top of the pristine white tablecloth.

"He doesn't need to know," Stuart says, a level of constraint in his voice. "I don't work *for* him anymore, remember?"

"Yes, I'm sorry."

Roger lowers his gaze in shame, praying that Stuart will calm down.

"I'm ready for you to summon him," Stuart says between clenched teeth.

"But sir, is that wise?"

As soon as the words leave his lips, Roger realizes his error.

"Do not question me!" Stuart says. "Others have defied me, none of whom are alive to tell about it. You will do as you're told. Do I make myself clear?"

"Yes, sir."

"Call me by my real name. The name that's garnered me respect amongst my peers. When it's all said and done, they will all learn to fear me again. And that starts with you."

Roger keeps his gaze lowered, unable to make eye contact with the other man. "Yes, Collector."

Outside on the busy streets, cars pass by the restaurant honking their horns, and people stroll by on the sidewalk, paying no attention to the fine dining establishment with the "closed" sign in the doorway.

Sitting back smugly in his chair, the Collector brings his hand up again. Roger winces, expecting to be smacked. "Summon him."

The mouse-faced man raises a trembling hand and snaps his fingers.

Appearing suddenly in the empty chair at their table is a young man in his early to mid-twenties, with long, curly brown hair, a pointy nose and blue eyes. He looks around the room in startlement.

"What the hell?" the young man shouts. "Where am I?"

"Shh," the Collector says. "Please, lower your voice, Mr. Verner."

Simon looks at the man who had him summoned here. "How do you know my name?"

"Lower your voice. Please."

"He doesn't ask a third time," Roger warns.

Stuart places his hands on the tablecloth in front of him, keeping his posture upright and proper. Roger follows suit to the best of his ability, mimicking his boss' mannerisms. Simon's blue eyes glare piercingly at both men, darting back and forth between them.

"You're in Paris," the Collector says smoothly. "My associate and I have summoned you here using the power granted to us by Mwari. My name is Stuart, and this is my associate, Roger. However, I'd prefer it if you referred to me as *the Collector*."

Simon's cheeks appear drained of all color immediately as he registers that name, and he takes a deep breath. "What do you want?"

"What I want, Mr. Verner, is for you to listen, as you so eloquently stated while on the Seattle news station yesterday."

"How d –"

The Collector puts a hand up, silencing Simon. The two men lock eyes for a few moments in a battle of wills, while Roger sits idly by, hoping things don't get out of hand.

"What I want is simple. I need you to tell me where my son has gone. He goes by the name of 'Popobowa.'"

"He's dead," Simon says, crossing his arms. "He followed me into my future, and he paid the ultimate price."

Stuart sighs, shaking his head. "Is that so?"

"It's the truth. I sliced that demon bastard's head clean off. Popobowa is no more."

"That's a pity. In that case, I can assure you of this; I will take from you everything you hold most dear as a method of unpaid debt. You owe me."

"Like hell I do!" Simon roars back.

The Collector raises his hand again, staring silently at Simon. "I'll be in touch, Mr. Verner. Enjoy your time with your friends while you still can."

Roger snaps his fingers, and Simon disappears, sent back to his apartment with his boring friends.

The Collector stares straight ahead, trembling with rage.

As **Wayne walks** further away from the dying city and the remains of the fallen Structure, fewer people are seen on the streets.

After the building fell, in a monumental moment that everyone has referred to only as *The Fall,* he found a medical tent which had been previously intended to patch up the wounded from the war. A war that, once The Fall happened, ended immediately.

All androids that were being controlled by the building's main computer ceased operations as soon as the Structure fell, collapsing to the ground, leaving only the humans left standing. People rejoiced, embracing one another in heartfelt hugs. Citizens sent out from the Structure into the world for the first time were led to another site where they could be looked after. A *New Civilization*, they were calling it. *Looking forward to the future, for a brighter tomorrow.* To Wayne, it was all just hollow words. Once his arm was sutured up and the bleeding stopped, he left the medical tent and went on his way.

After searching around the rubble of the city and the older collapsed buildings, scouring frantically at the base of where the Structure once stood for his staff, he was forced to accept that there were no ways to generate portals back to Earth or the Dark Dimension. No clues for a way back to

Simon's world. A couple of days went by before Wayne, formerly known as Mubiru in his first life, fully accepted his fate; he was stuck in this reality. Once again, he was cast away, banished from his tribe and left to fend for himself in an unforgiving, barren wasteland.

He cursed Simon for leaving him here to die. He had sprinted toward the gateway, but Simon and his ragtag group of loser friends shut the door on him, severing his arm. Simon's mentally challenged friend had somehow used the Oracle's staff. Ridiculous. They probably laughed about it later.

Wayne missed playing the role of Brittany, toying with Simon's fragile and insecure mind, playing on the boy's fantasies and invading his dreams. There were many other previous lives where Wayne had messed with his former brother, burning those prior lives to ashes, leaving a trail of crumbs for others to kill the body temporarily housing the soul of Magdoo. Mubiru wasn't one to get his own hands dirty. Usually.

For the first time in seventeen thousand years, he feels…free. Popobowa's claws are no longer sinking into his brainstem, telling him what to do. Not that he would've listened anymore. The demon's master plan with the Soul Generator had failed, predictably. Everything that Popobowa had tried to escape the Dark Dimension, to bring his loyal followers with him, always ended in disaster.

Chuckling softly to himself, Wayne continues walking down the long and dusty road. Cracks in the sidewalk with weeds growing out of them prove to be an obstacle to his tired feet.

For the next six months, Wayne wandered the dying city, scrounging for scraps of food. Having only one arm made that task twice as difficult as it needed to be. He eventually built himself a little hut on the outskirts of the city, sometimes venturing out into the small "living" section where the majority of the lost citizens – those who had already lived outside the Structure – called home, in order to get the food and water necessary to survive through barter and trade.

However, Wayne eventually grew tired of the monotonous routine. The brain-dead, knuckle-dragging citizens grew weary of him, refusing to deal with him any longer. He needed to find somewhere else to live before he ran out of resources. So, one day he left his little hut behind and started journeying away from the dying city. He followed a long, cracked road out of town, walking as far as his feet would take him.

Which brings him to this moment; his aching feet, dragging along underneath him, his dry lips eager for some water.

Thankfully, up ahead, there appears to be salvation; an enclosed encampment of some kind, surrounded by a tall fence with barbed wire at the top. A perfect place to hide from the dangers of the world, to give him time to recuperate and recover.

"Hey there, stranger!" a woman calls from a little guard tower above the front gate. "You lookin' for a place to stay the night?"

"Yes," Wayne says, his voice dry. "Please, let me in."

"Hold your horses," the female says. "I'll be right down."

A few moments later, the front gate begins to swing open, and the woman leans through the opening to get a better look at him. She's wearing dirty overalls, and her short, red hair appears that it hasn't been washed in quite some time.

"Come on in, handsome," she says.

"Thank you kindly."

The gate closes behind them, and the woman steps in front of Wayne.

"Let me show you the layout. Name's Collette, by the way. What's yours?"

"I go by many names. But you can call me Wayne."

"Alrighty, *Wayne* it is," Collette says, chuckling.

While leading Wayne around the grounds, she explains that they haven't allowed any newcomers in since a rogue androids came through several months ago and killed her husband, Ted.

He tries to patiently follow the talkative woman around the yard while she gives him the tour, but Wayne eventually succumbs to his exhaustion and collapses against the side of the chain-link fence.

"Water," he says hoarsely. "I need water."

"Well shoot, mister," Collette says innocently. "We all need water. That's why we let you in."

Wayne squints his eyes, unsure of what this mad woman is going on about. She steps away from him over to a gate. Three big dogs approach on the other side of the chain-link fence, licking their lips.

"We found these pups a little while back on a hunt in the city," Collette explains as the dogs begin growling. "Poor little puppies. They were on the verge of death. Their momma must've abandoned them. We're sure glad we took 'em in." Without warning, she opens the gate. "Dinner time!"

Snarling viciously, the three dogs bound out of the open gate, pouncing on Wayne before he has a chance to defend himself. They bite into his shoulder, his cheek, his legs, blood oozing out of him from the wounds. Men and women emerge from the shadows, creeping forward and digging into his flesh, slowly consuming him piece by piece. Wayne's screams can be heard for miles.

The soul of Mubiru, the entity who often chose to go by the name X, leaves his body. With no place to go, now suspended in a reality beyond the known boundaries of all time and space, the soul winks out, never to return to any known plane of existence again.

A PILE OF unfinished work rests on Detective Erickson's desk; all the files and documents pertaining to the missing former crime boss William Marcini, as well as the mysterious woman named Loretta. On top of the pile are files pertaining to Simon Verner.

Erickson has been trying to get in contact with Lenny Marcini for weeks, with no luck. The number on the business card Lenny left for him sends him straight to a full voicemail box. Why would the guy just pop into his office in a show of force, leave a business card, then ghost him? For the life of him, he can't understand it.

Last week, he went to visit Jill Verner, the ex-wife of disgraced Sergeant Doug Lewis. She's also Simon's mother. Erickson finds that connection to be awfully suspicious, but his investigation has simply led him to believe that it was truly just a mighty big coincidence. Jill was very open and honest with Erickson and was very concerned for her son. She had just spoken with him not too long ago, the day after Christmas, and said everything sounded fine. She was excited for his upcoming interview on a news station in Seattle.

Erickson already knew about Simon running off to the Emerald City with Jessica Williams and Ronald Douglas. The detective had contacts within the King County Sheriff's Office keeping an eye on their shared apartment. Apparently, Verner works at a sushi restaurant now. He's kept his nose clean. He's stayed out of trouble. His credit score has improved. Outside of a viral online video where he beats up some criminals, a video that now has millions of views, nothing about Verner seems out of the ordinary. Except that now both

William and Lenny Marcini have gone missing when they got near the guy.

The Marcini disappearances both appear to be cold cases. For now. But like always, something will eventually be dug up; a missing piece of the puzzle that he's just not seeing. Perhaps it has something to do with this mysterious Loretta…

Detective Erickson leans back in his chair, rubbing his eyes. He hasn't taken a day off in weeks. The grind and mental strain of working these relatively high-profile missing persons cases has him beat. Not to mention his Sergeant is up his ass, wondering what's taking him so long to track down any viable leads. The Marcini crime family still has a lot of pull on this city after all these years. A dirty, rotten pull.

A knock on the door.

"Come in," Erickson grumbles.

A blond woman opens the door, letting in that annoying racket from outside; the phones ringing, a woman screaming frantically, high-heeled shoes clacking past on the hardwood floor. He wishes this woman would just shut the damn door, regardless of where she was standing in relation to it. *In or out lady, make up your mind,* Erickson thinks to himself.

Thankfully, she walks in and closes the door quietly behind her without being told. She slowly approaches the desk and takes a seat, straightening her short-sleeved blazer. On one wrist a gruesome burn mark is visible, but she seems to wave it out in the open freely, begging others to look at it, to witness her prior pain, beckoning others to show her a shred of sympathy.

"What can I help you with, miss…"

"Garry," she says softly. "Doctor Angela Garry."

Finally, a lead. Erickson remembers this name. Simon was a patient of hers for over four years, recovering from the trauma of being kicked out of his house by his stepfather, forced into a life of homelessness for the better part of nine months because he was too stubborn or stupid to seek aid and assistance while on the streets. In his psych profile of the young man, Erickson concluded that Simon is simply mentally weak, unable to cope with his surroundings, unwilling to listen to those who don't agree with him. He doesn't jive with those that don't speak his language. A young man who has a fragile ego. Soft.

"I received a call from Jill Verner not too long ago," Angela continues. "It sounded like you had some questions about Simon, is that right?"

"Nothing that would concern you much, Doctor Garry."

"Please, call me Angela," she says, flicking back a strand of blond hair behind her ear. "I just wanted to see if you've found anything out. He was a patient of mine once, but I can't get him to return my calls. I understand he moved out west, but that's all I know."

Erickson sits back and crosses his arms. *Wouldn't she like to know*, he thinks to himself.

"After your involvement with Dr. Scholinsky, and your complicity in the tortures that Simon endured under his care, Dr. Garry, I'm surprised you're still interested in him. Isn't he what you'd consider a 'lost cause?'"

Angela looks down at the floor. "I know. I've felt so guilty ever since I gave into his ex-girlfriend's demands and had him sent there. I didn't realize how far over the line Dr. Scholinsky had gone. If I'd known that he was treating Simon with those unnecessary drugs, I would've stopped it all immediately. I cared for him. He was always a sensitive, confused boy. Young man, now."

"So, you're here out of guilt more so than your concern for him."

Shaking her head, Angela abruptly stands up. "I'm sorry for wasting your time, Detective."

Just as she's about to open the door, Erickson says, "He's doing fine, Dr. Garry. He's living in Seattle with those two friends of his. Apparently, he's a sushi chef now."

Angela turns toward Erickson. "Thank you. If you get a chance to talk to him, please tell him that I'm sorry, and that I wish to speak with him."

She opens the door and leaves.

Before the door can close completely, a man enters the office in a rush. He's out of breath, holding a USB stick in between his thumb and index finger.

Erickson sighs. "Jesus Christ. What is it now, Tommy?"

"I found her!"

Without warning, Tommy walks around the desk and slides the drive into the USB port of Erickson's computer. He places a hand on the back of the detective's chair, something that's always annoyed Erickson. Looking up at Tommy, Erickson grumbles before turning his attention to the monitor where Tommy is eagerly pointing.

"What is it?" Erickson asks. "What're you showing me here?"

"Look!" Tommy exclaims. "Just… just look. Right here…"

The image is slightly grainy, but thankfully in color. It's security footage of a parking lot of some kind. The security feed speeds up as Tommy fiddles with the keyboard. He places his finger on the monitor, creating what will become an annoying smudge on the new flatscreen, and holds his greasy, pudgy finger there for several moments.

"There!" Tommy shouts in Erickson's ear.

Erickson leans forward, focusing his attention on a black woman with a large afro, wearing an arm sling. In her other hand, she's using a strange looking walking stick as a cane, although it's difficult to tell if the woman actually walks with a limp. Suddenly, the camera distorts for a moment. When the footage returns to clarity, the woman has disappeared.

"Did you see it?" Tommy asks excitedly. "She just…poof! Vanished!"

"And why the hell should I care?" Erickson says, raising his voice. He's had just about enough of Tommy and his antics for one day. For one year, actually. The worst partner a guy could ask for.

Tommy rewinds the security footage to the point just before the woman vanishes. "This is footage from a car rental lot at SeaTac Airport. And *that*, my dear friend, is Loretta. She owns Sweet Loretta's shop here in the city. Some hippy trippy place. She broke her arm when Lenny Marcini confronted her about his dad. And by confront, I mean he hired some goon to ram her car off the road. Messed her up for a while, put her in the hospital. But for some reason, he stopped pursuing her, then he took off to Seattle. And then *she* goes to Seattle? Too much of a coincidence here, partner."

Tommy now has Erickson's full attention. He's not that bad of a partner after all, scrounging up information like this. Detective Erickson can smell a revenge story from miles away. This deranged woman follows Marcini Junior to Seattle, then kills him. He has to tell himself to pump the breaks before he starts jumping to conclusions. *But this is as clear as day. Right?*

Something on the security feed catches the detective's attention.

"Freeze at 38.4," Erickson says, leaning forward. "Right…there. Stop. I said *stop*, damn it!"

The security footage pauses just at the moment the camera goes blurry. Barely distinguishable is a large arm grabbing her by the shoulder. Circled around the base of this mysterious arm appears to be what can only be described as a hole. A hole that appears seemingly out of thin air in the middle of the airport parking lot in broad daylight. Nobody else seemed to be around the moment she was grabbed. Seeing this footage makes Erickson's back itch. *Loretta has some sort of a connection to the supernatural.* This case has taken a different turn.

"Where did you go, Loretta?"

"I'll keep working on that," Tommy says, ejecting the USB stick.

"Good work," Erickson says, leaning back in his chair and resting his arms behind his head. "We find her, and that'll take us right to Marcini. Verner was involved somehow. I just know it."

About the Author

Jeremy Howe was born and raised in Spokane, Washington to two loving parents. He enjoys his free time spending time with his wife Galixie, reading, playing video games and watching sports, especially his favorite team, the Seattle Seahawks. Taking trips to the Oregon Coast with his wife is something that Jeremy also enjoys doing once he and his wife get the time off work to do so. He graduated from Eastern Washington University in 2016 with a Bachelor's Degree in Business Administration.

Recently, he's taken up the hobby of writing as a form of relaxation before bed. His first book, *Simon's Dream*, was self-published in June 2023. He intends on making the *Simon's Dream* series into a total of five books, with the outlines already completed for the overall story arc.